An Opponent for Johnny

"Wolf was here askin' about you," said George.

"That so? Well, that ain't no crime."

"Can he shoot better'n you?" queried the cook. "He says he'll shoot against anybody in this country with six-guns, any fashion, for a dollar a shot. Does it sound like money?"

"If I could shoot that good I'd be too rich to be restin' up between cow-punchin' jobs," gurgled Johnny through a double handful of water. "Reckon he knows what he's talking about, or he wouldn't risk bein' took up."

Clarence E. Mulford

JOHNNY NELSON

A TOM DOHERTY ASSOCIATES BOOK
NEW YORK

This is a work of fiction. All of the characters, organizations, and events portrayed in this novel are either products of the author's imagination or are used fictitiously.

JOHNNY NELSON

All new material in this edition copyright © 1997 by Tom Doherty Associates, LLC.

A Forge Book
Published by Tom Doherty Associates, LLC
175 Fifth Avenue
New York, NY 10010

www.tor-forge.com

Forge® is a registered trademark of Tom Doherty Associates, LLC.

ISBN 978-0-8125-6766-3

Forge books may be purchased for educational, business, or promotional use. For information on bulk purchases, please contact Macmillan Corporate and Premium Sales Department at 1-800-221-7945 extension 5442 or write specialmarkets@macmillan.com.

First Forge Edition: July 1997

Printed in the United States of America

0 9 8 7 6 5 4 3 2

CONTENTS

CONTENTS

CHAPTER I

A Rolling Stone

THE HORSE stopped suddenly and her rider came to his senses with a jerk, his hand streaking to a six-gun, while he muttered a profane inquiry as he swiftly scrutinized his surroundings. Had it been any horse but Pepper he would have directed his suspicions at it, but he knew the animal too well to do it that injustice. The valley before and below him was heavily grassed, and throughout its entire length wandered a small stream. Grazing cattle were scattered along it, and riding up the farther slope were three men, who appeared to be peaceful and innocent of wrong intent. These his eyes swept past, and they passed a small cluster of boulders down on the slope below him, but instantly returned to them, a puzzled look appearing upon his face. In that nest of rocks a woman lay prone, peering at the distant horsemen, and she slowly brought a rifle to her shoulder, cuddling its stock against her cheek. What he did not see, and could not, at that angle, was the menacing head of a rattlesnake not twenty feet from her, the instinctive fear of which put a chill in her heart and urged her to shoot it, even at the risk of being heard by the men she was watching. Johnny Nelson unconsciously estimated the range and shook his head. He could do it with his Sharp's single-shot, a rifle of great power; but he had yet to see any repeater that could. Knowing the futility of a shot, he coughed loudly, and had the satisfaction of seeing a flurry below him, and a rifle muzzle at the same instant. Slowly he raised his hands level with his shoulders, spoke to the horse and, mustering all the dignity possible under the circumstances, rode slowly down the slope.

"That's far enough," said a crisp voice, pleasant in timbre even though business-like and angry. "Haven't I told you punchers to keep off this ranch?"

"Never to my knowledge, Ma'am," he answered.

"Have you the brazen effrontery to sit there and calmly tell me that?"

"I don't know, Ma'am; but I never heard about no such orders."

"Who are you? Where do you come from? What are you doing here?"

Johnny smiled apologetically. "Fifteen hundred shore would strain that gun, Ma'am. An' mostly a shot wasted is worse than none at all. I'm here to offer you one that bites hard at that distance, 'though I can't say I generally recommend it for ladies—it kicks powerful hard, heavy as it is."

"Answer my questions. Who are you?"

"A stranger, Ma'am; a pilgrim, seekin' what I can devour. But now it's nearer sixteen hundred," he suggested, lowering a hand to get the Sharp's from its sheath under his leg.

"That will do!" she warned. "The range which interests me is ten yards. You may rest them on your hat," she conceded.

He locked his fingers over his head and grinned. "Why, I'm a rollin' stone from Montanny, Ma'am. So far I've rolled into trouble all th' way, an' it looks like I'm still a-rollin'. I want to apologize for bustin' up your party—they've done faded."

" 'Done faded' never was born in Montana," she

retorted, suspicion glinting in her eyes. She lowered the gun until it rested on her knees, but its muzzle still covered Johnny.

"Neither was I, Ma'am," he replied, smiling. "I was born in Texas, an' grew up there. My greatest mistake was goin' north—but now I'm tryin' to wipe that out. It's a long trail, Ma'am; an' I've wasted a powerful lot of time."

"You shall waste some more; after that the speed of your departure will doubtless largely compensate you. How do I know you are telling the truth?"

"As to that, not meanin' no offense, I ain't none interested. An', Ma'am, neither are you. I might say, as a general proposition, that no stranger has any business askin' me personal questions; an', also, that in such cases I reserve th' right to lie as much as I please, 'though I ain't admittin' that I'm doin' it here. Pepper warned me that somethin' was wrong, which it was by several hundred yards—an', Ma'am, shootin' across a valley is shore deceivin'. Also I saw that one young lady was goin' to mix up serious with three growed-up men—pretty craggy individuals, from what I know of punchers. That was not th' right thing for a lady to do—but I'm allus with th' under dog, I'm sorry to say, so I horned in an' offered you a gun that would fill them fellers with righteous indignation, homicidal yearnin's, an' a belief in miracles. I knowed they wouldn't get hurt at that distance—you see, there's little things like windage, trigger pull, an' others. But, Ma'am, th' sound of that lead an' th' noise of that gun shore would pester 'em. They'd get most amazin' curious, for men, an' look into it. An' when they found me with a gun on 'em they'd get more indignant than ever. Now, Ma'am, I've busted up yore party, which I had no right to do. If you wants them fellers right up close so you can look 'em over good an' ask 'em questions, say so, an' I'll go get 'em for you. I owe you that much. But I don't aim to be no party to a murder," he finished, smiling, and slowly and deliberately lowered his hands and rested them on his belt.

She was staring at him with blazing eyes, a look on

her white face such as he never had seen on a woman before; and he realized that never before had he seen an angry woman. His smile changed subtly. It softened, the cynicism faded from it and kindly lines crept in; and there was something in his eyes that never had been there before. He looked out across the valley, at the few cows, where there should have been so many in a valley like that. Then he gazed steadily at the point where the three horsemen had become lost to sight—and the smile gave way to a look hard and cold. Pepper moved, and Johnny drew a deep breath, squaring his shoulders in sudden resolution. Swinging from the saddle he walked slowly forward toward the threatening rifle muzzle, took the weapon from its owner's knees, lowered the hammer, and placed the gun against the rock at her side. Straightening up, he whistled softly. Pepper, advancing with mincing steps, shoved her velvety muzzle against his cheek and stopped. He swung into the saddle, wheeled the horse and rode around a nearby thicket, soon returning with a saddled SV pony, which he led to its owner. Mounting again, he backed Pepper away and, removing his sombrero, wheeled and sent the horse up the slope without a backward glance, sitting erect in the saddle as a figure of bronze until hidden by the crest and well down on the other side. Then he pulled suddenly at the reins with unthinking roughness and dashed at top speed to the left until the crest was again close at hand. With his head barely on a level with the top of the hill, he sat staring across the little valley at the point where the horsemen had disappeared; and there was a look on his face which, had they seen it, would have turned their conversation to subjects less trivial.

CHAPTER II

Bit by Bit

THE SUN was near the meridian when Johnny rode into Gunsight, a town which he took as a matter of course. They were all alike, he reflected. If it were not for the names they scarcely could be told apart—and it would have been just as well to have numbered them. A collection of shacks, with the overplayed brave names. The shack he was riding for was the "Palace," which only rubbed it in. Out of a hundred towns, seventy-five would have their Palace saloon and fifty would have a Delmonico hotel. Dismounting before the door, he went in and saw the proprietor slowly arising from a chair, and he was the fattest man Johnny ever had seen. The visitor's unintentional stare started the conversation for him.

"Well, don't you like my looks?" bridled the proprietor.

Johnny's expression was one of injured innocence. "Why, I wasn't seein' you," he explained. "I was thinkin'—but now that you mention it, I don't see nothin' th' matter with your looks. Should there be?"

The other grunted something, becoming coherent

only when the words concerned business. "What's yourn?"

"A drink with you, an' some information."

"Th' drink goes; but th' information don't."

"I take it all back," soliloquized Johnny. "This town don't need a number; it don't even need a name. It's different. It's th' only one this side of Montanny where the barkeeper was hostile at th' start. I'm peaceful. My han's are up, palm out. If you won't give me information, will you tell me where I can eat an' sleep? Which of th' numerous hotels ain't as bad as th' rest of 'em?"

Davis Lee Beauregard Green slid a bottle across the bar, sent a glass spinning after it, leaned against the back bar and grinned. "Gunsight ain't impressin' you a hull lot?" he suggested.

"Why not? It's got all a man needs, which is why towns are made, ain't it?" Johnny tasted the liquor and downed it. "I allus size up a town by th' liquor it sells. I say Gunsight is a d—d sight better than I thought from a superficial examination."

Dave Green, wise in the psychology of the drinking type, decided that the stranger was not and never had been what he regarded as a drinking man; and even went so far in a quick, spontaneous flash of thought, as to tell himself that the stranger never had been drunk. Now, in his opinion, a hard-drinking, two-gun man was "bad;" but a coldly sober, real two-gun man was worse, although possibly less quarrelsome. He was certain that they lived longer. Dave was a good man with a short gun, despite his handicap; but a stirring warning instinct had told him that this stranger was the best who ever had entered his place. This impression came, was recognized, tabbed, and shoved back in his memory, all in a mechanical way. It was too plain to be overlooked by a man who, perhaps without realizing it, studied humanity, although he could not lay a finger on a single thing and call it by name.

Dave put the bottle back and washed the glass. "Well," he remarked, "every man sizes things up accordin' to his own way of thinkin', which is why there are so many different opinions about th' same thing." Letting this ponderous nugget sink in, he continued: "I reckon th' bottom of it all is a man's wants. You want good liquor, so a town's good, or bad. Which is as good a way as any other, for it suits you. But, speakin' about eatin'-houses, there's a hotel just around th' corner. It's th' only one in town. It butts up agin' th' corner of my rear wall. Further than sayin' I've et there, I got no remarks to make. I cook my own, owin' to th' pressure of business, an' choice."

"It ain't run by no woman, is it?" asked Johnny.

"No; why?"

Johnny grinned. "I'm ridin' clear of wimmin. It was wimmin that sent me roamin' over th' face of th' earth, a wanderer. My friends all got married, an'—oh, well, I drifted. Th' first section I come to where there ain't none, I'll tie fast; an' this country looks like a snubbin' post, to me."

"You lose," chuckled Dave. "There's one down here, an' some folks think she's considerable. What's more, she's lookin' for a good man to run her dad's ranch, an' get an outfit together, as will stay put. But if you don't like 'em, that loses th' job for you. An' I reckon yo're right lucky at that."

"Shore; I know th' kind of a 'good' man they want," said Johnny, reminiscently. " 'Good,' meanin' habits only. A man that don't smoke, chew, drink, cuss, get mad, or keep his hat on in th' house. Losin' th' job ain't bendin' my shoulders. I ain't lookin' for work; I'm dodgin' it. Goin' to loaf till my money peters out, which won't be soon. You'd be surprised if you knowed how many people between here an' Montanny think they can play poker. Just now I'm a eddicator. I'm peddlin' knowledge to th' ignorant, an' I ain't no gambler, at that!"

Dave chuckled. "There's some around here, too. Now, me; I'm different. I can't play, an' I know it; but, of course, I'll set in, just for th' excitement of it, once in a while, if there ain't nothin' else to do. Come to think of it, I got a deck of cards around here some'rs, right now."

The rear door opened and closed. Johnny looked up and saw the worst-looking tramp of his experience. The newcomer picked up a sand-box cuspidor and started with it for the street.

"Hi, stranger!" called Johnny. "Ain't that dusty work?"

The tramp stiffened. He hardly could believe his ears. The tones which had assailed them were so spontaneously friendly that for a moment he was stunned. It had been a long time since he had been hailed like that—far too long a time. He turned his head slowly and looked and believed, for the grin which met his eyes was as sincere as the voice. It made him honest in his reply.

"No," he said, "this here's sand."

"But ain't yore throat dusty?"

Two-Spot put the box down. "Seems like it allus is. If these boxes *get* dusty, I'll know how it come about, me bendin' over 'em like I do, an' breathin' on 'em."

Johnny laughed. "I take it we're all dusty." He turned to Dave. "Got three left?"

Two-Spot walked up to the bar. Usually he sidled. He picked up his glass and held it up to the light, and drank it in three swallows. Usually it was one gulp. Wiping his lips on a sleeve, he pushed back the glass, dug down into a pocket and brought up a silver dollar, which he tossed onto the bar. "Fill 'em again, Dave," he said, quietly.

At this Dave's slowly accumulating wonder leaped. He looked at the coin and from it to Two-Spot. Sensing the situation, Johnny pushed it farther along toward the proprietor. "Our friend is right, Dave," he said, "two *is* company. Make mine th' same."

Two-Spot put down his empty glass and grinned. "I'll now go on from where I was interrupted, Gents," and, picking up the box, went toward the door. As he was about to pass through he saw Pepper, and he stopped. "Good, Lord!" he muttered. "What a hoss! I've seen passels of hosses, but never one like that. Midnight her name oughter be, or Thunderbolt." He turned. "Stranger, what name do you call that hoss?"

Johnny looked around. "That's Pepper."

Two-Spot grinned. "Did you see that?" he demanded, tilting the box until the sand ran out. "Did you *see* it? She knows her name like a child. Well, it's a good name—a fair name," he hedged. "But, shucks! There ain't *no* name fit for that hoss! How fur has she come today?"

"Near forty miles," answered Johnny.

"I say it ag'in—there ain't *no* name fit for that hoss. She looks like she come five," and he passed out.

"Don't mind him," said Dave. "But where did he git that dollar? Steal it? Find it? Reckon he found it. I near dropped dead. Pore devil—he come here last winter an' walks in, cleans my boxes an' sweeps. Then he goes 'round to th' hotel an' mops an' cleans th' pans better than they ever was before. He was so handy an' useful that we let him stay. An' I've never seen him more than half drunk—it's amazin' th' liquor he can hold."

"Sleep here?"

"No; an' nobody knows where he does sleep. He's cunnin' as a fox, an' fooled 'em every time. But wherever it is, it's dry."

Johnny produced a Sharp's single-shot cartridge. "Where can I get some of these Specials?" he asked.

Dave looked at it. " '.45-120-550'—you won't get none of 'em down in this country."

"Post office in town?"

"Not yet. Th' nearest is Rawlins, thirty mile east, with th' worst trail a man ever rode. Th' next is Highbank, forty mile south. We use that, for th' trail's good. We get mail about twice a month. Th' Bar H an' th' Triangle take turns at it."

"Then I'll write for some of these after I feed. I'll tell 'em to send 'em to you, at Highbank. What name will I give?"

"Dave Green, Highbank-Gunsight mail. But you better write before you eat. This is goin' away day, an' th' Bar H will be in any minute now."

Johnny arose. "Not before I eat. I ain't had nothin' since daybreak, an' it's afternoon now. I hate letter writin'; an' if I don't eat soon I'll get thin."

"Then don't eat—'though I wasn't thinkin' of you when I spoke," growled Dave. "Wish I was in danger of gettin' thin."

"What you care?" demanded Johnny. "Yo're healthy, an' yore job don't call for a man bein' light."

"That's th' way you fellers talk," said Dave. "I'm short-winded, I'm in my own way, an' the joke of th' country. I can't ride a hoss—why, cuss it, I can't even get a gun out quick enough to get a hop-toad before he's moved twenty feet!"

"Pullin' a gun has its advantages, I admits," replied Johnny, who had his own ideas about Dave's ability in that line. Dave, he thought, could get a gun out quick enough for the average need—being a bartender, and still alive, was proof enough of that. He walked toward the door. "If you was to get a big hoss—a single-footer, you could ride, all right."

He went around and entered the hotel, mentally numbering it. Arranging for a week's board and bed for himself and Pepper, he hurried out to the wash bench just outside the dining-room door, where he found two tin basins, a bucket of water, a cake of yellow soap, a towel, and two men using them all. Taking his turn he in turn followed them into the dining-room and chose the fourth and last table, which was next to a window. The meal was better than he had expected but, hungry as he was, he did not eat as hurriedly as was his habit. Fragments of the conversation of the two punchers in the corner reached and interested him. It had to do with the SV ranch, as near as he could judge, and helped him to build the skeleton upon which he hoped to hang a body by dint of investigation and questioning. The episode of that morning had occurred on the SV ranch if the brands on the cattle he had seen meant anything. The woman's name was Arnold, and she had a father and a brother, the latter a boy. There was a fragment about "th' Doc," but just what it was he did not hear, except that it was coupled to the Bar H. Also, something was afoot, but it was so cautiously mentioned that he gained no information about it. Finishing before him, the two men went out, and soon rode past the window, mounted on Triangle horses.

He rattled his cup and ordered it refilled, and when the waiter slouched back with it, Johnny slid a perfectly good cigar across the table and waved his hand. "Sit down, an' smoke. You ought to rest while you got th' chance."

The waiter lost some of his slouch and obeyed, nodding his thanks. "Are you punchin'?" he asked.

"When I'm broke," answered Johnny. "Just now I'm ridin' around lookin' at th' scenery. Never knowed we had any out here till I heard some Easterners goin' mad about it. I've been tryin' to find it ever since. But, anyhow, punchin' is shore monotonous."

"If you can show me anythin' monotoner than *this* job, I'll eat it," growled the waiter. "It's hell on wheels for me."

"Oh, this whole range is monotonous," grunted Johnny. "Reckon nothin' interestin' has happened down here since Moses got lost. But there's one thing I like about it—there ain't no woman in thirty miles."

"You foller Clear River into Green Valley, which is SV, an' you'll change yore mind," chuckled the waiter. "She'll chase you off, too."

"I'll be cussed. An' she's suspicious of strangers?"

"Don't put no limit on it like that; she's suspicious of everythin' that wears pants."

"How's that?"

"Well, her cows has been wanderin' off, lookin' for better grass, I reckon, an' she thinks they're bein' drove."

Johnny pictured the valley, but hid his smile. "Oh, well; you can't blame the cows. They'll find th' best. Any ranches 'round here run by men?"

"Shore; three of 'em. There's th' Bar H, an' th' Triangle, an' over west is th' Double X, but it's ranch-house is so fur from here that it's a sort of outsider. It's th' biggest, th' Bar H is next, an' then comes th' Triangle. Th' Triangle don't hardly count, neither, 'though it's close by."

"What about th' SV you mentioned? An' what's yore name?"

"My name's George. Th' SV has gone to th' dogs since it was sold. It ain't a ranch no more. Of course, it's got range, an' water, an' some cows, an' a couple of buildin's—but it ain't got no outfit. Old Arnold, his gal, an' his kid—all tenderfeet—are tryin' to run it."

"But they've got to have punchers," objected Johnny.

"They can't keep 'em, though I ain't sayin' why," replied George mysteriously.

"Does th' Doc own th' Bar H?" asked Johnny.

"Lord, no! It owns him—but, say; you'll have to excuse me. I got work to do. See you at supper. So long."

Johnny left and rode back the way he had come that morning, lost in meditation. Reaching the rim of the valley he looked down over the rolling expanse of vivid green, here and there broken by shallow draws, with their brush and trees. He noticed an irregular circle of posts just south of him and close to the river. Experience told him what they meant, and he frowned. Here was a discordant note—that enclosure, small as it was, was a thing sinister, malevolent, to him almost possessing a personality. Turning from the quicksands he sat and gazed at the nest of rocks below him until Pepper, well trained though she was, became restless and thought it time to move. Stirring, he smiled and pressed a knee against her and as he rode away he shook his head. "Yes, girl, I'm still a-rollin'—an' I don't know where to."

After supper he talked with George until they heard the creaking of wheels and harness. Looking up they saw four heavy horses slowly passing the window, followed by a huge, covered wagon with great, heavy wheels having four-inch tires. A grizzled, whiskered, weather-beaten patriarch handled the lines and talked to his horses as though they were children.

"Now I got to make a new fire an' cook more grub," growled George, arising. "Why can't he get here in time for supper? He's allus late, goin' an' comin'."

"Who is he, an' where's he from?"

"Ol' Buffaler Wheatley from Highbank. He's goin' up to Juniper an' Sherman."

"He come from Highbank today?" demanded Johnny, surprised.

"Shore—an' he must 'a' come slow."

"Slow? Forty miles with *that* in a day, an' he come *slow*?" retorted Johnny. "He was lucky to get here before midnight. If you'd 'a' done what that old feller has today, you'd not think much of anybody as wanted you on hand at supper time."

"Mebby yo're right," conceded George, dubiously, as he went into the kitchen.

Johnny arose and went out to the shed where the driver was flexing his muscles. "Howd'y," he said. "Got th' waggin where you want it?"

"Howd'y, friend," replied Buffalo, looking out from under bushy brows. "I reckon so. 'Most any place'll do. Ain't nothin' 'round'll scratch th' polish off it," he grinned.

Johnny laughed and began unhitching the tired, patient horses, and his deft fingers had it done before Buffalo had any more than started. "Fine hosses," he complimented, slapping the big gray at his side. "You must treat 'em well."

"I do," said Buffalo. "I may abuse myself, sometimes, but not these here fellers. They'll pull all day, an' are as gentle as kittens."

"How do you find freightin'?" asked Johnny, leading his pair into the shed.

"Pickin' up, an' pickin' fast," answered Buffalo, following with the second team. "It's gettin' too much for one old man an' this waggin. An' top of that I got th' mail contract I been askin' for for years. So I got to put on another waggin an' make th' trip every week 'stead of only when th' freight piles up enough to make it worth while. Reckon I'll break my boy in on th' new waggin."

"I'll leave th' feedin' to you," said Johnny, leaning against the wall. "You know what they need."

"All right, friend; much obliged to you. I just let 'em eat all th' hay they can hold an' give 'em their measures of oats. I have to carry them with me—can't get none away from Highbank, everythin' up here bein' grass fed."

"I feed oats when I can get 'em," replied Johnny. "I allus reckon a corn-fed hoss has more bottom."

"Shore has—if they're that kind," agreed Buffalo.

"Travel th' same way all th' time?"

"Yes. I won't gain nothin' goin' t'other way 'round," answered Buffalo, busy with his pets. "You see I allus come north loaded. Th' first stop, after here, is Juniper, where I loses part of th' load. That's thirty miles from here, an' th' road's good. Then I cross over to Sherman, lose th' rest of th' load, an' come back from there light— it's fifty mile of hard travelin'. Goin' like I do I has th' good, short haul with th' heavy load; comin' back I have a light waggin on th' long, mean haul. If I went to Sherman first, things would just be turned 'round."

"What do you do when you have passengers for Sherman?"

"Don't want none!" snorted Buffalo. "Wouldn't carry 'em to Sherman, anyhow. Anybody with sense that can sit a hoss wouldn't crawl along with me in th' heat an' dust on that jouncin' seat. But sometimes I has a tender-foot to nurse, consarn 'em. They ask so many fool questions I near go *loco*. But they pays me well for it, you bet!"

"Anythin' else I can give you a hand with?" asked Johnny, following the old man out of the shed.

"No, thankee; I'm all done. Th' only man that can give me a hand now is that scamp, George. I'm goin' in to eat, friend. Got to be up an' be on my way before th' sun comes up. I get th' cool of th' mornin' for my team, an' give 'em a longer rest when she gets hot. If you see Jim Fanning, tell him I'm buyin' hides as a side line now. I pays spot cash for 'em, same price as Ol' Saunders would pay, less th' freight. He has quit th' business an' went to live with his married da'ter, ol' fool!"

"Fanning sell hides?"

"No; I just want him to know so he can tell th' Bar H an' th' Triangle an' mebby th' Double X. I want to have a good load goin' back from here. There ain't no profit in goin' all th' way back with an empty waggin. Well, good night, friend! I'm much obliged to you."

"That's all right," smiled Johnny. "I'll tell him. Good night; an' good luck!" he added as an afterthought, and then drifted around to the saloon, where he found several men at the bar.

Dave performed the introductions, and added: "Nelson, here, says he ain't goin' back punchin' cows as long as his money lasts. He's a travelin' eddicator in th' innercent game of draw—or was it studhoss, Nelson?"

"Draw is closer to my heart," laughed Johnny. "My friend, Tex, told me I might learn draw if I lived long enough; but I'd have to have a pack of cards buried with me an' practice in th' other world if I aimed to learn studhoss."

"It grieves me to see a young man wastin' his time in idleness," said Ben Dailey, the storekeeper. "Th' devil is allus lookin' for holts. Young men should keep workin'. Might I inquire if you feel like indulgin' in a little game of draw? You'll find us rusty, though."

"We don't play oftener than every night, an' some afternoons," said Fanning.

"I'm a little scared when a man says he's rusty," replied Johnny. "But I reckon I might as well lose tonight as later. I hope Dave is too busy to cut in—he said he don't know *nothin'* about it."

"Dave's still cuttin' his teeth," chuckled Jim Fanning; "but he uses my silver to cut 'em on. When he learns th' game I'm goin' to drift out of town while I still got a cayuse."

Two punchers came stamping in and Dave nodded to them. "Here's yore victims; here's them infants from th' Double X. Boys, say 'Howd'y' to Mr. Nelson. Nelson, that tall, red-headed feller is Slim Hawkes; an' that bow-legged towhead is Tom Wilkes. They ain't been in here in three months, an' they've rid twenty miles to rob us."

"An' we might walk home," retorted Wilkes. "Let's lay th' dust before we starts anythin'. Nelson, yo're in bad company. This gang would rob a church. You want to get a kneehold an' hang onto th' pommel after *this* game starts. Here's how!"

As the game progressed the few newcomers who straggled in felt their interest grow. As each finished his drink, Dave would lean forward and whisper: "There's what I call a poker game. Four highwaymen playin' 'em close. To listen to 'em you'd think they never saw a card before."

Johnny was complaining. "Gents, I know I'm ignorant—but would you advise me to draw to a pair of treys? Shall I hold up an ace, or take three cards? I'll chance it; I never hold a sider. Gimme three."

"Ain't that just my luck," sighed Ben. "An' me with three of a kind."

A little later Johnny picked up another hand and frowned at it. "Well, seein' as I allus hold up a sider, I'll have two, this time."

Hoofbeats drummed up and stopped, and a voice was heard outside. Dave looked at the calendar. "Big Tom's a day ahead—he ain't due for his spree till pay-day. Hello, Huff! What you doin' so fur from home?"

"Hello, Dave! Hello, boys!" said the newcomer. "I feel purty good tonight. Just got word that McCullough wants two thousand head from us fellers up here. He'll be along with his reg'lar trail outfit in a few weeks. Sixteen men, a four-mule chuck waggin, an' nine saddle hosses to th' man. I'm sendin' word that I can give him a thousand head, an' th' Triangle is goin' to give him five hundred; so he'll want five hundred from th' Double X, which Slim an' Tom can tell Sherwood."

"Shore," growled Slim, and his ranch mate nodded.

"Goin' up to Dodge again?" queried Dailey.

"He didn't say," answered Big Tom. "Who's doin' the scalpin'?" he asked, going over to the table, where he gradually grew more restless as he watched.

"Some of these days, when I grows up," grinned Wilkes, "I'm goin' up th' trail with a herd, like a reg'lar cow-puncher. Dodge may be top-heavy with marshals, but I'd like to see it again, with money in my pockets."

Slim grunted. "Huh!" He looked over his hand, and

drawled: "Th' last time you went up you put on too many airs. Just because Cimarron let you play *segundo* once in a while when he went on ahead to size up th' water or some river we would have to cross, you got too puffed up. I'm aimin' to be th' second boss th' next trip, an' I'll hand you a few jobs that'll keep you out of mischief."

Big Tom watched the winner rake in the chips and could stand it no longer. "Say," he growled, "anybody gettin' tired, an' want to drop out?"

Dailey looked up. "I only won two dollars in two hours, an' I got some work to do. Everybody bein' willin', I'll go out an' bury my winnin's."

Big Tom took his place. "I'm shore of one thing: I can't lose th' ranch, for I don't own it."

A round or two had been played when Big Tom drew his first openers. Johnny raised it and cards were drawn. After it had gone around twice, the others dropped out. Big Tom raised and Johnny helped it along. The betting became stiffer and Big Tom laughed. "I hope you keep on boostin' her."

"You can't get me out of this pot with dynamite," replied Johnny, pushing out a raise.

Big Tom's gun was out before he left his seat. His chair crashed backward and he leaned over the table. "Meanin'?" he snarled.

Johnny, surprised, kept his hand on the chips. "What I said," he answered, evenly.

"Tom!" yelled Dave. "He don't mean nothin'! He's a stranger down here."

Big Tom's scowl faded at the words. "I reckon I was hasty, Nelson," he said.

Johnny spoke slowly, his voice metallic. "You was so hasty you come near never gettin' over it. Put down th' gun."

"I'm a mite touchy at——"

"If you has anythin' to say, put—down—that—gun.

"No offense?"

"For th' third time: Put—down—that—gun."

Big Tom shook his head and appeared to be genuinely sorry. He slid the gun back and picked up his chair. "You raised?"

"I did. I advise you to call—and end it."

"She's called. Five little hearts," said Big Tom, lying down his cards.

"They're hasty, too. Queen full, count 'em. Let's liquor."

The foreman paused in indecision. "Nelson——"

"We all get touchy," interrupted Johnny, scraping in the winnings. "Will you drink with me?"

"I'll take the same," said Big Tom, and he bought the next round, nodded his good night and went out.

Johnny turned to Dave. "Will you oblige me by tellin' me what Mr. Huff got huffy about?"

Dave hesitated, but Slim Hawkes laughed and answered for him, his slow drawl enhancing the humor of his tale, and wrinkles playing about his eyes and lips told of the enjoyment the picture gave to him. "Clear River crossed our range, flowed through Little Canyon, made a big bend on th' Bar H, passed out of East Canyon, an' flowed down the middle of th' SV. Three years ago a piece of Little Canyon busted loose an' slid down, blockin' th' river, which backed up, gettin' higher an' higher, an' began to cut through its bank about three miles above. Big Tom got busy, *pronto*. He sends for a box of dynamite, sticks it around in th' *débris* an' let's her go—*all* of it. When th' earthquake stopped there was a second one in th' dust an' smoke—we all thought it was a delayed charge. It wasn't. It was a section of th' canyon wall, near a hundred feet long an' almost two hundred feet high. There was a shale fault runnin' down from th' top, back about forty feet. Everythin' in front of that was jarred loose an' slid. Th' canyon was choked so hard an' fast that it won't never get open again. Clear River kept right on a-cuttin', an' it now flows on th' other side of Pine Mountain, which means th' Bar H ain't got no water of its own, except a few muddy holes south an' west of th' ranch buildings. That's why he's touchy. But that's a long speech, an' a dry one. Let's all liquor again."

CHAPTER III

An Objection

JOHNNY LOOKED forward eagerly to the coming of the out-fits for their monthly celebration, and he was not certain that he would not make enemies before the night was over, which impelled him to visit the Bar H and the Tri-angle while he would be welcome. He had familiarized himself with the SV valley and the country close to the town. Therefore he mounted Pepper after an early breakfast and rode south, passing the shack occupied by the Doc, about two miles south of Gunsight. The Doc was squatting on SV land, had a small corral, a hitching post, and a well. Johnny stopped at the latter and had a drink while he mentally photographed everything in the immediate vicinity. When he started on again he had the choice of two trails. One wound up over Pine Moun-tain, a high, wooded hill, and was the more direct route to the Bar H; the other followed the river bed around the base of the mountain, and was the trail used by the Tri-angle. Deciding on the shorter, if more difficult route, he gave Pepper her head and started up the slope. The trail was fair, following, as it did, the line of least resistance and threading through rocky defiles, rocky clefts, and skirting steep walls.

Riding down on the south side he found himself in a deep ravine and when he left it he came to the old bed of the river, and a grin came to his face as he pictured the episode of the dynamiting. Following the dried-up bed he entered East Canyon and found its north wall to be perpendicular and remarkably smooth; the other side sloped more, showed great errosion and was scored by clefts and wooded defiles running far back. Emerging from the canyon he rode over a hilly, rolling range and some time later recrossed the old river bed and arrived at the Bar H ranchhouses. Two men were in sight, one mending riding gear and the other had just fixed the fence around the wall. They nodded, and he asked for Big Tom.

"He's around some'rs," said "Squint" Farrell, whose name had been well bestowed.

"Git off an' set down," invited the other. "He won't be long. Ridin' fur?"

"Gunsight," answered Johnny.

Bill Fraser's eyes were on Pepper. "Ever think of swappin' cayuses?" he asked.

"Not this one," smiled Johnny. "She's too dumb— won't learn nothin'. But I had her since she could stand up, an' she's rapid for short distances."

"Meanin' several short distances hooked together," suggested Squint. "I can see she's dumb—it's writ all over her."

"I don't care," said Fraser. "I'm a great hand with th' dumb ones. I'm doin' wonders with Squint."

"Shore," grunted Squint. "He owes me so much money I got to do what he says. Here comes Tom, now. He's some touchy this mornin'. Must 'a had a session with them poker deacons last night."

"He holds 'em too long," chuckled Fraser. "He figgers that if three little deuces are worth a dollar, why two aces an' two kings is worth a hull lot more."

"Does sound reasonable," said Squint, "three deuces makin' only six, an' th' others makin'—a king is thirteen—

twenty-six, an' two more is twenty-eight. That the way you been figgerin' all these years, Tom?"

Big Tom smiled. "Howd'y, Nelson. What brings you down here so early?"

"Curiosity, mostly," answered Johnny. "That an' not havin' nothin' to do. An' I'm grievin' about them two dollars Dailey took away from me last night."

"Nobody that wiggles away from Dailey an' only leaves two dollars behind can associate with me steady," objected Fraser. "I got my rights."

"Mebby we'll see him get two more tonight," said Squint. "We're ridin' in with money in our pockets."

"An' you'll travel light returnin'," said Big Tom.

"An' most amazin' noisy," laughed Squint.

After a little more idle conversation Johnny pulled his hat more firmly down on his head. "Well, I just thought I'd drop in an' say hello. Any place else to go?"

"Don't be in no hurry," said Big Tom. "But if yo're set, you might get acquainted with th' Triangle—it's only an hour's ride. They'll be in town, too, tonight."

Johnny nodded all around and rode off the way they pointed. He looked carefully at the brands of the cattle he passed, stopped at the Triangle for a drink and a few minutes' conversation with a puncher who was saddling a fresh horse and returned by the trail around the eastern end of Pine Mountain, to Gunsight, where he spent the afternoon playing seven-up with Dave, with indifferent success.

Night had scarcely fallen when a whooping down the trail heralded the approach of an outfit. It was from the Triangle and they stamped in eagerly. Dailey, Fanning, and several more of the townsfolk followed them, and it was not long before liquor and cards vied with each other for the honors of the evening.

Johnny, declining cards, and going easy with the liquor, watched the games and became better acquainted all around.

"I'm losin' my holt," mourned Dailey. "Reckon I'm sick."

"When you get so sick you can't move," grunted Hank

Lewis, foreman of the Triangle, "I'm comin' in an' take yore clothes. You'll be left like you was born."

"You ain't got a chance, Hank," asserted Fanning. "I live next door to him, an' I'll get him first. Here's a little more to freeze him out."

"No man with three jacks ought to sit in this here game at all," muttered Gardner, sorrowfully, "But I'm trailin'."

"Now that I know what Sam's got, I'll trail, too," grinned George Lang. "Here comes Huff an' his angels."

The Bar H arrived tempestuously. Big Tom's voice could be heard above the noise and he was the first to enter, followed closely by his outfit. He nodded to the crowd and ordered drinks all around. Exchanging a few words with Dave, he approached Johnny.

"Reckon you can hold onto that last pot, Nelson?" he asked.

"I'll do my best," replied Johnny. "I'll have a better chance with Dailey out of our game."

"Let's make up another table," said Big Tom, looking around.

Fraser joined them, followed by Lefty Carson. "I'm after more'n two dollars," he laughed. "Dailey allus did play a kid's game."

"Somebody else is pickin' on me," came Dailey's voice. "If that Fraser'll come in some evenin' I'll try to suit him. Hey, Dave! What's th' matter? Somebody tie you to th' bar?"

Dave's retort was not what fiction attributes to a fat man. He was not genial; he was stirred up. "You go hang! I'm so cussed busy I can't see. *I* ain't no jack rabbit!"

"He says so hisself!" shouted Squint, roaring with laughter. "If I ever sees a jack rabbit lookin' like Dave, I'll give him all th' trail!"

"Hey, Two-Spot!" yelled Dave, with a voice which shook the bottles. "He's allus around when there's nobody here—but when there's a crowd to be waited on, he flits. Hey! Two-Spot!"

Dahlgren held his hand over the bar. "Gimme a glass

of liquor, Dave, an' I'll trap him," he laughed, looking at his foreman, who had forgotten all about cards and was drinking steadily.

Dave looked at him, grinned, and complied. Dahlgren turned, glass held up. "'Order, Gents! Order! Less noise! I'm goin' to trap a bum-bum an' have him on show right before you for two bits a head."

The crowd took it as a wager and would not let him explain. "All right, you coyotes; let it go that way, then: Two bits apiece that I do," he cried, and, the cynosure of all eyes, pranced to the door where he placed the glass on the sill and then lay down along the wall, his hand raised to grasp his quarry. Laughing, he faced the crowd. "They are 'lusive animals, Gents; but they can't—oh! ho!—resist th' enticin' smell of——"

Another roar went up as a hand stole around the glass and whisked it from sight. All oblivious to this, Dahlgren took the shout as a tribute to his humor, and when he could be heard, continued: "They can't resist th' smell of liquor, Gents. When th' wary bum-bum scents this here glass of fire water," pointing—he stopped as another roar went up. "Well, I'm d—d!" he grunted. Scrambling to his feet, he plunged out into the night as Two-Spot entered the rear door, carrying the liquor at arm's length. Two-Spot stopped, gulped down the fiery liquid and, placing the glass on the bar, started to serve the card players, his face grave and serious.

The place was in an uproar when Dahlgren returned and he was met by a howling mob of creditors. Shaking his fist at Two-Spot he exhausted his change as he bobbed around in the crowd, got more from Dave and at last managed to pay off. Emitting a yell, he jumped for Two-Spot, grabbed him and began to manhandle him playfully. Others joined in and the sport grew fast and furious, rougher and rougher. Johnny, seeing how things stood, and thinking that Two-Spot was in danger of being hurt, plunged headfirst into the mass of merrymakers, grabbed Two-Spot and, at the first opportunity, threw him reeling toward the door. Leaping after him, he grasped the confused tramp, whispered: *"Vamoose!"*

and then yelled out: "I *can't*, huh? We'll *see*!" There was a flurry and Two-Spot shot out of the door as though he had left a bow. Johnny turned and faced the crowd. "Did you *hear* him?" he demanded. "I showed him if I could, or not. Blast his nerve, to talk like that to *me*!"

"Wish he'd said it to me," growled Big Tom, whose liquor was making him surly and uncertain. "I'd 'a' busted his cussed neck. This here country is gettin' too d—d independent. That's it—too independent. Th' Bar H runs this country, an' *I* run th' Bar H," he boasted, resting against the bar. "That's it, an' it's got to learn it. It's got to learn that th' Bar H runs this country, an' *I* run th' Bar H. Anybody say I don't?" he demanded, looking around.

Just at this auspicious occasion, Squint was unfortunate enough to step on the foot of a man who had little use for him and who, several times in the last few years, had been restrained only by force from carrying out his thinly veiled threats. Wolf Forbes, the deadliest man on the Bar H, more than disliked Squint, and only their common interests had averted bloodshed. Now he snarled and reached for his gun, but found it held in the holster by Little Tom Carney, who hung to Forbes' arm like a leech until others came to his aid and succeeded in taking the killing edge from Wolf's anger.

Wolf struggled, gradually getting free. "I don't want him *now*," he panted. "Let go of me! I'll get him when he's sober." He wrestled free and went over to his foreman. "You heard what I said?" he demanded. "There won't be no interference this time!"

Big Tom rocked back on his heels and scowled down at his gunman. "I heard you," he replied. "An' I says yo're makin' a fool of yoreself. *I*'m runnin' this ranch, an' I'm tellin' you that I'll see that he is *good* an' sober an' gets an even break, if it ever comes to gunplay between you two. Take my advice, an' forget about it." He pushed Forbes to one side and waved his arm. "Everybody have a drink with Big Tom Huff, th' boss of th' Bar H. Set 'em out, Dave."

They responded, but the soberer heads began to feel uneasy. Dave looked at Dailey, who exchanged glances with him; and at Johnny who, lounging against the farther wall near the card players, was missing nothing. Johnny allowed a faint smile to show, and winked at the proprietor, a knowing, significant wink. If it was meant to bring ease to Dave's troubled mind, it failed utterly. Worse than that, it acted the other way.

"D—n it!" thought Dave. "He's sober as a hoss an' cold as h—l!" which anomaly did not strike Dave's too-busy mind. "Is he aimin' to get Huff? Is he nursin' last night's play? Here I was hopin' none of th' Double X would ride in, an' Trouble was campin' under my fat nose all th' time! H—l will shore pop at the first shot—they'll shoot him to pieces, an' no tellin' who else!"

The card game died gradually and the players nearest the crowd shoved their chairs back. Dave noticed it and shook his head imploringly, trying by sheer willpower to force them back to the game. He failed, and his fears looked to be justified. Big Tom, turning ponderously, looked at them and then stared as their strange inactivity slowly impressed itself on his befuddled mind.

"Go on an' play!" he roared. "I run th' Bar H—an' Bar H runs th' country."

Dave leaped into the breach. "They can't. Dailey's got all th' money."

"Dailey's got—Ha! Ha! Ha!" roared Big Tom. "He's th' ol' fox. Goin' to shake han's with th' ol' fox!" He weaved across the floor and shook Dailey's hypocritical hand. "An' he's got Nelson's two pesos! Me an' Nelson's goin' to play a two-hand game for th' limit—an' th' winner'll tangle up with Dailey."

That plan did not suit Dave at all. He refilled a glass and slid it across the bar. "Hey, Tom!" he called. "Hey, *Tom!*" As the foreman turned clumsily and stared at him, Dave held up the glass. "I never thought you was so stuck up as to ask th' boys to drink with you, an' then throw 'em like that!"

"Who's stuck up?"

"Then why didn't you drink with 'em?" demanded Dave, severely.

Huff looked at him and lurched forward. "Beg boys'

pardon. I'm with th' boys. I allus drink with th' boys, an' I ain't stuck up!" He gulped the liquor and, spreading his feet, leaned against the bar. "Th' Bar H runs this country, an' *I* run th' Bar H. I'll learn 'em, too!" He threw off two of his men who tried to quiet him, fearing he would say too much. "I'm all right," he assured them. "I'll learn 'em," he continued. "There's that minx on th' SV. I'll learn her, too. I've been layin' low; but I'll learn her. I'm not stuck up; but *she* is. First night I called she tried to sneak out an' leave me holdin' th' sack. But I showed her who was runnin' this country. She's a wiry minx, but I kissed——"

"That'll do!" snapped Johnny, the words sounding like the crack of a whip. He leaned forward, away from the wall, his hands hanging limply at his sides. The crowd jumped, and Dave's heart was severely taxed. "I don't know th' woman, but I objects. The Bar H may run this country, an' you may run th' Bar H; but if I hears any more about wimmin I'll take th' job of runnin' you, an' th' Bar H, an th' country besides, if I has to! I've got some rights an' I ain't goin' to have my evenin' spoiled by wimmin! An' that goes as she lays!"

Big Tom had pushed away from the bar and swung around unsteadily. He blinked, and focused his eyes on the man who had interrupted him, and who spoke about running him. Steadily the meaning of the words hammered at the liquor-paralyzed brain cells, and at last was recognized and understood. His blood-red face wrinkled like the muzzle of an angry dog and the red eyes blazed with murder. Memory tried to inflame him further, and succeeded. He snarled an oath and reached for his gun.

There was a flash, a roar, and a cloud of smoke at Johnny's hip and before the crowd could move they were facing two guns, from one of which trailed a thin wisp of smoke. Big Tom, holding his benumbed hand against his body, looked from it to his gun, which slowly ceased sliding and came to a stop on the floor at the other end of the bar. He appeared to be stupefied.

"I didn't touch him!" snapped Johnny. "I hit his gun.

You all saw him draw first. I'm aimin' to make this personal between him an' me—an' so far's *I'm* concerned, it's over now. But if anybody has any objections, I'll hear 'em." Receiving no reply, he continued, looking out of the corner of his eye at the Bar H foreman:

"Tom, I don't aim to do you no injury, an' you can palaver all you wants, an' have all th' fun you wants, regardless. That is yore right. But I've got rights, too. An' so has all th' boys. An' we ain't goin' to hear nobody talk about wimmin. Wimmin is barred, all th' way to th' ace. I ain't goin' to listen about 'em, at all. They lost me th' best job I ever had, on the best ranch I ever saw. They drove me clean out of Montanny, to h——l an' gone. All my troubles have been caused by wimmin—an' you hear me shout that there ain't goin' to be no palaverin' about 'em where I got to hear it. That's flat; an' I got two six-guns that says it is. I ain't holdin' no grudge ag'in' you— no more'n yo're holdin' ag'in' me for my mistake last night. We all of us make 'em, not meanin' to.

"This is a man's town, a man's saloon, an' we're all of us men. We ain't goin' to be follered around by no wimmin in talk or otherwise. All in favor of barrin' wimmin, have a drink with me."

The invitation was accepted, and Dave followed it by a treat on the house. Then he mopped his head and wearily let his hands hang down at his side. He looked at Johnny and heaved a sigh. "D——d if you ain't a he-wizard!" he muttered. "A reg'lar sheep-herder!"

Johnny walked over, picked up the gun and handed it to its owner, slapping him on the back at the same time. "Here, Ol' Timer," he grinned, "take yore gun. She's a beauty an' ain't hurt a bit. Don't it beat all how me an you get all mixed up without meanin' to? I says it's funny—cussed if it ain't!"

Big Tom fumbled at the holster, slid the gun into it, and a grin crawled across his face. "Seems like we *are* allus buttin' our fool heads together," he replied. "I'm with you, Nelson. I'm with th' boys. Th' h——l with wimmin. They're barred, an' I won't listen about 'em. We're all men—ain't we, boys?"

"I reckon so," said Dave. He motioned to Squint and Fraser, nodding at Big Tom, and then at the door.

"Hey, Tom," called Fraser, "let's go home!"

"Won't—won't go home!" objected Big Tom, lurching forward. Reaching a chair in a corner he fell into it and in a few minutes was snoring sonorously.

Dave slid his elbow on the bar and rested his head in his hand. His pose bespoke great weariness. He looked at Johnny and shook his head in bewilderment. Johnny dragged a chair up to the unused second table, made a face at the fat proprietor, and piled up a sizable stack of coins in front of him.

"Any Bar H or Triangle *hombre* think they can get any of this?" he demanded, grinning. Four men thought so at the same time; and soon a third game was going on beside them.

Two-Spot poked his face up to the window again and looked in. Then he came in with an air of nonchalant confidence. Having seen all that had happened he believed the stormy weather to be over and if it wasn't, why Nelson seemed to be a friend of his, which sufficed. Dave slid him a partly filled bottle.

"Take it away and don't bother me," said the proprietor. 'I'm restin' up for th' next storm."

Two-Spot looked around. "You can go to sleep, Dave," he said. "I'll tend bar for you. There won't be no more. My friend over there is like his black cayuse—everythin' in this country is hid back in his dust." Turning away, he glanced quickly around, stuck out his tongue at the snoring Mr. Huff, put his bottle on a chair, sat down on another one, rested his feet on the recumbent form of Squint, who snored tenor to his boss' bass, and appeared to be well pleased with himself.

CHAPTER IV

With His Shadow Before Him

THE FOLLOWING morning was a quiet one in Gunsight and a stranger entering the town would have thought an epidemic of sleeping sickness had raided it, for yawns would have met him wherever he turned, and quite some headaches, the owners of which were short of temper and ugly in words. Dave dozed in his chair and his countenance was not a smiling one. He opened his eyes from time to time and fell asleep again with a scowl. Ben Dailey petulantly cursed everything his clumsy fingers bungled, and it can be said that clumsiness was not the normal condition of those digits. Art Fanning, whose hired man could run the routine affairs of the hotel as well without him, turned and tossed on his bed, finally getting up and poking his head out into the hall. Thinking he heard a noise in Nelson's room, he went to the door and hammered on it.

"House afire?" demanded Johnny, sleepily.

"No; but my head is," growled Fanning. "What you say about a bucket of roarin' strong coffee for us sinners?"

"I say yo're shoutin'. Comin' in?"

"Naw; I got to put on some clothes—an' find some

socks; these here are roundin' my heels an' climbin' up my laigs. I'm shore hard on socks," he growled. Leaning over the stairs he let out a bellow, "Hey, *George!*"

"I'll swear he heard you," said Johnny. "Mebby th' Bar H did, too. I never saw nobody go under so quick from liquor as Big Tom an' Squint."

"Hey, *George!*" yelled Fanning. "Oh, they was well ribbed before they hit town. Where th'——"

"What you want?" asked a voice from below.

"What you think I want!" retorted Fanning. "Yore gran'mother's aunt? You brew us a quart of coffee apiece, and brew it *my* way. I been bit by a snake."

"*I* don't want none of that paint," objected George, surprised.

"Who said you did?" snapped Fanning. "Who cares what *you* want? Nelson an' I'll handle that. Jump lively or I'll shoot down th' stairs."

"Shoot, if you wants. They don't belong to me. You can shoot down th' house, if you wants!" George slammed the door with vim. " 'Bit by a snake!' Bet it was a hydrophoby skunk. I'll brew him some coffee that'll stunt his growth, blast him!"

After breakfast, during which his companion found fault three times with everything in sight, Johnny wandered around and dropped in to see Jerry Poole, the harness-maker. Jerry's mouth tasted of burnt leather and alum from his night's indiscretions and he was so unendurably ugly that his visitor, twiddling his fingers at him, dodged a chunk of wax and departed, going into Dailey's.

"Hello, yoreself!" growled Dailey. He fumbled a ball of cord, dropped it, and kicked it through a window. "Now look what you done!" he yelled.

Johnny wheeled, slammed the door, and wandered to the Palace. Peering in, he assayed a test of Dave's hospitality.

"How do you feel?" he asked, loudly. "You was goin' too fast with th' juniper."

Dave straightened up, glared at him for a moment and found a more comfortable position. "You can go to

Juniper, or h—l, for all *I* care!" he grunted, and went off to sleep again.

Johnny leaned against the wall in momentary indecision. Hearing shuffling steps, he looked up to see Two-Spot rounding the corner. His face brightened. Here was someone with whom he could talk.

"Howd'y, Ol' Timer," he said, cheerily.

"Howd'y," grunted Two-Spot, and passed into the Palace. There was a noise within, a crashing of chair legs, and a thunder of words. Two-Spot came out again in undignified haste, crossed the street in three leaps and, turning, shook his unwashed fist at Dave, Johnny, Gunsight, and Creation, and told his opinion of them all.

Johnny shook his head and went around the corner. "Pepper's th' only company fit to 'sociate with; an' a ride won't do me no harm. Reckon I'll go down an' wander around that hill between th' SV an' th' Triangle. I ain't been south of that valley yet." He looked up at the sun. "Cussed if it ain't noon already!"

While Gunsight slept or swore, the day's work was going on as usual on the SV. Arnold had finished a hurried breakfast and ridden out to the north boundary of his ranch, at that point not more than a mile from the house, to continue setting posts for a fence. His boundary ran along the foot of hills heavily covered with brush and timber and he had grown tired of turning his cattle from them. Having found several rolls of wire left by the former owner of the SV, he determined to use them and make them go as far as they would. If they reached no farther than across the Devil's Gulch section and the creek, he would be repaid for his labor.

Reaching the gulch, he started to work and found the task disheartening. The ravine was rocky and boulder-strewn and he had difficulty in finding places for the posts. More than half of the morning had passed when he reached the bottom of the gulch and began to look for a place where his shovel would do more than scratch rock. After a fruitless search he abandoned the idea of digging and determined to build a cairn around the post. Taking a crowbar, he attacked the side of the gulch and sent several rocks rolling down. He was prying at a small boulder with indifferent success when the rock under it, giving way unexpectedly in a small slide of gravel and shale, freed the boulder suddenly and sent it crashing downward before he could get out of its way. It passed over his left leg and he dropped in agony, the leg broken below the knee. There was only one thing for him to do and he tried it, despite the excruciating pain. He had to drag himself to his horse and get into the saddle somehow. There was no way to call for help with any chance of being heard, for he did not pack a gun, believing himself safer without one. Not being able to use a six-gun well, he knew he would have no chance against men who used them as though they were an integral part of themselves; and to carry a weapon under those circumstances would be suicidal, for he then would become an armed man and have to assume the responsibilities of one.

After what seemed to be an age, he finally reached the top of the gulch, and saw his horse. Resting for a few minutes, he again dragged himself forward. The horse wheeled, pricked up its ears and stared at him in panicky fear. Snorting, the animal dashed away at top speed, the injured man calling after it in despair.

Back in the ranchhouse Margaret set the table for the noon meal. The dinner was nearly cooked when she glanced out of the window and saw her father's saddled horse standing at the corral. Going to the door, she called out that dinner was ready, well knowing her father's habit of not coming until the food was nearly spoiled. Her brother appeared from the tool shed and splashed with the wash basin, which he firmly believed was all that was necessary; but his sister, wise in the ways of boyhood, thought otherwise.

"Don't you dare to touch that towel," she warned. "If you want any dinner, wash your hands and face with soap—get them wet, anyway. Charley, for a ten-year-old boy you are hopeless!"

"An' for a twenty-year-old woman you are a nuisance," retorted Charley. "You women don't do nothing but find fault. Where's dad?"

"I don't know. When you have washed go tell him that dinner will be spoiled if he doesn't hurry."

Charley growled something, made a creditable effort at revealing his face, and departed to find his father. After a short but fruitless search, he returned and reported his failure. "Wonder where he went?" he demanded.

Margaret felt a chill of apprehension. Fears of this kind were not strangers to her, for she had felt many of them in the last two years. "Perhaps Lazy wandered home without him," she suggested. "It wouldn't be the first time. You would better saddle Pinto, and go see. Take Lazy with you."

"Go yourself."

"If you want any dinner you'd better be starting. The sooner you return, the sooner you will eat," she declared, with vexation. "You know that I cannot leave now."

"All right!" growled Charley. He slouched to the corral, saddled Pinto, caught Lazy, and loped toward the gulch.

Margaret's impatience gave way to a nameless fear as the minutes passed without sign of the "men." Going to the door again, she looked out, caught her breath, and then ran toward the corral. Her father, supported in the saddle by her brother, was riding slowly toward the house.

"Dad's broke his leg, Peggy; a big rock come down on it," said Charley, gloomily. "Help me get him into the house."

Between them they soon had him on his bed and Margaret told her brother to ride to Gunsight for the doctor.

"He won't come," groaned the injured man. "If he wouldn't come when you needed him, he won't come for me. Don't waste any time with Reed—I wouldn't have the blackguard if he would come! Charley, you'll have to make that ride to Highbank again. I hate to ask it of you, but there is nothing else to be done. Forty-five miles is too long a ride for Peggy, and besides, I need her here. Eat your dinner, sonny, and then start as soon as you can. I only hope Doctor Treadwell is sober enough to sit a horse when you get there."

"Gee, Dad! I can do it!" Charley asserted. "I did it before in five hours—I'll do it in less this time. Pinto can run all day, for she's a good little horse. Take good care of him, Sis; I'm off."

Grabbing a chunk of meat, and stuffing his pockets with bread, Charley dashed out of the house, climbed into the saddle, and rode off. "Come on, Pinto!" he pleaded. "It's goin' to be a long, hard wait for dad!"

Fording the river, he took the slope of the hill beyond at a walk and, reaching the crest, shot down the other side. Soon he came to a better trail, where the Triangle punchers rode when they went out to their north line. He had not gone far along it before he saw a horseman ahead of him, and when the rider turned and looked back, Charley felt a thrill of fear. It was Squint Farrell.

Squint was still going home from Gunsight and he was not yet sober. Worse than that, he was in a savage mood. When his outfit had started for the ranch, in the early, dark hours of the morning, he had fallen behind them, stupid with drink. At the end of one of his spells of mental oblivion he suddenly realized that he was alone, and urged his horse forward in hope of overtaking his friends. If left to itself the animal would have followed the trail to the ranch; but in his sodden frame of mind the rider knew better. "G'wan!" he ordered, pulling savagely on the reins, and barely managing to ride out the ensuing bucking. "Where you—goin'? I'm boss of this—here outfit an' I'm goin' home. I'll—point this here herd. G'wan!" The result was that when day broke and Squint aroused himself and looked around he had no idea of where he was. "It's further'n I reckoned," he muttered. "Don't care: I'm goin' to sleep." He dismounted, made the horse fast to a sapling, and soon was asleep. When he awakened he looked around in bewilderment and began to take note of his surroundings. Mounting his horse, he rode around and finally got his bearings. He was miles east of the ranchhouse and, with a savage burst of profanity, he turned the horse and started for home. As he crossed the SV-Triangle trail he heard the rapid drumming of a horse's hoofs and, drawing rein, waited to see who it was.

"Wonder if he got lost, too?" he muttered, and then the hard-riding horseman turned the corner and shot into the narrow defile. "Cussed if it ain't that brat from th' SV," he exclaimed, and became instantly though hazily suspicious. "Here, you!" he shouted. "What you doin' on this range? Where you goin' so fast?" He turned his horse across the narrow trail, effectually blocking it. "You speak up, an' don't give me none o' yore lip! Where you goin'?" He reached for the pinto's bridle, but missed it as Charley pulled the pony back on its haunches and backed away.

"I'm going to Highbank for the doctor; dad's broken his leg," answered the boy, trying to get past.

"Oh, are you?" snarled Squint. "Wish he'd busted his neck! Go 'round an' git on th' trail where you oughter; you can't cross this ranch."

"You don't belong to it," argued the boy. "This is the Triangle; and I haven't got time to go back now. Please, Mr. Farrell, let me past. I can't waste any time!"

"Can't you?" sneered Squint. "I say yo're goin' 'round th' way you should. G'wan, now! Turn 'round, an' d—d quick, before I does it for you! D—d brat!"

"Please, Mr. Farrell," pleaded the boy. "Let me past. Dad's suffering, and I've got to hurry."

" 'Please, Mr. Farrell,' " mimicked Squint, savagely. "You goin' to do what I say?" he demanded, drawing his Colt and waving it menacingly. "I got a notion not to let you go at all, no way. You turn that cayuse, an' move fast. Hear me?"

In his desperation Charley forgot his fear. There was only one way to save the precious miles, and he took it. The sides of the defile were steep, and studded with boulders, but he dug his heels into the pony's sides and sent him scrambling like a goat up the left-hand bank. He was ten feet above Squint before that surprised individual realized what had occurred; but with the realization came a burst of drunken rage. The heavy gun chopped down and flamed. Pinto rose straight up on his quivering hind legs, stood poised for an instant, and then crashed backward and rolled down to the trail, his rider barely having time to throw himself from the saddle.

"Now you can hoof it!" shouted Squint, brandishing the gun. "Next time you'll listen, an' do what yo're told. G'wan home, now!"

"D—n you!" blazed Charley, groping his way down the bank, and kneeling at the side of the little horse. Realizing what was at stake, he flung himself down on the dead pony and sobbed as though his heart would break.

Squint kneed his horse forward. "Don't you cuss me!" he warned. "Don't you do it, you brat! Serves you right: now you can hoof it!" He urged his horse into a lope and rode down the trail, arguing with himself, and finally burst into uproarious laughter at the trick he had played.

Johnny, riding as quietly as possible along the side of the big hill, just below and south of the SV-Triangle boundary, looking for rebranded cattle and other signs of range deviltry, pulled up short at the sound of a distant shot. It fitted in very nicely with his suspicious frame of mind and, thinking that he might catch some one redhanded in some of the things he had been searching for, he sent Pepper tearing down the slope and arrived at the trail shortly after Squint had departed. Rounding a turn, he saw the defile and the pitiful scene it held, and he pulled Pepper to her haunches and leaped from the saddle.

"Well, sonny," he said, cheerfully, "yo're in tough luck, but cryin'—" then he saw the wound in the horse and his eyes narrowed. "Who shot that cayuse?" he demanded.

Charley told him between sobs.

"Tell me all about it," demanded Johnny, but when the tale was half over he sprang into the saddle and started down the trail at top speed. "Stay there, sonny," he shouted over his shoulder. At the speed he was making he did not have to ride long before he caught sight of his quarry and he loosened his rope, shook it free, and leaned forward in the saddle.

Squint, still arguing, had a Colt in his upraised, waving hand, and was making so much noise with his mouth, and was so interested in and spellbound by his own eloquence that he failed to hear the rolling hoofs behind him until too late. As he turned, the sailing loop dropped over his upraised arm, tightened and pulled him from his horse which, slowing down, soon stopped and fell to grazing. Squint landed on his back, the gun exploding and flying from his hand, his sombrero going to the other side. Johnny came up along the taut rope, swung down, and scooped up the gun, and then released the lariat, recoiling it for future use. Squint opened his eyes, considerably more sober than he had been for twelve hours, and sat up, dazed and angry.

"What th'—" he began.

"Shut yore face!" snapped Johnny. "Pick up yore hat an' hoof it to yore cayuse. You was headed wrong, so I stopped you. Move rapid, or I'll provide some dance music!"

Squint tried his legs and arms, found them still to be working, and sullenly plodded to his horse. Mounting, he surrendered his rifle in compliance to orders, and then loped back the way he had come, Johnny riding one length in his rear.

"Squint," said his captor in a hard, level voice, "if you give me th' least excuse I'll blow you apart. I've seen some mangy humans, but I never run across a two-laigged polecat like you. I hate to tell you anythin' that'll save yore life, an' I'm hopin' you'll forget it. I'll tell you just once: You behave yoreself like you never did before, an' move lively when I speak. *Keep lookin' ahead!* You don't have to look around to hear, do you?"

Squint preserved an unbroken silence and soon they reached the scene of his outrage and stopped. Johnny ordered him to ride on for a hundred feet.

"That's him, Mister!" excitedly cried Charley. "That's th' big bum!"

"I agree with you, buddy," answered Johnny. "Now you tell me all of it, over again." He listened in grave silence until the pitiful tale was told and then pointed to

Pepper's back, behind him. "Climb up, sonny. Squint an'
me are passin' close to yore house an' we'll take you
as far as we can. You don't mind walkin' a few miles,
do you?"

"But I can't go!" protested Charley. "I got to go to Highbank for th' doctor. I only hope he ain't drunk when I get
there."

"How you goin'?" quizzically demanded Johnny.

"Don't know; but that don't make no difference—I just
got to go, *somehow*! Mebby I could take Squint's horse,"
he suggested, emboldened by desperation.

Johnny shook his head. "You don't never want to ride
a Bar H cayuse; 'tain't healthy. But, say, bud, we don't
have to go to Highback at all—we can get th' Doc at
Gunsight. You been eatin' loco weed?"

"He won't come," said the boy, whispering, and
looking at Squint.

"Did you ask him?" asked Johnny in a low voice,
taking the cue.

"No; but he wouldn't come when Peggy was sick—
an' dad says to get Dr. Treadwell from Highbank."

"He wouldn't come when—when *Peggy* was sick?"
demanded Johnny.

"No, sir; he said he'd treat cows an' horses, but he
wouldn't sling a leg across a saddle if the whole SV was
dying."

Johnny sat up very straight. "Climb up here, sonny. I'll
get th' doctor for you—I can get to Highbank on this
cayuse so quick you'd be surprised. First, I'll take you
nearer home. *Pronto*, buddy. Yo're holdin' up th' drive.
That's th' way; up you come!" He picked up the reins.
"Squint," he called, "lead th' way, an' don't stay too
close. We travel along th' foot of th' hill, on th' other
side, goin' east after we get there."

"That ain't th' way to Highbank," said the boy.

"I know," replied Johnny. "When you grow up an' ride
around th' country as long as I have, you'll find there's
lots of ways gettin' to places. I'll have th' doctor at yore
house by ten o'clock tonight, which is some hours
before you could get him there. Now, don't you tell any-

body who it was that helped you out. Plumb forget what me an' Pepper looked like. An' one thing more—if you say anything about what happened to that drunken coyote ahead, be sure an' tell 'em that he wasn't goin' to be killed, an' that they'll do th' stranger a great favor if they says nothin' about th' whole thing to nobody, nobody at all. Will you do that?"

"Shore, Mister," assured Charley. "Ain't he gettin' pretty far ahead?"

"Not as far as I'm hopin' he'll try to get. But he's got a most unpleasant memory, he don't forget nothin'—not nothin' you tell him."

Reaching the edge of the valley, they turned east and soon afterward Johnny checked his horse. "Here's where you get down, buddy. I hate to make you hoof it, but it won't be near as hard as ridin' down to Highbank an' back. Tell your sister to look for th' doctor at ten o'clock: I can't get him there any sooner. So-long, buddy."

"Thanks, Mister, but my name's Charley. I'm Charley Arnold."

"Glad to meet you, Charley," gravely replied Johnny. "I'll see you again some day, I hope. So-long, an' don't forget nothin'."

"No, sir. Thank you."

Johnny pushed forward until he was close behind his prisoner. "Hit it up, you!" he ordered. "Nice, easy lope; I ain't got all day, if I'm goin' to Highbank. That's something else I owe you for, you coyote. An' I'll have to wear out my cayuse, an' come back on a strange one. Oh, if you'll only make a break, or give me half an excuse to throw lead!"

The trail grew slowly but steadily worse, and when they finally reached the bottom of a long, rough slope Johnny ordered a halt.

"I figger we're twenty miles from Gunsight, near as I can judge," he said, "which leaves only ten to Rawlins. Get off that cayuse. You heard me. *Yes; get off!* Now, any man as shoots a fine little pinto pony an' tells a kid to walk, ought to do some of that walkin' hisself. Rawlins is ten miles; it's twenty to th' Triangle, an' with a lot of hills, an' a bad trail. Also, there's my six-guns. If I ever hear of you comin' back, or see you this side of Rawlins I'll *get* you. I want to make that plain. If it's th' last thing I do on earth, *I'll—get—you!* I ain't got no love for th' SV, but h—I ain't good enough for th' man that'll shoot a fine hoss to keep a kid from gettin' a doctor. Thinkin' as mebby you forgot last night, I'll give you another sample of my gunplay." He jerked out a gun and a hole appeared in the crown of Squint's hat. "When I say I'll get you, you know what it means. Turn around, an' keep yore shadow before you. *Vamoose!*"

Watching the hurrying Squint until satisfied that he intended to keep on in the right direction, Johnny turned back, leading the Bar H horse. He had watched the animal closely while driving Squint, and believed it to be in good enough condition to answer the demand he wished to make upon it. He could tell better when he got back to the SV range, in a certain woody draw near the main trail. This point was reached at dusk and he examined the horse, nodded his head, and picketed the animal to a tree with Squint's lariat. The two hours would do wonders for it. Leaving the Bar H horse, he led his own farther back in the draw and tied it to a tree with his lariat. Returning to Squint's mount, he took the slicker from behind the saddle and unrolled it, picking up the worn gloves which rolled out of it. Finishing his preparations, he went on a reconnaissance on foot, smiled as he saw the dim light in the Doc's house, and quickly returned to the horse.

CHAPTER V

A Lesson in Medical Ethics

DOC REED, finding his tobacco pouch nearly empty, led his horse around to the door and went in to replenish the pouch. He plunged his hand into the big tobacco jar—and let it remain there, the tobacco slipping from his fingers, for a guttural, muffled voice suddenly said:

"Hands up! Shut up! Come here, backwards!"

An argument in one's own mind can be exhaustive and reach a conclusion in a very short space of time. It took the Doc about a second to weight matters and abandon the idea of hurling the jar, and with the decision his hand came slowly out and went up, with the other, above his head. While he was doing this his eyes had not been idle and they saw everything there was to be seen, for he was trained in observation. They saw: A man of his own height, dressed in an old, well-worn, yellow slicker; a sombrero so covered with gray dust as to resemble a hat only in shape and function, its brim pulled well down in front; a pair of common black trousers reaching from the slicker down to common boots, so thickly covered with gray dust as to resemble the hat in everything but the above-mentioned characteristics; a common cotton kerchief, of a pattern found on half of the kerchiefs on the range, was tied across the caller's face, hiding it from chin to eyes; a narrow strip of the intruder's face, so indistinct in the shadow of the hat brim as even to hide the color of the eyes; a pair of gloved hands, the right of which was held in front of the intruder and on a level with his eyes; and last, but emphatically not least, a heavy, common-calibered Colt, with ivory grips yellowed by use and age, which weapon was firmly gripped by the upraised hand. The hammer was up, and a crooked, gloved finger lay in the trigger guard. As the Doc moved to obey, as he turned around, he caught a glimpse of a heavy, black line running from the lower edge of the ivory grip uncovered by the curling fingers. It looked as though it was a crack filled with dirt, which was a little thing, but not too small a thing to be forgotten.

"Whoa!" growled the man in the door.

The Doc obeyed. "What do you want?" he asked coolly.

"Nothin' you can lose," came the answer. "Back up a little more!"

The Doc backed, stopped when the gun pressed into his back and stood motionless while a heavy hand felt him over. It took a Colt out of his shoulder holster, and then the victim felt the gun at his back move a little. He smiled slightly, for the fact that his captor had shifted it to the left hand so he could use the right to empty the captured gun and then toss it across the room onto the bed was no clue, for the reason that all of the men he knew were right-handed. The pressure changed again as the right hand went back on the offensive, and then the intruder gave him his second surprise.

"Pack yore tools—broken laig—take everythin' you need. Hurry!"

The Doc stepped forward and picked up a satchel, glancing out of the corner of his eye as he did so. Only a hand, a foot, and part of the hat and face were in sight, the rest of the visitor's body being behind the outside wall. Filling the bag with what he would require, he took a bundle of splints from a shelf, for he was a methodical person, usually had plenty of time on his hands, and believed in having things to suit him.

"It was not necessary to go to all of this trouble," he smiled, as he reached out to turn down the lamp.

"Stop! Let it burn!" warned the visitor.

"Very well, although I only intended to turn it down. As I said, it was needless for you to go to all this trouble and risk. I am in the habit of going on professional calls at any hour, in any weather, merely upon a simple request, or a statement of fact. If this is a practical joke I may or may not enjoy it—usually the victim doesn't—but I really don't mind, if you are careful with this bag and its contents. You might be the man to need it first—*quién sabe?*"

"I shoot at th' first false move," warned the other. "You are goin' to th' SV—now—with me—an' fast. I'll lead yore hoss—mine's out yonder. Go ahead of me, an' don't look back."

The Doc obeyed and his captor, feeling around the saddle for weapons, grasped the bridle and led the animal to where his own was picketed. Mounting, he ordered the Doc to do likewise, and soon they were pounding along at a good pace, too good to suit the Doc, considering how dark it was.

Their coming had been prophesied by the stranger that afternoon, and now it was heralded by the rolling hoofbeats; and as they neared the house two figures, one considerably shorter than the other, appeared in the lighted doorway, while behind them a clock slowly struck ten.

The captor growled a command and, surprised, the Doc pulled up quickly. "There won't be no charge for this call," he said, "an' remember that I'm stayin' outside, near th' window. You make a false move an' I'll shoot you through it. If th' job ain't well done, I'll shoot you when I find it out. You don't know me, so you won't know who to watch for; but I know you well—all h—I can't save you. Don't talk more than you have to, an' then only about yore trade. Get off, an' go in—hurry, before they come out here!"

The Doc dismounted, turning for a look at his captor's horse and saddle, and walked forward, adjusting his hat and pulling at his coat sleeves. Handing the bag to the boy who ran to meet him, and who seemed to be very much surprised, he led the way to the house, bowed to Margaret and went inside. The boy, looking back reluctantly, slowly followed him, and as the man in the saddle tied the Doc's horse to a sapling and swung around to leave, he saw the slender figure of Margaret reappear, softly outlined against the mellow, yellow light of the room and framed by the darkness, for all the world like a jet cameo against an old ivory background. She looked without moving while the horseman in the dark, the glint of whose brass saddle ornaments barely reached her, bent low in the saddle and removed his hat. She could not see this, nor his slow departure, 'though she faintly heard the soft tread of his horse on the sod, steadily growing fainter. A voice from within called her, and turning, she shook her shoulders as if to throw off a restraining force, and hastened to answer the summons.

Reaching the main valley, Johnny rode at a lope, and when he believed himself to be well past the quicksands, he entered the river, following it close to the bank. Leaving the water at the main trail, he dismounted, removed the saddle and bridle and, slapping the horse on its rump, sent it homeward. Picking up the saddle and seeing that the stirrups did not drag, he stepped only on rock as he went up the mountain, where he stopped at the base of a great pine. When he came down again to go to his own horse he had left behind him everything belonging to Squint, the saddle in the brush, and the weapons and gloves well-wrapped in the slicker and buried in a sand drift.

Some time later, in Gunsight, Two-Spot heard a rider and, waiting a few minutes, slipped into the horse shed, where he spoke softly to Pepper before running his hand over her.

"Huh! What made Dave say he went to Juniper?" he muttered. "She's warm, but not much; her back is near dry. Juniper?" he scoffed. "Thirty miles there, an' thirty mile back, since noon? He was *some* place; but I'll bet my jewels he ain't been to Juniper. There's deviltry afoot—but I ain't talkin', little hoss."

CHAPTER VI

Information Wanted

TWO-SPOT RESTED on the broom. "Wonder what happened to Nelson?" he queried. "Ain't seen him since you
went on th' prod yesterday."

Dave held up the glass he was polishing and looked at
it. "What you mean, on th' prod?"

"When you chased me, at noon."

Dave picked up another glass, breathed on it and
rubbed it vigorously. "He stuck his head in th' door an'
said he was goin' to Juniper. Ain't he got back yet?"

"Don't know," grunted Two-Spot, going to work again.
"Ain't his hoss back?"

"Don't know." He listened. "Mebby this is him, now,
comin' up th' trail." He looked out and shook his head.
"Nope, it's only that d——d pill-roller from the flats. What's
he comin' here for? He's got more liquor in his shack
than we've got. I don't like no man that swizzles it
secret. As I was sayin', it ain't every—why, hello, Doc!
What brings you up here so early in th' mornin'?"

"My horse," grunted the Doc, passing him without a
glance. "Hello, Dave! How are things?"

"Smoother'n h—l, as th' old lady said when she slipped on th' ice. What'll yours be?"

"Cigar apiece," said the Doc; "for you an' me," he amended.

Two-Spot turned back and resumed his sweeping.

"Dave, I was kidnapped last night," said the Doc, bluntly. Waiting for Dave to get his expression part way back to normal, he told the story. Dave's expression was under control again and bespoke surprise and sympathy, gradually assuming a stern, uncompromising aspect at the thought of such a grave breach of law and order. Two-Spot, after the first shock, did not dare to look around, for his grin was unholy and altogether too sincere for his health, should the victim of the unheard of atrocity see it. *Swish! Swish!* went the broom; *he! he!* went his throat, low and in time with the sweeping. Doc finished and hammered the bar with his fist. "It's a d—d outrage!" he declared, with heat.

Dave nodded emphatically. "It shore is! Do you know who did it?"

"No; if I did I'd be on his trail."

"See anythin' that might identify th' coyote?"

"Perhaps; I'll know more about it before the day is over," answered the Doc. "Big Tom has some of his men out now looking for tracks on the Double X. Those fellows don't like me very much."

"Blast their eyes!" commented Two-Spot, sweeping with renewed vigor.

Doc glanced at him, frowned, and went on. "Some things lead me to think one way; other things, other ways. It's complicated by Squint's disappearance."

Two-Spot assimulated the second shock with avidity. He was beginning to be glad that he was alive, and his brain was putting two and two together at top speed. His ears fairly ached for more, and he waited for the third. When there were two, there should always be a third, he hopefully assured himself.

Dave's face showed real surprise again and then marched to orders and revealed his sympathy and disapprobation. "Why, there won't be nobody safe!" he exclaimed. "Do you mean he's missin'?"

"He is. Have you seen him since the night they were all here?"

"No; I ain't."

"Sorrers an' calamities never come singly," said Two-Spot, energetically digging a match stick out of a crack.

"Mebby it was Squint," suggested Dave, "as captured you."

"Well, the evidence points that way, but it isn't reasonable," replied the Doc, going to a chair and sitting down. "Squint wasn't the sort of a man who would go out of his way to do anyone a favor, especially if it was for someone he did not like; and most especially if it involved a large element of risk. But this man had on Squint's slicker, rode Squint's horse and saddle, and even had Squint's gloves and gun."

"He must 'a' et Squint," suggested Two-Spot, spitting violently at the thought.

"Shut up, you!" said Dave, sternly. "But, Doc, he was shore petrified when he left here; an' what he had in his person would stay with him for a long time. He allus was economical in his drunks: he made 'em last quite a spell. Now, when a man's full of liquor he'll likely do anythin'—no tellin' what."

"This man was not drunk," asserted the Doc in his best professional manner, "and he had not been drunk for over a week. His hand was as steady as mine, and he did not make a single false move. I'm sure it was not Squint; Big Tom cannot make up his mind; Wolf Forbes swears it was, but Wolf was no friend of his, as we all know. Some of the boys suggested the Double X, knowing the strong dislike some of that litter has for me. Three of the boys are over there now lookin' for tracks."

"What good will that do 'em?" demanded Dave. "A man has a right to make tracks on his own ranch, an' they're allus ridin' around over it. But, then, if they found tracks leadin' from th' Double X to yore place, or from th' Juniper trail to th' Double X, why, then you'd have somethin'."

"There are none of the first category," replied the Doc, "and there will be none of the second: I told you that this man rode Squint's horse, and any tracks on the Juniper trail could have been made while we rode over it together. We can't find where he got onto the horse, or where he got off of it; but it must have been in the river somewhere. He was a fiend for riding on rock—he knew this country like a book. We've tried trailing, but it got us nowhere. So, Dave, I rode up here to ask you a plain question: Who were in here last night between quarter of nine and, say, a quarter after ten? You may save some innocent person from a lot of trouble."

"Well," said Dave, pursing his lips. "Th' poker gang was here. Two-Spot an' I was here. Jerry Poole came in to set his watch—that was just at nine-twenty. Nelson poked his head in th' door about ten minutes after Jerry, wriggled his fingers at me, cuss his impudence, an' disappeared. Where he went I don't know. I guess that's all."

Two-Spot gripped the broom convulsively and then slowly relaxed. The third shock had arrived. The problems of his sorely taxed brain were jammed by the sudden arrival of more. Never before had he heard Dave deliberately lie; and here the proprietor was lying coolly and perfectly, with trimmings to make it stick. In turn surprise, wonder, and satisfaction swept across his boiled countenance like driven clouds across the coppery sun. He gradually worked closer to the Doc and soon his stroke became longer and harder. When he began trying to sweep a tobacco stain out of the flooring the Doc suddenly leaped from his chair.

"What—the h—l do—you think—you're doing?" he coughed.

"Huh?" said Two-Spot, looking up.

"What do you mean, sweeping like that, over here?"

"I was only sweepin' where th' dirt was," answered Two-Spot.

The Doc regarded him keenly. "Oh, is that it? Well, hunt for it somewhere else, or I'll kick you through the window!"

Two-Spot flared up. "You got my permission——"

"Shut up!" snapped Dave. "Now, Doc, as I was sayin'—what'n h—l *was* I sayin'? Well, anyhow, I said it,'" he asserted, belligerently. "What you aimin' to do now?"

"Dance on th' quicksands, I hope," grunted Two-Spot, savagely. Then he listened, and said: "Here comes Nelson on that fine little hoss." Under his breath he muttered, "I bet he'll be surprised to find out he was in here at nine-thirty, last night." He straightened up. "Huh! Mebby he won't. Mebby he fixed it with Dave. Well, if he's wise, he'll tip me off next time—I might tell th' truth, an' make a lot of trouble, if I didn't know."

Johnny walked in. "Hello, Ol' Timer!" he said, jabbing Two-Spot in the ribs.

Two-Spot grasped the broom handle firmly. "Hello, yoreself! An' you lookout who yo're punchin'," he grinned. "Squint's dead," he said, mournfully.

"What?"

"Oh, well; he's missin', anyhow," amended Two-Spot.

"Missin' what?" asked Johnny.

"Missin' hisself!"

"Then he's drunker than I thought," replied Johnny. "I never heard of nobody bein' so far gone in liquor that they missed themselves."

"Oh, you go to th' devil!" snorted Two-Spot, turning around so he could snicker in safety.

Johnny glanced casually at the Doc, walked up to the bar and bought a cigar, which he lit with scrupulous care.

"Meet th' Doc, Nelson," said Dave.

Johnny turned. "Glad to meet you, Doctor. I've heard of you, an' passed yore place."

"Saw you," replied the Doc, "and I coveted that black mare."

"Nice little cayuse," admitted Johnny.

"The Doc was kidnapped," said Dave, watching closely.

"That so?" replied Johnny, politely. "An' how old was you, Doctor?"

"What do you mean?"

"Why, when you was kidnapped," Johnny explained.

"I was kidnapped last night," replied the Doc.

"You—last night?" demanded Johnny, incredulously. "Well, I'm d—d! What did they get?"

"They got me."

"I mean, what did they get that was valuable?" persisted Johnny.

Two-Spot turned away again and missed the floor twice.

"They stole th' Doc," explained Dave. "They was takin' him away just about th' time you looked in at me. They took him over to th' SV, to set Ol' Arnold's busted laig."

"What you talkin' about?" snorted Johnny, seating himself across from the Doc. "I never heard of a doctor bein' kidnapped to set a busted laig. What am I supposed to say? I'll bite, if it does cost me th' drinks."

"No, Nelson, that's the truth," earnestly asserted the Doc, and he told the story over again.

"You say he was on Squint's cayuse, wearin' Squint's slicker, an' usin' Squint's gun?" asked Johnny. "Then where was Squint? A man don't just drop things like that without knowin' it. What was that Two-Spot was tryin' to tell me?"

The Doc explained the matter and finished by saying that he felt sure that it had not been the missing puncher who had visited him.

"I don't think so, neither," asserted Johnny. "He'd be a fool to go like that. No, sir, I'll bet it wasn't Squint—but, wait a minute! If he counted on leavin' th' country right after, why, he might a' done it, at that. If it wasn't Squint, then where was he?"

"Sleepin' off his liquor," said Dave. "Why, that's it! While he slept somebody took his outfit an' kidnapped th' Doc. H—l, it may all be a joke!"

"You wouldn't think so if you observed that man as I did," replied the Doc. "He was in deadly earnest. I could *feel* it."

"Well, there's two ways to start at it," said Johnny, ordering drinks all around, including Two-Spot. "He had a grudge ag'in' you, an' he was extra friendly to th' SV. Run back in yore mem'ry for somebody that hates you enough to want to get square. If that don't work, then hunt for th' feller that likes th' SV. Anybody 'round here that's sweet on that Arnold gal, that you knows of?"

"No; not that we know of," answered the Doc. "Big Tom was the last one who called there; but he quit, quite some time ago."

"Got throwed so hard he still aches," gloated Two-Spot.

"Well, I can't help you," said Johnny. "I don't know anythin' about th' people around here. An', bein' a stranger, an' likely to be suspected of any orphaned devilment, I'm shore glad I looked in here, last night. But I ain't worryin' about Squint," he deprecated. "He's an old hand at takin' care of hisself, if I'm any judge. He'll turn up with a headache, an' yell fit to bust for his saddle, an' gun."

"I hope so," said Dave. He turned to the Doc. "Did you fix up th' laig?"

"Certainly; it was a simple fracture," answered the Doc. He paused. "Cussed if I know what to think," he growled, arising. He had observed Johnny closely, saw that he was left-handed, found the voice not quite what he had hoped for, and Dave's statement cinched the matter. He nodded good-by and went out, but he looked at Johnny's saddle, where he found silver ornaments instead of brass, and plain stirrup guards instead of the fringed ones he had noticed the night before. Shaking his head he mounted and rode homeward.

Two-Spot placed the broom across a table and sat down. "Dave," he said, almost reverently, "what made you say that?"

"Say what?" demanded the proprietor, belligerently. "You hearin' things?"

"Mebby; but I ain't *seein'* 'em."

"What did I say that's ridin' you so hard?" demanded Dave.

"What you did about Nelson lookin' in last night."

"What was that?" asked Johnny, with pardonable curiosity.

"Why, Dave up an' tells th' Doc that you poked yore head in at that there door at nine-thirty *last night*," explained Two-Spot.

"Well, suppose I did?" asked Johnny. "What about it?"

"Well, now," mourned Two-Spot, "if I ain't got th' cussedest mem'ry! It's got Texas fever; a tick must a' crawled up my ear. Of course you did; and didn't you say 'Two-Spot, when I sees you tomorrow I'll buy you a drink?' "

"I reckon I might 'a' said somethin' like that," laughed Johnny. "She's yourn, Ol' Timer—with a cigar to punish me for forgettin'."

Two-Spot enjoyed his drink and pulled contentedly on the cigar. Then he turned toward the rear door. "Time for me to give George a hand. Shall I take Pepper around out of th' sun?"

"Why, yes; an' much obliged," answered Johnny.

Dave pointed his finger and his whole arm at the broom lying across the table. "That yourn?" he demanded.

Two-Spot looked. "I told you that my mem'ry was bad," he chuckled. Putting the broom away where it belonged he went out and led Pepper around to the shed.

Johnny looked hard at Dave. "That was a good turn, Dave," he said. "What made you do it?"

Dave rumpled his hair. "Squint's missin', which means one customer less. Bein' a stranger down here I reckoned they'd pass th' buck to you. That meant they'd likely do it here—th' Doc come up to locate you, I figgered. Besides losin' a lot more customers I'd have to clean up a slaughter-house. I just made up my mind I wouldn't do it. Anyhow, I'd like to shake hands with th' coyote that lugged th' Doc off to fix that laig. I would so."

"Don't blame you," said Johnny, holding out his hand. "We can shake on that, all right. I say a doctor is a doctor an' ought to go where he's needed."

Dave looked him full in the eyes, a quizzical smile playing around his mouth, and shook hands gravely, solemnly. It was almost a ceremony. "My sentiments, exactly," he responded. "Wonder if Squint was hurt?"

"I'd bet he wasn't," answered Johnny. "I'd even bet he went to a different part of th' country. Mebby he got caught in some devilment. Punchers are great for roamin'—just look where *I* am." He shook his head sadly and went out through the rear door for the hotel, leaving Dave with a grin on his face which threatened to disrupt it. He had not gone more than a few steps when he turned and went back. Poking his head in at the door, he said: "Dave, when I'm drinkin' in here, an' it can be done easy, just see that mine is some watery. I like th' delicate flavor it has that way; th' delicater, th' better."

Dave chuckled and nodded. "Yo're drinkin' it. If yo're satisfied, I am. I can't do it at th' bar, where th' bottle passes; but it'll be easy if yo're playin' cards."

CHAPTER VII

Hunting with the Hounds

JOHNNY ENTERED the kitchen, looked at the stove and went into the dining-room, where George was playing solitaire. "That's a bad habit, George," he said, shaking his head. "It don't get you nothin'."

George made a play and looked up. "Aimin' to get me into a two-handed game of somethin'?" he queried.

"No; I ain't," answered Johnny. "I was just wonderin' how long you was goin' to play it."

"I'm goin' to play it till I have to start cookin'," said George, determinedly.

"Then you ain't goin' to stand over that hot stove for more'n an hour, are you?"

"No, sir; I ain't."

"You talk like it was somethin' to dodge!" snorted Johnny.

"I'd like to see *you* do it!" retorted George.

"Huh!" sniffed Johnny. "I got a good notion to do it."

George made another play. "Notions!" he sneered. "Notions ain't doin' it!"

"Then I *will* do it," said Johnny, going into the kitchen and throwing wood into the stove. He took down a lid made up of rings, substituted it for one of the stove lids, lifted out the middle section and put in its place an iron ladle.

A chair scraped out in the dining-room and George poked his head in. "What you think yo're doin'?" he demanded.

"Callin' yore bluff. Go on back to yore solitaire. I'm goin' to run some bullets."

"Why, cuss yore nerve!" said George. "Who told you to mess up my kitchen?"

"You said you'd like to see me stand over this stove," answered Johnny. "Run around an' get me two pounds of lead from Dailey."

"Get it yoreself!" snapped George. "You clean up when you get through," he warned.

"Shore," replied Johnny, and he went out to get the lead.

Dailey looked up. "Hello, Nelson!"

"Howd'y, Ben! Got two pounds of lead, an' some Kentucky powder?"

"Shore, answered Dailey. He slid a bar of lead onto the counter and took a can from a shelf. "This ain't Kaintuck—but it's as good. How much?"

Johnny put a few grains in the palm of his hand and rubbed them with a forefinger. "I don't want this at all," he said, showing the black smudge. "I want th' kind *you* use."

Dailey grumbled, but felt under the counter and produced another can. "Here's th' best made," he said.

Johnny tested it, and nodded. "Half a pound will do."

Returning to the kitchen he used George's axe to cut the lead into smaller pieces, and dumped them into the ladle, after which he paid a hurried visit to his room for tools.

Two-Spot shoved his head in at the door. "What you doin'? Runnin' slugs?"

"Shoein' a hoss," said Johnny.

Two-Spot grinned. "Where'd you get th' lead?"

"Dailey's," answered Johnny, punching out old primers.

"Buy primers, an' powder, too?" demanded Two-Spot.

"Powder," grunted Johnny.

"Off'n th' shelf behind him?"

"Under th' counter."

"Yo're lucky; he must like you. Well, then some of 'em will go off," said Two-Spot. "But if you'd bought his primers, none of 'em would." He looked around and started to resize some of the shells. "These here ain't shells. They're—they're kegs." He picked up the mold and opened it. "My G—d!" he snorted. "Yo're a bloody-minded cuss. Yore gun got wheels an' a limber?"

"It'll make th' other feller limber gettin' out of th' way."

Two-Spot hurt his finger and quit. "Reckon Dave wants me," he observed.

"I'm shore *I* don't," grunted Johnny, beginning to reprime the shells.

"*Do* it yoreself, then!" snapped Two-Spot, going out. He looked carefully around and, going into the narrow space between the kitchen and the rear of the saloon, disappeared from sight.

Around in front of the Palace four punchers were dismounting. They were disgruntled, but in one way they felt relief. After a morning's search for tracks on the Double X, along its eastern line, they had given up the job and had started to Gunsight to carry out a task which they felt would require a great amount of tact to keep it from becoming a shambles. But on the way they had stopped at the Doc's and found that it would not be necessary to cross-question Johnny. There remained one further duty to perform and they decided to slake their thirsts before attempting it. Big Tom wanted information from those who he felt would be able to give it, since they were directly benefited by the kidnapping of the Doc. He felt sure that the committee he had appointed were qualified to get it for him, especially if they had a proper amount of liquor before they started after it. Hence he had supplied them with the funds and told them that it was his treat. Carson and Dahlgren had fat blanket rolls behind their saddles; "Smitty" and Fraser, nothing but their usual paraphernalia.

They stamped in to the bar and lined up. To Dave's inquiry, they replied that their morning's work had been in vain, but boasted that the afternoon would not be wasted.

"We're goin' where th' information is," said Carson, "an' we're goin' to get it. If it comes easy, all right—*but* we're *goin' to get it*, savvy?"

"An' when we *do* get it, it will be forty feet of rope an' a sycamore tree for th' coyote that got rid of Squint an' kidnapped th' Doc," boasted Dahlgren.

"Nobody gives a whoop about th' kidnappin', 'cept th' Doc," said Fraser; "but this was a poke at th' Bar H, an' that's where we set in. If we finds out who got rid of Squint, we know who kidnapped th' Doc; an' if we learns who kidnapped th' Doc, we likewise finds th' coyote what got rid of Squint. An' I'm tellin' *you* that we're goin' to find out who he is. Doc said he done a good job on that busted laig, an' it would be a mean trick on him to undo it; but we're goin' to find out! Give us another round."

"I got to laugh about th' Doc," said Smitty, "a growed man, lettin' hisself be stole that way. An' what's he doin' now? Is he out a-huntin'? He ain't. He's settin' in that shack of his'n waitin' for *us* to get his kidnapper. Fill 'em again, Dave."

"Forty feet of rope an' a sycamore tree," repeated Carson. "If he puts up a fight we'll give him *this!*" He yanked out his gun and fired at the floor.

Could they have seen the result of the shot they would have been greatly surprised. Two-Spot, under their feet, lying on his pile of stolen blankets and discarded clothing, and drinking in every word they said, had just shifted to a more comfortable position when the gun roared and the bullet, ripping through the flooring, cut a welt on his cheek. Panic stricken, he started to roll and crawl toward the hotel, and was too excited to notice the pair of legs at the wash bench, where Johnny was cooling bullets in the basin, but rolled out and against the bench, upsetting it and Johnny, too, as well as the basin, bullets, and the water bucket. There was a mad scramble for a few seconds and Two-Spot lost a tooth before Johnny saw who it was. Then both leaped to their feet, Two-Spot angrily spitting blood and dirt.

"What you think yo're doin'?" blazed Johnny, reaching for Two-Spot's collar. "Playin' earthquake?"

"Who you hittin'?" snarled Two-Spot. "Leggo my shirt; I got somethin' to tell you!"

George came running and stuck his head out of the door. "Go it, Ol' Timer!" he encouraged. "Serves him right for th' mess he's made!"

Two-Spot thanked him by kicking backward, guided by sound and instinct. George, receiving one whole foot just below his short ribs, doubled up forthwith and disappeared. There was a crash and the sound of falling stove wood, and George had interest in nothing outside of himself.

"They're goin' to th' SV, an' make 'em tell who's raisin' th' devil on th' range," said Two-Spot in Johnny's ear. "If they ain't told easy, then they'll take th' splints off'n th' ol' man's laig. G——d only knows where they'll stop, for they're gettin' full of liquor."

"Who are they?"

"Carson, Dal, Smitty, an' Fraser," answered Two-Spot. " 'Forty feet of rope an' a sycamore tree,' they says," he mimicked, "an' shot through th' floor. I got it in th' cheek, d——n 'em." A frightened look came to his face. "Don't tell 'em where I was," he begged, for the hiding-place was his only refuge and without it his life would be miserable.

"I'll swap secrets," said Johnny. "Keep mum about tellin' me this. Take Pepper around front an' mix her in with their cayuses. Then pick up th' slugs an' keep 'em for me."

A piece of firewood whizzed past his ear, and then a stream of them. George, still throwing, emerged from the kitchen, blood in his eye. Johnny grabbed him.

"We was playin' a joke on you, George," he said, hurriedly. "Two-Spot kicked you accidental. Here's somethin' to square it," and George opened his hand to see a coin nestling therein.

"Joke!" he muttered, feeling around his belt. "Accidental! *You* may think so, but I'm cussed if *I* do! My G—d, his relations must be mules!"

Dave and the committee looked up as the door flew back and slammed against the wall, to see Johnny enter, a little too erect, stepping a little too precisely and wide, his mind obviously concentrated on his legs. His face was owlishly serious and he nodded to each in turn with great gravity. Describing a wide curve he stepped carefully to the bar, where he stopped, sighed, and braced himself.

"Dave," he said, waving an arm, "th' best in th' house for us. Didn't know what to do with m'self; but now we can have some 'citement. Here's how. Here's to pore Ol' Squint."

"Here's to pore Ol' Squint," repeated Dave. "I allus liked Squint."

"Everybody liked Squint," responded Johnny. "Everybody, 'cept—'cept what's his name? Pore Squint, kidnapped; an' the Doc, kidnapped; nobody's safe no more. *You* might get kidnapped—*you*—an' *you*—an' *you*—an' Dave! No, not Dave!" he burst into laughter. "Not *Dave*! He! He! Less'n it was Ol' Buffalo an' his waggin!"

Smitty rocked to and fro: "He! He! He!" he roared. "Ol' Buffalo an' his four-hoss team! Freight for Juniper!"

Carson slapped Johnny on the shoulder. "Nobody's safe but Dave!" he shouted. "Ol' Buffalo would have to *roll* him in, like a bar'l."

"Don't you care, Dave," said Fraser. "I'm yore friend, an' nobody's goin' to kidnap you, waggin or no waggin. Not while Bill Fraser's around'. No, sir. Give us another. Big Tom's blowin' his boys."

"Couldn't get along without Dave, not nohow," said Johnny. "Here's to Dave—everybody's fr'en'. Just th' same I ain't forgettin' pore Squint. I'd like to know who kidnapped him—just so I could get my rope on him.

That's all. Jus' that. Got notion to go find him. Come on, le's *all* go!"

"Forty feet of rope an' a sycamore tree," burbled Smitty. "Forty feet of——"

"We're goin' to find him," boasted Dahlgren. "Goin' to righ' now. Le's have one more drink, Dave. Just one more, an' then we go git him."

"That's th' way!" cried Johnny. "Come on—one more, Dave, ol' kidnapper. Then forty feet of sycamore rope. Want to come, Dave? Come on! Come on with us!"

"I better stay here," said Dave, earnestly. "I better be right here when you bring him in. *Somebody* ought to be."

"That's Ol' Dave, all righ'," cried Smitty. "Good Ol' Dave."

"Give us a bottle, Dave," said Johnny. "Give us *two* bottles. Nothin's too good for my fren's."

"If pore Squint was only here," burbled Smitty, eyeing the bottles. "Pore Squint. We'll bring that coyote in for you, Dave. We'll drag him to town."

"Him an' Ol' Arnold," supplemented Carson. "*Both* of 'em!"

"That's it!" cried Johnny. "That's where we'll go—come on, fellers! Goo'-by, Dave; goo'by!"

They surged toward the door, milled before the opening, and then shuffled to the street. Fraser threw an arm around Johnny's neck and slobbered about poor Squint. Johnny slipped the six-gun from Fraser's holster, dropped it on his own foot to deaden the fall, and then pushed it under the saloon. He staggered, with Fraser, out toward the horses and bumped into Dahlgren, who grabbed them both to save himself. Fraser's other arm went around his friend's neck and he protested his love for them both. Dahlgren's gun also struck Johnny's boot and was quickly scraped over with sand.

Under the saloon Two-Spot changed from all ears to mostly ears and some eyes, for his view was limited to below the hips of the maudlin gang. When Fraser's gun slid under the floor he became, for an instant, all eyes, and wriggled in greedy anticipation. Then he saw the second gun strike Johnny's boot and become covered over with sand, and he rocked from side to side with silent mirth, his boiled countenance acquiring spots of mottled purple, especially his nose. As soon as the crowd mounted, he crawled forward, wriggling desperately when the space became too small for hands and knees. He had to get those guns before the proprietor got them, for Dave would not allow him to own a weapon. When he had gone as far as he dared, he stopped and waited until the bunched group whirled away up the trail, and then wriggled more desperately than ever. Suddenly he stopped and writhed sideways behind a pile of dirt, for the heavy steps above his head ceased as a pair of enormous legs waddled into his field of view. Dave kicked around in the sand, found the weapon, and laboriously picked it up. The huge legs remained motionless for a moment as their owner watched the cloud of dust which rolled eastward on the trail.

"He's takin' chances," muttered Dave. "An' I can almost smell him from here. Six glasses of whiskey down his sleeve—great guns, but he must feel comfortable! Well, boys, I don't know where yo're goin', but nothin' would surprise me." He paused a moment in indecision, thoughtfully regarding the Colt. "I reckon I ought to lose this gun down th' well—but I'll wait till he comes back."

The fat legs waddled out of sight and the floor creaked again. Two-Spot wriggled forward, snatched the Colt and backed to his nest, where he looked at his prize and gloated.

"Dave never saw you fall," he chuckled. "Oh, yo're a beauty; an' only two are gone. Cuss it! This is th' gun that shot *me!*" He considered a moment. "Now I got to get some .45's from th' store when Ol' Eagle-Eye ain't lookin'."

Meanwhile the exuberant committee tore over the trail until Fraser, wishing to let off some extra steam, felt for his gun. He reined in so quickly as almost to cause a catastrophe. Dahlgren now discovered his own loss and there was a wrangle about going back to look for the missing weapons. Their insistence won out and the committee wheeled, spread out, and cantered back almost to Gunsight, wrangling all the way. Yielding at last to the acrimonious suggestions of the other three, they gave up the search and set out again, beginning on the second bottle. When they finally arrived at the SV ranchhouse the afternoon was over half gone and they were so under the influence of liquor that it was all they could do to get to the door of the house. Staggering in, they went to Arnold's room and all began talking at once. There were no preliminaries—Margaret and Charley, caught in the room, were forced into a corner and had to hear the brutal threats. Johnny was the loudest of them all, but there was no profanity in his words; and he took the first chance that offered to wink at the helpless man on the bed. Arnold, ignorant of what he was supposed to know, pleaded in vain. Carson rolled up his sleeves and announced his intentions, staggering toward the bed. He collided with Johnny and they both fell. As Johnny scrambled to his feet he caught Margaret's eye and winked slowly. Then he let out a roar and blamed Carson for the fall. His eye caught sight of a calendar on the wall and he objected to the red numerals representing Sundays. Jerking out his guns he shot the numbers out, the bullets passing so close to Smitty that that valiant committeeman nearly broke his neck falling over a chair he backed against. A glass of water was shattered and then the guns became wobbly, covering everything in sight. Boasting that he could shoot out a fly's eye without touching the rest of the insect, he shot a spur off of Carson's boot and put a hole through Dahlgren's hat when he presumably aimed at the lamp on a shelf. Roaring and jumping, he accused Arnold of doing the kidnapping himself, and fired at a knot in the floor, missing it, and clipping a button from Fraser's vest. The committee was very drunk, but it was not so far gone that all instincts of self-preservation had fled, and it made haste to get out of the room. Smitty, finding the door blocked, and being in a hurry, went through the open window with remarkable directness for one in his condition.

"He ain't here!" shouted Johnny. "He's got away! Come on, fellers; we got to get him—*pronto!*"

"Where'd he go?" shouted Carson, stumbling over a chair. He kicked it across the room and sat down suddenly. Being assisted to his feet, he staggered out toward the horses, the rest stringing after him. "Where'd he go?" he demanded at the top of his voice.

"Don't know," answered Johnny, hanging onto Dahlgren. "But he'll come back. Let's ambush him!"

"A'right; I'm tired of ridin'," declared Smitty. "Got forty feet of rope an' sycamore tree. Where'll we go?"

"Up on th' Juniper trail," said Johnny. "We know he don't hide in th' south; we'd a' seen him long ago. I know a good place, come on!"

It was a wonder how they ever mounted, but they managed it, all but Smitty, who had to be assisted to the saddle. Once seated, they were fairly well at home and followed Johnny along the ranch trail. An hour later Johnny and three of them were lying in the bushes at the edge of the Juniper trail, Smitty having been lost on the way. The sun was still warm, and the liquor potent, which was in no way checked by their inactivity, and snores soon arose. Johnny, smiling cynically at the prostrate figures, made a soft bed out of Carson's and Dahlgren's blankets and lay down to see it through. The night passed quietly and the early morning light showed four soundly sleeping figures. Higher and higher climbed the sun and one by one the men awakened, consumed by raging thirsts. Johnny raised himself on one elbow and looked around.

"I want a drink," he announced. "Gimme a drink, Fraser!"

"Ain't got none; I'm dyin' of thirst!"

Staggering to their feet they looked around, got their bearings and made a rush for their horses; and soon a miserable, sick committee pounded along the trail at its best speed, bent only on one thing—to get to Dave's.

Dave heard them coming and knew what would be wanted. He met them at the door and passed out a bottle; consuming it eagerly, they straggled off toward their ranch, ugly and profane.

Johnny watched them go. "I was in desperate company, Dave," he said. "They was all primed to raise h—l out there, but I saw that nobody belongin' to that ranch knew anything about Squint, or th' Doc, that we didn't know, so I sort of coaxed 'em away. An' would you believe it, Dave, we was so petrified we got lost an' finally climbed down an' went to sleep right where th' idea struck us?"

"I allus was a great believer, Nelson," answered Dave. "That's mebby why I'm a pore man at my time of life. An' I admits that you has persuadin' ways. Now, I figgers it this way: Th' Doc up an' kills Squint; Squint gets even by kidnappin' th' Doc; after which th' Doc buries th' corpse an' throws away th' grave. But, I says, an' it's th' 'buts' that raise th' devil, how does Big Tom figger it? He ain't got my trustin' nature. An' how will Wolf figger it? An' all th' rest, after they get together an' wrestle things out? I'm glad you got a fast hoss, an' a clear trail. Where's Smitty?" he demanded.

"He was a weak brother," Johnny sorrowfully declared. "Th' last I saw of him he was fallin' off his cayuse about five miles northwest of th' ranch. First he fell back over a chair, backwards; then he fell out of a window, frontwards; an' when he fell off his cayuse he was goin' sideways. When it comes to fallin' I'll back him against anybody. What do I owe you for them two bottles of whiskey? They was amazin' medicine."

"Whiskey?" queried Dave. "Did you taste it?"

"I didn't," confessed Johnny. "I handed th' first bottle to Dahlgren, an' by th' time it got back to me there wasn't nothin' in it. Th' second bottle I gives to Smitty, an' I got left again. If I'd had a couple more I might a' got a drink. What makes you ask?"

"The first was brandy, an' th' second was gin," said

Dave. "I reckoned mebby they'd like a change. Sorry you didn't get none of 'em."

Johnny looked at him reproachfully. "*I* ain't," he said. "Good Lord! Come, Pepper, there ain't no tellin' what this man'll do next. Mebby we won't see Smitty till next week—come, little hoss!"

CHAPTER VIII

A Man's a Man

HAVING EATEN enough to arouse the unqualified admiration of George, Johnny went to the kitchen and became busy with patch paper, tallow, and loading cup, and had just finished the twenty-fifth, and last, cartridge, when Two-Spot wandered in. George was out attacking the wood pile.

"Got 'em done, huh? Ain't it better to buy 'em?" asked Two-Spot, looking into the dining-room.

"It is, Ol' Timer, when you can. Just now I can't get 'em, so I got to make 'em."

His companion looked at the belt full of .45's. "Gimme a couple of them? I want to try somethin'."

Johnny complied. "Want to see if they fits?" he asked.

"What you mean?"

"Carson dropped his gun under Dave's floor. Who got th' one in th' road?"

"Don't say nothin'," begged Two-Spot. "Dave's an old woman, an' I don't want nobody to know I got it. He got th' other."

"What you goin' to do with yourn?"

"Keep it in my bunk. I might need it, sometime. I ought to have a rifle, though."

"I'll get you one," promised Johnny.

"What you goin' to do this afternoon?" asked Two-Spot, his face beaming at the thought of owning a rifle.

"Don't know yet."

"It's time you knowed about things out here. You ride up th' Juniper trail to th' second draw, in about an hour, an' I'll fix yore case rack so you'll know what cards are out. Yo're guessin' good, but Faro ain't th' only game where keepin' cases is better,"

"Why go up there?"

"Well, purty soon it ain't goin' to be healthy for anybody to be too friendly with you," said Two-Spot, reflectively. "Anyhow, I'll be worth more if I ain't suspected of bein' too talkative."

"Th' best way to get suspected is to hide out when you don't have to," said Johnny. "You wander over to that grass spot across th' road from Dave's an' Dailey's in about an hour, an' lay down to rest yore lazy bones, with yore head toward th' saloon, so nobody can see that yo're talkin' steady. I'll try to get there first. It'll be innocent as sheep. Pepper hankers for live grass—an' she deserves what she hankers for."

"She does," responded Two-Spot. "Big Tom was in yesterday talkin' to Dailey. I heard him say somethin' about no supplies. They had an argument, an' finally Dailey says: 'All right; if you say so.' "

Johnny nodded. "I'll see you around front in about an hour."

About the time agreed upon Two-Spot stopped sweeping and looked out of the door. "Things look plumb peaceful, Dave," he said. "There's Nelson lyin' on his back over there in th' sun. He's too comfortable. Got a notion to stir him up."

"You stir up that broom an' get through," replied Dave. "You're sweepin' later an' later every mornin'."

The sweeper sighed and went to work again, with a vigor so carefully figured that Dave was on the verge of speaking about dust several times, but thought better of it each time. Finishing his chores, Two-Spot shuffled out and threw a can at the recumbent figure over on the grass. It stirred and raised its head.

"I'll turn you inside out," it threatened.

"You couldn't turn a glove inside out," retorted Two-Spot.

Johnny grunted. He was silent for a moment, and then inquired, "What you doin', Feather Head?"

"Workin'."

"Then you can't do it," regretted Johnny.

"What?"

"Bring over a couple of cigars."

"Show me yore money."

Johnny rolled over on his side and produced a coin, which he held up.

"Chuck it over," said Two-Spot.

"Yo're too busy," jeered Johnny.

"Chuck it, an' see."

Johnny sat up and sent the coin glittering through the air, Two-Spot making an unexpected catch. He went into the saloon, soon reappeared, and shuffled across the road. Sitting down at Johnny's side with his back to the buildings, he lit his cigar and lazily reclined. "I shore appreciates this rest," he sighed.

Johnny laughed outright. "Yo're worked to death," he jibed.

"Ol' Simon Verrier," began Two-Spot, "was th' first owner of th' SV. He run it for twenty years, an' there wasn't nobody in all that time done any devilment an' wanted to repeat it. He was testy, big, an' powerful, an' he reckoned th' gun he packed was made to be used. He had Buck Sneed for his best man, an' an outfit what believed th' same as he did about guns. At that time there wasn't no boundaries, not fixed. Th' ranches sort of mingled along th' edges. Then th' Bar H got notions. It sort of honed for that valley, an' made a play or two for it. There wasn't no third. Ol' Simon an' Buck rid down to th' Bar H house an' spoke plain. Failin' to have any lines didn't bother them two. They picked th' ridges of th' dividin' hills an' says: 'Them's th' lines; stay on yore own side.' "

Johnny laughed for the benefit of any of the curious on the other side of the road.

"Ol' Frank Harper owned th' Bar H in them days. Poker an' drink was his failin's. His poker took Dailey out of th' saddle an' put him into th' store, an' it did th' same for Dave. It also put a mortgage on th' Bar H. More'n that, it kept him drinkin' harder an' harder—an' he was found dead one day in East Canyon; he had fell off his cayuse an' busted his neck. Th' mortgage was foreclosed an' th' present owners of th' ranch bought it in an' hired Big Tom to run it.

"Th' first thing Big Tom did was to forget all about them boundary lines. Ol' Simon an' him had words, an' when th' smoke cleared Big Tom had four slugs out of five into him; but he's got th' strength of a grizzly an' pulled through. About th' time he was ridin' around ag'in, on his own side of th' lines, Simon got his feet wet an' died in four days. I says that is downright funny. He had weathered stampedes, gunplay, northers, an' th' Lord only knows what for sixty years, an' then he goes an' dies from wet feet!"

Johnny nodded and pushed Pepper's muzzle from his face. "Keep a-feedin', girl," he ordered; "I won't sneak away."

"Well," continued Two-Spot, "Buck buried th' ol' man, an' went right on runnin' things for th' heirs. He kept th' outfit together, an' th' ranch was payin' fine. Then th' heirs, eastern mutton-heads, didn't like his spellin', an' his habit of writin' letters when he was mad. They fired him, an' th' outfit, feelin' insulted personally, quit th' ranch an' went with him."

"I've knowed outfits just like that," murmured Johnny, reflectively.

"Th' new foreman came, an' went. Likewise th' second. They had a mark to live up to—it lays along th' top of them hills—an' they wasn't big enough to do it. Meanwhile th' SV was goin' to th' dogs. Then Ol' Arnold bought it an' came out to run it. He was a tenderfoot, an' came out for his health. Things was happenin' all th' time. His herds was shrinkin'. Rustlin', shootin', maverick huntin', an' them quicksands kept a-cuttin' his herds. Just about that time Big Tom dynamites th' rock slide in Little Canyon, an' forthwith loses his water. Then things happen faster than ever. He makes a play toward th' Double X; but th' Double X talks plain an' he reckons he better get th' SV."

Johnny sat up and stretched. "Let's play mumble-peg," he suggested, producing a clasp knife. "This steady talkin' is lastin' a long time, though I don't believe they hear you. I better cut in an' ask fool questions for th' looks of it."

"That'll come easy to you," retorted Two-Spot. "Well, things was goin' from bad to worse on th' SV. They couldn't keep an outfit. Them that wasn't scared away was bribed to quit. Dahlgren, Lang, an' Gurley all was SV men. Ol' Arnold borrowed three thousand dollars on his note in Highbank two years ago. Big Tom bought it an' holds it now. I think it's due next spring. Arnold has had to sell cows in small bunches to buy grub. There ain't no nat'ral increase, an' th' Bar H has a lot more calves an' yearlin's than Nature gave it. For th' last year th' SV ain't been bothered very much. It's so close to dyin' that I reckon Big Tom would rather wait a little longer an' have somethin' left to take when he does get it."

"Pleasant sort of a buzzard, Big Tom," said Johnny. "You missed then—gimme th' knife."

"Once in a while Lang or Gurley drive a cow into th' quicksands, just to keep their hands in. They work for th' Triangle, but really for Big Tom. They're handy for him, seein' that they has th' Triangle range next to th' SV."

"Them names are easy to remember," observed Johnny, surrendering the knife.

"Big Tom wants th' SV for its water," said Two-Spot. "That's what most folks think. *I* think him an' some friends he's got somewhere aim to get it cheap an' run it themselves."

"What's th' Doc doin', squattin' where he is?" queried Johnny.

"There was some talk about th' SV's title to that end of it lyin' west of th' main trail, an' I reckon he's there to file a homestead claim if it's needed; but I really don't know."

"An' these other ranches are settin' back an' watchin' a sick man, a woman, an' a kid get robbed?" asked Johnny.

"Th' Triangle is scared of th' Bar H," answered Two-Spot. "It had its lesson ten years ago, an' ain't forgot it. Hank Lewis ain't got no nerve—it's only gall. Sam Gardner is sore about th' game, but he's all alone. Lefferts an' Reilly don't care much, an' Lang an' Gurley are in Big Tom's pay."

"What about th' Double X?" demanded Johnny.

"They are so far off they don't take no interest. They keeps over there purty much an' don't meddle, an', besides, they has troubles of their own, with th' rustlin' goin' on along their west edge."

"How do you know all this?" said Johnny.

"I worked for Ol' Simon fifteen years ago. I drifted back last winter, an' I've been here ever since. Nobody knows me."

"Why are you tellin' me?"

"I hears a lot under th' floor, before you come, an' after," said Two-Spot. "My ears are good, an' I got some brains left—not much, but enough to put two an' two together. Likewise I'm feelin' sorry for them Arnolds. I don't like to see a gang of thieves robbin' helpless critters like them. An' there's more. When I was comin' down here I got ketched in a storm an' like to froze to death. I would have, too, if that Arnold gal hadn't rid across me, pulled me out of a snowbank, an' toted me to th' ranch. They took care of me till I was strong ag'in, an' fed me up. I was near starved when th' storm got me."

"But why are you tellin' all this to me?" demanded Johnny.

Two-Spot stretched and handed over the knife. "I'm an ol' man, now," he said, "but there was a time when I wasn't. You are a young man, an' square, fur's I know.

You been hangin' 'round here playin' a lone hand against a bunch that'd cut your throat if they knowed what you've been doin'. There's a purty gal over on th' SV. She's square, too, an' helpless, an' lonely. She don't know what to do, nor where to turn. She layed in a nest of rocks one day an' was watchin' three Bar H punchers. A rattler showed up close to her, in a dead line with th' men. Scared to death of snakes, she was drawin' a bead on it, when a stranger offers her his cannon, an' his help. Then he gives her h—l about murder, an' goes away. But he don't go fur, only to Gunsight. He drives Squint out of th' country, kidnaps th' Doc, an' keeps a bunch of hoss thieves from killin' her ol' man. I never saw you before; I don't know how many cattle you've rustled nor how many trains you've stuck up. What's more, I don't care. I know a white man when I sees one, an' I'm not gamblin' when I shoots off my mouth to you. I'm only a two-spot; but even two-spots has their good points. You can allus remember that there's a two-spot holdin' a six-gun under that there floor any time you need him."

Johnny sat up: "I'm sayin' you ain't no two-spot, neither."

"Before I forget it, I want to tell you th' rest of it," went on Two-Spot, anger heightening his color. "As I was sayin', th' gal's white, an' square. She's plumb different from some I've seen in th' cow-towns. Big Tom wants th' SV, but he wants her, too; an' 'though he ain't pesterin' her now, I know him too well to think he's give up th' idea. He never lets loose. Th' only reason he's let up is because he figgers he's got a better way; an' he's patient. Can you imagine a whiskey-smellin', big brute like him courtin' *her*? Can you imagine how he'd do it? An' lemme tell you, Nelson: I *am* a two-spot, for if I'd been any good at all I'd 'a' put a knife into him an' then took my medicine, like a man. I was near sick with disappointment when you shot th' gun out of his hand."

"How do you know anythin' about that nest of rocks, an' th' three men?"

"I know lots of things I ain't supposed to, an' one of 'em is that Big Tom ain't give up th' notion of gettin' th'

SV, nor her, neither. There ain't no parson in thirty miles—an' Big Tom is terrible lazy. Sometimes I near sees red!" He glanced up the trail. "Here comes little Charley, leadin' a pack hoss. He's after supplies at Dailey's—" he stopped short and looked at Johnny, who was looking at him through narrowed lids. The same thought had come to them both at the same time. "I'm bettin' he don't get 'em," Two-Spot prophesied.

Johnny arose and stretched. "I'm bettin' he does," he drawled. "Reckon I'll go over an' swap gossip with Dailey," he explained, striding away.

Two-Spot watched him and also arose, going across the road and around the saloon. "I called it wrong," he muttered. "I'll copper that bet: *I* bets he does." A grin stole across his face as he shuffled toward Dailey's back door. "This'll be worth hearin', an' mebby I can get me a box of .45's; Ol' Eagle-Eye may be too cussed busy to pay any attention to *me!*"

Johnny sauntered into the store and seated himself on a box. "Howd'y, Ben."

Dailey smiled a welcome. "Been sunnin' yoreself?"

Johnny yawned. "Yeah; I'm shore lazy." He glanced out of the door at the boy who had ridden up and dismounted. "Reckon this is that Arnold kid," he observed.

Dailey hid a frown, and nodded. "I'm awful short of supplies today," he said. "Ol' Buffalo didn't bring me any—now I got to wait till he comes again."

Charley entered and handed a paper to the storekeeper, who took it, studied it, and then shook his head. "Bud, if you'd hunted through th' store you couldn't 'a' picked 'em any worse. I ain't got nothin' this calls for."

Charley's face fell. "Gee!" he said, "Peggy's out of almost everything. She said she just had to get these today." He looked around inquiringly. "Ain't that flour?" he asked, pointing to several filled sacks behind the counter.

"Them's flour sacks," answered Dailey, "but there ain't no flour in 'em now." He handed the list back to the boy. "No use, bud, you'll have to wait till Buffalo comes

up again. He's too old to be of any account, anyhow, th'
ol' fossil: he's allus forgettin' somethin', allus!"

Johnny held out his hand, his right hand. "Let's see it,
Charley," he said, and looked it over. "I'll be cussed if
that ain't funny!" he exclaimed. "This here is th' very
same as I was goin' to get filled for myself, only mine
wasn't all writ down like this. How'd you come to pick
these things out, Charley?"

"Quit yore fooling," grinned Charley. "I didn't pick
them. Peggy wrote that."

Johnny reached out and put the list in Dailey's hand.
"Better begin at th' top, Ben, an' run right down," he suggested. "We won't get 'em mixed that way, or leave
nothin' out. Let's start with one of them flour sacks, no
matter what's in 'em."

Dailey flushed. "But I just said I was all out——"

"Yo're th' most forgetful man I ever knowed, except,
mebby, Buffalo," said Johnny. "You ain't got no mem'ry
at all. Don't you remember you found a lot of things
you'd poked away an' forgot you had? An' don't you
remember that nobody ain't told you, yet, not to sell me
nothin'? That there paper is mine, now. I'm borrowin' it
because I ain't got my own list writ out. That's writ so
pretty an' plain, that it's pretty plain to read. If anybody
gets curious, which they won't unless you tell 'em, you
say that I gave you that an' wanted it filled. Now, we'll
start with th' flour, like I was sayin'."

Dailey looked down the list and then up at Johnny. He
was asking Fate why Nelson had to pick that particular
time to visit the store. Johnny was smiling, but there was
a look in his eyes which made the storekeeper do some
quick thinking. He had no orders not to sell to anyone
but the SV; and if Big Tom became curious he could put
his questions to the two-gun man and get what satisfaction he could. In his heart he was in sympathy with the
SV, and he had argued against refusing to sell to it.

"Nelson," said Dailey, slowly going behind the counter,
"It's a good thing you remembered about that stuff. Are
you takin' it to th' hotel?"

"Reckon not," answered Johnny. "Reckon I'll borrow

Charley's pack hoss an' him to take it off to a place I knows of, where there ain't no mice. You'd be surprised, Ben, if you knowed how many mice there are in that hotel."

Charley looked from one to the other and, not knowing what to think or say, grinned somewhat anxiously.

"How's yore dad, an' yore sister?" Johnny asked him.

"Al right," answered Charley. "But they was scared half to death yesterday when you an' them fellers came tearin' in, 'specially when you started shooting. You was awful drunk, wasn't you?"

"I don't remember much about it," confessed Johnny, "so I reckon mebby I was. We all got lost an' had to sleep out in th' brush all night. We was after th' coyote what kidnapped th' Doc, but we couldn't find him."

Dailey forgot to continue filling the list. He was holding a sack of sugar in his hand and drinking in every word. Johnny turned to him.

"Say, Ben," he said, "did I ever tell you th' story about Damsight?"

"You never did," answered the storekeeper, "not if my mem'ry ain't playin' me false again."

"It was scandalous," began Johnny, drumming with his fingers on the butt of a gun. "There was a bunch of hoss thieves fightin' a lone woman an' her crippled dad. An' what do you reckon th' men in Damsight did about it? Nothin'. Nothin' at all. They was so miserable, so coyote-livered, so scared to death that they didn't raise a finger. No, sir; there wasn't a *man* in th' town. They were just yellow dogs, runnin' around in men's clothes an' pertendin' they was humans—a lot of yellow dogs, an' not a cussed thing more."

Dailey bungled a knot, and swore under his breath.

"Things went on like that for quite a spell," continued Johnny, "then a big storm come up, an' one by one them fellers who didn't see th' error of their ways was struck by lightnin'. They never knowed what hit 'em. It was just like th' miracles I've heard sky pilots tell about. Some of 'em did see th' error of their ways in time. They had a hard time in th' storm, but they pulled out alive. There seems to be a moral to that story; there ain't no use tellin' a story like that if th' moral is left out. An' I reckon th' moral of this one is: A man might be able to dodge lots of trouble, 'specially when it ain't near him all th' time; but when he's livin' right next door to th' lightnin', he can't dodge that. What do you think about it, Charley?"

"Gee! That's like the things Peggy reads to me out of the Bible," he replied. "Only it wasn't lightning, but floods, and pestilences, and things like that. Why, once a whole ocean opened up right in the middle and let a lot of people walk across it, but when their enemies got halfway over it, closed up, *smack!* and they were all drowned."

Johnny nodded gravely. "There's strange things happenin', even today, Charley, an' nobody knows when or where they *will* happen. Now, leavin' miracles out of it, let's put those packages on that hoss out here, an' see if Ben has forgot how to throw a diamond hitch. I'm bettin' a dollar he has."

"I'll take that dollar, parson," grinned Dailey. "Gimme a hand with th' stuff."

They filed out to the horse, loaded with packages, as Two-Spot slipped in the back door, and Dailey won the dollar. Watching the boy ride away, he turned and started for the store.

"Well," he said, over his shoulder, "I've put up my lightnin' rods, an' now I'm goin' to spit on my hands an' hold fast, for if this storm busts she'll be a whizzer. I'm aimin' to tell people right to their faces that Dailey's store sells to anybody that's got th' cash. You better look to yore tent pegs, young man."

CHAPTER IX

Rolling Faster

THE NEXT morning Johnny mounted Pepper and rode toward the SV. He had some thinking to do and chose the conditions which he had found were most conducive to clarity and continuity of thought—the saddle. As he left the town behind he took Pepper into his confidence.

"Little hoss," he muttered, "we've gone just about as far as we can go without stirrin' up active an' personal troubles. We can't play our hand much longer without folks knowin' what we are doin'. What you an' me has got to do is plan things, choose th' leads, an' then stick to 'em in spite of h—l an' high water. An' we ought to figger on doin' somethin' solid for th' SV. Any fool can tear around an' smash things, an' we've got to do that; but you an' me ain't satisfied with no worthless pile of rubbish; we got to smash so we can pan that rubbish, sort of, an' get somethin' out of it. An' when a feller pans free an' wide on a cattle range, he most likely will get cows. What else can he get? A man rocks gravel an' gets gold, if there's any gold in it. A puncher, rockin' ranches, ought to get cows. There ain't nothin' else *to* get. So we got to get cows, an' now we got to find out how many cows we want. We can't find out exact, but we can do better than guess at it. There's a limit to this pannin' of ours—an' it ought to be what was lost an' stolen. There's only one place where we can find that out, an' we're ridin' that way now. Havin' decided what we're aimin' for, we'll let it rest an' turn to somethin' mighty close to us, ourselves; somethin' plumb personal, an' terrible riled.

"You remember Tex Ewalt, don't you? You ought to, because he said some mighty nice things about you; I was scared he'd turn yore head. Now, Tex was a wise boy; he was amazin' wise. Do you remember what he told young Slim-Shanks, that there Baxter kid, who was all tangled up with tender feelin's? Mebby you don't; but *I* do. Slim-Shanks, he was fair wallerin' in misery, an' actin' like a sick calf. He hung around that gal's house like a dogie 'round a water hole. She must 'a' got sick of th' sight of him. Every place she looked, there was Slim-Shanks, an' his hope-I-die look. She couldn't get away from th' big calf. Tex never missed anythin', 'specially if it was under his eyes, an' one day young Slim-Shanks got bleatin' to him, moanin' an' groanin' about his busted heart. What did Tex tell him? I'll tell you. He says, slow an' deliberate: 'Slim-Shanks, some you got to rush; others you got to pique—an' th' best way to do that, in most cases, is to let 'em think you can look at 'em, an' not see 'em. It takes nerve—an' not one man in a hundred has got th' nerve. Make 'em keep a-thinkin' of you without chasin' after 'em. Yore medicine ain't no good—you might try th' other.' Now, just because Slim-Shanks didn't have th' nerve ain't sayin' Tex was wrong. I've got to decide which way is best, an' it's tough ridin'. Now you keep right still while I wrestle this thing out," and he became so wrapped up in the problem that he paid no attention to where Pepper was going; and she took him to the vantage point on the valley's rim from whence he had looked down at the posts and their enclosed quicksands; and arriving there, she stopped. Johnny was aroused from his abstractions by a voice which brought him back in touch with his surroundings, and with a jerk.

"Good morning," said Margaret.

He looked up, hauled off his sombrero and muttered something, his face in one instant giving up his secret. Then by an act of will almost brutal in its punishment, he mastered his feelings and nodded calmly.

"Good mornin', Ma'am," he replied. "You found me off my guard; I was miles away."

"Why aren't you?" she retorted, smiling.

"Meanin'?"

"If I were a man I'd stay near my friends as long as I could."

"I did, Ma'am; but there was too many wimmin', so I drifted."

"Ah! A woman-hater; or are you trying to forget?"

"They was all married," he grinned, "that is, all that had any chance to be. They married my friends, which took down th' bars on me. I was fair game when there was any blame which should 'a' been saddled on their partners. So I drifted. You can't use a gun on a woman, you know."

"So you came down here to be a mystery?"

"Mystery?" he laughed. "Me! Why, Ma'am, I'm so open I'm easy pickin' in every poker game I sets in. Folks know what I'm goin' to think before I start thinkin' at all."

"Then I must be even denser than I feared. I am very much interested in what you have been thinking, and haven't the slightest clue to it. Perhaps if I confess my helplessness you will take pity on me, and tell me what you are doing down here; and why?"

"Th' 'why' shows you ain't guessin' much, Ma'am," he replied, quizzically.

"Why did you join that crowd of drunken rowdies, and act worse than any of them?"

"Because when I acts bad, I'm harmless, an' they was not."

"Perhaps; but why did you join them?"

"I was afraid they might hurt themselves, or get lost."

"Father says that we owe you a debt of gratitude; I'm sorry that I shall have to disillusion him."

"I wouldn't give him no shocks, Ma'am, till his laig gets well. He ain't as young as he was."

"Why did you go to the trouble of seeing that we had supplies?"

"Invalids has got to eat, Ma'am."

"Why did you stop that—that brute—when he was entertaining his companions with his idea of humor?"

"A man would just naturally do that, Ma'am; it's an instinct."

"Why did you do what you did the day, and night, that my brother was stopped from going to Highbank for the doctor?"

"A man would do that, too; an' any doctor that forgets his duty deserves to be stole an' *made* do it."

"You realize, of course, that you are getting yourself into great danger?"

"I wouldn't hardly call it that, Ma'am," he replied, smiling. "There are different breeds. A man might get scared at a pack of wolves, an' not worry about coyotes, at all."

"Nevertheless, the danger exists; no man is proof against ambush. Why are you courting it?" she persisted.

"Folks don't ambush till they're purty shore about things; an' tryin' to keep 'em from gettin' shore is th' hardest part of it."

"Why are you courting it?"

"Ma'am, some things are so raw that they rile an honest man; I admits I'm riled considerable, which, of course, don't prove me to be honest. Even Two-Spot says he don't know how many cows I've rustled, nor how many trains I've stuck up. Th' number might surprise him."

"Somehow I feel that I should thank you for the favors you have done us," she replied; "but my opinion of western men, as *I* have found them, urges me to seek the motive first."

He flushed, and looked at her steadily. "Mebby that's th' motive yo're askin' about," he said gravely, and slowly continued: "You've asked me a lot of questions; can I deal a few?"

"It depends on what they are."

"They're personal—plumb personal. I'm wantin' to know if Big Tom holds yore dad's note for three thousand dollars." He waited a moment and, receiving no reply, asked two in one. "How many cows was on th' SV when you bought it, an' how many are on it now? Th' tally sheets ought to give that purty close—close enough, anyhow."

"Mr. Nelson, the first seems to be public knowledge. Mr. Huff holds my father's note for that amount. The number of cows, then or now, I do not know."

"Is th' note endorsed, an 'what security was given?"

"I endorsed it. The ranch is in my name."

"Uh-huh," commented Johnny. "Do you know where th' tally sheets are?"

"If you mean the books, they are on a shelf in the house."

"Ma'am," he said, earnestly, "I wonder if you would mind copyin' off what there is about th' number of cows on th' ranch after th' last trail herd left, th' year before you took possession? An' how many cows there was this spring, or th' number of calves branded then?"

"Why do you want this?" she demanded. "Why should I go to that trouble, or tell you such things?"

"I don't know," he answered, "less'n you want to. You see, I'm curious about things, *too*. It's a failin' most humans have, a bad failin'. An', before I forget it, I'm goin' to ask you another: Judgin' from them posts down there along th' river, that's quicksand. Why ain't there more wire strung to keep th' cows out of it?"

"Because it is torn off as fast as it is put up. We have given up the effort; it is useless. *If you only knew—*" she checked herself, but the tears of helpless anger in her eyes could not be kept from forming.

"That's just it, Ma'am—if I only knowed," he replied, nodding. "I know a lot about that, but not about th' number of cows you have lost. I'm what you might call morbid, an' like to grieve about calamities. Would you mind gettin' them figgers for me? I'll be here about ten o'clock tomorrow for 'em, if you will."

"Yes; but *why* do you want them?" she demanded.

"I'm aimin' to put th' fear of God where it ain't been knowed for a long time, Ma'am," he answered, "an' be rewarded by th' company."

"What company?"

"I'll tell you that later, Ma'am. It will be th' last thing to be told, an' you'll never guess it alone. You'll have to be helped. An' when I tell you, you'll be surprised, an' wonder how it was that you couldn't guess such a simple thing as that. I'll be leavin' you now, to keep on a-rollin'."

She looked after him longer than he was in sight, lost in the solving of the riddle, which grew more formidable the more it was attacked, unless the instinct of her sex was given a fairer hearing. It hammered and hammered for admittance and gained entry enough to cause a flush to steal across her face, and was instantly thrown out bodily. But if it was refused its day in court, it could at least stand outside the walls and make its plea, and so it did. Somehow, when she was in the presence of this man she felt a sense of security that was almost like a lullaby. His easy, graceful poise, the quiet reverence which lay smiling behind his eyes and crept into his voice, the unobtrusive but unwavering confidence he had in himself, and the feeling of tremendous reserve power which emanated from his every word, look, and movement seemed almost to bathe her with peace and security. And for one instant his eyes had looked at her and made her go suddenly limp: she had felt suffocated, and the feeling had not been rebuked. Turning her pony's head, she rode slowly homeward, knowing that she would do whatever he requested, in spite of herself—and, strangely, she felt no fear.

Johnny, the vortex of an emotional whirlpool, rode into Gunsight and dismounted before the Palace, the action purely a matter of habit. Suddenly he shook his head with savage energy. "You fool!" he growled. "Keep yore mind on yore job, or somebody'll find you easy pickin'!" He looked around and saw Two-Spot grinning at him, and felt a quick irritation. "Well," he demanded sharply, "what's on *yore* mind?"

Two-Spot rubbed the disgraceful stubble on his face and grinned wider than before. "I was just a-thinkin' you need a guardian," he retorted. "Through with Pepper?"

Johnny regarded him unfavorably. "A man usually gets what he needs, if he tries hard enough. Tote that away an' gnaw on it! I'm through with Pepper."

Two-Spot watched him enter the saloon, and reflectively scratched his chin. "Mebby there is some meat on that bone, but he didn't have to call me no dog, did he? Cuss him an' his trick of leavin' me knots to untie. He's crazy—crazy as a fox!"

CHAPTER X

Freight for Highbank

WHILE JOHNNY had been talking to Margaret there was being enacted a far different scene down on the Bar H. The foreman's anger at the condition of his three men when they had ridden in the day before was newly aroused by Smitty the following morning, when he arrived and shamefacedly slunk into the bunkhouse. Big Tom stormed about the room, demanding to know why he had to have such sheep in his outfit. He wanted to know what they had done, and they could not tell him; he asked where they had gone, and they replied to the SV. What had they done there? They could not recall. Dahlgren spoke vaguely of "going after th' feller," but had no idea who he was, or anything about it; but they all remembered that Nelson had been with them, in the same condition as themselves, and that he had terrorized the SV household. Smitty corroborated the last and rejoiced at the agility which had twice saved him. There were some things to which his memory clung.

Little Tom Carney and Wolf Forbes enjoyed their friends' discomfiture, at the same time sharing in some of Big Tom's disgust.

Wolf looked at them pityingly. "You make me sick!" he sneered. "Fine bunch of sage hens—all you think about is liquor. How many times have I told you to let th' stuff alone, as long as you couldn't drink like humans?"

"Parson Forbes has th' floor," growled Carson. "Bein' human, he——"

"That'll do!" snapped Wolf. "You know how much parson there is to me. Who shot you out of a lynchin' bee back in Texas?" he demanded.

"Who got me into it?" demanded Carson. "They was watchin' that bank, an' I told you so!"

"You said so because you got scared at th' last minute!" retorted Wolf. "If I didn't have to waste half an hour arguin' with you—oh, what of it! That ain't excusin' you from bein' a fool day before yesterday, is it?"

"Mebby you could 'a' done better?" ironically queried Dahlgren.

"If he couldn't, I'd fire him!" snapped Big Tom.

"You wouldn't have to fire me; I'd quit!" replied Wolf.

"Then why don't you *do* somethin', 'stead of loafin' along that northwest line, pertendin' you has got to watch for rustlers an' them Double X fellers?" sneered Fraser.

"I will!" shouted Wolf. "I'm goin' to watch one man—not everybody on th' range. There's only one man in this country that ain't got a good reason for bein' here—that's Nelson—an' I'm goin' to watch him till I get what I want. Then mebby you fools will be able to bury him for me. Think so?"

"I'm wishin' you luck," said Smitty. "You'll need it. You be careful who it is that gets buried."

Wolf looked at him pityingly. "You pore sheep!" he said, "I'm sorry you was so lively in th' SV house, cussed if I ain't!" He turned to Big Tom. "Do I go?"

"You do," said the foreman. "Somethin' is wrong, an' we got to fix it. Stay as long as you has to. I'm not worryin' about *you*—but I *am* scared th' cows will eat these four chumps. They shore is green an' tender. When you startin'?"

"Right soon," answered Forbes, going out.

Big Tom stood in the doorway and watched his two-gun man enter the corral. His confidence in the wiry killer was not built upon hearsay. Cold, venomous, and quick, he was more like a rattler than his namesake. Up to now every man who had faced Wolf Forbes had faced death, a death swift and certain.

In due time Wolf rode northward and arrived in Gunsight, where he loafed around exchanging gossip with everyone he knew. George was coaxed to talk, but his stupidity did what a mediocre cleverness might have failed to do. He yielded nothing that Wolf could use, and a few things which did not suit Wolf's needs. With Jerry, the harness-maker, the conversation was a husk without a kernel, and the second-hand saddles were of no value to Wolf, who was searching down things which were against his own convictions. Two-Spot smoked his cigar and rambled aimlessly in his garrulous monologue. He was hopeless from Wolf's viewpoint. Dave's admissions were barren of information of a constructive sort. Fanning did not know anything, and Dailey was as bad. Wolf finally gave up the effort and went back to the Palace, there to await the coming of Nelson.

Johnny entered the saloon some time later, nodded to its occupants, but kept on going toward the rear door. "Be back after I eat," he said.

George looked out to see who was washing. "This ain't no time to come in for dinner," he growled.

"There's never no time like th' present. Can't help it," retorted Johnny. "While I'm washin' you rustle th' chuck."

"Wolf was here askin' about you," said George.

"That so? Well, that ain't no crime."

"Can he shoot better'n you?" queried the cook. "He says he'll shoot against anybody in this country with six-guns, any fashion, for a dollar a shot. Does it sound like money?"

"If I could shoot that good I'd be too rich to be restin' up between cow-punchin' jobs," gurgled Johnny through a double handful of water. "Reckon he knows what he's talking about, or he wouldn't risk bein' took up."

"Well," said the cook, "I've heard somethin' from them that seen it. If you aim to go ag'in' him, let me know ahead of time, will you?"

"I ain't aimin' to," replied Johnny.

"Hey! Wait!" exclaimed the cook, disappearing. He returned with a clean towel. "Use this. That ain't fit for a dog no more."

Johnny looked at the old one and smiled. It was quite some distance from the condition which called for a change of towels at the Delmonico. "Thanks. Th' dirt won't come off this one. What about dinner?"

"Gosh! I forgot," said George, dodging into the kitchen.

Johnny had company while he ate, for the cook entertained him with an account of Wolf's visit, to all of which Johnny paid polite interest, but he hastened his meal. Then he slowed again, for George was beginning to get at the kernels.

"Has he lost his saddle?" asked the cook.

"Don't know."

"Must a' busted it. He asked me if I knowed where there was a good second-hand one, gold or brass trimmed. An' say, keep yore eyes on yourn; he asked me if you tote it up to yore room nights. I didn't tell him you keep it in th' kitchen, but I did say there wasn't no room in yore room for no saddle. He wants one, I reckon, because he went to Jerry's when he left here."

"He wouldn't take my saddle," said Johnny. "He was havin' fun with you."

"Mebby," admitted George. "He was in a jokin' humor, 'cause he laughed an' says he reckoned you'd get th' courtin' bug, like all th' rest, an' go callin' on that Arnold gal. An' he says he'll bet you get throwed as hard as th' rest of 'em. I gave it to him right back an' says that you an' me are both alike—we hates wimmin."

"They've got to hustle if they rope you or me," laughed Johnny. "What else did he say?"

"That's all, that an' what I told you before. Where you goin' now?"

"Round to Dave's for a game of cards, mebby. Wolf

an' Fanning are there," answered Johnny, taking his hat from the floor and arising.

"You ain't repeatin' what I said, are you?" asked George, somewhat anxiously. "He didn't mean nothin' by it."

"No; why should I? We all like to joke. I ain't got nothin' against Wolf. See you at supper," and Johnny went out the back door. As he neared the corner of the kitchen Two-Spot turned it and bumped into him. "Wolf's askin' about you all over town," he muttered, and then, louder: "Why'n blazes don't you look out?"

"Some day I'll chuck you over th' roof," retorted Johnny. "If you'd keep yore head up you'd see where you was goin'!"

"Keep yore own head up! You don't own this town!"

Johnny turned as he reached Dave's door. "If I did I'd run *you* out of it," and entering, he slammed the door behind him.

There was a laugh from the bar, where Wolf and Fanning were still chatting with Dave. Wolf swung the conversation around to the SV and kept it there as long as he could after Johnny joined them. He worked around to Squint, and to the kidnapping of the Doc, and endeavored to get a careless admission from Johnny; but the latter evaded the traps. He showed no disinclination to talk about Wolf's pet subjects and even helped the other to keep the conversation on them. He disposed of the committee's visit to the SV by saying that either the Arnolds knew nothing at all about recent events, or else they had been terrorized by the visitors' actions and had been unable to think clearly or even to talk. He admitted that the committee was in no condition to handle the situation, and that he was as bad as any member of it. As to what had really occurred out there the details were lost to him because he had been too drunk to know much about anything; and in this he was backed up by what Wolf, himself, knew about the other members of the committee. He remembered that he had got rough and that someone, he thought it had been Smitty, had yelled something about getting somebody, and they had followed him to do it.

"Give us another round, Dave," said Wolf. "I ain't losin' no sleep about th' Doc—" he began again.

Johnny interrupted him and led the way to a table. "Ain't no use standin' up all afternoon. We'll drink 'em over here, Dave."

Fanning and Wolf followed and the afternoon passed in cards, drinking, and talking. Johnny drank his liquor every round without losing his head, for which he was indebted to the proprietor. When supper time came around Fanning pushed back the table.

"I just can't make nothin' these days," he growled. "I never saw a game break so even; bet nobody's lost ten dollars."

"I won somewhere 'round four," laughed Wolf, arising.

"I'm out five," grinned Johnny. "Jim has played all afternoon to get that dollar. Goin' home, Wolf, or you aimin' to make a night of it?"

"Got to go," answered Wolf, "but I got sense enough to get my supper in town," he smiled. "Lead th' way, Jim."

"Hey!" called Dave,' "somebody gimme a hand with this keg?"

Johnny, who was last in the line, turned. "Be right after you fellers," he said, over his shoulder. "Where do you want it, Dave?"

"Up on th' buck, under th' bar. Easy, now! *Up!* Good."

"That was fine baby stuff I was drinkin' all afternoon," chuckled Johnny. "How'd you keep th' color?"

"Young man," smiled Dave, "yore business is punchin' cows; mine's sellin' liquor. Go on, now, an' eat. Keep yore wits sharp."

While they were at supper there was a commotion outside and four punchers from the Double X stamped in. "Hello, fellers!" said Slim Hawkes, throwing his sombrero on a table.

"It smells good," grunted Wilkes, and turned to the other two. "Boys, this is Nelson: Nelson, shake han's with Gus Thompson an' Bill Sage." He nodded coldly to Wolf, who returned it with reserve.

"What brought you hoodlums to town?" asked Fanning. "You fellers act scared of Gunsight. Ol' Dailey got you buffaloed?"

"I reckon it's th' twenty miles," said Slim, dragging a table up to the one then in use. "Hey, George! Can't you move faster'n that?"

"Go roll in a ditch," came the polite reply.

"Well," said Wilkes, "we was riding near th' east line when we discovers we was goin' to be late for supper, an' th' ranchhouse bein' near twenty miles, an' th' town only a couple, we votes for a *ho*-tel feed an' a session in Dave's." He turned toward the kitchen. "Hey, George! We saw dust above th' Sherman trail an' figgers it's Buffalo. Is he due tonight? Thought I'd tell you so you could get ready for th' old codger."

George stuck his head in the doorway. "Any more hard luck comin' this evenin'?" he demanded. "Can't somebody trail in after him so I can keep on a-workin'?"

"You get back in there an' go to work!" warned Thompson. "We're hungry!"

Wolf arose, paid his bill, and took up his hat. "Well, I'm off. So-long, fellers," and he strolled out.

"Which ain't causin' me no tears," muttered Slim. "He likes us 'bout as well as we like him. Here comes th' cook. Good for you, George!"

When the Double X squad had nearly finished, the rumble of a wagon was heard, rapidly getting nearer. Soon it passed the side of the hotel, and ceased.

"There's Ol' Allus-Late!" grumbled George.

"I'll give him a hand," said Johnny, arising and going out. "It'll save you time."

"Don't strain yoreself on *my* account," replied George.

"Hello, Buffalo!" said Johnny, starting to unhitch. "I'll put these boys in th' shed an' you go eat. George is ready for you. You can feed 'em later. If you'll trust me, I'll do it for you; I watched you last time."

"Much obliged, sonny," smiled the old man. "Yo're right

obligin', but I allus eat last. They've done good today, considerin' th' load, an' nothin's too good for 'em."

"Thought you came back light?"

"Got near a load of hides—can't you smell 'em?"

"I shore can; but I'm so slow witted they didn't mean anythin' to me. Green, too?" he suggested.

"Yep," replied the freighter. "Picked 'em up all along; but I won't get no more this trip. Th' Triangle won't have none—an' I ain't goin' to go out of my way to call at th' Bar H. Got enough, an' I'm goin' right through. I'm allus glad to git home."

"I bet you are," replied Johnny. "Ain't anythin' more I can do, is there?"

"No, sonny; thankee. I appreciate yore help. I ain't as young as I used ter be, nor as quick. Thankee; good night."

Johnny went to the saloon, where a sudden outburst of voices told him he would find Fanning and the Double X men. As he opened the door a roar of laughter greeted him.

"Cussed if that ain't rich!" shouted Slim, jumping up and down. "Th' Doc stole from his peaceful fireside. Oh! Ho! Ho! An' to 'tend to his *friends*, th' SV! By th' Lord! Mebby we'll do it over again, ourselves, sometime, when we feel extra good!"

"I'd give ten dollars to shake han's with th' man that done it," laughed Sage. "I bet Big Tom rolled on th' floor when he heard it—an' bit th' furniture!"

"But how'd he get Squint's outfit?" demanded Wilkes.

Dave told of Squint's disappearance and of the deep sorrow darkening the sun, whereupon an eager discussion took place. This lasted until Dailey came in and impatiently pounded on a table with the butt of his gun.

"Order, Gents; order!" he shouted. "My time's valuable—who are goin' to be th' victims?"

"Shore we'll order!" yelled Slim. "All up, boys! Dailey's treatin'," and despite his protests, he found that he was. Soon after this a six-handed game got into full swing.

Dave's vexation grew steadily and passed the anger point without stopping. He was tired, and now his labors were only beginning. Two-Spot was living up to Dave's opinion of him, for he had not been much in evidence around the saloon since noon, and had not appeared at all since the Double X punchers had come in. Dave went to the front door and called, and then he went to the rear door and yelled, but received no response. Thinking that he saw a shadowy figure skulking in the darkness, he yelled again, and with no honeyed promises as the burden of his message. Glancing around in the darkness as if to penetrate it by an act of will, he shouted a threat and stamped back to the bar, slamming the door so hard that the windows shook.

"Come on, Dave!" cried Dailey, cheerful in view of his ownership of the last pot. "What you so slow about?"

"If he'd quit pickin' on Two-Spot," said Thompson, "an' tend to business, folks would like it better."

"Anybody that don't like it can get out!" retorted Dave. "He's *never* around when there's work to be did!"

The evening passed swiftly and midnight was not far off when Dave found it necessary to draw on the contents of the new keg, and he disappeared below the bar for a few minutes. Hardly had his head passed from sight when Two-Spot, closely watching the bar, slipped quietly through the back door and went silently to Johnny, where he poked his face close to the puncher's ear and muttered for a moment. Johnny nodded and looked over his hand again, while Two-Spot scurried for the door and safety, being silently threatened by Fanning, who thoroughly enjoyed the situation. Two-Spot looked fearfully around and closed the door behind him. He barely had time to get under the saloon when Wolf Forbes, returning from his short tour around the buildings, turned the corner of the kitchen and peered in at the window.

Johnny folded his hand, pushed out the required number of chips and grunted. "I'm trailin'—but I shore wish that man would stop. He must have about thirteen aces."

"I'm limpin', but I'm there," remarked Thompson. "Th' dust back here is awful."

"There ain't no call for you to put on airs," growled Slim, pushing in what he was shy. "I got four kings, but you don't see *me* quittin', do you?"

"You must a' picked up what I throwed away," said Dailey. "Havin' felt yore pulses I'm buildin' a house right out there in th' middle, where you all can see it, an' get covetous."

"Th' coyote that wins this pot," said Slim, "will shore have to get Ol' Buffalo an' his freight waggin' to haul——"

A roar of laughter burst from Johnny and he pushed back from the table, lying back in his chair so his lungs could have plenty of room. Dailey put his hand over the pile of chips he had just shoved in, Slim jumped and stared at the roaring puncher, the others manifesting their astonishment each according to his own manner. There was a resounding *whack!* from the bar and Dave, holding the top of his head with both hands, moaned as he looked wildly about, and then, glaring at the convulsed puncher, he made several pointed, pertinent, profane, and personal remarks and slowly went down again to finish his task.

Slim scratched his head. "Well," he drawled, "I allus knowed I was bright an' witty, but I never knowed that I was *that* good. I likes a man that pays me a compliment like that."

"Th' loud an' screechin' roarin' of th' wild jackass is heard nightly over th' land," observed Sage. "It has scared me plumb cold—I'm layin' down as fine a pair of four-spots as I've ever held. I ain't got th' nerve to give 'em the backin' they deserves. Will somebody lend me their gun?"

"I cussed near shot," said Wilkes.

"What's that?" demanded Dailey. "Don't you do nothin' like that! He's a part of my profits. Now, if somebody will stuff a hat in that cave, I'll proceed from where I left off. I've raised her till she sags in th' middle—who's got any props?"

"I allus play poker by th' weather," said Thompson. "When it's dry an' hot, I calls, an' when it's hot an' dry, I raises. Bein' dry an' hot, I hereby calls. Dave, bring me a box to put it in."

"Don't you bother Dave," chuckled Dailey. "He's puttin' hoss liniment on his bald spot—from ear to ear, an' eyes to spine. I can tote this home in a couple of trips."

Johnny, weak and tearful, drew up to the table. "I was just a-thinkin'," he said. "Where are we now?"

"Was you?" queried Fanning. "Then don't you never do no thinkin' nights after I've gone to bed."

Dave emerged again, grinning. "Beats all," he muttered, "how our sins foller us around. Pore Squint; I reckon his mem'ry's with us. I won't rest till I knows what was done with him."

In the middle of the next game Johnny broke out again and Dave reached for the mallet.

"I ain't what you'd call superstitious," said Dailey, "but I lost that last pot to a man who didn't even know where he was. Every time I hears a jackass warble I has bad luck. I'm obeyin' th' warnin' an' gettin' out of this game while I have th' holes left in my belt. What's more, I'm goin' home; I know when it's time to let go."

"Pore Dailey," moaned Fanning, "we all got a little of it tonight—an' I'm sleepin' with a gun under my piller, you bet!"

"It's time we quit," said Slim, arising. "We got twenty miles to go—an' while mebby it ain't so dark as I've seen it, it'll be dark enough to keep us from racin'. But before I go I'd like to find out somethin': Will somebody please tell me what I said, that second time, that was so funny?"

"It wasn't nothin' you said, Slim," answered Wilkes; "it was yore face—but I holds that it's cussed unpolite for anybody to laugh right out loud about a man's misfortunes."

"Nelson, I begs yore pardon," said Slim. "You has a proper an' fittin' sense of humor. Let's have one more round before we ride home an' wake up th' boys to tell 'em what happened to Dailey. How'd you come out, Nelson?"

"I got plenty—a great plenty, thank you," answered Johnny, throttling the laughter which threatened to burst out again. "I'm heavy with it. Dailey will foller me around tomorrow tryin' to get me into a seven-up or Californy-jack game in his store, where he's got lookin' glasses an' cold decks. Well—here's how." Putting down the half-emptied glass he turned, nodded, and went out. When he closed the door behind him he became alert as a cat in a strange cellar and slipped around the kitchen, hand on gun. Once inside the hotel he began laughing again, silently this time, and went hurriedly up to his room, where he lit the lamp and began to undress. Removing his boots he stood up, and in such a position that the shadow on the wall would tell any watcher that he was removing his shirt. Blowing out the light, he hurriedly put the garment on again and, carrying the boots in his hand, slipped silently down the stairs and into the kitchen, where he took the lariat from his saddle and went swiftly to the front door, where he listened as he slowly opened it. Satisfied that no one was watching, he slid out sideways, closed the door gently behind him and, going along the side of Dailey's store, he slung the lariat around his neck, put the boot straps between his teeth and, dropping on all fours, crossed the road and disappeared into the darkness on the farther side.

The noise around at Dave's took on sudden volume as the Double X punchers went out to their horses. Laughing and joking, they swung down the trail at a lope. Fanning and Dailey said good night to Dave and departed.

Gunsight instantly grew quiet and soon a figure emerged from Dave's horse shed and was swallowed up in the darkness to the east of the main trail, and soon thereafter the hoofbeats of a horse were heard by one pair of listening ears in town. Two-Spot crept out from under the saloon and stood up, shaking his fist at the sound, which moved southward. Then the hoofbeats grew more rapid as Wolf increased the pace of his horse.

Down the trail, where it narrowed to pass between two clumps of bush, a coatless, hatless figure crouched in the left-hand thicket, the coil of rope in his left hand held low down. At irregular intervals he seemed to be suffering from an attack of ague, for he quivered and shook; and there came from him strange, subterranean rumblings and rusty wheezes which he tried to muffle with an arm. As the hoofbeats coming from town grew rapidly louder and nearer he tensed himself. The pounding rang out loudly now, the soft jingling of chain and ornaments distinguishable in the greater sound, and soon the vague figure of a mounted man burst out of the darkness and swept past the clumps of brush. The waiting man on foot straightened his body and arm at the same moment, and at the instant the rope grew taut he pulled it sharply and leaned back with all his strength. There was an exclamation and a crash, and the man who had waited ran swiftly forward, hauling the rope in hand over hand. Kneeling at the side of the prostrate figure he slipped the guns from their holsters and threw them into the brush, and then fell back to work with the rope and the victim's kerchiefs. With the gagged, bound, and blindfolded man on his back he went up the trail toward town.

Gunsight had been quiet for over an hour when a strangely shaped figure staggered across the road west of the hotel and steadily neared the shed. It came slowly around the corner and stopped at the side of the big freight wagon, where part of it went to the ground, while the remainder, appearing in the form of a man, worked at the ropes closing the tarpaulin at the rear of the wagon, and soon had it open. He stepped back for a moment as a reminder of what lay behind it struck his nostrils, and again he was seized with a recurrence of the peculiar malady which had seized him frequently in the last hour. At the muffled sounds which came from him, the figure on the ground writhed as if in sympathy and endeavored to repeat them. The attack passing, he drew a long breath and plunged his head and shoulders into the opening he had made and worked hard for a few minutes; and when he stepped back he had several pieces of rope in his hands, which he had taken from a bundle of skins. Drawing a few deep breaths he moved around the wagon and bent over the figure on the ground, exchanging the pieces of rope for his own lariat, but not without a struggle which made it necessary for him to sit on the figure and exert his strength. Tying good knots in the dark on arms and legs which writhed and twisted was slow work, but it was necessary that it be well done, and when he arose to his feet he was assured as to that. Bending over, he picked up the figure and carried it to the rear of the wagon, where he pushed it headfirst into the opening made for it, despite its contortions and gurgled profanity. Again his head and shoulders disappeared under the tarpaulin, and when he straightened up he knew that his victim was so securely lashed to the wagon box that it would be impossible for him to move around, no matter how much he bridged and wriggled, no matter how much the wagon jolted. It was a job which demanded care, and had received it. Satisfied as to the conditions inside the wagon, he now turned his attention to the outside, which must be proof against telling anything to the observing eyes of the old buffalo hunter. He carefully replaced the tarpaulin as he had found it, even to its folds, and he duplicated the knots he had untied. Pausing a moment to think, he dusted canvas and ropes, cogitated as to his own footprints, which Old Buffalo would not fail to notice, if the light permitted. He got his rope, coiled it, and with this for his tool he effaced the prints and then went to the horse shed. When he reappeared he was leading a horse whose color melted into the darkness like a lump of charcoal in ink. They passed in the dark like the passing of a cloud and it was not until some minutes later that the drumming of hoofs rang out on the trail, bound southward in search of a saddled, but riderless, horse, which should be found in that direction. It would not do for it to be seen by anyone but themselves while it bore the riding gear of Wolf Forbes.

A blot on the ground near the horse shed arose. Two-Spot was in pain and the tears were flowing down his unwashed cheeks, while spasm after spasm racked him. Holding a six-gun limply in his hand, he stumbled and staggered away from the buildings, to some place where he could give free vent to the agonizing mirth which threatened to choke him. Coming to a weed-filled gully he sank into it and lay with his face buried in his arms. Minutes passed before he got control of himself and then he rolled over weakly and stared up at the star-filled sky, inert and sore, for he knew not how long.

"If it was anybody but Wolf," he moaned, "it would be bad enough, but it's ten times worse as it is. Wolf Forbes, th' killer; Wolf, th' two-gun badman, th' terror of th' range; th' cool, deliberate, stuck-up Wolf, who walks with stiff-laigged dignity, an' holds his nose up in th' air! Wolf Forbes—oh, my G—d! Gimmie air! Snoopin' wise-like all over town, fillin' his ears; smart an' chipper, cold an' wise! Oh, me! Oh, my! Sneakin' 'round from winder to winder, listenin' at th' cracks—as if I didn't see his bow laigs passin' back and forth. Tryin' to learn if it was Nelson who stole th' pill-roller, an' did for Squint. Hearin' what them Double X fellers had to say about it, an' *him*; standin' there bilin' with rage! Oh, when this night's work gets spread over th' range there'll go up a laugh that'll shake th' sky! If he's got th' nerve to come back an' face that music he'll have to *use* them guns of his'n. An' he can't fight 'em all, good as he is. *Wolf*, huh? He started out as a wolf, but he'll change his spots afore he gets to Highbank, an' his scent, too! He! He! He! He'll turn into a polecat—a hydrophoby skunk! Oh! Me! Oh! My! Polecat Forbes, th' strong man! Oh! Ho! Ho!"

While he rested, his merriment slowly died and gave way to venom, and he sat up to shake his fist in the direction of the wagon.

"You earned it, cuss you!" he snarled. "Bound up like a bundle of rags, an' headed for Highbank, you are! Forty mile, it is; forty mile of sun, an' jolts, an' stink, an' flies, an' achin' bones, an' cuttin' ropes. Forty mile of heat an' dust an' thirst; forty mile of rage, of thinkin' it all over; forty mile of h—l on wheels—that's what it is— forty mile of h—l on wheels! Fourteen hours, says I, but I hopes it's twenty. Time enough for thinkin', you blackguard. 'Member th' time you kicked me off'n Dave's hitchin' rail? 'Member how funny it was, huh? 'Member how I said I'd get square with you, an' how you kicked me ag'in, an' made me dance to yore blasted guns? I was a harmless ol' man; but it was funny, just th' same. Oh, I'm wishin' I dast go over there an' tell you all I'm thinkin'—yore ears would bother you more'n yore nose if I could. If I only knowed you wouldn't come back; if I only knowed that! It was *me* that did it. I told Nelson about you, an' I was hopin' you'd get blowed apart; but this is better, cuss you! When yo're dead yore troubles are over—an' you'll wish you was dead when *this* story gets out. An' if you keeps yore nerve, an' finds out who done it, you *will* be! Wolf? Wolf? Huh? I got a better name for *you*!"

He arose and went back toward the saloon, and had not quite reached it when he heard the soft steps of a horse on the sand and he dropped to the ground, his gun lightly held and ready. In a moment he made out a man leading a horse and he arose, which turned the approaching figure into a blur of action. He could feel the menace of the other's gun.

"It's me—Two Spot," he whispered hoarsely.

The other relaxed and came nearer. "You tryin' to get shot?" came a low, tense voice. "What you doin'?"

"I had to be *dead shore* who it was that's tied up like a bundle of trash in th' waggin," answered Two-Spot. "You ridin' south bothered me. I'll never forget this, *never!*"

"That's th' first thing you got to do—till you hear about it from somebody else," replied Johnny, feeling at his saddle. "Here," he said, untying a Winchester and holding it out. "I promised you a rifle—an' this is somethin' else you want to forget. I got one of his six-guns tied under my slicker roll—you see that you don't forget that it belongs to me. I'll give you th' cartridges tomorrow—they're in th' belt over my shoulder. You rustle under that floor, it's near daylight."

A grin of delight swept over Two-Spot's face as he grasped the weapon, and he scurried to his nest. But there was one thing more to make his happiness complete—he had to see the start of the wagon. And he did not have to wait long. With the first blush of day Old Buffalo appeared, hitched up his horses and urged them to begin their long pull to Highbank. The wagon squeaked and rumbled and passed from the watcher's sight; and when the last sound died out in the south, Two-Spot went to his blankets to lie on his back and gloat over the miseries of Wolf as his vivid imagination pictured them.

Down on the Highbank trail, bound and helpless, and exhausted by his frantic efforts to free himself, Wolf Forbes seethed with rage, which later would burn itself out and bring an inert apathy to ease him; and two things seared his memory: The mirth of the man who had trapped him, and the sound of a horse's hoofs pounding at top speed down the trail. They had gone southward, toward the Bar H, the Triangle, and the faint trail leading to the Double X. With these meager clues he built several edifices of speculation, not one of which could be singled out in preference to the others. His friends were notorious practical jokers, and he had done his share at it. The Double X outfit hated him, and Nelson had cause to wish him out of the way if his suspicions concerning Nelson were well founded. Would his unthinking friends carry a joke so far; would the Double X think of and carry out the play; and if Nelson felt that he was in danger, would he be fool enough to do a thing like that? In his place Wolf would have killed. But he would hunt out the perpetrator, whoever he was, when he came back—*and he was going back!*

CHAPTER XI

"The Tinkling of the Camel's Bell"

JOHNNY HAD a late breakfast, according to George.

"You look like you made a night of it," said the cook.

"I reckon I did," replied Johnny, yawning; "I didn't get much sleep."

"Did Wolf make any remarks about shootin'?"

"When?"

"Last night."

"Didn't you see him start for home?"

"Thought mebby he come back to play."

"He didn't come back to play," replied Johnny. "I'm goin' for a ride an' see if I can wake up," he said, and he did.

As he loped along the Juniper trail he made a confidante of Pepper.

"Dearly Beloved," he muttered, "we are goin' to be th' center of a whole lot of eyes before long. People will pay attention when they sees us. We are going to be right popular—an' *un*popular. If you knowed all th' trouble I'm brewin' for us, you'd reckon I wasn't no friend at all. But I know yo're with me to a finish, an' not worryin' about whose finish it's goin' to be. I've got to do some thinkin'. You listen.

"Wolf was sent up to find out who's been ticklin' th' Bar H with a prong, an' he didn't have no luck. Knowin' he was losin' patience, I knowed what a man like him would do when he came to th' end of it. He'd pick a fight an' start shootin'. Now you know I ain't scared of Wolf, but you don't know that I wasn't ready to start no open war just yet. I'll admit I hope I don't have to start none, but I wouldn't bet two bits on *that*. So what did I do? I sent him away, Pepper, but he'll come back. Uh-huh, he'll come back if he's got th' nerve—an' it'll take some. An' if he does you an' me'll have to step around right lively. If he figgers right he'll come back a-shootin', for he'll be all riled up. I couldn't have him trailin' me wherever I went, could I? Th' man wasn't reasonable—he didn't allow I had any rights.

"Now, then: Wolf won't be back before tomorrow mornin'. I'm bettin' he won't be able to sit a saddle before mornin', an' that brings him here tomorrow afternoon. Th' Bar H won't hunt for him, thanks to what you helped me do last night. If they find his cayuse without his saddle they'll think he come down an' got a fresh hoss. An' all we want is to see that little Peggy girl, an' go over to th' Double X. Then we'll turn th' Bar H upside down, an' let Wolf square up for his buggy ride if he wants. An' I'll give odds that he'll want to."

When he reached the rendezvous he was early and he grinned as he realized his unusual impatience. "Pepper, things are shore happenin' to me. I'm what you might call sober-drunk. Just settin' here quiet, lookin' at that little valley is plumb thrillin', little hoss—an' *would* you cock an eye at that gent down there! An' cussed if there ain't a cow in them sands! I reckon, mebby, it's goin' to be *real* thrillin' before long."

He jammed his sombrero tight on his head and waited, tense and eager for the overt act he felt sure would come, and send him down the hill like the swoop of a hawk.

Down in the valley Lang looked searchingly around

and then, tying his rope to the remaining strand of wire, urged his horse ahead. He was standing up in the stirrups, his weight on one leg, leaning to one side to keep the rope from pressing against his other leg, his back to the hill, and he did not see the black thunderbolt dropping down the green slope; and so intent was he upon the work in hand that his ears did not give him warning of the charging enemy in time to attempt deliberate and well-sighted long-range rifle shooting. The wire had been torn loose from the first post and was straining at the staples in the next one before he had any intimation of the swiftly approaching danger. Surprised and galvanized into action by the sound of rolling hoofs pounding over a stretch of bare, hard ground, he turned in his saddle, flung a glance at the racing thoroughbred and jerked his rifle from its sheath. His horse, feeling the rope rub against one of its hind legs, kicked viciously and pranced. Twisting from one side to the other, rifle at his shoulder, Lang found himself in too awkward a position for well-aimed shooting against the racing enemy, who lay along the back of his horse and presented a discouragingly small target. Sliding the rifle back into the sheath, Lang worked desperately at the rope, trying to free it from the saddle. Cursing his clumsy fingers, he suddenly realized the trouble. "D—n my soul, if somebody ain't *knotted* it! Oh, th' cussed fool!"

Giving up the attempt, he reached again for the rifle, swiftly changed his mind and pulled angrily on the reins to back his horse so he could get the other end of the rope and free it from the wire. "Staked out like a calf!" he gritted. Hauling in the rope, he at last grabbed the knot, and swore again. It had pulled so tight that precious seconds were wasted before he could free it, and his temper was not sweetened any by the two bullets which Johnny, firing at long range, sent on a gamble. They missed him by feet, but had their effect. Dropping the freed wire, he spurred around to face the swiftly nearing danger and jerked out his Colt, firing hastily. Johnny now was standing up in his stirrups to offset the bouncing of the horse and his shots were coming nearer all the time.

Lang swerved his horse suddenly and fired again, but the animal was prancing. Johnny's reply struck the horse and the pain-racked animal, leaping convulsively, bolted for the gap between the posts, straight for the quicksands. Lang, frantic at this new danger, fought the animal with one hand, trying desperately to turn it, and used the gun with his other hand, doing neither well. Johnny, drawing his second Colt, replied to Lang's last shot and the Triangle puncher, dropping his weapon, sagged forward in the saddle and fell sideways into a grassy hollow, where he sprawled grotesquely as his horse, freed of his weight, leaped forward at greater speed and dashed out onto the treacherous sands, stopping only when it became mired beyond the possibility of further progress. It floundered and strained with frantic energy until exhaustion made it pause, and then stood trembling, doomed by the inexorable sands which slowly crept up its quivering legs and caused its eyes to become wide with terror.

Johnny flashed past the prostrate puncher and then suddenly became aware of his danger. Pepper, holding her speed, kept straight on for the sandy trap. Johnny tried to swing her and she responded, but not enough in the restricted space and when he had pulled her back on her haunches she had crossed the quicksands' edge and slid, wallowing and struggling, to a stop far from safety. Her instinct warned her of her peril and she struggled frantically to retrace her steps, but succeeded only in turning part way and had to give up the fight momentarily, with her side to the firm ground she had just quitted. Panting and shaking with terror, she looked around appealingly at her rider, who shook his head.

"No use, Pepper Girl," he said. "You'll only get in deeper. Rest yourself an' wait—I'm th' only one who can help you now—an' I never thought I'd do a thing like that to you; an' I ain't goin' to do it till I has to. Good little cayuse—th' best I ever laid eyes on, an' I've seen th' best there was. We've had our last ride together, little hoss, an' mebby we'll go down together, too. Easy, girl; easy," he coaxed, and not wholly in vain. "You just rest an' mebby we'll make another try after I see what there is to be seen. We got th' coyote that caused it, anyhow!"

His words were contradicted almost as soon as spoken, for a derisive voice from the grassy hollow rang out in exultant laughter. Johnny, fearing a shot, although the fear was from instinct rather than from reason, fired instantly at the sound, and then lowered the gun. Lang was unarmed and could not get to his Colt without exposing himself.

"He won't get it while I'm alive," muttered Johnny, reloading his other gun.

"Shoot!" exulted Lang; "but you better save th' last for yoreself. That's right, *shoot!*" he jeered, as Johnny, stung by the words, wasted another cartridge. "Yo're comin' as close as anybody could," he continued. "You can shoot like th' hammers of h—l, an' that makes it all th' funnier. Shoot again!" he invited, holding up his hat. A hole appeared in it, to his surprise, but he jeered again instantly. "Fine! *That's* shootin'. Shoot again!"

Johnny stroked Pepper's neck and then leaned over and looked down. "Not so deep," he muttered.

"Shore; look it over," shouted Lang. "That's what I'm aimin' to do. I'm aimin' to look it over, right to th' finish. I've allus wondered how a man would act in them sands, an' I'm goin' to find out now. Mebby if yo're polite I'll put you out of yore misery when yore chin gets wet. Then I'll ride over to th' Bar H an' tell 'em who kidnapped th' Doc, an' did for Squint. I've seen shows, but this here is goin' to be th' best of th' lot."

Johnny's eyes glinted and he fired twice in succession—then a third shot after an interval, endeavoring to force Lang to keep his head down while his other hand worked swiftly under his slicker roll. Emptying one gun, he slipped it back into its holster and used the other, still struggling with the slicker. At the last shot in the second weapon he worked Wolf's gun loose and slipped it into the holster on the far side from Lang. Standing up in his stirrups he gave vent to a burst of profanity and hurled his Colts, one after the other, at the hidden observer.

Lang looked up in time to see the first gun bounce

from the ground and then the second fell close to it. He laughed nastily and ducked down again as Johnny drew the heavy Sharp's from its sheath and sent an ounce of lead smashing into the sand and pebbles close to his head. Another, another, and another struck the top of the ridge, the last striking a rock and screaming high into the air. Then Johnny gripped the heavy weapon at its muzzle with both hands, stood up in his stirrups, whirled it around his head and sent it through the air toward the hidden man. It struck loose sand and slid ten feet in a little cloud of dust. The Triangle puncher looked out again, chuckled, and slowly emerged from his place of refuge.

"I calls that kind," he laughed. "There *wasn't* no use of lettin' good weapons like them be lost. I can use 'em all—an' just for that I'm goin' to end yore misery like I said I might. First," he said, going over to the nearest Colt and picking it up, "I'm goin' to load this gun an' do somethin' for my hoss an' that cow." He walked unsteadily toward the edge of the sands, pulling half a dozen cartridges from his belt as he advanced. Reaching the danger zone, he tried each step before putting his weight into it and slowly advanced to the last tuft of grass, where he stood, swaying slightly as it moved gently under his weight. The sand at its outer edges moved a little and changed color as the water flooded and receded in it. "Reckon this is th' jumpin' off place," he said. "You'd be plumb tickled if I fell in, wouldn't you?" he jeered. "Well, I ain't aimin' to. I'm figgerin' on loadin' this gun—*this* way: Number One," he said, sliding a cartridge into the cylinder, "is for my hoss; Number Two is for th' cow; Number Three is for a hole through yore hat; *this* one is for yore hoss when only its head is out, or as soon as you jump off. I'm givin' you that chance to help it—an' to save my valuable time; these two are for yore head when yore chin gets under. One'll be enough, but two will be dead shore—I might miss th' first to hear you cuss."

Lang raised the Colt and put his horse out of its misery; then he did the same for the cow. "That's what I call fair shootin'," he said. "Of course, you might 'a' done it faster—but I'm in no hurry. Now, this next shot has got to be dead shore if I put it high enough in yore hat to miss yore head—an' I ain't aimin' to hit that *yet*. So if I takes plenty of time, don't you get jumpy."

He raised the gun above his head to increase the torment and there was a flash and roar at Johnny's hip. The Triangle puncher's hand opened and the gun dropped behind him as a look of great surprise flashed to his face, and remained there. Twisting sideways, he fell face down, sprawled full length upon the greedy sands.

"There, d—n you!" gritted Johnny. "Th' show's over, for *you*!" He brought the gun back on its mark, but did not release the hammer again. There was no doubt, this time, about Lang. He let the hammer down on an empty chamber and slid the weapon back in his holster.

Reassuring Pepper, he glanced down and saw that her legs were being pulled to the sides, which sprawled them out. "Slow," he said, and looked again to make sure. "Mighty slow. This stuff is different in places—but d—d sure," he added bitterly. "You take it easy, Pepper Girl. I won't let it last much longer—'though it's goin' to take a lot of nerve. Good little hoss—good little Pepper Girl."

He now knew there was no hope of riding out. He knew quicksands—he had seen them on other ranges, but never such a one as this, for the others had been small—the size of this bed was far beyond his experience. He studied it and watched the tremors running through it—the sand seemed to be moving and new surfaces to be forming. Wet spots appeared, became covered with water and then were uncovered again as it drained away. Hollows slowly formed here, slight bulges there, but with no stability. Undulations showed frequently near the bodies, which were slowly sinking. The cow was nearly under. This trap had no definite edges, for it met and merged with the honest sands around it in such a way as to show no lines; but he knew, by looking at the tracks of his horse, which, strangely enough, had not been quite obliterated, that he was too far from firm ground to have any hope of getting out in that direction. He cogitated upon the possibilities of escape in other directions, for it was possible that along some other course he might find firm earth closer to him. To his right was a grass tuft, not as far from him as was the place where Lang's body marked the other edge, but it lay too far away. Behind him the nature of the sands was evident for a like distance, and questionable for half as far again. To his left was the Triangle horse, which he could gain by leaping from his saddle; beyond that, half as far, was the cow, still useful if used soon enough and not rested on for too long. He believed that the cow could not have crossed much of the sands before becoming mired, and this gave him renewed hope. It was the only way worth trying with a chance of success. At the best it would be a gamble, but while those two bodies remained above the surface they would serve as stepping stones. From the body of the horse he would do the last kind act in his power for Pepper, and then, throwing away the gun to save its weight, jump to the cow. This would be easy; but from there on he would need all his strength and wits and will. Looking beyond the cow, he searched for something to put his rope on, and found nothing nearer than the fence posts, which were too far away. And then, while he looked, he saw water ooze up and cover the sand some distance beyond the cow, and he admitted that his case was hopeless; and as he admitted it the cow disappeared from sight.

Hopeless, but not to be submitted to without a struggle. He would neither sit apathetic nor frantic, nor turn the gun on himself. Hope had gone as a matter of reasoning; but something had taken its place which in power transcended hope—cold rage, and a savage, defiant hatred for that deadly, silent trap; a rage such as he seldom had felt before, which urged him to tear and rend the sands as though they were a sentient enemy. Hope, living in him, had been faint-hearted when he thought of how ghastly the thing was; how he, a man with all a man's strength of body and mind and will, mounted on the finest horse for hundreds of miles, armed with a weapon, the use of which no man knew better; how he could not do a thing to save his life. What is hope but a wish? But the dynamic rage which crept through him was a force of another kind—defiant, savage determination to cheat the workings of that mobile bed of horror, or go down to a death made glorious by the fight.

He shook his fist at it. His thin lips drew back over set teeth in a snarl primitive in its timbre and in the savage nature behind it. "D—n you! You may win; but I'll make that winnin' hard!"

Gripping the pommel he climbed up onto the saddle and poised for the leap. Could he believe his ears? Glancing around, he saw a woman tearing down the valley toward him, the drumming roll of her horse's pounding hoofs growing ever louder. What a sound! What music ever was so sweet? What sight had ever been so beautiful as that trim figure mounted astride a horse which seemed to spurn the grass in its arrowy flight? Hatless, her hair streaming behind her like a glorious battle flag of Hope, came Margaret, and her voice rang out like a trumpet.

"Wait!"

Hope returned again to bulwark Rage and give Determination a better footing and stronger lever.

"Pepper Girl," choked Johnny, "I'm glad I waited. There's mebby many a mile we'll do together, better friends than ever. I'm tellin' you that if there's any way outside of h—l to get you out of this, yo're goin'. Hear me, little hoss? An' that thoroughbred girl has brought us th' way. Cheer up—we're goin' out, you an' me. But we'll have bad dreams—plumb bad dreams—for many a night to come." He suddenly raised a warning hand. "Look out!" he shouted. "Don't come too close!"

"I know this grisly thing like a book," she replied. "What shall I do?"

"Don't come too close!"

"This is the edge; tell me what to do!" She looked at Lang's partly submerged body and shuddered.

"Hold your cayuse fast by th' reins an' get off, so I can

put my rope around that pommel. But I'm afraid it's a little too far," he replied, swinging the braided lariat carefully around his head. She quickly obeyed, but led the horse to another point on the edge, and gained a few inches. The rope shot out and up, struck the saddle and then the sands. Jerking it back again, he coiled it carefully, and then looked up, and nodded. Margaret was holding to the pommel with one hand and leaning out over the sands, her other arm extended toward him. The second cast went over her wrist and she caught the rope, drew back to the saddle and made the loop fast around her pommel.

"Get up in th' saddle an' pull this rope tight—*tight,*" he said, and at a word from him Pepper braced herself, as well as she could, as if a cow were at the other end. He slid from the saddle, touched the sand for an instant, and pulled himself at his best speed along the lariat, moving too rapidly to be caught, and soon stood at the side of the woman who had saved him.

"Can't we save that darling?" she asked, tears in her eyes.

"We're goin' to try mighty hard," he said. "Start ahead, *slow*— a little more. You watch yore cayuse an' stop instanter when I says th' word. I'm scared we'll break Pepper's laigs, 'though if it's done easy we may get along all right; it looks soft, right there. Ready? Then, *pull.* Come, Pepper! Come on, little hoss! Come on! Come on!" he cried, and then he whistled the well-known signal. "Come on! That's th' girl! That's th' girl! Keep a-churnin', tear it up! Come on! Come on, you black darlin'! That's th' way! Keep a-comin', keep a-comin'!"

Slowly Pepper went sideways, Margaret fearing that its legs would snap under the strain, but the struggling animal fell on its side, and then came the tug of war. Johnny added his strength to the rope and slowly, an inch at a time, they gained, and then had to rest for a moment because flesh and blood could not stand such a continued effort. Johnny breathed deeply and relaxed.

"Once more, Ma'am," he said, getting a fresh hold on

the rope. "I'm glad that saddle is a rim-fire—I'd mistrust a center-fire, with its one cinch. An' I'm glad it was made by Ol' Hawkins—that pommel can stand twice th' strain. Now then—*pull!*" Again they rested, the blood pounding in his ears. "Yo're comin' fine, little hoss! We ain't handlin' you very gentle; but yo're *comin'!*" A few minutes later Pepper slid across sand that was dry and honest, and with the slackening of the rope she scrambled to her feet and trembled, weary but safe.

Johnny hung the lariat on his saddle and then rubbed the velvety muzzle which sought his cheek, and stroked the quivering shoulder. Impulsively he buried his face in the wet, sandy, roughened coat on her neck and flung an arm around it; and when he turned away his face was drawn and wet, and there were tears in his eyes despite all effort of will.

"Ma'am," he said, huskily, "Pepper an' me owe you a debt we never can pay; but we can try right hard to square up some of it. I'll never forget th' last half-hour, never."

"How did you come to get in it?" asked Margaret, glancing where she last had seen the body of Lang. It was gone, and so was the horse. The sands, still undulating, were slowly assuming their mask of innocence.

"Pepper got goin' so fast she couldn't stop quick enough, which was my fault. I didn't try to turn her in time."

"And that—that other—man. Who was he, and what happened to him?"

"I reckon he got tangled in th' wire, an' got his rope mixed up with it. An' somehow we got to shootin'. When th' excitement stopped he was there, an' I was where you found me."

"Who was he?" she demanded.

"He was a Triangle puncher, Ma'am; Lang was his name."

"He was one of the men whom I ordered to stay off our range—we couldn't keep the wire on those posts, and I suspected them strongly. Are you sure he was only tangled in the wire?"

"Well, I wouldn't just say nothin' about that. Mebby he was tryin' to help th' cow that was mired, an' got afoul of th' wire. But that don't make no difference, anyhow, now. Have you got any wire at th' ranch?"

"I think so," she answered.

"We'll put it up some day soon, so it'll take some time, an' more trouble, to get it loose."

She nodded and took a paper out of her waist. "Here are the figures for the year we took possession."

He looked them over. "Uh-huh," he said, "they're what I want."

"It is surprising that we have as many left as we have," she said. "We are about ready to give up, admit our failure, and go back East."

"Ma'am," said Johnny, with great earnestness, "don't you do it. Just sit tight an' see things come around yore way. Luck allus turns. Stick it out, an' see."

"Do you believe in luck?"

"I do; when somebody's behind it pushin' hard. Now, Ma'am, I reckon we hadn't ought to stay here no longer, where folks can see us. They might talk, an' there's no tellin' what harm it might do. Besides, this little Pepper hoss needs a bath an' I'm aimin' to take her into th' river as soon as she gets a little quieter—she looks like she mixed up with a tornado." He walked around collecting his guns, blowing sand from them, and cleaning them as well as he could. "There's shore some guns around here," he grinned, getting Lang's Colt and throwing it into the quicksand. "This here gun," he said, reloading Wolf's Colt and tying it under the slicker roll, "shore come in handy. Some folks would call that luck—mebby it was, as far as totin' it is concerned—but I'm tellin' you there wasn't no luck in th' way it was used. But as for totin' it, I reckon that was luck, even if I did carry it to fool somebody, sometime. Now, Ma'am, I'll be ridin' west. There's a regular bath tub near th' main trail, where th' river runs over solid rock: an' solid rock is th' only kind of river bottom I have any use for today.

Pepper an' I won't forget what you did for us—an' I'm tellin' you to sit tight, an' watch th' luck swing yore way. I'll be leavin' now—good-by, Ma'am."

She spurred her horse and shot even with him. "Why are you doing this?" she demanded. "You can't fool me about that—that man's rope fouling the wire. I know what he was doing. Why are you running such risks for total strangers?"

"Ma'am," he replied, smiling quizzically, "I don't know, unless it's because I can't keep out of trouble. I'm allus gettin' mixed up with it, somehow, an' th' habit's set, I reckon. I'm gettin' so I like it. But we shouldn't be ridin' like this. You have no idea how much folks can talk, or figger from a little thing like this."

"Can't you stop them, as you did that Bar H foreman?"

"Reckon so; but I ain't ready to," he grinned. "There's a time for everythin', an' I'm not shore th' time has come for that. When it does I'll know it without no doubts. I'm askin' how you learned all th' things you said yesterday?"

"I suppose it is a natural curiosity, even in a man; but I prefer to say nothing about the matter." She drew rein and he took off his sombrero. "I'm tempted to see if the luck will turn," she smiled. "Good-by."

"I'm thankin' you again, Ma'am," he replied. "It shore will, an' you can bank on it," and he pressed Pepper's sides. The horse struck into a stride suggestive of a wish to put miles between her and the scene of her torture, but he pulled her down to a walk. "Yo're entirely too willin', little hoss of mine," he reproved, patting the roughened coat. "I was aimin' to do somethin' today, but it can wait, Wolf or no Wolf. If he horns in I won't waste no more time on him, none at all. There's a nice little wooded draw over there, an' we're goin' for it. You got to get rested up an' quieted a little—th' bath can wait a couple of hours. You got to keep in good shape, because th' time is comin' when I'll have to ride you like I had a *remuda* to draw on—an' I ain't worth a cuss unless yo're in good shape. Yo're my laigs, Pepper, an' no puncher is better'n his cayuse. An' mebby Two-Spot, th' tattle-tale, won't be surprised when he sees you!"

Margaret looked after him and smiled, and then turned and stared at the innocent patch of wet sand under whose hypocritical surface lay grisly death. Shuddering, she sent her pony into a sharp gallop and set out for home, a color in her face which might have been due to the exhilaration of horseback riding.

CHAPTER XII

"Coming Events ——"

JOHNNY ENTERED the draw, found a small clearing, and let
Pepper wander, watching her closely, while he went
over his guns again, cleaning them thoroughly. The
afternoon had half gone when he whistled her to him
and rode her down to the rocky pool he had mentioned.
Stripping himself, he removed the saddle and its blanket
and, mounting bareback, rode her into the stream,
where he found a place deep enough to swim her.
Crossing and recrossing this several times, he took her
out and started to dress; and no sooner was she free
than she trotted to a dry, warm patch of sand and rolled
to her heart's content, grunting with pleasure.

"Now look at what you've done," he grinned. "After
me gettin' you all washed up, you go an' blot yoreself
just like a common cayuse. I've been wastin' sympathy
on you—there ain't nothin' th' matter with you. An'
there's somethin' I want to ask you, before I forget it:
Was you ever in a quicksand just like that one? I bet you
wasn't. I've crossed some rivers in my time, an' had
cattle bogged in several—but this was different somehow. Mebby it's because it wasn't under water; but I

don't know. I was scared we'd bust yore laigs; mebby we didn't because we pulled you sideways, an' you raised so much h——l when you felt th' rope tighten, an' heard me call you. Just th' same, I'm sayin' we had a close call. An' we mustn't forget it. Come here, now, an' let me throw this saddle on you. We're goin' to town, an' yore goin' to get rubbed till you shines. I'm as stuck-up about you as a gal is over her first beau."

In a few minutes they were on their way to Gunsight, but they did not reach the town without incident. They had ridden to Pine Mountain and Johnny, wishing to see if Squint's saddle had been discovered, hid Pepper in a clump of brush and scrub timber well back from the trail and, taking his rifle, crossed the beaten road at a rocky place and worked his way into the brush on the mountain side. When he had climbed about eighty feet he reached a little rock shelf and rested a moment. As he was about to go on he heard hoofbeats down the trail and he flattened himself behind a tuft of grass growing in a crack. Looking down the trail he saw a horseman round into sight from the arroyo leading from East Canyon.

"Smitty," he muttered. "I don't think much of him, an' I reckon he'll scare. An' mebby if he's scared near to death a few times he'll figger he ain't wanted around here, an' hit th' trail out. Mebby I'm wrong, but here's where Mr. Smitty gets a jolt he won't forget. It will be Number One. Whether or not he gets any more will depend on how he takes this one. I'm bettin' he don't stalk me for it—here he comes, ridin' lazy an' tryin' to sing. I ought to be able to come awful close at this distance, with a rifle layin' on a rock rest."

Mr. Smith, of the Bar H, rode at a walk, singing a song, the words of which should never appear in print. He had a message to deliver to the Doc and was in no hurry. His hat, a Mexican sombrero with ultra-fancy band, and a high crown, which appeared to be even higher because of the vertical dents which pushed the top into a peak, was tilted rakishly off-center and looked rather ludicrous to the man on the mountain, who noted that there appeared to be plenty of hat and horse, but very little man. When just across a short stretch of rocky trail there rang out over the rider's head a roar such as only black powder can make, and the tilted sombrero flew into the air and struck the ground. The horse and its rider heard the roar at the same instant and each acted as their instincts prompted. The horse shot forward, clearing a dozen feet in the jump, sprang back, wheeling in the air, and bolted for the arroyo it had just left, where it quickly recovered its poise and stopped to search out succulent grass tufts. Mr. Smith's instincts seemed to have come to him through generations of acrobatic ancestors, although he was not aware that any of his family tree claimed any such accomplishments, at least since they had forsaken arboreal surroundings. Certainly he never boasted, even in his maddest sprees, of being in any way gifted in acrobatics. Nevertheless, he performed a creditable exhibition when the roar smashed against his ears. As the horse leaped, he grabbed at the pommel, missed it, and in his haste to jerk his head back from the screaming lead he lost his balance. His feet left the stirrups, and then came swiftly upward as he pivoted on the saddle. They swept up past the horse's neck, kept on and described a half-circle, the saddle as the center. As they went up Mr. Smith's head went down, and as the horse leaped back and whirled, he was jolted into a position rarely seen in horseback riding except in exhibitions. For a moment he stood on his shoulder against the cantle of the saddle and then turned a pretty, if unintentional, back flip onto the ground, landing squarely on his hat. The whole thing happened in a flash and the sound of the shot was still rumbling among the hills when, grabbing his sombrero, he started on a dead run for the horse and the ranch. When he reached the animal he leaped into the saddle without touching the stirrups, and urged a speedy departure, which his spurs obtained.

Johnny rolled over on his back and laughed heartily. Finally he sat up, put the empty shell in his pocket, reloaded the rifle and went up the mountain to hide

Squint's saddle in a better place, for he now believed such a precaution necessary. It was more than probable that Pine Mountain would be searched as soon as the indignant puncher could lead his friends to the scene of his discomfiture. He found the saddle where he had left it and carried it to a narrow, shallow split in the mountain's rocky side and dropped it in, after which dead branches and grass and rocks covered it and hid it securely. Scrambling back to the trail he looked cautiously along it and then dashed across and made his way to his horse, stepping on rock whenever possible. Not long afterward he rode down the Juniper trail and went to the hotel shed, where he led Pepper inside and prepared to groom her. He hardly had begun work when Two-Spot sidled in, and there was wrath in his eyes.

"What you been doin' to that hoss?" he demanded, as his gaze swept over her. "She looks like she's been rolled in th' river."

"Mebby she has," replied Johnny, rubbing briskly. "She likes a swim as well as I do—an' we both had one, which is somethin' I can recommend to you."

"What did you do with them rifle ca'tridges of Polecat's you was goin' to give me?" asked Two-Spot, going to work on the other flank.

"I hid 'em," answered Johnny. "Look out she don't hand you a stomachful of hoof—she don't like strangers."

"Huh!" snorted Two-Spot, "what do *I* care about strangers? Where'd you hide 'em?"

"In them sweepin's, under th' manger," replied Johnny. "Wait till after dark."

"What you figger I'm goin' to do—show everybody that Two-Spot's startin' an arsenal?" He rubbed for a moment in silence, and then began to chuckle. "Ol' Chief Smell-Um-Strong had a plumb fine gun—I got a laugh comin'; you gave th' best one away."

"I'm satisfied," grunted Johnny.

"Dave was on th' prod this noon when I showed up," continued Two-Spot. "What did you say you was swimmin' in?" he demanded, curiously, examining one of Pepper's hocks.

"Water," answered Johnny. "What did he say?"

"Mebby it was," observed Two-Spot. "How'd you get out?"

"Swum."

"At th' end of a rope? Why, Dave, he wanted to know where th' this, that, an' th' other thing I was last night. Reckoned, mebby, I'd got full of berries an' hibernated. What was you doin' in th' SV valley?"

"What did you tell him?" asked Johnny, grinning.

"Told him that I was rustlin' a passel of cows an' that they went so fast I had to run to Juniper before I could head 'em off. You must 'a' had one h—l of a time gettin' out. Shore Pepper ain't hurt?"

"It ain't th' first bath she's had—she's a good swimmer, 'though for much of it I'd ruther have a cayuse with a bigger barrel. She won't shrink."

"Why in h—l don't Dave set out th' bottle, like he used to?" growled Two-Spot. "There ain't no sense in totin' it by th' glass to a crowd of blotters. They'll hold more liquor than a gopher hole—an' I've broke my back carryin' water to drown them fellers out when I was a kid. How long is your rope?"

"Dave's a friend of mine, that's why," answered Johnny. "My capacity is so limited that ol' Dailey could clean me out after my fourth drink. Them leather-bellies can drink me into a heap on th' floor, an' never know they'd been drinkin'."

"Shore," said Two-Spot, chuckling; "yo're a teethin' infant, a reg'lar suckin' calf—I've seen you put away a dozen an' not bat an eye. An' it's bad medicine; look at me. How long's that rope?"

"Eighty feet."

"Yo're another. There ain't a man livin' can throw such a rope an' ketch anythin'. I've seen some good uns, but I've never seen even a sixty-foot rope. Who fastened to you?"

"Yo're loco—plumb loco," said Johnny. "You want to forget them hallucernations—somebody might believe 'em."

" 'Hallerlucinations'—humph! I'll have to remember that an' throw it at Dave. Where was you today?"

"Mindin' my own business," retorted Johnny. "What ever put you hangin' 'round a saloon, emptyin' boxes?"

"Whiskey," said Two-Spot. "I was smart, like you, an' liked to hold up my end, drink for drink. Here's some more of that water you swum in—looks familiar."

"I'm goin' to drag you out to a ranch some of these days," threatened Johnny, "an' give you a job—an' whale th' skin from yore bones th' first time I see you takin' a drink. You got brains an' that ranch needs 'em."

"You can't learn an old dog new tricks," grunted Two-Spot, and then burst out laughing; "but you can change a wolf inter a skunk if you goes about it right. He! He! He!" In a few minutes he threw down the brush and went to the door. "Seein' as how yo're playin' fresh-water clam, do it yoreself!" he snorted and, dodging the other brush, he scurried around to Dave's.

Down on the Bar H, Smitty's arrival made a ripple of excitement. Big Tom was mending a shirt and cursing the clumsiness of his fingers and the sharpness of the needle, when there came the clatter of hoofs outside and he looked up to see Smitty leap from the saddle and jump through the doorway, holding a much-abused Mexican sombrero out at arm's length. It was trampled and soiled and there was a fuzzy-edged rip an inch long in the brim where a 550-grain bullet had ploughed before passing through. Eight years before Smitty had paid twenty-five dollars for the hat, perhaps entirely too much, and next to his saddle it was his most prized possession. It had seen hard service, but he fondly regarded it as being as good as new.

"Lookit my hat!" he cried, jabbing it under the foreman's nose, which caused the needle to find the finger again.

"D—n th' hat!" growled Big Tom. "Take it away from my nose!"

"Lookit it!" insisted Smitty. "Some coyote shot at me from up on Pine Mountain an' plumb ruined it! He came so close I could feel th' slug—cuss it, I *smelled* it! It fair grazed my nose. Lookit it!"

Big Tom threw the shirt away and took the hat, turning it over in his hands. "I'd say it was close—plumb close," he admitted. "How far off was he?"

"Right over my head—couple dozen feet," answered Smitty. "Here! Don't poke yore blasted finger in it like that! Cuss it, it's bad enough now! That's more like it. I could feel th' concussion an' smell th' smoke. I was ridin' along at a walk, when *whango!* It near stunned me, it was so close. An' lookit what he done to that hat! There ain't another hat like that on th' whole range!"

"Yo're right, they throw 'em away long before that," retorted Big Tom, an idea coming into his head. "Did you pick up his trail?"

"How could I?" indignantly demanded Smitty. "My cayuse fair went wild, an' before I could get him under control he was clean out of th' canyon—I tell you I did some highfalutin' ridin', stickin' to a crazy hoss among all them rocks."

"How'd you get yore hat? Didn't it go off yore head?"

"Shore it did! I scooped it up as my cayuse wheeled—an' talk about turnin' on a saddle blanket—that jack rabbit can wheel on a postage stamp if he's prodded enough. He just simply climbed up straight an' swapped ends."

"You should 'a' gone back an' stalked that feller," said Big Tom, using plenty of salt on what he heard. "Or at least rustled to Gunsight to see who might come ridin' in. Where did all this happen?"

"Right on them benches on th' east end of th' mountain—at that rocky hump in th' trail. How he ever missed at such close range is more'n *I* can understand—why, a kid oughta be able to make a hit, every time, as close as that. An' it was a rifle; th' roar was deafenin'."

"He missed because he wanted to miss," said Big Tom. "One of th' boys is playin' a joke on you—you know what they've said about that tent. He come closer than he reckoned on—I'll bet you rocked forward in th' saddle as he shot."

"Yes, I reckon I did—you know what ridin' is over that hump," Smitty said. "I remember that when I jerked back as it passed my nose I went quite a ways—my neck is sore from th' jerk. But I'm tellin' you I ain't nowise shore it was any joke. An' I says, if it was, it was a cussed pore one. I'll nat'rally skin any fool *I* ketches playin' any more jokes like that on *me*. Cuss it, it skun my nose!"

"A skin fur a skin, huh?" chuckled the foreman. He handed the hat back to its owner. "There ain't no man on th' range that would miss yore head, hat or no hat, from them benches. It ain't more than seventy-five or eighty feet from up there. They aimed to miss you; an' they shaved it a little too fine, not allowin' for you bobbin' forward. I says it was one of th' boys. You lay low an' use yore eyes an' ears, an' if you find out who it was I'll give that fool a dressin' down he won't forget. A joke's a joke—we all play 'em; but there's such a thing as ridin' 'em too hard. Did you give th' Doc my message?"

"What message?"

The foreman stared at him and slowly raised his hands. "I'll be cussed—it was more of a joke than I thought. Didn't I tell you to ride up there an' tell th' Doc that we wanted to see him tonight? Didn't you leave here to tell him that, an' for nothin' else?" he demanded, his voice rising.

"Yeah, I reckon mebby you did," admitted the puncher, uneasily. "You want to see him tonight, shore."

"I do. Now you fork that cayuse an' get goin'. Good Lord! That bullet must 'a' hit yore mem'ry." He glanced at his puncher's thigh. "An' where's yore six-shooter? Did you forget that, somewhere?"

Smitty's hand went to the holster and he cursed heartily. "D—n these open sheaths! It must 'a' fell out when that jack rabbit did th' fancy swappin' of ends. Now I got to go get it, but I'm borrowin' a gun to wear, or I stays here. Somethin' tells me it's unhealthy to go ridin' around this God-forsaken country without no six-gun."

"Take that spare one of mine, hangin' up over my

bunk," offered the foreman. "She's in good shape. Now, yo're plumb shore you didn't lose nothin' else, more valuable than earthly belongin's?" he grinned. "Yo're shore yo're goin' back for yore gun?"

"Shore I am; what you mean?" replied Smitty, suspiciously.

"Nothin' worth mentionin'," smiled Big Tom. "I reckoned mebby you'd take th' over-mountain trail, seein' as it's shorter."

"Then how could I get my gun?"

"That's what I was wonderin'."

"I'll get it," Smitty assured him. "I'll get it unless yore fool joker picked it up. Mebby he's a-settin' on it, waitin' to hand it to me, an' 'pologize for missin' me."

"He won't be within miles of here by this time," said Big Tom. "He dusted quick. If he was jokin' he'd get away *pronto*, an' if he wasn't, he'd do it quicker. I reckon you'd better climb up on that bench an' see what you can find—an empty shell might help us a lot. But don't forget to see th' Doc, this time. After that you can go to town an' find out what you can learn. Now get started. An' take good care of that hat—that ain't no way to treat it, nohow."

Smitty growled, took down the six-shooter, strode out to his horse and swung into the saddle. "Hope nobody picked it up," he said. "Twenty dollars is twenty dollars, an' I ain't got th' twenty. Anyway, it's a better gun than they're makin' nowadays."

"Don't lose that one while yo're pickin' up th' other," laughed the foreman.

When he was out of sight of the ranch Smitty wheeled sharply and rode eastward. "I got to get it," he muttered, "or I'll never hear th' last of it; but there ain't no reason for ridin' through th' canyon an' th' arroyo, along th' side of th' mountain for no four miles. It was too cussed close for a joke. An' mebby he aimed to spatter me all over th' trail. I just can't figger it, nohow. But I'm free to remark that any more of them jokes will send Smitty dustin' along th' trail, no matter what way he's pointin' at th' time, an' he won't never come back no more."

Somehow, I just can't help thinkin' of pore Squint. Cuss it, I can feel it yet!"

Getting near the scene of his discomfiture, Smitty dismounted and went on a reconnaissance, viewing the benches from every angle, and after some time he located his gun lying in the grass near the trail. Returning to his horse he mounted and rode forward, striking into a dead run as he approached the rocky hump in the trail and, leaning down, he picked up the weapon as he swept past, no mean feat when the grass is considered. In a few minutes he pulled his mount to a lope and soon drew rein at the Doc's door, where he delivered the message, gossiped for a few minutes, and then went on to town.

The first person he saw was Two-Spot, leaning against the front of the Palace and who accepted, with alacrity, Smitty's invitation to drink. Two-Spot saw the condition of the hat before its wearer had dismounted, and his curiosity burned strongly within him. The puncher engaged him and Dave in conversation but his efforts at these sources of information were futile. What knowledge he gained had no bearing on Johnny. Two-Spot casually remarked that Johnny had been loafing around most of the afternoon, pestering him and said that he was a nuisance. Buying another round Smitty sauntered into Dailey's, where he learned nothing at all. Having taken the census and found that everyone had been rooted in town all day, he began to accept his foreman's view of the mystery, and set out for home, burning for an opportunity to observe his bosom friends and listen to their careless conversation. But if he had not received any information, he had not given any, and Two-Spot's curiosity about the hole in the hat was still raging.

"Th' doin's on this here range are scandalous," observed Dave's factotum to Dave, himself. "They're gettin' worse an' worse, an' somebody's goin' to get hurt afore long. Now I wonder how th' devil Smitty's hat got abused like that?"

"What makes you think things is gettin' worse?" asked Dave.

"That Greaser tent never come by that hole from bein' used; an' Smitty was shore askin' a lot of questions; an' Nelson ain't swimmin' hisself an' that hoss for fun—I know *I* wouldn't."

"Which is an abidin' sorrer to all them as gets down wind of you," said Dave. "Was Nelson's saddle wet?"

"No-o; I reckon it was dry," grudgingly admitted the other.

"Was his clothes wet?" continued Dave.

"No-o-o," more reluctantly admitted Two-Spot.

"You got a head like a toad," contemptuously rejoined the proprietor. "Trouble with you is, yore imagination is on th' rampage. You got too much time on yore hands—suppose you 'tend to th' sand boxes? They ain't been touched in three days."

Two-Spot sighed and obeyed. "Huh!" he grunted, emptying a box into the road. "Mebby; but I saw somethin' about that hole that reminded me of some gosh-awful ca'tridges I seen lately. Cuss it—I'd *bet* on it!"

He chuckled, set down the box, slipped around the side of the saloon and poked his head in the hotel shed. "Don't she shine, though?" he remarked in congratulatory tones.

"She does," admitted Johnny, finishing the job.

"Say," said his visitor, "gimme an empty rifle shell."

"What for?"

"I want to keep matches in it. I'll get a cork from Dave an' have a waterproof matchbox."

"You need it," countered Johnny. "Aimin' to fall in th' crick? You need that, too."

Two-Spot ignored the insult, the second on that topic within five minutes. Evidently there must be some real or fancied foundation for it. "Got one?" he asked.

"I'll save you one," replied Johnny; "but mebby you'll have to wait quite a spell. I still got them I loaded," he said, truthfully.

"Well, there ain't no hurry," admitted Two-Spot. "Thought mebby you had one in yore clothes."

"I might go out an' shoot one off; but I reckon I won't, seein' that it ain't goin' to rain for a day or two."

"Don't shoot none for that," replied Two-Spot. "Smitty was in town a few minutes ago."

"Yes?"

"Uh-huh, he was. He was projectin' around tryin' to find out who spoiled his twenty-year-old Mex. sunshade. He was het up about it."

"Don't blame him. Was it spoiled bad?"

"Plumb sufficient. Looks like th' railroad thought it was a tunnel. He acts like he's got hal—hallerlucerations," grinned Two-Spot.

"But you can't wear them on a hat," reproved Johnny. "That is, not till after you open th' can, anyhow."

"Huh?" Two-Spot scratched his frowsy head, "mebby not, but that's th' safest place to tote 'em—on th' outside, leastawise. Did you think they was like a—a shirt?" he demanded with great sarcasm.

"Mebby; they covers a lot of ignorance. Yo're not goin' out, are you?" asked Johnny.

"I am," retorted his companion, shuffling toward the door. "You think yo're d—d smart, don't you? You an' yore hullercations? Well, you can go plumb to h—l!" and Two-Spot made haste to get around in front of the saloon, where he refilled the box and carried it inside.

"Cuss it, Dave," he complained, "nobody 'round here treats me like I deserve!"

"An it's d—d lucky for you that they don't," retorted Dave. "You 'tend to them boxes, or I'll make a start at treatin' you like you deserves. What's th' matter with you, anyhow? You've been chucklin' all day like you've lost what little sense you had. You ought to take somethin' for them spasms—they're too frequent to do you any good."

Two-Spot sighed and carried out another box. He dropped it and shook his head. "I don't care a cuss; I'm still bettin' that hole was made by a Sharp's Special. But what gets me is, how could he perforate th' brim while that there pinched-up peak waves defiance, an' courts destruction? You gimme a shot at it, and I'd blow th' hull top off'n it. But I dassn't think about that, now that I've got a gun; it's so fascinatin' I'll be takin' a shot at it some of these days—an' I reckon I'd get more'n a hat. Shucks! that'd be all right; it's only Smitty." He leaned up against the building and laughed until Dave came out to see if he could get in one healthy kick, but Two-Spot avoided him and went back to the box. "Polecat is near High-bank now," he muttered. "I'd give his gun to read his thoughts! He! He! He!"

CHAPTER XIII

Highbank Makes a Discovery

AT THE other end of the Highbank-Gunsight trail the warm afternoon was drawing to a close and the shadows of the buildings were reaching out across the dirt streets when a dust-covered, four-horse freight wagon rolled down the steep bank across the river to an accompaniment of rattling trace chains and grinding brakes, passed the end of ford, followed the road along the river's edge and crept out onto the big, flat-bottomed ferry which awaited it.

"On time to a tick," smiled the ferryman, poling off and shifting the lengths of the trolley ropes leading to the block which ran on the great, sagging cable overhead. The current struck the side of the craft at the changed angle and sent it slowly across.

"I got an extra early start," explained Buffalo. "Got a fine load of hides."

"You young fellers are h—l on branchin' out," said the ferryman, grinning.

"Well," replied the freighter, "they was lyin' there; I only picked 'em up."

"Here we are; hold tight," laughed the boatman. He used his pole deftly and the ferry struck the bank squarely. Making it fast, he lowered the short gangplank. "All ashore, an' good luck!"

The quartet strained and the wagon rumbled up the bank and then up the road in the wide ravine, and in a few minutes struck the level at the top and entered the main street of the town.

"Brazos" Larkin, town marshal, pushed away from the Highbank bank and rolled out to the wagon, stepped on a hub and then up to the footboard, as was his custom.

"Judgin' from th' way those no-'count hosses was pullin' when they come over th' hill," he said, "I reckoned you got th' hides; but now I'm dead shore of it."

"Yep," chuckled Buffalo, "they smells good to me."

"Dodge th' Injuns all right?" asked Brazos, indulging in a time-honored jest.

"Dodged 'em ag'in," gravely nodded the driver. "Here comes th' postmaster. Hello, Jim!"

Jim Hands walked up to the wagon and alongside as it turned the corner and stopped before a frame building bearing in weather-bleached letters across its front: "Wheatley's Express." As it stopped, a tall, lean young man came out and smiled.

"Everythin' all right, Pop?" he asked.

"Right as a dollar. Can't you smell 'em?" chuckled the old man.

"Jerry," said Brazos, "I hears yo're quittin' th' office for a wagon next week?"

"I am; I wanted to swap jobs right along with Pop. Now that we're goin' to run two waggins I'll get a chance to bust out of this jail; an' Pop can still see his friends along th' trail, too. I start in a day or two."

A small group came up and joined them. In it was Rod Wilson, the liveryman; Reb Travers, the railroad freight agent; and Pete Wiggins, the owner of the hotel. They all were cronies of the same vintage as the driver and formed a closed circle into which, however, they had admitted Brazos.

"Bet you didn't git a load," said Rod.

"Bet you didn't git *half* a load," amended Reb.

"I'll show you scoffin' mossbacks what I got," retorted Buffalo, rising to the bait. He clambered down and went to the rear of the wagon, untied the knots and threw back the canvas. As he paused to wonder how the bale had become spread out, the top skin moved up and down, and he jerked back his hand. "There's some kind of a varmint in there!" he cried in pardonable amazement.

Brazos left the group with a leap and reached for the hide as his gun slanted down on it. Giving it a quick, hard jerk, he threw it behind him and then gazed in astonishment at a pair of boots which moved energetically, while strange, strangled gurgles were heard in the wagon box. "I'm d—d!" he muttered. "What th'—who th'—how th'—" He grabbed hold of a boot and pulled heartily. It resisted and tried to kick. Following his gun under the canvas, he moved another skin and then emerged and stared at Buffalo.

"What is it?" demanded the freighter. "*Who* is it? How'd he git there, hey?"

"It's Wolf Forbes, blind-folded, gagged, hog-tied, an' lashed to th' box," accused Brazos. "Was you aimin' to skin him when you had more time?"

"Skin him?" indignantly retorted Buffalo. "You can't skin him; he's so tough a plough wouldn't scratch his hide. How'd he git in there, an' tie hisself up like that?"

"Mebby you can tell that to a jury," retorted Brazos, slying winking at the dumbfounded group. "However, unless we want to call on a coroner's jury first, we better git him out," and, slipping the gun into its holster, he plunged back under the canvas.

Pete Wiggins was the first of the group to recover. "After all these years we done found you out!" he exulted.

"What's wrong?" demanded Jerry, from the office.

"Yore Pop is bringin' in hide on th' hoof," declared Reb.

"Kidnappin' innercent punchers like Wolf Forbes," accused Pete.

"Cuss it!" snorted Buffalo. "What I want you fools to tell me is how he got there?"

"You can't slip out that way," asserted Rod.

They listened to what Brazos was saying under the canvas. "Tied up four ways from th' Jack," he announced. "Rolled up in a stinkin' hide, he was, all but his head an' arms. Cuss me! this is somethin' new to me; an' I reckoned I'd been up ag'in' everythin' in human cussedness. How fur did he come this way?"

"How in h——l do *I* know!" blazed Buffalo, his thin chin whiskers bobbing pugnaciously. "I didn't even know he was *there!*"

"You can't never tell," said a voice back in the crowd. "Sometimes it comes out in a man when he's even older'n Buffalo. Reckon it's th' breed."

"I'll show you what's in my breed!" shouted the freighter, pushing into the press. "Let me git a-holt of th' skunk as said that an'——an'——an'——" he faltered.

Pete grabbed him and pulled him back again. "None of that!" he warned. "You stay right here till we find out more about this!"

"Startin' a passenger business, too, I reckon," said the same voice. "Bein' an old hand on th' cattle trail he knowed a herd will often foller if one cow crosses a river."

"He got so used to skinnin' buffalers that he's itchin' to try it on a human," said another. "I says he shows spunk, pickin' Wolf to try it on."

"There's tricks in all trades," said Jim Hands.

" 'Cept freightin'," laughed Jerry.

"Somebody pass in a knife," requested Brazos. "Mines's in my other pants where it allus is when I wants it. My sacred cow! I'm near choked! Them hides must be full of maggots." Receiving the knife he soon backed out. "Phew! An' hot! Now, as I pull him out, some of you grab holt under him so he won't drop. Don't try to stand him up; he can't do that for all th' money in th' country. Here he comes; stand by!"

Ready hands went under the puncher as he appeared, and lowered him to the ground. Wolf could not speak; he could not even move his jaw; but there was nothing the matter with his eyes and they served as points of concentration for his rage. They almost sparked.

"Jerry, get a bottle of liquor," ordered Brazos. "Get it sudden, too. Reb, you an' some of th' others rub his arms an' laigs. He ain't nowhere near goin' to die, but he's in bad shape, temporary."

Jerry appeared with a bottle of brandy and Brazos poured a thin trickle of it into the open mouth. When a fourth of it was used he started to rub the jaw muscles, whereat the eyes sparked furiously and the gurgling became more emphatic.

"He says he likes that," chuckled the marshal, "but he likes this better," and he gave another dose of brandy. "You can't kill these fellers," he remarked, rubbing the jaws with rhythmic strokes. "They're steel, rubber, an' rawhide—tough as hickory knots. In administerin' a stimulant"—he paused, liked the words, and repeated them: "In administerin' a stimulant, as I says before, you got to consider what effect it will have on a liquor-drinkin' patient. This here feller looks like he was used to it, so we'll give him all six chambers. There ain't no harm in gettin' a man drunk, not if it's good for him, an' if I was him I'd ruther be drunk than sober when th' blood starts a-flowin' ag'in. Dose Number Three—it's fetchin' him; an' he ain't coughed once. Didn't I tell you he was brought up on it?"

Buffalo, holding back his laughter with all his will, shook his fist at the prostrate puncher.

"Think yo're smart, hey?" he demanded fiercely. "But I want my pay! Nobody can steal a ride with me without payin'. I want five dollars. You hear me? *Five dollars!* These fools act like they think it's a joke, but I ain't swallerin' it; no, sir! How do *I* know you didn't plan this all out, an' get yore friends to help you beat an old man out of his fare? There you was, snug in my skins, like a tick in a cow's hair, layin' there for forty miles, snickerin' at me! You wouldn't pay, an' ride alongside me, up in th' dust an' th' heat; but you got poked away on them soft hides, out of' th' dust an' th' sun, takin' it easy while I was drivin' them four wild horses for forty miles! Dozin' off, mebby, while I was doin' all th' work. I don't see no joke." He choked, controlled himself, and shouted: "But you can't do it! I want my pay! An' what will folks say up in Gunsight when they hears about you?"

"Oh, Lord!" yelled Pete. "What *will* they say? It'll never be forgot!"

"Life must be pleasant," said Reb, "livin' with *that* outfit! There's allus somethin' to pass away th' time. I reckon they must 'a' saved up a long time for this feller."

"Can you imagine what he's been through today?" asked Pete, his imagination becoming active. "It was plain, common h—l!"

Buffalo suddenly let out a whoop, draped himself on a wheel and burst into laughter, and when he could get control of himself he looked around at his audience. "Fellers," he groaned, "it wasn't *his* outfit! It was them Double X fellers. There was four of 'em in Gunsight last night, an' they was feelin' good. They've got th' nerve to tackle a joke like this, too; an' there ain't no love lost between them two ranches. When I was goin' into th' hotel after puttin' up my team, I heard a lot of laughin' in Dave's saloon, an' I remembers some of them Double X fellers howlin' 'bout a kidnappin'. That's it! They done it! An' I tell you it took nerve, tacklin' this two-gun man for a joke! It won't be no joke when he gits back—there'll be killin's over this. But, killin' or no killin', I can't help it—Oh! Ho! Ho! Oh! Ho! Ho! An' me settin' up there, drivin' like a dodderin' old fool, with this feller tied up in them odorous skins! Wolf Forbes, two-gun badman of th' Bar H! Oh! Ho! Ho! There'll be killin's; but I got to laugh—Oh, Lordy! Lordy! Lordy!"

"Forty mile! Forty mile!" senselessly repeated one man, weaving around, stepping on everyone in his path. "Forty mile! Forty mile!"

"Playin' mummy on a pile of stinkin' hides!" cried another.

"Tied up like a—like a—I dunno what!"

"Bouncin' an' jouncin' under that tarp on a day like this!"

"Forty mile" came around again, chanting his passwords, stumbled over Reb and flopped, still chanting.

Brazos held up the bottle, and put it down again, not daring to give the last dose for fear of spilling it, and rocked back and forth on his haunches: "Wrapped in a stinkin' hide—forty mile—mummy—oh, my sacred cow!"

"Forty mile" gasped and sat up. The bottle took his eye, and his hand took the bottle. Putting it back empty he slowly arose; and when last seen he was trying to walk on both sides of the street at once, still chanting his lay.

Wolf stirred, tried to get up and, falling, rolled over.

" 'Oot 'ell out ah th'," he muttered. "No dah 'an." He desisted, since he could not pronounce labials, and tried his arms and legs. They responded somewhat, but there was a great uncertainty about them.

Brazos wiped his eyes, picked up the bottle, looked at it and then around at the crowd, and arose. "Come on, boys; give me a hand. In another hour he'll be petrified. After which, I'm takin' a drink—two of 'em—*three* of 'em! I needs it bad."

The cronies picked Buffalo off the wheel. "Give us a hand, ol' kidnapper," ordered Reb. "We'll lug him into Pete's. Come on—git a-holt, all as can find room."

A procession formed, with a line of dogs acting as skirmishers, and tramped to Pete Wiggins' Highbank hotel and bar, into which all but the small boys and dogs disappeared. Any stranger entering Highbank later that night would have carried away a very unfavorable impression about the sobriety of its citizens. And had he seen the innocent and unassuming cause of it all he would have marveled how a man could get so drunk, and live. And for a day or two Wolf did not draw a sober breath, but staggered, when he was able to walk, from place to place, muttering dire threats and drinking steadily while his money lasted. There is no telling where a periodical drinker will stop when once he gets started—and he had been started on more than a pint of brandy.

CHAPTER XIV

Enough Is Sufficient

THE FOLLOWING morning Johnny rode toward the northwest corner of the Bar H, the hilly, wooded section which had been presided over by Wolf Forbes. On his ride from the Bar H bunkhouse to the Triangle he had seen numerous unbranded cattle and wondered what he would find on the difficult section over which Wolf was wont to hold jealous guard. Riding to the west of the town he then turned and went south, passing behind the Doc's cabin, and parallel with the over-mountain trail. Reaching Clear River he followed it onto Double X range and then let Pepper pick her way over the mountain, and soon came to his objective, where he found large numbers of cattle, with an unusually high percentage of mavericks among them.

"Pepper," he said, alert for signs of Bar H riders, "th' SV has lost a lot of cows—an' folks can't make cows. So if it's goin' to make up its losses, it will have to do it with cows that are livin' this very minute. Now, it ain't reasonable to go on a ranch an' round up a lot of unbranded cattle, 'specially if it ain't willin' for 'em to be rounded up. On th' other hand, there ain't no harm in ridin' around an' sizin' things up. We want to find out where th' mavericks are, an' get some idea of how many there are of 'em.

"Mebby you don't know it, but a lot of mavericks means, generally, a lazy outfit, not to say nothin' worse. An' when a ranch reckons it's fenced off by natural barriers from other herds, that don't excuse 'em. A dishonest foreman or outfit, or a couple of dishonest men in it, can get rich with mavericks, if they know their business, an' don't work too hard. An' if th' whole outfit is dishonest an' workin' for its ranch, mavericks belongin' to surroundin' ranches are awful temptations.

"Now, th' SV don't earnotch its calves. They don't have no sleepers, at all; an' I know that calves will wander from their mothers after they are weaned, an' get notions of their own; an' they can be cut out an' drove to another range an' grow up to be big cows. On a ranch like th' SV, that ain't had no round-up in three years, all calves will be mavericks. There won't be a sign on none of 'em to tell where they belongs.

"Now then: We'll say th' Bar H is dishonest, but its foreman an' outfit is workin' for th' ranch an' not for their own pockets. If they drove SV calves to their own ranch, they'd put an iron on 'em as soon as they could, after which they wouldn't have to bother with 'em no more. They wouldn't have to be guarded jealous by th' best man of th' outfit, an' turned back when they tried to get off th' ranch. When I heard how Wolf almost lived out here, I got suspicious, Pepper; an' when I saw too many mavericks on this ranch, I got more suspicious; an' you've mebby heard that I was brought up in a plumb suspicious outfit. Of course, all ranches are goin' to have some mavericks, 'specially if it has a wild, rough range. Brush, timber, scrub, an' broken country hides cows that don't get combed out in a round-up; we had some, ourselves, down on th' old Bar-20, along our west line—but th' numbers out here are scandalous. I'm keepin' cases on these cattle, an' I says it's so scandalous that it just can't be true—but it *is* true, so far.

There's folks down here that are careless an' lazy, or crooked an' I've got my suspicions about which it is.

"Now, we'll say that th' outfit is crooked, an' workin' for its own pockets. They wouldn't want to brand any mavericks, not with th' ranch mark. There's two ways of dividin' that conclusion. First: That they're doin' it for their own pockets, th' foreman not knowin' about it. But no foreman is so dumb that he'd overlook so many mavericks—he'd raise h—l, an' weed out his punchers an' get new men. There wouldn't be many cows unbranded if he was workin' for his ranch. Th' second is: Foreman an' outfit are workin' for themselves, dividin' up th' profits accordin' to some plan. Then nobody would care how many mavericks there was, for th' more th' merrier. They'd have a right smart herd to brand with th' mark of some friend's ranch, road brand, an' throw on th' trail for some shippin' point up north, near th' railroad. Or mebby they figger on stockin' a ranch of their own that they has in some other part of th' country. Rustlers plumb love mavericks—an' if I was one, an' wanted to get rich, I know where I'd start out. An' if it wasn't for th' Double X layin' between this ranch an' th' Snake Buttes country, them rustlers over there would give this outfit sleepless nights. Them Double X punchers bein' on th' job all th' time is all that saves these here mavericks from swappin' ranges. Th' Double X is workin' for this passel of thieves, an' don't know it.

"Now, then: These mavericks out here are mostly all three years old, or younger. There's some four-year-olds, an' others, of course. An' th' SV ain't had a calf round-up in three years. Ain't that remarkable? Th' Bar H owners get good reports every round-up. Th' new calves keep right up to th' factor of natural increase, an' there ain't nothin' to make anybody jump out here for a good look at things. An' when th' drive figgers go on, an' show five hundred cattle on th' beef trail, an' really there is a thousand, th' books balance just right; an' Big Tom gets a Christmas present from th' owners for bein' such a good, honest foreman. Where that extra five hundred head goes to nobody knows but th' outfit. I've heard that

Wolf is th' *segundo* down here, an' is trail boss on every drive. Do you wonder he's jealous of his mavericks out here, an' watchin' day an night for some of them Snake Buttes rustlers to bust through th' Double X riders an' pay this section a visit? Him bein' so alert was another reason why I packed him off to Highbank for a day or two, where he can have excitement, an' there's things to do an' see. An' while he's enjoyin' th' hilarity of town, we'll have a good look around. *Pull up,* Pepper, there's hoss tracks—fresh, too. They was made while th' mornin's dew was heavy, which is told by th' little chunks of dirt his hoofs picked up an' turned over. You stay right here while I go ahead. *Lay down!*" He slapped the horse and gave a low, peculiar whistle. Pepper laid her ears back, but slowly obeyed the signal and went down, "playing dead" on her side. Taking his rifle, Johnny slipped into the brush, following a course parallel to but some distance from the tracks. For an hour he trailed, seeing numbers of mavericks and but few branded cattle, and twice he was in danger of being charged by crusty, old long-horned "outlaws" who, while having a due and well-founded respect for mounted men, evidently regarded a man on foot as being a different and less dangerous species of animal. These he eluded by taking to the brush and swiftly getting out of sight, detouring and picking up the trail again farther along. Suddenly he stopped and laughed silently. On the farther side of a clump of brush a conical, vertically dented Mexican sombrero loomed against the sky. Waiting a moment to be sure that he had not been heard, he raised the rifle and took long, deliberate aim. With the roar of the gun the peak of the hat flipped up and over, reversing itself as if on a hinge, and hung down on the side of the high crown like a cup. There was a yell of surprise, the hat dipped down below the shielding brush, and the sudden noise of pounding hoofs rolled toward East Canyon. Johnny reloaded and ran to a place from where he could see the fleeing horseman. It was Smitty, and he was mounted on his own horse, a long-legged, big-barreled roan, and it was fresh from a three day's rest. The speed it made awakened a surprised admiration in the laughing rifleman, who watched the departing horseman until he dashed into East Canyon.

"Thanks, Smitty," chuckled Johnny. "I'm glad you ain't headin' for th' bunkhouse. Now I won't be bothered by no curious outfit combin' these hills, lookin' for me. Reckon Smitty is goin' to town—or he never would 'a' rode for th' canyon. Just th' same, I'm leavin' for th' Double X. I've seen all I wants out here, an' now I'll try to fix up a round-up for th' SV, an' get the rest of th' figgers I needs." He returned to the horse and rode into the northwest, giving vent to occasional bursts of laughter.

"Pepper," he chuckled, as he rode down the other slope of the watershed, "we're havin' more fun down here than we had up around Twin Buttes, but th' show ain't hardly begun. However, we'll laugh while we can, an' meet trouble when it really comes."

Smitty pounded into and through East Canyon, busy with his crowded thoughts and harrowed feelings. His horse from habit chose the left-hand turn at the other end of East Arroyo, and swung around the bend toward Gunsight.

"Twice!" he soliloquized. "Twice in th' hat! He was close up, th' murderin' coyote—sneaked up on top of me when I was so far away from th' mountain I had plumb forgot him. Sneaked up to th' other side of that brush—couldn't 'a' been forty feet away—an' he missed *again*! You can't tell me he didn't aim to miss, not *this* time. An' I'm dead shore he aimed to miss me that other time. Why? Because he didn't want to hit me, *yet!* It was a warnin', it was. He says plain: 'Smitty, you ain't wanted around here no more. I'm warnin' you th' second time. But, mebby, th' third time I won't miss.' I'm sayin' there won't be no third time. Practice makes perfect, an' *I* ain't no target. He won't score no bulls-eyes on *me*! Big Tom says it's a joke; all right; but if it is, it ain't goin' no further. An' th' reason is, *I* am. I'm goin' further, an' I ain't comin' back. I ain't even wastin' time to go back to th' house for my war bag, an' have to give em' an argument about quittin'. There ain't much pay a-comin' to me—none, when I pays up what I owe—an' I'm callin' everythin' square, all around. Pore Squint! Huh; I'd rather be able to say 'Pore Squint' than hang around here till somebody up an' says 'Pore Smitty.' This here country ain't fit for a dog no more an' I'm goin' to find one that is. Keep a-goin', you long-laigged rabbit!"

He whirled over the rock hump below the historic stone benches on Pine Mountain and streaked toward Gunsight, seeing the Doc come to the door of the shack and wave at him. The Doc was haggard and sallow, nervous and poorly nourished after an unfavorable bout with his worst enemy, and leaned weakly against the door casing as he watched the hard-riding puncher whirl toward him. He made up his mind that if Big Tom wanted to see him, Mahomet could come to the mountain, for he was in no condition to go afield. To his surprise and great relief, Smitty followed the bend in the trail and headed to ride past. Then it was that Doc waved again.

Smitty's hand went to his nose and he shouted a greeting and prophecy in three words. The Doc, unstrung and highly irritable, took enraged umbrage at the insulting greeting, jerked the Colt from its shoulder holster and took three erratic shots at the derisive rider, followed almost instantly by three more. Smitty's anger flared up and centered on this tangible escape valve. Shooting at him seemed to be the fashion these days, but it had to stop. There were five rapid reports and five puffs of smoke, spaced at regular intervals along the trail behind his horse. He was lucky in his off-hand shooting, for all of the bullets found a target. One smashed the Doc's window, already cracked; one drilled a hole through the edge of the door behind him; one turned his water bucket into a sprinkling can, and the other two screamed past him into the room and accounted for a dishpan and his lamp. The owner of the aforesaid articles waxed wrathy and indignant, and jumped up and down, making strange noises; then, running after the irritated puncher, tried in vain to find the chambers of his six-gun with the wrong ends of a handful of cartridges, at the same time indulging in a spirited monologue, which was jumpy and spasmodic from shortness of breath. Smitty tuned in the saddle and let loose an insult which cannot be excelled in words, wig-wagged again, and flashed up the gentle slope toward town.

Gunsight heard him coming, and those inhabitants who suspected that strange things were likely to happen, made haste to look out and see what it was. Dailey chose his doorway, Dave an open window, while Two-Spot wished to be unhampered by walls and roof, and chose his favorite hang-out, the front of the saloon.

"Where you goin' so fast?" shouted Dailey, pleasantly curious. He became instantly indignant at the gesture which answered him, and the words which followed the action left no doubt in his mind that he had interpreted it correctly. He reached for his gun, thought better of it and, shaking a fist, shouted instead: "All right! But you'll be comin' back, cuss you!" and forthwith reached toward the gun again at the shouted answer he received.

Two-Spot saw the felt cup flapping up and down at the edge of the sombrero's peak and he let out a howl of pleasure at the sight, whereat Dave discreetly ducked back from the window, fearing Smitty's reply; but the puncher kept on ahead of his dust cloud and whirled over the trail toward Juniper.

Two-Spot shouted with laughter. "Did you see th' hat? Did you *see* it? Just what I was sayin'," he cried, delighted by the idea that his humorous conception had appealed to another. "Number Two, an' Smitty pulls his stakes. Hey, Dailey!" he shouted, "you says he'll be comin' back; *I'm* sayin' he won't. I'm bettin' we won't see Smitty no more. He's takin' what's left of his hat where it won't be spoiled no more. Did you notice th' hoss he's on? That ain't no Bar H critter; that's his *own*! I'm givin' you two to one he won't come back—two to one, you gapin' jackass!"

Dailey's open mouth closed suddenly, and he stepped

forward, feeling for his gun again; but Two-Spot went around the corner of the saloon, kicking his heels together. "He won't come back! Squint, Polecat, an' Smitty! Wonder who else will be missin'? Three in a row—if Polecat stays away. But Polecat won't, cuss him. I know him too well for that. He won't—and I'll be glad of it, too, th' coyote. Who's next?"

CHAPTER XV

A Diplomatic Mission

RIDING NORTHWARD after he had left the hills which lay along the line between the Double X and the Bar H, to find and follow the trail used by the Double X punchers when they rode to and from Gunsight, Johnny was nearing it when he saw a horseman far to the north, riding at speed down a hill and headed straight for him. Keeping on, Johnny turned into the trail in the direction of the Double X bunkhouse, whereupon the other changed his course and rode as if to head him off. From the way in which the other stuck up above the horse, Johnny thought him to be Slim Hawkes, and he pulled Pepper to a walk, rolling a cigarette while he loafed along. His surmise was correct, and soon Slim joined him, his look of suspicion having some time back given way to a smile.

"Hello, Nelson!" he cried. "Lost?"

"Not quite," answered Johnny, smiling in turn. "How are you?"

"Cheerful, if not handsome," grinned Slim. "Judgin' from th' way yo're headed, I reckon yo're headed my way. Wolf Forbes chase you away from his pet mavericks?"

"Didn't see him down there. What's he doin'—trainin' 'em?"

"Keepin' 'em from strayin' over on us," growled Slim. "If he'd 'a' seen you there he'd 'a' been plumb nasty."

"Then I'm glad he didn't," replied Johnny. "I don't like people to be nasty to me. It hurts my feelin's; I'm what you might call tender."

"Lookin' you over, I'd say you was," retorted Slim.

"I'm aimin' to pay you fellers a visit," said Johnny. "Bein' so tender, I won't stay long if I ain't treated nice, or if yore cook is worse than George."

"Yo're welcome if you has money with you," laughed Slim. "We make it a point to entertain visitors with plenty of poker. Which reminds me that this must be visitors' week on th' Double X. Larry Hallock's three brothers is visitin' him, an' Pete Wiggins' boy, Arch, dropped in last night. Arch quit th' Circle 4 an' was goin' to Highbank to see his dad, an' spend his month's wages. He's still able to go an' see his dad, but there ain't no danger of him spendin' any of them wages in town. He can't leave us, now. We got him interested in our entertainment an' he ain't got no money left. He aims to stay around an' get it back. We aim to get his hoss an' fixin's, an' then lend 'em to him so he can go down an' strike old Wiggins for enough to redeem 'em. Th' Hallock boys are doin' a little better, but we have hopes. Now that yo're headed for our web, I'm shore everythin' will be real cheerful. Anyhow, we'll make you welcome, little stranger, for we've got ideas about you that have kept grins on th' faces of our outfit. Th' boys are honin' to pump you. Has th' Doc been kidnapped again, or has Squint come back?"

"Neither of them calamities has happened," chuckled Johnny. "How much can th' Double X scrape up, in case I makes up my mind to stay a week?"

"Four dollars an' two bits. I'm aimin' to play 'em so that you'll have to put up that black wonder yo're ridin'. I shore can use her for my very own ridin' hoss."

"This cayuse won't never put no interest in gamblin',"

said Johnny, stroking a glossy shoulder. "She's my pardner."

"I'd say she was northern raised," guessed Slim. "The, north ranges shore do make a difference in stock. I've heard of Texas ponies puttin' on a couple of hundred pounds, 'an' even growin' higher, up there. 'Tin-Cup,' " he read. "Where's that located? I never saw that brand before?"

"Up in Montanny," replied Johnny. "I worked for it, an' bought this cayuse while th' brand was still red. She's got *blood* in her, I'm tellin' you."

"I knowed that as fur as I could see her," replied Slim. "But you ain't no Northerner. Did you go up with a trail herd, an' stay over?"

"No, I went up by myself. Went up to help a friend spread th' gospel over his ranch, which was done proper. It's fine country, but it's gettin' crowded."

"See many Texas an' Greaser cattle up there?"

"Shore; we wasn't so far from th' Musselshell. They're on th' trail all th' time. An' they ain't loved a whole lot, neither. Th' northern punchers try to keep their herds from grazin' too close to th' trails. They're plumb scared about Texas fever. Sometimes a trail herd will pick up quite a lot of local cattle, an' when they're cut out they're mostly held on a range by themselves over a winter, until th' danger is reckoned to be past. You can't blame 'em, for th' fever raises th' very devil in northern herds. I know what I'm talkin' about, because some fever cattle was throwed over on th' Tin-Cup by some two-laigged skunks, an' we had one busy time, I'll admit. It went through our cattle like fire through dead grass; an' if it hadn't been for an Englishman, with plenty of brains in his deceivin' head, it would 'a' been good-by Tin-Cup. It was a squeak for us. How's everythin' with you fellers?"

"Our troubles are periodics," replied Slim. "We'll have a long stretch of peace an' quiet, an' then things will happen in bunches, an' keep us crow-hoppin' all over th' range. We got our southeast section tamed, but our west section boils over every once in a while. Even when it ain't boilin', or even simmerin', we have got to watch it close. An' it's generally on th' simmer. If you go broke a-visitin' us, which I hopes you do, you can earn quite some cash. All you got to do is to go over in th' Snake Buttes country, just west of us, an' get Nevada for us. We'll pay five hundred dollars for his body, an' a hundred apiece for each of his men. I've heard tell about th' Hole in th' Wall, up north, but I reckon we've got its first cousin down here, right next door to us. We have to keep four men on our west section day an' night. Don't you never ride out there for fun—we shoots first, an' then finds out who it was."

"Nevada!" mused Johnny, "who is he?"

"Some say he's white, others, a half-breed," answered Slim. "Nobody I ever met knew anythin' about him, except that he come from Nevada. While I never saw him, I shore heard an' felt his lead one night; an' if he can shoot that good in th' dark, by ear, I ain't honin' to meet him for fun an' excitement in th' daytime when he can use his eyes. He skinned my ear, put one through my arm, another cut my shoulder, one went through my hat, th' fourth grazed my side, an' th' fifth killed my cayuse. It sounded like a loud *r-i-i-p!* Since then I don't make no noise at night out there. I imitates a ghost when I move around, an' I'm on full cock, with a hair trigger, every minute, which is some strain."

"How'd it happen?" asked Johnny.

"We was roundin' up last fall, an' had a beef herd we was holdin'. Th' night come on windy an' rainy, but there wasn't no lightnin' or thunder. Four of us was ridin' th' middle trick an' singin' plenty as we went around. Th' herd had fed heavy an' was well watered, an' tired, an' we wasn't worryin' much about it. Just after midnight we heard a rumble from behind us, an' th' whole herd was on its feet like one cow. It was a small bunch of stampeded cattle, an' when it hit our herd everythin' went that had hoofs. Th' cook, back in th' waggin', was awake because of a leak over his bed-roll, an' as soon as he heard th' rumble he let out a yell an' woke up th' off-shifts. The had their cayuses tied to th' waggin, or staked out close at hand, an' they forked 'em quick. Tom Wilkes saw my six-gun flashes an' he joins me. We lean against one end of th' front rank of our bunch, tryin' to turn 'em, an' get 'em to mill; but it wasn't no use. Th' herd had split up into bunches, an' our bunch run for half an hour southwest. When we finally got 'em millin', an' then busted that up, they figgered they had all th' runnin' they wanted an' behaved themselves. I rode back to take th' rear when I heard what sounded like another bunch runnin' west, quite a ways north of us. I sung out to Tom that I'd be back, an' streaked up to give a hand with th' other herd. When I got to it I rode right up front an' sung out that I was givin' a hand. My mouth wasn't hardly shut before I got in th' way of that stream of lead I told you about. I got my gun workin', but I was afoot an' had to hear th' herd leave me behind. Managin' to get my saddle off, I hoofed it for th' cook's fire, which was blazin' high when I got to where I could see it. By th' time I got there th' rain was comin' down in sheets, an' I was done up. They got away with over forty head, as near as we could figger it, an' th' rain had smoothed them sandy valleys over in th' Buttes so they didn't show a print. We wouldn't 'a' follered far, anyhow—Nevada likes ambushes, an' that country was made for 'em."

"I've been through it," growled Johnny. "There's th' fourth muley I've seen in ten minutes," he said, nodding to the right.

"He was made a muley by a saw," replied Slim. "That feller was a bloody-minded terror. He's cost this ranch a dozen times what he was ever worth. We don't know what was th' matter with him—just born savage, I reckon. He killed an' ruined a lot of young steers before we got onto him. At first we was goin' to kill him; then we said he had been so all-fired mean that he ought to be punished. So we sawed off his horns an' turned him loose to play with th' rest of th' longhorns. He got some good lickin's before he learned that he wasn't dangerous no more. He got mauled so much before he quit his mean ways that we sort of felt sorry for him. Here comes Quantrell. He's our *segundo*, an' boss of our trail outfit. Good man, all around. Hey! Look at that old reprobate go for him! What do you think of that? Cimarron was th' man who sawed off his horns, an' cussed if he don't remember it!"

The approaching rider evaded the charge, fired close to the steer's nose as the animal went past, which turned its chain of thought, and rode up laughing.

"Did you see th' old boy?" he chuckled.

"Reg'lar friend of yourn," laughed Slim. "Here, shake han's with Nelson. He's comin' out to show us how to play draw—an' his pockets are full of money."

"Yo're welcome," said Cimarron, grinning, his handclasp solid and sincere. "Better put yore rope on him, Slim, in case he gets scared off."

Laughing and chatting they rode westward until about mid-afternoon when, hungry as wolves, they arrived at the bunkhouse, where Cimarron dared the sanctity of the cook shack to rustle warm, if rather dried-out food, from the back of the stove; and they ate to the frank and personal comments of several loafing onlookers. The rest of the afternoon was passed in discussions and reminiscences of things concerning range activities and in telling stories about men they had known. It was not long before other men began to come in from the range and the cook showed signs of activity. When he was ready he let out a yell: "Are you all a-comin'?" They were, and ate hungrily, for the most part in silence, listening to the three who had enjoyed a late dinner and who could take time to talk. Four men soon arose and exchanged banter as they looked to tobacco, guns, and other things requiring their attention and, saying good-by, went out to the corral. They had the first night shift on the west section and soon were riding away. Hardly two hours later another four-man group came in, fell upon the second meal the cook had prepared in less than three hours, and then loafed, joining in the conversation.

"How's things over Gunsight way?" Cimarron asked Johnny.

"Just th' same, I reckon," came the answer. "Everythin' is all right, a cussed sight better than they are further east. It's a shame, too; a cussed shame."

"Meanin'?" queried Lin Sherwood, the foreman, a tall, wiry man of about forty years, whose broad, sloping shoulders suggested great strength. His face was frank and kindly, and his steel-blue eyes twinkled from their frames of wrinkles in a manner to win Johnny the moment he had looked into them.

"I'm meanin' that old man with th' busted laig, over on the SV," answered Johnny; "an' that kid, an' that helpless girl. Do you know they ain't had no round-up in three years, neither calf nor beef?"

"What's that?" exclaimed Cimarron in surprise. "That ain't no way to run a ranch. Ain't they done no brandin' at all?"

"Ain't had an iron hot in three years," replied Johnny.

"What's th' matter with 'em?" demanded Matt Webb.

"They can't keep an outfit," answered Johnny. "Every time they hired a man he was either scared off or bribed to quit. After a while they gave it up. Three of their men are workin' on th' Triangle, or th' Bar H right now."

"Then they didn't lose a whole lot," snorted Art French.

"If they don't round up, how do they know where they are?" asked Bud Norris. "How do they know how many cows they got, or if they're runnin' at a profit or a loss?"

"They don't," answered Johnny. "But there ain't no round-up necessary to tell 'em about profit an' loss. They can see th' herds skrinkin', it's so plain; an' when they has to sell off a few head every time they needs chuck, I reckon they know about th' profit an' loss. They want to have a round-up just to get a tally of th' cattle now on th' ranch. Knowing how many there was from th' tally th' year they took possession, they could tell what their losses are. But how can they hold one, without punchers?"

"They ought to know," said Slim. "But that wouldn't help 'em much, at that. It would only make 'em feel worse, I reckon."

"Their herds ain't got no business to shrink, not on a range like theirs," said Bud. "If they ain't throwed many on th' trail they ought to have more now than they had three years ago. Cattle don't stop multiplyin' just because they ain't rounded up once in a while!"

"Mebby their cattle are different, then," said Johnny. "An' there's one thing shore: I never saw so few mavericks on any ranch as there are on th' SV; nor so d——d many as I saw on th' Bar H. Why, when I was on th' Bar-20, down in th' Pecos Valley, we wouldn't 'a' let no ranch close to us hold so many unbranded cows."

"Where did you say?" quickly demanded Bill Dusenberry, who answered to the name of "Deuce."

"Bar-20," replied Johnny, "down in th' Pecos."

"Did you ever hear of Lacey?" excitedly asked Deuce.

"Lacey? Why, he run a saloon, over in Perry's Bend; an' he was a white man clean through."

"Holy mackerel!" cried Deuce. "Was you one of Peter's outfit?"

"I was near since I was old enough to throw a rope," answered Johnny, a pleased grin coming to his face. "Did you know Lacey, or Buck?"

"Lacey is my cousin," exclaimed Deuce. He turned to his friends. "We ain't goin' to have no poker tonight. This feller is goin' to entertain us with th' doin's of th' cussedest he-man outfit that ever lived under one roof. Lacey has told me just enough to get me on th' prod—an' here's a man who was one of that outfit. You can begin with that cow-skinner you fellers went to Perry's Bend after. I'm tellin' you that if you can show us that you belonged to that hair-trigger outfit there ain't nothin' Bill Dusenberry an' his friends won't do for you. What was that cow-skinner's name, an' where did he die?"

"I'm glad to meet a relative of Lacey's," replied Johnny, smiling. "Lacey turned a buffalo gun loose on that gang of rustlers when they had me in Jackson's store after they had killed Edwards. As to Jerry Brown, he died in some sort of a church, or mission, or somethin' like that. He shot me in Harlan's saloon, shootin' through his coat pocket, th' skunk. Speakin' of mavericks, you fellers all know that if th' natural increase ain't branded yo're goin' to have a fine crop of unbranded cattle; an if there ain't no calves branded for three years, yo're shore goin' to have one slashin' big herd of mavericks. Now, if them mavericks wander off th' ranch there ain't no tellin' what'll happen to 'em. An' if they ain't allowed to git back again, or ain't kept off some other ranch, somebody's goin' to have a fine lot of cattle that can be marked with any brand they feels like puttin' on 'em. They won't even have to be vent branded: they can be sold, an' th' first an' only brand they start with can be th' sign of th' man that buys 'em. With a road brand to take 'em over th' trail, there ain't nobody can question 'em, is there? At least not down in this country, where there ain't no laws to question 'em."

"Yo're right!" exclaimed Slim, his eyes glowing with a sudden inspiration. "Where have our brains been, all this time? Reckon we was too busy out on our west line to do much thinkin' about other things."

"Yes, an' none of 'em will be much more than three years old," said Cimarron, looking around the room, where various expressions met his eye. "A plumb fine lot of unbranded cattle, runnin' up to three-year-olds, ready for any iron. I've been as dumb as a locoed dogie!"

"Lin," said Gus Thompson, turning to the foreman, "I'm tellin' you that when folks get th' maverick habit, an' ain't bothered, they get so, after a while, that they don't care a whole lot *where* them mavericks come from; an' you know that there are *some* parts of our ranch that are plumb heavy with scrub timber, brush, an' rough ground."

"Tell us about Perry's Bend," impatiently demanded Deuce.

"Tell us about yore gran'mother's cat!" snorted Bill Sage. "That can wait: Nelson's goin' to stay here a couple of nights, anyhow." He looked around. "I'm beginnin' to see through th' holes in th' ladder; an' I'm honin' to listen to why th' SV don't show no mavericks, when it ain't had a spring round-up for three years. Does it sleeper?"

"Not an earnotch," interjected Tom Wilkes. "You ought to know that, you flathead; you've seen enough SV cattle, anyhow."

"Mebby Nelson can explain it," suggested the foreman.

"I'm willin' to talk it over, anyhow," said Johnny. "In th' first place, there's natural enemies."

"Then you can leave 'em in th' first place," laughed Slim. "There ain't none, that I knows of, down here."

"Well, then, there's them quicksands," continued Johnny, gravely. "Cattle are plumb fascinated by quicksands——"

"Huh!" snorted Cimarron, "you ain't figgerin' them sands are takin' th' increase of three whole years, are you?"

"Or pickin' mavericks, as a choice?" grunted Matt Webb.

"They'd be so full of bones if they got three years' calves," said Bud, "that you could build a shack on 'em, an' never feel a quiver."

"Well, then, there's th' freezin' cold an' th' ice on th' grass," suggested Johnny, grinning. "We all know that cattle ain't got sense enough to paw through ice to get at th' grass under it."

"Shore!" snorted Slim. "Did we have a freeze-up last winter?" he asked the crowd.

"Not so no cows was killed," replied Cimarron. "An' I didn't see no driftin' herds at all."

"What's th' matter with you fellers?" indignantly demanded Johnny. "Here I'm tryin' to explain a mystery, an' you keep pullin' me out of th' saddle as fast as I climb up. That ain't fair. Then how about this one: Th' SV wasn't no good for winter range, bein' all et off?"

"Yo're down again," laughed Art French. "Th' SV is good winter range, an' summer, too."

"An' spring an' fall, an' th' Fourth of July, as well as Christmas," supplemented Bud.

"You fellers are shore ornery," complained Johnny. "Then mebby th' mavericks, bein' different than marked animals, all got th' travel itch an' left that arid valley for th' thick, green grass down south of 'em, or for th' juicy scrub an' clean rocks north of 'em."

" 'Arid valley' is purty near as good as 'thick, green grass south of 'em,' " chuckled Cimarron. "Was you ever over on that luxuriant south range?" he asked, ironically.

"I wasn't, but Ol' Buffalo was," answered Johnny.

"Shore, but he don't eat grass," retorted Cimarron; "an' what's more, he don't stop on it at all."

"Well, I'll try once more," said Johnny, in simulated desperation. "Mebby cow-hawks flew away with 'em seein' that there wasn't no brands to prove nothin'."

After the laughter quieted down, Cimarron jammed his fist into an open palm with a resounding smash. "I'm thinkin' we got more interest in th' way them SV cows are handled than we ever thought. I'm gettin' interested in seein' that th' SV runs itself some better than it has. There's ideas millin' around in my head that some folks might say are scandalous an' unpolite. You all heard *me*—lemme hear somethin'."

"An' I'm wantin' to know," said Johnny, "what kind of barb wire is sold down in these parts?"

"Mean, cussed mean," replied Slim.

"Then mebby that's why it won't stay up," muttered Johnny. "It keeps a-comin' down from off them posts around th' quicksands, pullin' out double staples, an' draggin' itself all over th' valley. A couple of them posts set fire to themselves, too, an' burned till they busted themselves off, close to th' ground. I'm shore doin' a lot of guessin'."

"Lacey told me—" began Deuce.

"—to rope yourself," interrupted Cimarron. "We got lots of time, later, to hear about what Lacey told you."

"I believe in bein' neighborly," said Matt, "an' givin' folks a hand when they deserve it."

"Is th' Doc a friend of you fellers?" asked Johnny.

"We ain't weepin' none over his kidnappin', if that's what you mean," chuckled Matt. "He mebby will be kidnapped ag'in, sometime—an' hoof it back home. Why?"

"Well, I didn't want to hurt you fellers' feelin's," replied Johnny.

"What you mean?" asked Cimarron. "You'll have to be plumb rough to hurt any feelin's out here."

"Matt was sayin' he believes in bein' neighborly," explained Johnny, "an' I happened to think of somethin' about th' Doc, what stirred me a-plenty. That's why I asked."

"What was that?" asked Slim.

"Why, that Arnold girl was took sick about a year ago, an' they sent for th' Doc. He said he would doctor cows an' horses, but he wouldn't sling a laig across a saddle if th' whole SV was dyin', an' he refused to go. That kid had to ride to Highbank for that drunken doctor down there."

"Th' h—l you say!" snapped Thompson. "Is that right?"

"It is," answered Johnny. "An' it made me wonder what kind of country I'd got into. I maintains that no doctor like that measures up to th' standards of cow-country men; an' when th' old man busted his laig I says it was plumb proper that th' coyote was kidnapped an' made to do his plain duty."

"I'm admirin' that kidnappin' more every day," exclaimed Slim. "Th' dog wouldn't have to be kidnapped if he was needed on th' Bar H."

"Huh!" snorted Cimarron. "If Big Tom had a sore toe th' Doc would bust his neck an' kill a hoss gettin' there."

"Will somebody tell me what's th' matter with that coyote?" asked Larry Hallock. "One day he's as bright as a new dollar an' witty as blazes; th' next, he looks like somebody had dragged him by th' heels through th' hottest parts of h—l. Talk about quick changes! He's a wonder. What's he drinkin', anyhow?"

"I reckon it ain't drink," said the foreman, reflectively. "I once knowed a gambler, up in Dodge, that could play longer than anybody in town—hours longer—but when he went to pieces he shore hit hard. An' he'd rather lie than tell th' truth. However, th' devil with th' Doc; I'm wonderin' about somethin' else."

"Lacey knowed a man like that," said Deuce, but got

no further, for Cimarron balanced a gun in his hand and seemed to be considering.

"I'm itchin' for to shoot Lacey," Cimarron remarked, "but as he ain't on hand any of his tribe will do. You shut up about Lacey till th' time's ripe to talk about him!"

"It'd look too set, too plain, an' sort of hintin'," soliloquized the foreman, "to send a Double X bunch over there. If we could make it universal, sort of free-for-all, with others joinin' in, it would be better. It would look like a surprise party an' not point too strong in one direction. They should have a round-up an' get a tally. Even a little iron heatin' wouldn't be out of place, as long as it was done by them as didn't belong to th' SV. Nobody could hardly blame th' SV for brandin' mavericks, an' say they was stealin' cows that didn't belong to 'em, if punchers from other ranches did th' brandin'. How many men do you reckon we'd need, Nelson?"

"More than you could spare if you kept a good watch on that west section," answered Johnny, seeing the drift of the foreman's thoughts. "Quite some few more. An' you got to count me out of it, 'though I'd be glad to stay here an' take some man's place while he's gone. I don't aim to be hobbled in th' future by comin' out strong an' plain. That may sound funny, but I got things to answer for if they're found out an' laid to me—which I ain't aimin' to have found out, positive. It ain't that I'm gun-shy, or tryin' to slip out of trouble, but I just ain't ready to smoke up, right now. It's shore a puzzle."

Arch Wiggins slapped his thigh with stinging emphasis. "I'm seein' th' drift of this here conversation, an' I ain't declarin' myself in because th' wool is bein' pulled over my eyes at all; but I *am* declarin' myself in, clean up to my hat, because I'm a cowman, through an' through, first an' last; an' because I'm a human bein'. If any round-up gang needs a first-class hoss wrangler for a few days, or a week, without pay, an' willin' to feed hisself, I'm speakin' for th' job. An' I ain't too lazy to keep irons hot, neither. Do I hear anythin'?"

Jim Hallock leaped to his feet. "I come down here to visit, an' get a rest," he declared, grinning. "I've had all th' visitin' I wants with a bunch of cold-deckers; an' I ain't had no rest since I arrove. My fingers ache from dealin' an' cuttin' an' drawin'; an' I can see deuces an' treys in my sleep, when I get any. Speakin' for myself, I'd enjoy seein' that lazy Wiggins wranglin' cayuses for me every mornin' before sunup. I'll do my cussedest to wear him to a frazzle. How about you, boys?" he asked, turning to his brothers.

"I ain't got no love for Arch Wiggins," announced Wood, "but I'm swallerin' my pride. If he wants an assistant wrangler that knows more about th' job than he ever will, I'm ready to take orders, an' sacrifice my independence an' self-respect."

"Where you find one Hallock," chuckled George, "you finds more. We was brought up like that. I can use an iron with any man on th' range, no matter who says I'm lyin'."

Larry burst out laughing. "I never let my cub brothers put on no airs," he declared; "an' some older member of th' family ought to go along to keep 'em from gettin' into trouble. I'm signin' this pay-yoreself-pay-roll, with Lin's permission."

"I can't give no permission to anybody in my outfit to brand mavericks, or run another man's ranch for him," said Sherwood, "but I reckon I can give some of you boys a few days off, in case you want to go fishin' over in Green Valley, or chase them cow-hawks Nelson was tellin' about. Do you chase 'em, or trap 'em, Nelson?"

"You put a hunk of maverick meat on th' end of a rope, an' tie knots in it," said Johnny. "Th' cow-hawk swallers th' whole thing, an' th' knots get caught in his innards. Then you shoot him through th' epizootic with a hunk of lead. Didn't you ever go huntin' 'em?"

"No, but I've heard all about it," replied Sherwood, apologetically. "Now, lemme see: some of you fellers have got to stay here. There's twelve, not countin' me, which nobody ever does, anyhow. Twelve, thanks to them Snake Buttes coyotes, on a ranch that shouldn't have more'n eight. Well, after all, sizin' up th' twelve an' lumpin' 'em, an' dividin' it by one real, shore-enough puncher, they only come to eight, after all. I figger I can do without four of th' laziest—five, if Nelson stays to show somebody how his job ought to be done. Now, that makes nine goin' to Gunsight to spend their time an' money. Somebody ought to remember about a cook, for I'm sayin' right out loud an' flat, that our cook ain't gettin' no time off."

"You can't make me sore," chuckled Lem Curtis, culinary artist of the ranch." It'd only be out of th' fryin' pan an' into th' fire for me. Thanks, Lin."

"I can cook good enough for any bow-laigged coyote that ever set foot on this ranch," declared Art French. An' besides, I got some scores to settle up. I'll cook."

"Well," said Sherwood, "I promised Cimarron sometime ago that he could have a few days off, to rest up from them poker parties. He's a good foreman an' round-up boss, only he ought to do some work hisself. But I'm bettin' our wrangler ain't got enough saddle stock within a day's ride to give you fellers a *remuda* apiece—say about five to a man."

"If you wasn't th' foreman an' keeper of th' payroll," retorted Rich Morgan, "I'd say you was a cross-eyed fabricator. Cuss yore nerve! I'm th' best hoss wrangler, barrin' Arch, of course, that ever took a cussin' from a fool outfit. What th' devil is a little matter like a herd of forty-five saddle hosses to a man like *me*?"

The foreman leaned back and laughed contentedly. "You would think we was wantin' 'em to go to a dance," he said to Johnny, his eyes twinkling, "instead of goin' out of their way to do some hard work. I'm bettin' th' SV has a proper round-up. Who's goin' to be tally man?"

"That takes a good man away from work, when anybody can count knots or make a pencil mark," growled Cimarron. "We ought to have somebody that can't do nothin' else like that Two-Spot over in Gunsight."

"That's th' tally man!" shouted Arch.

"He's ourn, if we has to do some kidnappin' ourselves," exulted Larry. "We won't let him have a smell of liquor till we drop him off at Gunsight on th' way back. An' then we'll pickle him so he'll keep for a week."

"He won't do," asserted Slim. "He can't keep a tally straight."

"I'm sayin' he can," contradicted Johnny, smiling. "Seems to me I've seen him do little things that showed me he was a-punchin' once—an' punchin' for a long time. I'll bet he can keep tally as good as any man in this outfit, an' count 'em as they pass, too. Mebby he wouldn't suit a buyer, or a seller, but he's good enough for me. Anyhow, you can call th' figgers when yo're countin' herd. There won't be a new brand get away from him if you let him alone. It's time he was put to work."

"Mebby he won't work on th' SV?" suggested Arch.

"Th' Doc didn't want to, neither, did he?" demanded Slim; "but he did. What's th' use of kidnappin' anybody that wants to be took? He'll work, all right—or he won't eat."

"Hey," said Cimarron, turning to Johnny. "We got a lot of gall runnin' a round-up on another man's ranch. What'll we say to 'em? We got to say *somethin'*!"

"Tell 'em it's a neighborly act," replied Johnny. "Say you'd 'a' done it before if you'd 'a' knowed about things."

"They got any wire?" asked Wood. "I'm aimin' to run a fence around them posts that'll make some thief cuss some dark an' stormy night, as th' books say. Staplin' is fine, but takin' a couple of turns around th' posts an' staplin' all around is better."

"I reckon so," answered Johnny. "If they ain't tell Dailey to give you a spool an' charge it to me."

"Not bein' in on this personal I'll pervide a spool," offered the foreman. "I'd like to see this crew at work over there—a man allus works harder for somebody as a favor than he does for th' man that pays him. It would give me a line on how hard I could crowd you fellers. Wood, if you throw about three half-hitches over them posts before you staple 'em, you'll bother anybody that tries to unwind it from a hoss. Try it an' see."

"Yo're talkin' gospel," said Wood, grinning. "It'll just

wind up th' other way, an' before he knows what he's doin' he'll have one plumb, fine job on his hands."

"I'll give two bits, purty near," chuckled the foreman, "to see some faces in this country when th' news gets out about this here high-speed round-up. But I don't reckon there'll be no trouble about it. I'm sayin', however, if you'll listen to me, don't nobody start none. Yo're job is takin' care of SV cows, an' not gun-fightin', 'though I know there ain't no danger of anybody chasin' you off th' range."

"There won't be no trouble, Lin," assured Cimarron, "not if I has to shoot up th' whole blasted country. An' I'm aimin' to have some of them Triangle riders join hands with us: we're roundin' up wide an' regardless, an' it stands to reason that we'll have to cross their boundary line. But we'll be polite an' fair; we'll tell 'em three times, smiling. After that it'll be their own bull-headed fault."

"There's one man on th' Triangle I hope is hard of hearin'," chuckled Tom Wilkes; "that's Gurley. Can *I* ask him, Cimarron?"

"You'll stay right here," replied the *segundo*. "We'll have trouble enough, mebby, takin' things as they come, without luggin' along no canned grudges."

"You watch me stay here!" retorted Wilkes.

"I'll do that very thing," chuckled the foreman. "Yo're goin' to show Nelson over our west range tomorrow night, an' cover more ground out there on account of there bein' fewer of you. Nelson," he said, turning, "have you any choice of men for this here party that's goin' to celebrate their freedom over in Gunsight?"

"I ain't sayin' a word—not one word."

"All right, then," continued the foreman. "Now, boys, them that are goin' to have a few days off are: Cimarron, Larry, Art, Slim, an' Bud. I ain't lendin' no cayuses, wire, or no chuck waggin, for they ain't needed goin' to Gunsight on a spree; but, I'm sayin' that I don't expect to go in th' storeroom, nor th' waggin shed, nor have no time to bother about my hoss wrangler's job. If

he wants to keep a lot of saddle hosses away off somewhere where they can't be seen, that's his business.
He's doin' th' wranglin' for this ranch, an' nobody else is.
An'," he grinned, turning toward the cook, "Lem, here,
has a pore mem'ry an' never would miss no pots an'
pans."

"I has; likewise I'm blind," said Lem. "But lemme
make a prophecy: If there are any cookin' utensils that
gets misplaced an' can't be found for near a week, an'
they ain't as clean when they're found again as they was
when they got lost, there'll be some h—l-roarin', excitin'
times on this here packet. You all here me chirp?"

"Now, then, Nelson," said Deuce, "tell us about Lacey
an'—" he broke off his request as he dodged Cimarron's
boot, for the *segundo* was a man of set ideas, and he
was going to turn in.

"If I hears any more about that cousin of yourn,
tonight," quoth Cimarron, pulling off a second boot and
balancing it, "there is goin' to be weepin' in th' Deusen-
berry family. I'm turnin' in, an' I only turns in when I
want to go to sleep. I got plenty of work ahead of me for
a few days. An' I'm sayin', further, that if there's any
poker playin' tonight, it's goin' to be held in th' kitchen,
an' played by a lot of dumb men."

"An' if I ketches any poker parties in my kitchen,"
announced Lem, arising and flexing his muscles, "I'll
heave 'em out again. I ain't goin' to clean up after no
pack of bums. You hear me real plain?"

"Couple of grouches," growled Slim, looking around.
"Get th' cards an' beans, Tom. We'll pull th' waggin out
of th' shed, an' play in there, out of th' wind. Somebody
else get th' lanterns."

"An' what are *you* goin' to get?" demanded Rich,
pausing as he started to take a lantern down from
its peg.

"I wasn't goin' to say nothin' about that," answered
Slim, grinning; "but as long as you asked, I'll tell you. I'm
goin' to get th' money. Come on, Nelson; we'll move th'
waggin for them suckers."

"I don't mind lookin' like a sucker," retorted Rich, getting the other lantern, "as long as I don't play like one. Who'll buy Slim's watch from me tomorrow?" he asked from the doorway.

"Yo're blockin' th' door, an' talkin' foolish," said Thompson, shoving him aside. "Anybody wants that watch'll have to come an' see *me*. Don't forget them beans," he called over his shoulder.

"He ain't got time to get 'em," muttered Tom, "but he'll have to wait for *me*, if *I* get 'em. Can you figger him?"

CHAPTER XVI

A Neighborly Call

AT DAYLIGHT there was hubbub, horseplay, and banter on
the Double X. Art French climbed up into the chuck
wagon (the cook's supply list in his pocket), banged on
a huge pot, and announced that the race was on. Arch
Wiggins, on this part of the journey, at least, had plenty
of assistant horse wranglers, for the eight riders,
Cimarron with the rest, herded the horses and started
for the SV, happy as schoolboys on a lark.

Reaching Gunsight, they caused quite some commotion, and fired into the air to give zest to the occasion.
Dave mopped his beaded brow several times before his
share in the festivities slackened, and Two-Spot, burning
with a fever of curiosity, shuffled from the chuck wagon
being loaded in front of Dailey's to the saloon, asking
shrewd questions and making pertinent observations.

"An' why th' waggin?" he asked Slim.

"To put Juniper in," answered that cheerful disciple of
George Washington. "We reckoned we'd like to have a
town closer to th' ranch, an' Gunsight ain't good
enough."

Two-Spot wandered around and put the question to Cimarron.

The *segundo* regarded him with level gaze. "It's for th' widder's mite," he answered. "We're on th' rustle, which ain't to be told."

"Huh!" snorted Two-Spot, "you might be aimin' for some widder, at that; but I'm sayin' that if she sees you first, you'll need more'n eight men an' a waggin to take her away from her home an' fambly. What are you aimin' to rustle?"

"Every cow on a certain ranch between here an' Juniper," whispered Cimarron, looking stealthily around.

"Then don't you waste no time hangin' around here," warned Two-Spot, also looking stealthily around. "Big Tom's gettin' up early these mornin's, I bets."

Cimarron gravely shook his head, whereat Two-Spot remarked carelessly, apropos of nothing, "Smitty has left th' range for good. He had two holes in his hat, th' upper hole like a coffeepot with th' lid back. He rode his own hoss, an' was goin' strong when he passed here. But nobody was chasin' him, then."

"Hey, fellers!" shouted the *segundo*, joyously, "Smitty has follered Squint, with a couple of gun-shot wounds in his Mex. hat!"

Laughter and cheerful remarks greeted the news, and Dave had to verify it.

"Bar H: mark *two*!" cried Norris. "Bring 'em up, you ropers—th' irons are hot!"

Two-Spot, despairing of gaining any real information in Dave's, shuffled out and went to Dailey's where Art French was putting the last of the provisions on the wagon.

"Hello, French!" greeted Two-Spot, putting a foot on the spokes of a wheel. "Where are you fellers headin' for?"

"Up th' Juniper trail," answered Art. "Want to come along? Have you got th' nerve to take a chance with somebody else's cattle?"

Two-Spot looked at him intently. "What are you aimin' to do with 'em?" he asked.

"What do folks usually do with cows that don't belong to 'em?" countered Art.

"Holy mavericks!" muttered Two-Spot. "These here ijuts ain't carin' a whole lot who knows about it! What you got th' waggin for? Aimin' to squat out there an' steal 'em as fast as they grows up?"

"That's for th' hides of them that gets killed. We're goin' to round up every hoof, clean and prompt."

"You didn't stop at th' Doc's on yore way up, did you?" asked Two-Spot, paying no attention to the noise made by several men who had mounted and were riding toward the wagon at a walk.

"Why?"

"Oh, nothin', only I reckon'd mebby you'd got some of them little white pills he shoots into hisself."

"Can you keep a tally?" asked Art, carelessly.

"I can; but I won't."

Art waved a hand at him. "He can tally; but he won't." Three ropes dropped over the surprised ex-tally man and were drawn not unpleasantly tight. He thought it might be a joke, so he grinned; it would not do to let anyone think he took it seriously, because it might cause them to take it that way. "Takes three men on hosses to rope me," he jeered, chuckling. "Better get th' rest of th' gang before I gets rough an' boisterous."

"Can you set a horse?" asked Slim.

"I shore can't," regretted Two-Spot. "It's one of th' sorrers of my life."

"Then we'll have to tie him on," said Wood. "Chuck us out a couple of hobbles, Art."

"I can ride any hoss you can," boasted Two-Spot. "I was bustin' 'em before you was borned."

"Then we'll hobble th' hoss," laughed Wiggins.

"Loosen 'em up; I hears Dave a-callin'!" exclaimed Two-Spot, suspiciously eager to answer duty's call.

"Where you aimin' to have him swing?" demanded Art. "Squint has got to be revenged."

"Th' first tree," growled Slim. "We gives you one chance to save yoreself an' help rid this range of law-breakers. Who got Squint?"

"You go to h——l!" blazed Two-Spot as the ropes tightened. "Take 'em off me!"

"Who got Squint?" repeated Slim, threateningly.

"If I tells, will you let me out of these cussed ropes?" asked the shivering victim.

"We will!"

"Smitty got him," chuckled the captive. "Ask him if you don't believe me. Take 'em off, now!" As soon as he was freed he danced away, wary and anxious, and bumped into Cimarron, whose muscular arms held him as in a vice. "*Now*, what's th' matter?" blazed Two-Spot, wriggling in vain. "What you reckon yo're goin' to do?"

"We need a tally man on this rustlin' expedition," said Cimarron, "an' we like yore looks. Bring up a cayuse, an' he can go bareback; either that or ride with Art."

"I'm ridin' with Art if I goes, which I ain't aimin' to!" snorted Two-Spot. "I can't count up to more'n ten," he protested.

"You won't have to count at all," Cimarron assured him. "All you got to do is make little pencil marks like a picket fence on a piece of paper, or drop a pebble in yore hat for every cow. You can drop pebbles, can't you?"

"Not very good," deprecated Two-Spot. "I'm too oncertain."

"Well, when yo're oncertain," chuckled Slim, "yore chuck will be oncertain. Th' oncertainer you are, th' less you'll eat."

Cimarron picked Two-Spot up and put him in the wagon, whereupon Slim and Wood rode up close to it, ropes in hand. "There ain't nothin' oncertain about Slim's ropin', or Wood's, neither," warned Cimarron. "You better stay right in that wagon." He turned to go to his horse. "Come on, boys! We're startin' *now*!"

Dave went to a window to see them off, caught sight of Two-Spot's appealing face in the wagon, and hastened to the door and out toward the vehicle.

"Hi!" shrilled Larry, his rope darting from his hand.

"Hi! Hi! Hi!" yelled the others, their ropes going to the mark.

"What'n h—l!" shouted Dave, struggling, and glaring around. He was the center from which four rope radii pointed to the cardinal points of the compass. "Leggo me! Loosen 'em up, you coyotes! Loosen up!"

"Does Two-Spot go with us?" asked Larry.

"Can we borrow him for a few days, to keep tally for us on th' SV, Mr. Green?" politely inquired Bud, tightening the rope.

"You can; an' go to blazes, for all I cares!" snorted Dave. He loosened the ropes and lost no time in getting back to his window. "Cuss 'em! All right; *take* him!" he yelled at the noisy cavalcade. "But if anythin' happens to him, you'll settle with Dave Green! You hear me?"

They did not.

Margaret, responding to her brother's excited summons, went to the door and her hands flew to her breast. A wagon, loaded with packages, pulled up at the dilapidated corral and eight rough-looking men, driving a herd of horses, stopped near it. One of them kept on at a walk and approached her. Removing his sombrero, he pulled up and bowed.

"Ma'am," he said, slowly and kindly, a smile wreathing his weather-beaten face, from which genial gray eyes twinkled at her; "Ma'am, we have come out to round up for you. We understand that this ranch ain't' been combed for three years—an' it shore is time it was. I saw a wire fence north of th' trail: how far does it run?"

"Why, why—I didn't know—we were not expecting any round-up. Isn't there some mistake?" she faltered.

"I don't reckon there is, Ma'am," Cimarron assured her. "Mr. Nelson was tellin' us about th' SV, an' we all reckoned it was time there was a round-up run over here. You ought to know how many cows you got; an' mebby there's some as should be branded."

"I hardly know what to say—how to thank you," Margaret replied. "Won't you come in and speak to father? He doesn't want to leave his bed for a few days more."

"Shore, Ma'am," said Cimarron, dismounting and

throwing the reins over the head of his horse, and following her into the house.

"Father, this is Mr.—Mr.—?" she looked at Cimarron inquiringly.

"Quantrell—Cimarron Quantrell," he smiled. "I was born on th' banks of th' Cimarron when they wasn't exactly safe for bein' born on, but our fambly was lucky."

"This is my father, Mr. Quantrell," smiled Margaret. "I'll leave you men to talk by yourselves. If you want me, please call."

"Arnold," said Cimarron, with simple directness, "we've come out here, nine of us, from th' Double X, to round up for you. Nelson said you hadn't held none in three years, an' we reckoned it was time we was payin' you a neighborly call. When you get an outfit of yore own some day you can give us a hand. By helpin' each other we'll both be helpin' ourselves. How far does that wire fence run, up north of th' house?"

"Mr. Quantrell, I don't know how to thank you," replied Arnold. "I was growing to think there were no human beings in this country, but I'm beginning to change my mind. Even Doctor Reed has had a change of heart."

"Don't you bank on th' Doc changin' his ideas," warned Cimarron. "He come out here because he was made to come. He shore was plain kidnapped that night."

"You amaze me! Surely you are mistaken. Who would force him to come here?"

"That ain't known," answered Cimarron, "but everybody knows he was forced, all right. Th' fool says so, hisself."

"This is astonishing!"

"How long did you say that wire was?"

"Oh, yes; I forgot. It's nearly a mile; why?"

"I'm aimin' to hold a herd ag'in' it; it'll save men. Now, we're aimin' to start on th' west end first, before anybody knows what's up," and the *segundo* sketched the operations as he had planned them. Leaving as soon as he could, he was crossing the kitchen when Margaret stopped him.

"You told father about Doctor Reed coming against his will?" she asked.

"Why, yes, Ma'am; did I trample on anythin'?"

"It doesn't matter—only I hoped to keep that from him. It pleased him so to think the hostility was dying out."

"Ma'am, I'm shore sorry, but I didn't know that. An' it's all right, too, for th' hostility *is* dying out."

"It's perfectly all right. Where do you expect to cook; and what are you doing with Two-Spot?"

"We aim to cook on th' range, Ma'am; an' Two-Spot is goin' to be our tally man. He was plumb tickled at th' chance to help."

"Can't you cook here? Or, better yet, can't I cook for you? I would like to do something."

"Well, at first we'll not be near enough to th' house for th' boys to have time to ride in for meals," Cimarron replied. "You see, as we move over th' range, our cook moves with us, which saves time. Mebby when we work close at hand you can cook a meal for us—but I'm sayin' that you don't know what yo're tryin' to get into. I'll be leavin' now, Ma'am. If you hears anythin', or sees anythin' that you don't understand, don't you worry none. I'm goin' out to start th' boys. Good afternoon, Ma'am."

She watched him join the riders and saw them, with chuck wagon and horse herd, drive down toward Green Valley, noisy with cheerful laughter and shouted jests. They passed around a hill and became lost to her sight, and soon the voices could be heard no more.

"Margaret!" came an excited, impatient call from the front room.

"Yes, Father; I'm coming," she answered, turning and entering the house.

"It begins to look like people are getting friendly," he exclaimed, smiles playing on his drawn face. "Perhaps things will change, and we can make the ranch a success!"

" 'Luck always turns,' " she smiled.

"Are you getting to believe in luck?" he demanded.

" 'I do; when somebody's behind it pushing hard,' " she replied, turning her face away.

"Are you crying my dear?" he exclaimed, but she had left the room.

While events were moving smoothly and swiftly on the SV, a new freight wagon rumbled north over the Highbank-Gunsight trail; and about the time that a circle of tired but happy punchers sat around a roaring fire on the west end of the SV ranch, the great wagon rolled around the corner of the hotel in Gunsight and the weary driver got down stiffly to put up and attend to his four-horse team. After becoming acquainted with George, and eating a hasty supper in the hotel, Jerry Wheatley went around to Dave's to make the acquaintance of that person and whoever else might be in the saloon, and to tell about Wolf Forbes and his trip to Highbank. He found the place quiet, but he left it full of hysterical laughter, wet eyes, sore sides, and some hiccups. And before he had gone to sleep, Dave's patrons were emulating some of the substantial citizens of Highbank in the avidity with which they sought strength from Dave's merchandise. An occasional burst of uproarious laughter brought the freighter back from the shadowy boundaries of sleep and set his bed shaking as he silently joined in. Realizing that Wolf's miseries were going to do more for him in the matter of getting acquainted along the way than a dozen ordinary trips up the trail would accomplish, he smiled contentedly and fell asleep.

CHAPTER XVII

News All Around

AT DAYLIGHT Jerry went on his way rejoicing; the round-up started again in full swing on the SV, crossing the line onto Triangle range, to the later astonishment and vexation of Frank Gurley, Triangle rider on that section, whose hasty visit to his bunkhouse aroused a lively discussion, fortified him with Sam Gardner and Jim Lefferts to protect the interests of their ranch, and upon their return to the scene of activity, fortified Cimarron's smiling, but firm outfit, with three more men. In High-bank, Wolf Forbes, penniless now, was beginning to go without liquor and drift toward soberness, and the lambent flame of his reawakened anger burned constantly stronger; while out on the Double X, Johnny and the sleeping members of that outfit awoke to a new day's work, and to a firmer and warmer bond between them. The Bar H awakened to a new puzzle; the mysterious disappearance of Smitty and the discussion which followed his inexplicable absence resulted in Dahlgren being dispatched to Gunsight to see if the erring puncher had yielded to his well-known thirst and might be found snoring in that vicinity. Also, he was to keep an eye out for Wolf, and to make cautious inquiry concerning him.

Dahlgren was most successful in his mission, accumulating a fund of information staggering in its total and barren of reason. His first accretion of wisdom came when he left East Canyon and descried numerous punchers zealously bent upon an operation well known to him, and he rode up for what information he might be able to obtain. Hoping for a full loaf, expecting a half, he left with a few crumbs which only increased his appetite for more. In Gunsight his appearance caused unnecessary hilarity, and his questions as to Smitty's location were received with impolite guffaws, followed by an explicit description of Smitty's riding, looks, words, and actions, coupled to various prophesies, variously stated. When he mentioned Wolf, a veritable gale of laughter deafened and confused him, and the roundabout, cryptic, and fragmentary references to Wolf taxed his brain. He gathered the information that Wolf was wrapped in hides as his preference in perfumes; that Wolf was in the skin business, without competitors; that he had descended in the social scale to the point where he traveled as freight; that he took an arduous, unnecessary, and uncomfortable journey and was to be known, henceforth and hereafter, as Polecat, a name being better suited to his habits and preferences. It was explained that he was not expected back, which accounted for the half-masted flags and the black bands on the hats. He learned that Smitty was on the trail of Squint and would catch him if he went far enough in the right direction, and that Polecat was on the trail of Smitty, but would have to ride hard; and a further suggestion postulated the belief that Squint was on the trail of Wolf. Gunsight was as generous in its liquor as it was in its explanations; it was open-handed and lavish, and insisted that the distinguished Bar H ambassador imbibe freely, which he did; and when he was helped into his saddle and started for home, he tried to repeat what he had heard so that he would not forget it; and by the time he reached the bunkhouse he had not forgotten anything but the relations between the various parts of each thing to be remembered, and his account was verbal hash. Big Tom learned, among other things equally lucid and valuable, that Polecate Forbes went after Squint hunting Smitty's holy hat rounding up SV cows on the Double X part of the Triangle journey and would not be back until forty miles of hides went up toward Juniper with Two-Spot keeping tally on Cimarron's wagon.

In the presence of such loquacity, Big Tom lost the power of speech, choked with feelings of a murderous kind, and used the flat of his foot as a propulsive agent, which Dahlgren found helped him in getting to his bunk, where he sprawled out on his back and snored through a cloud of flies foregathered for their share of what had dribbled.

The foreman strode to the horse corral, swearing at every step, caught, saddled, and mounted his best horse and rode off to see and hear for himself. The first man he met was Cimarron, who was expecting visitors after Dahlgren's departure, and had placed himself where he would be seen easily. The *segundo* had been thinking things over and had about come to the conclusion that it would be foolish to try to deny the part the Double X was taking in the round-up; and when he caught sight of Big Tom riding toward him a feeling of contempt swept over him and decided the question.

"There's more excitement on this ranch than I've seen in some time," smiled the Bar H foreman. "Makin' a clean sweep of everythin' that's got hoofs?"

"Clean is th' word," answered Cimarron, his smile as friendly as the visitor's. "I reckon Lin is mebby thinkin' more about beef, though."

"Aimin' to start a herd up th' trail?"

"I don't just know what dickerin' there may come out of this," answered the round-up boss. "He says for me to take some of th' boys an' round up over here. There's no tellin' what he may do. I know that I can report that there's quite some four-year-olds, an' a few three-year-olds. Where th' devil th' cattle under four years old are keepin' themselves I don't know. But if he's aimin' to throw in a herd for Arnold an' send 'em up th' trail with some of ours they'll be numerous enough to make a showin'. He may be gettin' sweet on this ranch, because of them Snake Buttes thieves. If he is, I reckon Arnold wouldn't turn down a fair cash offer for grazin' a couple of herds over here through th' fall an' winter. He's got room for three times th' number feedin' here now."

"There ain't no doubt about that," answered Big Tom. "When are you aimin' to round up for strays on our north end?"

"Why, there can't be many over there," replied Cimarron. "Th' natural barriers would keep 'em back. Have you noticed any?"

"Nary a one; but if you want to make shore, I'll lend you a couple of th' boys, 'though I'm shore gettin' short of men."

"If you say you ain't seen none, that's good enough for me until th' spring round-up, anyhow; an' then we can start combin' at the same time, if we do th' work for th' SV, of course."

"What's Arnold askin' for th' SV, lock, stock, an' barrel?" bluntly asked Big Tom.

"Don't know," answered Cimarron, surprised. "I don't reckon Lin would consider buyin' it, 'less, mebby, he could sell th' Double X. But what's th' use of you an' me talkin' about that? I don't know, nothin' except orders, an' th' only orders I got was to run this round-up an' get back as soon as I can. I'll be leavin' you now, for I'm workin' harder than any man here, which shore is sayin' somethin'."

"An' I got to be ridin' on," said the Bar H foreman, and he made the words good. Reaching the Doc's shack, he dismounted and went inside, where he remained for nearly an hour, came out, glanced at the bullet holes and then went on to town, where he found the saloon deserted except for the proprietor.

Dave looked up and let his hand rest on the cap-and-ball under the bar, said cap-and-ball being .44 caliber, with the annoying habit of often sending one through the barrel, and igniting the caps on the nearest chambers and sending their contents along each side of the barrel with roving commissions.

"Well, Dave!" smiled Big Tom, motioning for a drink that he did not want, "I'm lookin' for strays—two-laigged strays."

"What you wants is another outfit to ride herd on this one," sympathized Dave. "Lookin' for Smitty?"

"He's one of 'em. Have you seen him?"

"I have. He didn't stop here, so I don't know where he got it," said the proprietor, grinning; "but from th' way he acted, insultin' folks, I reckon he must 'a' been bit by a passel of snakes, an' took too much cure."

"That's th' worst of them sponges," regretted Big Tom, a scowl going over his face. "I don't mind a periodic if there's plenty of time in between; but Smitty's periodics are like th' days in th' week durin' a round-up—they come too close together. Have you seen any others?"

"I ain't—not since Wolf was in here one afternoon last week," answered Dave. "Let's see: that was th' day Ol' Buffalo come down from Sherman, which would make it on a Friday. But," he said sorrowfully, "I has had distressin' news about Wolf. Young Jerry Wheatley, who's freightin' now, stopped in here only last night an' says Wolf was down in Highbank drinkin' 'em out of everything but water. He says yore puncher was on th' worst bender he's seen in months, which I says means somethin', comin' from a town like Highbank."

Big Tom's fist crashed on the bar. "Cuss it!" he exclaimed wrathfully, "that's th' worst of them periodics! You can't never tell when they'll start, an' nobody knows when they'll stop!"

"You lose, both ways," nodded Dave. "Jerry says he didn't have no hoss, saddle, or guns; an' a man can travel rapid on what they'd sell for."

"They wouldn't buy th' cayuse," reflected Big Tom, "seein' as he ain't supposed to own no Bar H animal. But I reckon it might 'a' strayed th' Lord only knows how far. We ain't noticed no cayuse missin', so far, but that don't mean nothin'. All right! He can come back when he goes broke an' sobers up an' he can walk, d—n him! Was Lang with him?"

"Lang? Is he missin', too?" Dave's astonishment was genuine.

"Disappeared like th' earth swallowed him," growled Big Tom. "They've hunted all over for him, an' can't find nothin' at all. I'm sayin' this country is goin' *loco*; an' I'll give a hundred dollars cash to find out what's at th' bottom of it all. Why, cuss it! Sherwood is roundin' up for the SV—what's th' matter with *him*? Is he *loco*, too?"

"Mebby he figgers on makin' them idle punchers of his'n bring in somethin' besides appetites," guessed Dave. "I don't blame him at all."

"Mebby; but they acts like they was havin' a picnic out there. Have you heard anythin' about th' Double X startin' a herd of their own up on th' trail?"

"Not a word; but ain't they throwin' their cattle into McCullough's this year?"

"They're supposed to; but you can't never tell," answered the foreman. He glanced around and then looked fixedly at his companion. "Yo're not forgettin' what I said about a hundred dollars' cash, are you?" he asked.

"That's somethin' I ain't likely to forget," replied Dave ambiguously, "if you mean it, shore."

"I'm meanin' it 'though I ain't wantin' you to have no rivals," replied Big Tom, significantly. "You hears an' sees a lot in here an' there ain't no use of lettin' anybody else in on it, an' splittin' up with you."

"There ain't nobody else goin' to get in on it," truthfully assured Dave.

"Nelson got over his grouch ag'in' wimmin?" laughed the foreman.

"Don't reckon so; but he ain't seen her yet, I guess," replied Dave, grinning. "When he does, there ain't no tellin' what's goin' to happen to him. Don't it beat all? You better look out, Tom; he may edge you out of th' game."

"Me!" demanded the foreman. He let out a roar of

laughter. "I ain't got no interest thataway at all. I passed, cold." He turned away. "Don't forget Dave."

"Goin' so soon?"

"Yes; I'm ridin' back. *Adios*."

Dave stared out of the window for a few minutes, his face slowly getting redder. "Yo're lyin', Big Tom," he muttered. "Yo're aimin' to get that girl more'n ever you was. An', d——n yore shriveled soul! Do I look like a Judas?"

Down on the SV, Cimarron was weighing something in his mind. Perhaps he had said too much to the Bar H foreman. Coming to a sudden decision he rode over to Bud Norris.

"Hello, Boss!" said Bud, grinning from ear to ear. "Big Tom's visit ridin' you?"

"Bud, we've got enough men here for this toy round-up," replied Cimarron. "There ain't no use of robbin' th' ranch of a man that ain't really needed here, an' I'm wishin' to send word to Lin by somebody who won't shuffle it. Now, you listen close," and the round-up boss gave him the facts of Big Tom's visit. "Tell him that, an' what I said. He ought to know my leads in case that big coyote rides out to th' house an' gets curious. Now you tell me what I've just told you." Bud complied, and when he had finished, his companion nodded. "Big Tom ain't seen you. You go north, foller th' Juniper trail back, an' don't pass within sight of th' Doc's place. Tell Lin to keep you with th' outfit—I don't need you here, an' he's too short handed. Get a-goin'."

Bud obeyed and in due time he came within sight of Gunsight, where a growing thirst lured him to ride in for a visit at Dave's. The proprietor still was smarting under the sting of Big Tom's attempt to bribe him and was glad to see someone who would help him get his mind on pleasant subjects. Dave regarded the story of the kidnapping of Wolf as being in that category, and when Bud left he was howling with laughter, and drove his horse toward home at a speed which awakened a resentful surprise in that animal.

"Th' locoed sons-of-guns!" repeated the delighted rider at intervals. "I knowed we had some locoed sage hens under our roof, but I thought they had limits! Why th' devil wasn't *I* in on that? *I'm* stickin' too close to home nights; but not no more. Any future Double X parties goin' to Gunsight will shore have little Buddie right in their midst! Th' nervy coyotes! Th' stem-windin' fools! Ha! Ha! Ha!

Farther on he gave vent to another burst of laughter as a new thought struck him. "It's all Nelson's fault. Cuss it! *now* I know why there has been so much hilarity about th' kidnappin' of th' Doc! They was plannin' to go it one better—an' I'm sayin' that they shore succeeded. They aimed purty high, but they done it, an' without even a scratch. I wonder who put th' sand burr under Smitty's saddle? Cuss that west section! I'm goin' to change an' ride our southeast line!"

When he pulled up at the bunkhouse door he found Lin and two other men who had ridden the last trick on the west section and he delivered Cimarron's message as soon as he dismounted. Answering the foreman's few questions, he let out a whoop and unburdened his news about Wolf and Smitty, painting the word pictures in a way which did him credit, and he felt the thrill of pride of an artist in the responses he obtained. After the greater pressure of their hilarity had escaped they began the puzzle of trying to name the jokers, and their foreman did that for them.

"Friday night," mused Lin. "Huh! Th' last that went to town was Slim, Tom, Gus, an' Bill. An' it was Friday night, too, because they said somethin' about hearin' Buffalo rumblin' in. That *makes* it Friday night, an' puts 'em in town when th' wagon was there. Well, I'm d—d! I can believe it of Slim and Tom, purty near, but not Bill an' Gus; still, there ain't no tellin' what any man of this fool outfit will do after he's been in Dave's all evenin'. I'm sayin' that mebby they got a tail holt on a mean varmint; that's their business, 'though, an' they ain't helpless kids."

"Mebby Wolf don't know who done it, but blames us

all," suggested Rich Morgan, unconsciously resting his hand on the butt of his gun. "In which case I'm all eyes an' ears from now on."

"He knows who was in town that night," replied the foreman. "But if he goes shootin' promisciously like, I'll have to take my rifle an' go get him, an' any way will do." He thought for a moment. "He knows who to look for. Well, they started it, an' nobody's got any right to help 'em out, not if he goes about it open an' above-board. Now, if Big Tom Huff comes a-visitin', you don't know nothin' at all. Cimarron sort of declared us in an' I'll play our cards, myself. You better fix that horse corral. There's five posts loose near th' northeast corner. Set 'em tight an' bind around th' corner with a couple strands of wire. Keep it outside as much as you can so th' barbs won't do no damage. Th' locoed fools—kidnappin' a man like Wolf!"

"Wait till Nelson comes in tonight," exulted Deuce, who by this time had learned quite a lot about the old Bar-20 outfit. "We got somethin' that beats th' kid-nappin' of th' Doc every way!"

"Huh!" muttered the foreman thoughtfully. "That was th' night Dailey played in such hard luck, wasn't it? Shore it was. Then Nelson was there, too." He paused and looked out of the window for a moment. "Well, go out an' wrestle with them posts. Bud, you go on day shift with Tom an' Nelson. I'm takin' th' second night shift with Bill an' Gus."

Darkness had fallen when Johnny and Tom Wilkes rode in from the day shift after being relieved by the first night shift. They had heard the bare outlines of the joke, and now got it as completely as the foreman could give it to them while they ate their supper. Johnny looked serious and did not laugh as much as they had expected he would.

"What's th' matter, Nelson?" bantered Matt. "Jealous?"

Johnny pushed back. "Boys, you've forced my hand. I wasn't goin' to say nothin' to nobody about some few things till I had made all th' plays I was aimin' to make. But this here joke on Wolf, gettin' out like it did, shore forces me to lay down my cards, face up. An' I want th' whole range to see 'em—to spread th' news before it's too late. It ain't my way to sneak out of anythin' I've started an' let some innocent party take th' comeback. I freighted Wolf away; I shot th' holes in Smitty's hat; I drove Squint out of th' country; I kidnapped th' Doc, an' I killed Lang in a fair fight, his wits ag'in' mine, in fair sight of each other, when I was mired in them cussed quicksands. I can prove what I say by showin' where Squint's things are hid, by Wolf's six-gun, that I kept to remember him by, an' by describin' what them holes in Smitty's hat looked like. I was savin' Wolf's gun to show it to him, sometime, an' ask him if he couldn't take a joke. Now I ain't apologizin' to nobody for nothin' I've done. I claim I was justified—an' I'll leave it to you if th' joke on Wolf wasn't a hummer? Wasn't it a three-ringer with a side show? I says it was; an', further, I says I'll do it over again if I feel like it. No cussed man can spy on me without riskin' a comeback. An' I says there wasn't nothin' I could do to him that would 'a' been as good a joke as what I did do. Now, Sherwood, I better be ridin' to tell Cimarron's boys about it, so they won't be caught off their guard in case Wolf gets to them before he looks anywhere else. I'm wantin' to warn Slim 'specially—he was in town that night. Then I'll rustle to town an' stay there. I reckon he'll come to Gunsight, an' I'm aimin' to be there when he does, to ask him if I ain't the cussedest practical joker he ever knowed. If he's gone an' got on th' prod about a little joke like that, then I'll have to look out for myself. I'm startin' now."

"No use goin' now," said the foreman quickly. "That's a bad trail for a stranger to tackle at night, an' that cayuse of yourn is too good to risk bustin' her laigs. If you leave here before daylight—say half an hour before—tomorrow mornin', you'll be in plenty of time. Them boys ain't kids. I'm honin' to hear about these jokes, an' so are th' boys. You stay here, with us, tonight."

"Lin's dead right," earnestly endorsed Tom Wilkes, the others unanimously backing him up. "You ain't goin' till we hears about 'em—that is, of course, if you feels like tellin' us."

Johnny looked from one to another and then sat down again, and for the rest of the evening he had an audience which expressed its appreciation of what it heard, and in unrestrained enthusiasm. When he had finished and started to turn in, the foreman strode over to him and held out his hand.

"Nelson, I'm proud to know you. Put it there!"

The others shook his hand with an enthusiastic sincerity which warmed Johnny's heart, and he fell asleep with a smile on his face.

CHAPTER XVIII

Whom the Gods Would Destroy

IN GUNSIGHT, Dailey rubbed his eyes and cursed the slowness of his breakfast fire, and then padded in his stocking feet to the window and looked out in time to see a black horse go past with a reach and swinging smoothness which brought an appreciative glow into his blinking eyes. The rider sat his saddle with a supple grace and erectness which harmonized with the beautiful leg action of his mount.

"He ain't stoppin'," muttered Dailey. "Must 'a' been up to Juniper. I'm sayin' again that if that pack of coyotes lets him start ahead of 'em out of rifle range, there ain't nobody from down here as will ever get close enough to see him again. There's mebby purtier things on earth than a hoss like that, but I'm admittin' I never saw 'em. Cuss that fire—it's smokin' again!"

The Doc heard the rhythmic beat pass his shack, muttered drowsily, and turned over to go to sleep again. "Hope it's that Smitty, blast him!" and his snores grew steadily louder.

Leaving the Double X quite some time before daylight, Pepper had been sent over the upper trail, which joined the Juniper trail north of town. Now she spurned the Highbank-Gunsight road beneath her flying hoofs with an eagerness and power that belittled the twenty-five miles she already had put behind her.

Johnny stroked the satin skin under which the powerful muscles of her sloping shoulders rippled and bunched, and pride surged through him.

"I used to think Hoppy's Red Eagle, an' Red's Ginger was th' real thing in hossflesh," he told her, "but they was cows compared to you, Pepper Girl. There ain't nothin' on four laigs has any right to look at you—an' some few on two laigs, too." Swinging around the hill where Green Valley met the trail he patted her again. "There they are, little hoss, ridin' off to comb th' range. See that tied-in pinto Slim's a-ridin'? Show it what runnin' is—I want to talk to him."

Slim glanced around, drew rein and had a brief argument with the pinto, which did not like Slim, or his habit of stopping suddenly. "Changed yore mind?" he asked, smiling.

"In quite some ways," replied Johnny, forthwith explaining the situation in terse sentences. Slim's mouth opened and forgot to close until his groping mind at last mastered what his ears fed to it, when the mouth opened wider and gave vent to loud, sustaining laughter. Finally subsiding, he demanded the story in detail, but Johnny wheeled around.

"I'm warnin' you, not amusin' you, you human rope," retorted Johnny. "If Wolf comes back he'll mebby come a-shootin'—pass th' word along."

Slim shoved his hat well back on his head and jammed his gloved hands against his sides. "Th' h—l he will!" he rejoined. "Let him, then. He ain't th' only man out here as packs a gun; I mebby got one, myself. Havin' been kindly warned, now I'm all ready to be amused. Tell it slow. If you can't talk it, sing it. Wait! Here comes Cimarron."

The round-up boss rode up wearing a grin, in sympathy with Slim's far-reaching guffaws. "What's th' scandal?" he demanded.

"Th' cussedest thing you ever heard," laughed Slim,

putting his hand on Pepper's bridle. "Nelson is in a hurry to go somewhere, but he's got to give us all of it now that he's whetted my appetite with th' mustard."

"I want to get to town an' give Wolf his chance," objected Johnny.

"If he's achin' to smoke up he'll come here, won't he?" demanded Slim. "This is th' place to wait for him—right here."

"All of which I admits is interestin'," said Cimarron; "but what is it all about?"

"Slow now," prompted Slim. He looked around. "Would you listen to that dickey bird up on th' hill?" he asked.

The dickey bird was Larry Hallock, whose voice barely reached them. "What do you reckon yo're doin'?" demanded Larry, but in far different language. "Gettin' married?" Further inquiries not receiving the attention he felt they were entitled to, he suspected trouble and made haste to get where he could hear about it. "Hello, Nelson!" he smiled as he joined them. "Lookin' for Two-Spot?"

"No; where is he?" demanded Johnny.

"I reckon he's downin' liquor in Dave's about now," answered Cimarron. "He's been raisin' th' devil for a drink which he didn't get. Slim, th' fool, owns up that he gave him a dollar last night—an' when we woke up this mornin' our tally man had disappeared. But that ain't tellin' me what Slim was hee-hawin' about, or about Wolf."

"Slow, an' deliberate, with everythin' in," chuckled Slim. "Go ahead."

Johnny complied, to their hilarious enjoyment, and when the tale was ended, Slim wiped his eyes, pointed out over the range, and said: "You can stay right here an' do somethin' worth while. Not one man in a thousand would come back with that pinned on his shirt tail—an' I'm sayin' Wolf ain't that man. He blames th' Double X—an' there's *only* twelve of us. He's shore about four bein' in town that night, but I ain't lettin' my modesty stop me from sayin' that, barrin' Cimarron here, he knows that th' four who was there are th' best six-gun men on our ranch; an' that we ain't takin' lessons from nobody when it comes to throwin' lead. He might get one of us, mebby two, an' I'll stretch h——l out of that word probability an' say he might get three; but he won't get us all, an' he knows it. But worse than shootin' it out is what he'll have to face; an' he hates ridicule worse than a rattler hates a king snake. You ain't goin' to set in Dave's, takin' it easy, while we're sweatin' out here——I got a nice little place where you'll fit in an' stop th' gaps that Larry is allus leavin' open."

"Gaps!" snorted Larry, indignantly. "Trouble is, you drive 'em so hard they gets stubborn an' go on th' prod. Anybody'd think you never saw a cow before, th' way you acts. You ought to know you can't crowd 'em too hard."

Cimarron cogitated. "If yo're aimin' to meet with Wolf, Nelson," he said, judicially, "I reckon you'd do better to stay here. He ain't got no reason to want anybody in town——nobody there has done anythin' to him. An' he knows none of us boys hang out there, except once in a while. What's more, he ain't likely to want to face Gunsight till he's squared up for his kidnappin'. As to him comin' back, I ain't nowise shore he won't. Some fellers are so full of th' idea of revenge that everythin' else plays second fiddle when they go on th' prod. They go fair mad an' don't care about nothin' else. Wolf's bad——bad as a mad rattler. I figger this is th' place for you. I'm sayin' this, too: If Slim had worked that razzle on him I wouldn't take a hand; but, knowin' Slim didn't, if that venomous reptile comes tearin' around here with his guns cocked, I'll just nat'rally puncture him at long range with my Remington. I ain't sympathizin' with no man that shoots till he knows why he's doin' it."

"Stay here till this afternoon, anyhow," said Slim. "We'll be needin' our tally man before night, an' you can ride to town, look around, an' bring Two-Spot back with you. I'm sayin' Wolf won't come back—I'm cussed shore *I* wouldn't in his place."

"Shore," endorsed Larry. "Turn yore cayuse loose an' get one from Arch—take that bay gelding—he's near human at this kind of work. Anyhow, he's got more sense than Slim."

Dawn in Highbank found a sobered Wolf, unarmed, penniless, and hectic, with a steadily growing rage. He went to place after place in search of a horse, finally borrowing one from a saloon-keeper who knew the foreman of the Bar H. Promising to use the animal only as far as the ranch, and to send it back behind the freight wagon, he threw the saddle on it and then rode around in search of a gun. Knowing about the joke, and feeling the man's murderous rage, no one would lend him a weapon. He had about decided to leave without one when he chanced to pass the small horse corral and shed behind Pete Wiggins' hotel, and espied a sodden figure asleep against the palings. Stealing the puncher's gun he rode away and in a few minutes was cursing the ford, of which a few yards was swimming water. Emerging on the other bank he pushed up the bluff trail at a walk and then, reaching level ground, set off for his ranch at a pace which might have killed a poorer horse.

As he rode, his mind became clearer and clearer, and he began to unravel the tangled skein of his abduction. Like his kind who, accustomed to hours of solitude, often talked their thoughts, he did his thinking aloud.

"Double X, says Buffalo. Mebby. First we'll accuse everybody else in town. Dave?" he laughed sneeringly at the thought. "Dailey? Fanning? Jerry? George? Why them? They ain't th' kind to stack up ag'in' such a risk for th' fun of it; an' they ain't none of 'em got any other reason. Dailey an' Fanning was in Dave's all evenin'— they never left th' table. Jerry was snoring in his shop when I went around th' buildin's, an' he wouldn't dare try to kidnap a blind pup. George is another without nerve, an' he was snorin' worse than Jerry. Nelson? He was with th' others. Mebby he did it, but I'm thinkin' there was more'n one man mixed up in that. If my senses hadn't been knocked out of me I'd know more about it. We'll put him aside as a possibility.

"Them Double X coyotes ain't lovin' me, 'specially since I've been ridin' sign along their line. There was four of 'em, an' they was all primed for a good time; an' from what I heard 'em say about th' Doc an' Squint an' me an' th' rest of our outfit, they wasn't needin' much urgin' to tackle a job like that. But they was in Dave's too; still, they left before I did.

"That leaves my own gang of practical jokers. They knowed that I was in town, but they didn't know I was goin' to ride home that night because I didn't know it myself. They might 'a' done it, but I'll find that out cussed quick when I get back.

"Who else was there? Dailey, Fanning, Jerry, Dave, Nelson—*Two-Spot!* He wasn't in sight at all. Dave was raisin' th' roof about him not bein' around. But h—l! Twenty Two-Spots wouldn't 'a' tackled a play like that; an' he couldn't sling a rope, nor carry a man as heavy as me *that* distance. Slim can rope—he's the best down here. I don't remember much about it till I was put down near th' waggin; but I'm shore that th' man that throwed that rope was an expert.

"Two-Spot? I don't see how he could fit in—*cuss him! I* got it! Somebody must 'a' seen me movin' 'round or else nobody would 'a' knowed I was in town. None of them fellers could 'a' seen me; but Two-Spot could have. Whoever did that job had to be told I was there; an' I'm sayin' they *was* told. That bum hates me; he'll never forget my kickin' him off'n th' tie-rail an' makin' him dance th' tenderfoot's fandango. I'm goin' to see Two-Spot after I stop at th' ranch—an' if he don't talk fast and straight, he'll dance to h—l this time!"

It was not yet noon when Wolf swept up to his bunkhouse and rode in through the door leaning forward in the saddle to clear the rafters, his gun freezing Big Tom and Dick Carson as stiff as statues.

"Don't you move till I says so!" he snarled. "Who was in town th' night Buffalo stopped there on his way home? Think quick; an' talk straight!"

"What are you doin'? Goin' *loco*?" demanded the foreman. He stopped in his tracks when he saw the look on his puncher's face.

"I'm askin' th' questions!" snapped Wolf, his rage climbing anew. "You answer 'em, an' *pronto*! Who was there that night?"

"Don't know; but none of our boys was."

"Nobody left here at all that night?" demanded Wolf.

"Not one."

"How do you know? That was near a week ago. How do you know they was all here?"

"That was th' first night you went on Nelson's trail," answered the foreman somewhat angrily. "I told them to stay home, an' give you plenty of room. They did it."

"I reckon they was glad to do it," sneered Wolf. "Coyotes don't go cougar huntin', less'n th' pack is big."

"They might as well stay home as go on a drunk in Highbank," retorted Big Tom, coldly.

For a moment Wolf was balanced on a narrow edge, but controlled himself because of genuine liking for his foreman. "Don't you ever come that close again," he said, almost in a whisper. "Do you know *why* I went to Highbank? You ought to, for I reckon everybody does by *this* time," he grated.

"I'm listenin' to you," answered Big Tom. "I don't know *why* you went."

Wolf dismounted, drove the horse out of the house, and paced up and down the long room in a frenzy of energy.

"I was roped off my cayuse ridin' home that night. I must 'a' fell on my head, for I don't know nothin' about it till I got to town. When I came to my senses I was bound, blindfolded, an' gagged, an' my head was spinnin' an' near bustin' with pain. I was dumped into Buffalo's wagon, pushed in among a load of hides, an' staked out so I couldn't move. All that day I lay here under that tarp, joltin' over that long trail, near faintin' with th' pain of th' lashin's an' th' gag, swelterin' in th' heat an' stink, sick with th' pain in my head, parched an' burnin' with thirst, ragin' with my thoughts, mile after mile. There was times I must 'a' lost consciousness; but I can remember a-plenty!

"Down in Highbank I was hauled out by a gang of cacklin' sage hens who thought it was a joke. If I'd had a gun, an' could 'a' used it, I'd 'a' showed 'em what kind of a joke it was!" He flew into a burst of rage which awed his companions, and he nearly wrecked the room before he subsided, his words one quivering stream of profanity. "An' what have I got to face?" he shouted. "What have I got to live down? I'll be th' laughin' stock of this whole country till I die, an' after! But I can show 'em that it costs somethin' to make a fool of Wolf Forbes; an' I will, if I dies for it! I want a six-gun, an' a rifle, an' yore pet hoss. I'm ridin' to town to see th' one man who can tell me where to start, an' I'm ridin' alone."

"Think it was Nelson?" asked Carson.

"Mebby; but I'm not sayin' till I know," snapped Wolf, pacing again. "I'm askin' you: Do you figger ropin' an' kidnappin' Wolf Forbes was any one-man job? Is there any man in this country that would tackle that job, alone, for th' fun of it? Yo're right. I says not, too. An' if he didn't do it for th' fun of it, would he 'a' dared tackle it, at all? What I mean is, if he did it to get rid of me, wouldn't he 'a' killed me from that ambush. I'm tellin' you he'd 'a' figgered it would be a lot safer to shoot me, for there wouldn't be th' risk at th' time, an' th' dead shore danger of th' comeback. One man, alone, would 'a' shot; three or four might 'a' took a chance with th' rope. I'm ridin' to town to learn for shore; an' I'm ridin' now. Carson, saddle me that hoss, while I get th' guns I want. Gimme a drink of yore flask, Tom."

"You shore you want it?"

"Gimme a drink. I know what I want."

In a few minutes he rode north at a dead run, headed for the over-mountain trail, and it was not until he was gone that the foreman realized that he had not told his puncher a word about the events which had taken place during his absence.

Wolf crossed the mountain, turned to the left, and went around Gunsight on the west, heading back toward town to approach it on its blind side. He rode up behind the hotel shed, dismounted and crept along it, and as he passed a crack in the warped boards his eye caught a movement, and he stopped to peer through the crack. Two-Spot was crawling out from under the saloon. Arising to his feet, the tramp looked carefully around for signs of any of Cimarron's outfit who might have come after him, and then slipped through Dave's rear door.

The watcher stiffened, and a sudden thought sent his rage up to the border line of madness. Two-Spot's mysterious sleeping quarters were no longer a mystery to him. His eyes swept the side of the saloon, and the narrow space between its foundation sills and the ground. This open space ran along three sides of the building and he knew that a man under the floor could see the feet and ankles of anyone who passed along the building. Returning to his horse he mounted and rode off the way he had come, careful to keep the shed between him and Dave's rear wall. Reaching an arroyo, he dropped into it and followed it until far enough from town, and then, keeping under the cover of hills and brush, he emerged upon the trail and loped along it into Gunsight. Dismounting in front of Dailey's, he walked swiftly and quietly toward Dave's, bending low to keep under the two front windows, and paused at the door to listen.

"He! He! He!" shrilled Two-Spot, warming to the liquor he had taken. "I'd 'a' liked to died when Jerry told about him. I could smell them hides before they turned th' corner of th' hotel that night. They was so odorous they near made me sick. An' if he went into 'em a Wolf, I'm sayin' he come out a Polecat; this range never will forget it. He can't never live it down—never! An' Jerry's tellin' it all along th' way, too. I'm wonderin' if he'll come back."

Dailey laughed sarcastically. "I'm bettin' he won't. *No* man would."

"I'm shore *I* wouldn't," chuckled Fanning. "I'd ship off to South Americky, *pronto*—an' I wouldn't care what happened to th' ship while I was on it, neither."

"I'll take three to one he *does* come back," said Dave.

"Is twenty dollars too much?" asked Dailey.

"Twenty to my seven suits me," replied Dave. "I'll take th' same from Jim, too."

"Yo're on," chuckled Dailey.

"Me, too," replied Fanning.

A man slipped through the door, a gun in each hand. "Dave wins!" he snarled. "Keep 'em both on th' bar!" he snapped at Dave, who forthwith forgot, for the moment, all about the cap-and-ball. The little group in front of the bar stiffened into whatever postures they had been caught in, their eyes on the muzzles of the steady guns. Death hung poised on Wolf's thumbs like a hawk balanced in the blue, ready to strike. The only sounds in the room were the hushed breathing of four men facing destruction for the slightest slip, the insistent buzzing of a bee cruising across the ceiling and the soft *slip! slip!* of the gunman's feet as he slid them forward a few inches at a time. His face was ghastly and working with rage, his power concentrated in his dull, threatening weapons. He jabbed one of them at Two-Spot.

"Step over there, on th' end!" he snapped. "I'll shoot at th' first move," he warned them all, feeling the hostility which he faced. Three of them were armed and needed only an instant's carelessness or indecision on his part to prove that their courage was only held in leash by calculating reason. "Not a move, cuss you!" he warned, his eyes not for a moment leaving the three armed men. Dailey's face was tense, but his body had slouched into a relaxation, the danger of which was well known to Wolf. Fanning's eyes were glinting and his lips were hard and thin, while enmity leered out of his eyes as though it were a living thing. Dave, his face paling after the redness of his first flush of anger, stood as a cat stands in the presence of a foe. Not for a fleeting instant did Wolf dare to take his eyes from this crouched danger.

"You'd 'a' done better if you hadn't come back," said Dave, quietly, but the timbre of his voice sent a chill up Two-Spot's spine.

"Don't move yore paws," snarled Wolf. "Two-Spot, come over here, by th' bar."

Two-Spot obeyed, sullen and fearful, taking a place which shortened the arc of danger for Wolf.

"Where was you that night?" demanded the gunman.

Two-Spot stared at him and tried to moisten his throat.

"Where was you?" snapped Wolf, venomously. "Talk fast!"

"I don't remember," answered Two-Spot.

"You was in yore hang-out under this floor," accused Wolf. "Did you see me?"

"It was too dark," answered the tramp, flashing an appealing look at Dave, whose face was growing red again.

"Not with th' light streamin' out of them side windows! Who did you tell?"

"I didn't see you."

"Who did you tell? Th' Double X?"

"No; it was too dark."

Warned by a premonition of impending disaster, and feeling that they were unawed, and restrained only by reason, Wolf ordered the three armed men to turn their backs to him, which they did with a slowness which in itself was an insult. He took the guns of Dailey and Fanning and ordered Dave to come out and join them. Dave took time enough to keep his dignity unsmirched. Free from the necessity of keeping a high-tension vigilance, Wolf walked up to Two-Spot and struck him on the face with the heel of his hand.

"Did you tell th' Double X?" he demanded. "D——n you, answer me!"

"No," whispered Two-Spot, and in his bleared eyes there smouldered the sparks of a fire long dormant.

"Did you tell Nelson? Quick!"

Dailey and Fanning hung on the slow answer, for they remembered that little incident with startling clearness.

"No!" snarled Two-Spot.

Wolf kicked him on the shins and, dropping one gun into its sheath, grabbed the skinny throat, gripping it cruelly. "Who did you tell?" he growled, shaking his victim, and quivering with rage at such resistance where he had expected to encounter none.

Some ghost of a former stalwart courage, shaken awake by desperation and rage, came back to its forsaken habitation and spoke through a mouthpiece for too long a stranger to it. Two-Spot tried to speak and Wolf, a gleam of triumph burning through the madness in his eyes, loosened his grip and stepped back.

The voice which answered him was not Two-Spot's, although it came through his lips. It was level, cold, self-possessed, and biting. "You ask somebody who's a-scared of you, you three-card flush. An' keep yore paws off'n me—they stink of hides an' maggots."

The crashing roar sounded like a thunderbolt and the acrid cloud of smoke swept forward and shrouded the falling man. Wolf leaped back, out of it, and stopped the instinctive advance of the horrified and enraged onlookers, who had turned at the shot, his two guns barely sufficient for the task. Dave's expression took his instant attention and he snapped a warning, venomous as the jet from a copperhead's fangs: "Don't you try it, Green!" He flashed a look at the other two, and nearly fired in instinctive answer to the malevolent looks in their eyes.

"Anybody that itches to take this up will get their chance: I'll be back!" he promised, and retreated swiftly to the door. Shoving his guns forward in a silent, final warning, he slipped from their sight and dashed for his horse, firing several shots behind him past the windows and door. Leaping into the saddle, he wheeled around the store and rode at a dead run for the cover of an arroyo several hundred yards beyond.

Dave started toward his bedroom for the rifle hanging

on the wall, reconsidered and looked at the huddled heap on the floor. "We'll take care of th' best man first," he said, picking up the limp figure and carrying it to the base of the front wall. Getting a blanket, he went back again, and as he stood up he drew a deep breath and faced his companions, a look almost reverent coming to his face and softening the malignancy of its expression.

"He died like a man—I hope I do as good. Let's liquor."

The afternoon shadows were beginning to lengthen when the low voices in the saloon ceased to allow the speakers to catch the sounds of a horse coming up the trail. Dave, moving with surprising celerity for one of his build and habits, grabbed a rifle and hastened to the front window, where he peered out cautiously, and then, walking to the bar, he reached over it, stood the weapon behind it, and replied to the unspoken inquiries of his companions.

"It's Nelson," he said, quietly.

The hoofbeats ceased abruptly and Johnny's voice was heard promising the horse some sugar. He entered and strode straight for the bar, nodding cheerily at the three, and then smiled quizzically.

"You shore look glum," he remarked, "glum as a funeral. Come up an' take somethin' for it. Well, th' SV is bein' cleaned neat an' proper. Cimarron knows his business, an' that crew of his is goin' at full speed. I come in to get Two-Spot. They're needin' a tally man, an' he ought to go through with it. Seen him around, or is he hidin' out, layin' low?"

"He's layin' low," replied Dave.

Johnny looked at him curiously, puzzled by the proprietor's manner. "Meanin'?"

"He's dead," said Dailey, bluntly, staring fixedly at the front wall.

Johnny flashed him a glance and looked back at Dave, who nodded significantly at the front of the room. Johnny turned quickly and followed the other's stare. He straightened and walked slowly to the blanket, drew it back a little and then replaced it with reverent care. Arising to his full height, he turned and looked at them. The silence was oppressive, crowded with potentials. They could feel a tension which fairly crackled, and which made them shrink, guiltless though they were. The erect figure radiated a ferocity which numbed them and caused Fanning to lick his dry lips. Overhead the bee, which had buzzed monotonously for so long a time, increased its buzzing and bounced from point to point, its wings striking the ceiling with a dry whirring not greatly unlike the angry whir of a rattler. From an unrinsed glass on the bar came a buzzing from drunken flies renewing their efforts to escape from it. The measured breathing of four men sounded loud and unnatural, and from Dailey's forehead rolled a bead of sweat. They stared at the cold, motionless puncher, fascinated by what emanated from him, unable to look away from the glinting eyes which peered out between narrowed lids at each in turn, and back again. Outside a horse pawed restlessly and the intermittent sound of striking metal reminded them of the slow pealing of a bell. A board cracked suddenly as it contracted from the encroachment of a cooling shadow and sent a shiver up their backs. Fanning's nerves were on edge and seemed about to snap, and his clenching fingers cut into his palms. He suddenly slumped down into his chair.

"It was *Wolf*!" he shouted. "Two-Spot wouldn't tell!"

The others sat rigid, not heeding the words.

Slowly the puncher's hand went to his sombrero and slowly readjusted it with deliberate care and precision. He turned slowly, and slowly departed, the sound of the diminishing hoofbeats echoing in their brains long after the sound had ceased. The unrinsed glass became quiet, the bee blundered out through an open window, and a great peace, soothing and enfolding, stole over them. Fanning stirred, arose to his feet, and stumbled toward the door.

"Christ!" he whispered.

"Amen," said Dave. "Death's flyin' low."

* * *

The Bar H outfit, loafing near the bunkhouse, were deep in discussion when they heard a horse. Looking up, they saw Johnny Nelson coming toward them at an amble. He nodded gravely and soon stopped near them. Carelessly throwing the reins over Pepper's head, he lazily swung down, pushed his hat back on his head, and sauntered up to them, stopping when only an arm's length away, Wolf stirring restlessly and not taking his eyes from the visitor's face.

"Two-Spot was my friend," said Johnny in a matter-of-fact voice.

Wolf's slouching frame shifted slightly and froze.

"He never went heeled," continued Johnny's even, dispassionate voice. The open palm of his right hand struck Wolf's face with vicious force. There came two roars which sounded almost as one, and Johnny, leaping pantherishly aside out of the rolling smoke, held two guns on the paralyzed group.

"Wolf shot him," he explained, backing away behind his ominous guns. He whistled softly, and Pepper, despite the dangling reins, lifted her head high and came to him.

Big Tom recovered himself first and took his eyes from the figure sprawled on the ground. He was beginning to believe them. He glanced at Johnny and back to the prostrate figure. It was incredible that a man with Wolf's courage, and ability with weapons, should shoot down an old, helpless tramp, whose greatest offense could hardly be more than a verbal one, especially against a two-gun killer. Bad as he was, and hardened, the foreman could not stomach such a murder, and, snapping a warning to his companions, who still stared at what had been Wolf Forbes, he looked at Johnny, who was preparing to mount, and he called out in a voice ringing with sincerity: "Put 'em up, Nelson; an' ride off. I'll knock th' man down that pulls a gun!"

Johnny slipped the guns into their sheaths, swung up into the saddle, wheeled, and pushed Pepper at a lope over the trail toward town without a single backward glance.

Big Tom watched him for a moment and then wheeled and glanced down at the ground. "*Wolf*, huh? All right." He turned to the thoughtful group. "Dig a hole somewhere out on th' range an' dump that into it," he said contemptuously, and strode toward the ranchhouse.

CHAPTER XIX

"Give Eternal Rest ——"

THE DEATHS of Two-Spot and Wolf created a mild sensation over the range, particularly the manner in which each had occurred. The respect which Johnny had enjoyed in Gunsight and on the Double X was increased and the range enjoyed his other exploits. Dave was open in his sympathy for the SV and his growing contempt for the Bar H. Dailey said that he had a gun and could use it any time Johnny needed help, adding with a grin that he hardly expected to be called upon. The Double X was hilarious and brutally frank in everything concerning their neighbor on the southeast. On the Triangle, Frank Gurley became moody and silent, Sam Gardner and Reilly noisy and assertive. The latter, with Lefferts, took over the north end of their ranch and worked nearly as hard for the SV as they did for the Triangle.

Two-Spot's funeral was a holiday by tacit consent, and Gunsight was the Mecca for the surrounding country. Fanning offered the hotel, but Dave's eyes grew red and he declared that the saloon had been Two-Spot's home and that he would be buried from it, even if the cap-and-ball had to cast the deciding votes. Slim rode to Juniper half an hour after he had heard the news and brought a minister back with him. Cimarron sent Larry Hallock to the ranch with the news, George Hallock to the SV, and went down to notify the Triangle himself.

The day dawned clear and reasonably cool, and at an early hour the riders began to come in. The saloon was as clean as Dave, Johnny, and George could make it, and the rude box which had kept Dailey and Fanning up most of the night with hammer and saw, was covered by green boughs and a few wild flowers. As each newcomer rode up to the door he was quietly informed by Dave that the bar was closed and would remain so until after the funeral. There would be no instrumental music, for Arch Wiggins' offer to ride to the Double X for his fiddle was politely but firmly declined after he had been questioned about his repertoire; Jerry's harmonica was overruled, and Reilly's accordion was declined for the same reason which had barred the violin.

When Margaret Arnold rode up alone with a huge bouquet of old-fashioned flowers, Gunsight became tremendously interested and there was a great amount of surreptitious grooming going on in out-of-the-way places. Lin Sherwood regretted that he had not been more neighborly, and that he had decided against his new boots, tight though they were. He accused himself of being a poor sort of a grown-up man not to risk a corn or two under such circumstances. He frowned down Slim's sheepish remark about seeing Miss Arnold home after the ceremony as being unwarranted and too forward; and he kept Slim in sight thereafter. Dailey cursed Big Tom's warning about selling supplies to the SV and was gloomy because of the handicap it put him under, but it became him well in such an atmosphere and nearly gave him the place of chief mourner. Several of the rejected suitors formed a consolation circle and deeply reflected the sorrow expected at funerals, grumbling because the universal remedy for grief would not be obtainable until the return from the grave. There was a suggestion concerning a concerted rush on the bar, but the tender flower of hope was frostbitten by a glance at the cap-and-ball protruding from Dave's waist-band. The proprietor had no consideration for the sacredness of the occasion to hang around the walnut armed like a highwayman, and the amount of pugnacious confidence he exhaled and exuded was entirely out of place.

"He acts like a cow with its first calf," growled Sam Gardner.

"He acts like it was *his* funeral, which I'm sorry it ain't," snorted Pete Wiggins' young hopeful, still raw about the matter concerning his fiddle.

The minister walking around from the hotel was the signal for the groups to fall in behind him and file into the Palace. This sky pilot was a stalwart member of his cloth and acted as though saloons were not strangers to him. He looked about and nodded his appreciation of Dave's efforts and at once became the friend of every man there.

"Friends," he said, looking slowly around, "a good friend of the deceased, and one who knew him well and who cherishes his memory with gratitude and affection, will sing. Miss Arnold, if you please."

Margaret, tears in her voice and eyes, arose and began her favorite hymn, her rich contralto voice playing upon the heartstrings of the rough men until they dared not look around. Cimarron coughed, and received Slim's elbow in his side with unnecessary force. Dave developed a sudden cold and reddened with self-consciousness, wishing he had chosen a seat in the rear of the room instead of standing at the end of the bar, which was an altogether too suggestive place for one in his line of business.

The singer's voice grew slowly lower and lower and it was only by exercising all her will-power that she managed to finish the last verse. Her own emotion and faith throbbed in the beautiful words and gave them a power which brought tears to nearly every eye. Finishing, she sank down in her chair and sobbed softly.

The minister, arising, looked over the room.

" 'Nearer to Thee,' " he repeated softly, and then paused, and when he resumed, his voice struck through to the hearts of his hearers as a hand plucking the strings of a harp. " 'Greater love hath no man than this, that a man lay down his life for his friends.' Two-Spot. The name was lowly, and with thoughtless cruelty was given to Henry Travers, who once was under foreman for Simon Verrier, the former owner of the SV ranch. We have no knowledge of the interval between the days of his responsibility and strength, and that cold winter evening when Margaret Arnold found him, weak from hunger and exposure, freezing in a snowdrift not far from her home. Of the man's weakness we will not speak, except in charity and to show that the character which won for him the confidence and trust of old Simon persisted in spite of that weakness and blazed out gloriously, to win for him an honorable death. It would have been easy to betray the confidence of another, especially when he knew the ability of that other to protect himself. He could have saved his life by telling the truth, and I say to you that there are some untruths more glorious than those truths which mean danger, or perhaps death, to a friend. And if he had yielded to fear to save his life he would have found that life to be a thing without value. He would have lost to himself all that remained worth while. Two-Spot, weak with a weakness perhaps passed on to him by the thoughtless and vicious lives of those others who had preceded him, was, nevertheless, a man, and will live in your memories as a man, a man who at the threat of death, rallied the best within him and died to protect a fellow-man who had been kind to him. He was a lowly card, but even a two-spot has a value, as every man in this room can testify. A two-spot, at the right time and in the right combination, makes a winning hand; and I have it on the authority of two people here that he was given one spot too many. Hardly an ace of diamonds, but surely an ace of hearts, for in his breast beat a heart as true and sympathetic as that of any man in this room.

"There was not a thing coming to his knowledge which affected the welfare of a struggling, defenseless family on this range, that he did not tell them; and when

I say that for a man of his age and weakness to walk nine miles to warn them, and nine miles back again, in any weather, at the only time he could do so without being seen and arousing suspicion, required such a heart, and a fine quality of courage, I know that you all will agree with me. Many nights when the range was wrapped in sleep, Two-Spot made that journey. And I say that he was a man, and I pay him the respect which such a heart and courage merits. And no matter what his weaknesses were, no matter how unworthy you may have thought him to be, I say that this man whom you knew as Two-Spot was as good as any who sneered at him, as much a man in his last moment on earth as a material being as any man in this room! And I say that if we all, every one of us, can die as fearlessly and as honorably as this man died, we need not fear the Judgment Day. There may be some of you who do not give much thought to that Judgment Day, or to that Merciful Judge. There may be some of you who do not believe in God— but I say, that, no matter Who or What waits beyond the Open Door, He or It will deal gently with Henry Travers. And I say for those who do not believe in any divine faith, and say it aside from any viewpoint of religion, but purely as a question of ethics, of effort and reward, of right living or wrong, that every man in this room can find something in the strength of this weak man, something in the way he faced death, that can be taken with profit to himself and serve as an inspiration. Under all his fleshly weakness, with all his yielding to a dominant craving, there blazed the white flames of sympathy, affection, and loyalty. And I cannot find this occasion to be one for sorrow, or for grief. Rather, I should say it is one for congratulation: Two-spot, shorn of his weaknesses, saved from jeers and cruelty and injustice, and the misery coming with old age, which cannot but be tragic to such a one as he, found himself at the last moment, and died the man which circumstances would have refused to have let him live. Let us pray."

If his auditors had been impressed by his address, the

prayer reached down and gripped their very heartstrings, stirring into groping life the vague fear and
awe of the supernatural, by heritage firmly implanted in
each consciousness. Death, with its mystery and threat,
brought its awesome fear like a wave, with an impetus
acquired from rolling down past generations, to minds
prepared to quail before it in momentary surrender.
From the distant and impersonal, it suddenly loomed
out of the fog of the mysterious unknown real, and
made real by a mind trained to present truth as it is, and
became close and personal. And at the conclusion of
the gripping words, only the fresher, newer momentum
of the carelessness and indifference of their every-day
lives could offset the fear which spread like ripples over
their superstitions and set their religious instincts a-
quiver. But like concentric ripples, it grew weaker even
as it reached farther out; yet the reacting ripples endur-
ing for days, showing intermittently and intermittently
arousing vague unrest in their minds.

He glanced at Margaret and walked quickly to her,
placing his hand on her shoulder. "I would not attempt
it, my dear. Two-Spot would not allow another hymn, at
such a cost to you."

Dailey, Johnny, Dave, and Fanning moved slowly forward, feeling as they never had felt before, reverently
and carefully picked up the box and led the way out of
the building and across the street to a grassy knoll not far
from the road, where the warmth and brightness of the
sun rested from dawn to dark. The ceremony at the
grave over, they returned to Dave's, where they shook
hands with a parson who had jolted their ideas
regarding men of his calling.

"Friends," he protested, raising his hands at the coins
in the hat held out to him, "this is too much. I cannot
take so much for doing my duty. It is not reasonable."

"Parson," said Dave, a grin coming to his face, "we
ain't had no gunplay today, but if you don't take that
money, I can't promise that there won't be none. Some
of us leather-backs has been eddicated today, an' they
say eddication costs money. I reckon a parson livin' in

such a hole of iniquity as Juniper can find use for our offerin's. If you can't take it for yoreself, take it for yore church—it'll help you to build one all th' quicker. An' I'm sayin' that we'll allus be glad to see you in Gunsight, as a parson or as a man. Shake."

Margaret came forward and thanked him, and turned to Dave.

"Did you know that he slept under your floor?" she asked. "He was always wondering if you did."

"Ma'am," smiled Dave, feeling to see if his tie had slipped, "I knowed it th' very first time he snored, which was th' second night he was here. An' I've had many a laugh at him th' way he wiggled out of little slips he made. He heard a lot under here, an' sometimes he let things out that made him dig frantic to explain away. I reckon I'm goin' to be lonesome, 'specially this winter. Here comes Lin Sherwood—Miss Arnold, meet Mr. Sherwood, th' bashfullest man in this country. He don't mind a little thing like an extra eighteen miles in th' saddle— an' I'm admittin' that nobody will steal yore cayuse while he's along. Now that I've broke th' ice an' pushed him in where he was afraid to go hisself, I'll take th' parson around an' make him better acquainted with th' boys."

As they moved away, the minister noticed the restraint and restlessness visible around him and he turned a smiling face to the proprietor. "As soon as Miss Arnold leaves, open the bar. I'll take a cigar with the boys and then say good-by."

Dave stopped in his tracks, his jaw dropped, and then he beamed upon his clerical companion. "I'm repeatin' what I said about bein' glad to see you any time," he exclaimed, slapping the broadcloth shoulder. "Parson, I'm proud to know you! Put it there!"

Johnny, going over to say good-by to Margaret, and concealing to the best of his ability any sign of jealousy, received a distinct shock and one which made him wrestle hard to keep his dignity.

"Oh, here's Mr. Nelson, now," smiled Margaret. "I just told Mr. Sherwood that he was too late; but perhaps he will beat you the next time. I think we would better be riding, for these men feel a restraint while I'm here; and I'm getting anxious about father. So if you will excuse me, Mr. Sherwood, I'll say good-by to the men and ride on."

Sherwood stood on his foot and did foolish things to his hat, but was spared any further embarrassment by Johnny, who gripped his arm in a friendly way and escorted Margaret on her round of the room. And as the pair rode away Sherwood turned from the door, kicked Cimarron, and tramped to the bar.

The *segundo* stared after him. "Well, I'm cussed!" he muttered. "So *that's* it, huh? Well, you'd 'a' done better if you'd 'a' kicked Nelson."

The minister having left, Dave became very busy, and Dailey found a pack of cards and dragged out a table. "Havin' been generous to th' church, now I aims to get back some of it," he remarked. "He is a fine man—an' what he said is true; an' if I can get four little two-spots I'll show you all an inspiration that's stem-windin'. One at a time; don't push!"

"Yo're shore hard-boiled," reproved Slim, slightly vexed. "You ain't got enough reverence in yore saturated carcass to start a prairie dog out in life like he ought to go—an' G—d knows that ain't much."

"Which same I says is true as h—l," endorsed Cimarron, scowling. "Let th' old mosshead herd by himself. I'm goin' back an' pick up that round-up where we dropped it. We got to get that over with as soon as we can, for we'll be roundin' up for McCullough purty soon—an' he ought to be along next week."

Sherwood heard him and turned from the bar. "He ain't getting many from us," he said. "We'll send our own herd up th' trail next spring, an' take a gamble on gettin' more for 'em. I'm sayin' th' SV has got plenty of friends from now on, too. I'm ridin' home; who's comin' with me?"

CHAPTER XX

Plans and Preparations

ON THE last day of the round-up Johnny rode out to the SV and found a herd held against the wire fence. A branding fire was burning off to one side and Larry Hallock had just thrown a calf, its pitiful bawl turning its mother into a charging fury. The mother, being unbranded, was thrown instead of being diverted and received the same treatment being accorded to her sturdy offspring. Larry's helpers arose, let the calf up and grinned at its eagerness for maternal protection. They wiped their foreheads with wet sleeves and welcomed the visitor.

"There's some calves at that," said Larry, "but they're this year's crop. An' that's th' last brandin', I reckon, for here. Cimarron an' three of th' boys are startin' a clean-up north of th' east end in that grassy valley. I reckon today will finish it."

Slim nodded. "It wouldn't hurt to keep a few men ridin' well back, for a few days, pickin' up strays; but I'm sayin' this ranch has been combed to a T. We've cussed near branded even th' shadows. You'll never have no trouble tellin' them that Larry has branded. He paints

wide an' free like he was paintin' a house. Just look at
that yearlin' over there; an' them two weaners—they're
cussed near all brand."

Larry grinned. "Shore; it saves a lot of ridin' when you
can read 'em far off. I'm in favor of histin' flags on 'em
an' ridin' sign with a telescope hangin' from th' saddle."

Johnny laughed at the grinning pair, dust and sweat
from head to feet. "This ranch will have stampin' irons
as soon as it can get 'em, 'though Larry must hate 'em
like poison. I'm comin' out here, some of these days, an'
put that horse corral at th' house in better shape; an'
anybody that offers to help won't get insulted. Now I'm
ridin' to th' house. I got an idea an' want to see how it
sets with th' Ol' Man. See you later."

"I been scratchin' all day for an idea like that,"
chuckled Slim. "All I could think of was a drink of water;
an' Larry goes an' shoves out his canteen to me!"

"If I didn't," said Larry, "everybody would 'a' got
thirsty, an' then who would 'a' held this herd?"

Johnny laughed and rode off, his friends watching him
for a few moments. Then Larry went toward his horse,
Slim following him.

"Well," said Slim, "Nelson knows where he can find a
parson ten miles closer than Highbank, anyhow. After
he got her on her hoss th' other day in Gunsight an' went
off to get his own, she looked after him—an' I ain't no
fool. I'm in favor of holdin' it in town. An' I says this here
busted-down ranch needs a good man to take hold of it
an' run it. I reckon an outfit of four would swing it handsome. Yes, three good men could do it."

Larry swung into the saddle. "I got three brothers that
shore do love singin' since Two-Spot was planted. I'm
leanin' strong to th' melodious myself. An' I'm admittin'
that I never knowed what singin' was before. Well, you
maverick, let's go an' help 'em count that herd. You an'
me aim to stop in town tonight on our way home, don't
we? Then come on."

Johnny dismounted at the kitchen door and knocked.
Charley came running and acted as host.

"Gee!" he exclaimed, his eyes sweeping to the six-

guns and resting on them. "Come on in! Peggy's readin'
to dad. He's gettin' plumb ornery an' says he's goin' to
get up tomorrow, anyhow, come h—l or high water.
Here she is now: Hey, Sis! Here's Mr. Nelson—bet yo're
plumb glad to see him. Is dad still on th' prod?"

"Charley! What language! How you do pick things up!
How-do-you-do, Mr. Nelson?" she smiled, holding out
her hand. "I am so glad to see someone who may have a
good influence on father. Come in. Father, here is our
friend, Mr. Nelson."

"Which gun got Wolf?" demanded Charley.

"Glad to see you, sir!" exclaimed Arnold. "You have
been entirely too much a stranger to this house. Sit
down, and tell me what is going on. That Cimarron may
know how to talk, but he doesn't seem very anxious to
prove it. When I ask him how he finds the ranch he tells
me about everything else that he can in one minute,
pleads work, and leaves."

"I think a whole lot of Cimarron," replied Johnny. "He
and his boys have worked like slaves out here—they've
done an amazin' lot. They expect to have everything
cleaned up an' counted by tonight, or by tomorrow,
without fail. Then we can do some figgerin' ourselves,
an' see how many cows are comin' to you. What I called
for was to make a proposition to you, an' I think it's a
good one."

"Go ahead; I'm sayin' yes to it right now," smiled
Arnold.

"I reckoned mebby you would say that after you heard
it," said Johnny. "McCullough, trail boss for Twitchell
an' Carpenter, is comin' up from th' south with two
thousand head of mixed cattle. His deliveries call for
four thousand head, an' he is countin' on gettin' th'
second two thousand right up here around Gunsight. Th'
Bar H is throwin' a thousand over to him an' th' Triangle
has promised him five hundred. Th' other five hundred
was to come from th' Double X, but Sherwood has got
other ideas. He's got a good outfit an' hankers on gamblin' a little. He's made up his mind to sell McCullough
only a hundred head of older cattle an' keep th' other

four hundred for his own trail herd next year. He says Dodge, but I reckon he's fishin' for a government contract up north; an' if he is, an' lands it, he'll make a lot of money."

"I wish somebody would show me how to make some," replied Arnold, gloomily. "We are headed for some poorhouse, I'm afraid."

"Father!" exclaimed Margaret, reprovingly. "You should not say or think such things. Everything will come out all right. Our luck is turning."

Johnny glanced at her and smiled.

"Perhaps it is, but I can't see its face, yet," retorted Arnold. "We'll know how many head we have, and how many we have lost, but that knowledge won't keep us, will it?"

"Perhaps Mr. Nelson has something to say concerning that."

"I have, Ma'am," smiled Johnny, his eyes for an instant resting full on hers. "I'm goin' to suggest that th' SV sells McCullough that missin' four hundred head. That will be th' best way to turn some of yore cattle into money, an' it will bring you as much as you can hope to get without startin' an outfit up th' trail. If you put a herd on th' trail, it would have to be a small one this year, an' there ain't no profit in drivin' four hundred cows up to Dodge, 'specially th' kind you'd have to take. You'd have th' risk an' th' worry, an' th' spendin' of quite some money. This other way you'll get yore money, an' McCullough will have th' wrestlin' to do. Now, I suggests that you let Cimarron drive four hundred head home with him tomorrow, an' keep 'em handy on th' Double X for th' drive herd. They'll road brand 'em an' hold 'em with their own, and when Sherwood gets th' money, he'll send yourn to you, an' you'll have something to work on."

"And we will be four hundred head nearer bankruptcy," growled Arnold, more to give vent to his pessimism, which had become nearly chronic by this time.

"There will be more than that many turned over to you before winter," said Johnny. "Cattle stealin' don't go very long down here, even. Now, don't ask me nothin' about it; but I'm wishin' you'd give me authority to act for you in any little thing that might come up—I might not have time to ride out here for it, then."

"Why, certainly; and I'll be glad to have somebody act for me who knows what to do," replied Arnold.

"All right. I'm advisin' you to tell Cimarron to go ahead with that little trail herd. I'm goin' out that way now, an' I'll speak to him about it if you want me to."

"I think that is a splendid idea," enthused Margaret. "If we did not sell them, they will be a year older next year, and we will have to sell them then, anyhow."

"All right!" grunted Arnold. "Sell them. I don't care what is done, if only I can get out of this cursed bed. And I'll be out of it tomorrow or know the reason why!"

"We'd better have th' Doc come out an' look at it," said Johnny. "I'll be ridin' to town purty soon an' I'll drop in an' tell him. He shore ought to finish what he started."

Margaret's hand went to his arm. "Please!" she pleaded. "Don't—don't have any trouble—we—father can wait a little longer, I'm sure."

"I certainly can, Nelson," quickly spoke up the quasi-invalid, "if it will save you from any trouble. I don't know just how much I would do for you."

"There won't be no trouble, at all," Johnny gravely assured them. "Doc an' I know each other real well. You've got no idea how well we get along together. You'd be surprised if you only knowed how prompt he'll start for here. Why, trouble with me over a little thing like this is th' last thing he'd think of. You just stay where you are till he sees you an' says you can get up."

"That's the least I can do," replied Arnold. "D—n it, man! If I only were up and about, and could get a few good, honest men to work for me, I'd *make* something out of the SV!"

"You'll be up an' around before you know it," Johnny assured him. "An' you won't have no trouble gettin' three honest men to ride for you. That parson must 'a' had a good influence on this range, even before he come down to Gunsight. Did I hear Sam Gardner tell him he was tired of workin' for th' Triangle?" he asked Margaret. "Why, of course you didn't. Well, I'll have to ask Sam if I heard right. I'm going to ask you to send to Highbank for three SV stampin' irons—Arch Wiggins is ridin' down there tomorrow. They're real handy—an' chute brandin' shore saves a lot of time. They'll be needed in a month or so. Arch knows a blacksmith that can turn 'em out alike as three cartridges."

"You get anything you think we need," said Arnold. "How about some wire for those quicksands?"

"They're fixed to stay fixed," answered Johnny. "Arch an' that Wood Hallock are great boys when it comes to wire, an' I'm gamblin' on that wire stayin' up till it rusts, which won't be soon. There's six strands, an' they set quite some few more posts. Arch does things right. I reckon he'll be lookin' for a job when he gets through visitin' Highbank. He says as how he's quittin' th' Circle 4. An' from what I've seen of Arch, I like him a lot."

"Tell him to see me before he leaves the ranch," exclaimed Arnold. "Why, we're sailing along at a great clip. Look here, Nelson, there's a spare-room here—you come and use it until you ride south. You're better than a tonic. Quit that hotel—God save the word—and come out here."

"Well, I hardly think I can do that," smiled Johnny, " 'though I'm thankin' you, just th' same. I've got business close to Gunsight that'll keep me there for quite a spell, but afterward, I'll mebby spend a couple of days with you."

"Well, come when you can," replied Arnold. "If you think of anything else this ranch needs to get from Highbank, order it. You can tell that Arch that there's a job here if he wants it. I'll leave the question of wages to you."

"All right, but I'll send him in, anyhow," said Johnny, arising. "I'll be goin' now. You better stay where you are till th' Doc comes an' looks you over," and he followed Margaret out.

"You are sure that you will have no trouble with Doctor Reed?" she asked, as he stepped onto the porch.

"Why, no, Ma'am; th' Doc is seein' th' error of his sinful ways, an' I reckons he'll do purty near anythin' I tell him to if I tell him right. An' of course, I wouldn't tell him no other way."

"You are a puzzle to me," confessed Margaret, smiling. "I'm never quite sure about you."

"Puzzle?" He turned his hat over and looked into it as if to find something puzzling. "Why, Ma'am," he said, grinning, daring another deep look into her eyes, "I'm as simple an' easy to read as a—as a—Injun. Now if it was you I'd say there was a puzzle—but, pshaw! I never was no good, at all, figgerin' puzzles. I remember once I was watchin' some tenderfeet playin' billiards, when I was in Kansas City, after leavin' some cattle at th' yards across th' river. They did things to them balls that I never thought could be done, an' they did them easylike. Billiards is mebby an easy game, Ma'am, for them that knows how. It looked plumb easy to me, an' awful temptin'. I got me a table over in a corner an' took off my coat. I ain't never tried it since. Th' proprietor come a-runnin' an tells me that th' blacksmith-shop is down th' street a couple of blocks. That's me, Ma'am—my touch ain't gentle—I can't help smashin'. An' when somebody gives me a puzzle to figger out I allus look to see if I can smash through it. But puzzles ain't made that way I reckon."

Margaret stepped back into the kitchen, half closed the door and said, quickly, quietly, although somewhat breathlessly: "There is no puzzle worth the solving that the right man can't solve—if he tries hard enough."

Johnny started forward, but the door closed in his face and he heard the bar drop, and then the front door slammed. He tensed himself and then relaxed, a smile lighting up his face like a sunrise bathing a granite mountain. "This weather is bound to change," he said, loudly. "I can feel cyclones in th' air—an' I ain't th' only one that had better look to their tent pegs!" He reached Pepper in two leaps, the second of which put him in the saddle, and he dashed off to find Cimarron as though it were a matter of life or death.

The *segundo* looked up, a covetous expression on his face. The black whirlwind slid to a stop at his feet, a cloud of dust enveloping him and drifting slowly south with the wind.

"I'm solvin' puzzles with an axe," came the astonishing statement from the heart of the cloud. "I mean, have you got a match?"

The round-up boss put his fingers in a vest pocket and produced the desired article. "I got one; but mebby you ought to roll somethin' to smoke before you lights it."

Johnny scratched his head and burst into a roar of laughter, Cimarron joining him purely because it was infectious.

"Seein' where you come from, I'd say you was *loco*," chuckled Cimarron. "What's on yore mind besides matches an' axes?"

"Why, I was just wonderin' if you could take four hundred head of these cows over to th' Double X, road brand 'em with th' Question Mark, an' throw 'em in with Lin's hundred. McCullough shore is countin' on gettin' five hundred from you fellers, and he shouldn't be disappointed."

"I can do it unless I lose my health an' strength," answered the boss. "We ain't got 'em here—but on yore way to town stop an' tell Slim an' Larry to pick out as many as they can from that herd they're holdin'. If we're still short we can get th' rest easy enough. Where you goin' now?"

"To see Arch. I reckon he's got a new job if he wants it."

"That so?" replied the round-up boss. "He is a good man. You aimin' to be in Dave's tonight?"

"I am."

"Slim an' Larry will stop there with th' tally figgers on their way home. Are you reckonin' there'll be any blast tonight? They ain't in no hurry—an' I'd just as soon come with 'em."

"There won't be no blast—that'll come later," replied Johnny, smiling. "I only aim to light th' fuse tonight. Mebby it's a long one, an' mebby it's busted somewhere."

"You move cautious just th' same after tonight," warned Cimarron. "Some fuses hang fire; others get crossed, which cuts out some of th' waitin'. You've been packin' in quite some giant, off an' on. I'd say it's over-charged, with Squint, Smitty, Wolf, Lang, an' th' Doc all packed in together. Don't you get slack, son."

"I'll be hummin' like a fiddle string," replied Johnny quietly. "There's Arch, over there. See you later, mebby."

Arch tested an iron and put it back in the fire, and looked up. "Well," he said, smiling cheerfully, "We're near through."

"Glad to hear it," replied Johnny. "Are you aimin' to bum around Highbank, or get yoreself a new job an' keep out of mischief?"

"I knowed that parson wouldn't have no good effect on you," growled Arch, "'seein' how strong he affected me with my strong mind. What you want to know for? Found somethin' for my idle hands to do?"

"Arnold needs a good man out here steady; two of 'em to start with, an' mebby another later on. I told him that you wasn't worth a cuss; but bein' stubborn he says mebby you'll do."

"I ain't heard no offer yet," grinned Arch, impudently.

"You ought to be glad that folks will let you hang around," retorted Johnny. "What were you gettin' on th' Circle 4?"

"Forty-five," answered Arch. "I ain't no kid, an' I asks for fifty. They couldn't see it; so here I am."

"Fifty is yours; but you better see Arnold first. Are you goin' down to Highbank tomorrow?"

"I am, an' I'm shore set on it," answered Arch, firmly, "An' when I'm set, I'm set solid. I'm goin'; why?"

"I'm glad of it," chuckled Johnny. "You bring back three stampin' irons for this ranch; an' be shore that you can get both ends of 'em on a cow at th' same time."

"If I'm totin' 'em with me on my hoss, you can gamble they won't be no pets of Larry's," laughed Arch. "Anybody goin' to be in town tonight?"

"I reckon so. I'm dead shore that Fraser will be there. He's got a plumb affectionate disposition. He's been follerin' me around steady since Wolf cashed in. He's over there in that patch of scrub right now—don't look!"

"I ain't lookin', you ignoramus!" retorted Arch, indignantly. "I'm comin' in to have a little of Dave's fire water tonight, an' sleep in a bed once more. It looks like rain," he observed, scanning the cloudless sky, "an' I shore hate a blanket an' slicker roll when it rains."

"So I see," gravely rejoined Johnny. "I don't care where you go, of course, if you don't crowd me. I like plenty of elbowroom when I'm millin' around indoors keepin' out of th' rain. But I don't figger there'll be any trouble tonight."

"You'll have plenty of room," promised Arch. "In case you ain't got enough, sing out an' we'll bust th' front out of th' Palace." He considered a moment. "Mebby it'll be just as well to have a couple of friends hangin' 'round outside in th' dark watchin' th' weather. Dave hardly ever pulls down his curtains."

"It won't be needed—not tonight, anyhow," smiled Johnny, his heart warming to the cocky youngster. "I'm thankin' you just th' same, you flathead. Well, so-long!" and Johnny rode toward town. After he had spoken to Slim about the herd to be collected he sent Pepper into a pace that defied any horse on that range to equal. There was to be no third man present when he visited the Doc.

Arch looked carelessly over the range, stretched the kinks out of his back and let his gaze rest idly for a moment on the distant clump of scrub timber. "You pore jackass," he muttered. "You'll mebby be another one of them fellers that didn't know it was loaded."

The Doc glanced idly out of the door and resumed his packing. Big Tom had promised to send the chuck wagon for his effects on the morrow and to give him the extra room in the ranchhouse. The offer had been accepted with reluctance, for the Doc did not like to live in the same house with another, especially if the other was the boss of the house. Visiting was all very well, but he yarned for privacy, and there was good reason for it besides a natural inclination. He had little in common with the minds about him on the range, for he was a student and a reader, and his book shelves held a literature far above the understanding of those around him. He had no choice, however, for the time had come to get out of an impending storm. Being energetic, and impatient to finish a disagreeable task, he had kept at it and there now remained only a few odds and ends to be collected. He drew the corners of an old blanket over the bundle of clothing, extra bedding, and miscellaneous linen, pulled them tightly together and knelt on the bundle, straining at the rope. He had just finished the knot when a moving shadow on the east wall caught his attention and made him reach instinctively for the gun in its shoulder holster; but he checked his hand in mid-air, and just in time. There was only one man whom he had reason to fear, and that man had killed Wolf Forbes under the noses of his own outfit and in an even break; and what chance had he, a novice, against such gunplay? He let his hand drop to his side and slowly looked around.

"That was shore close, Doc," remarked a quiet but not unfriendly voice. "You don't never need to reach for no gun for me if you acts square. I ain't on th' warpath, at all; I'm peaceful, I am; an' I come down to ask you somethin' that nobody but you can tell me."

The Doc arose, anger glinting in his eyes from the memory of a former indignity. "Well, what do you want?" he growled. "Framing up another kidnapping?"

"There you go," accused Johnny in great disgust. "You shore hop on th' prod as quick as any man I ever knowed. I only come down to ask you how soon Arnold can get out of bed an' get some use of that laig of his'n."

"I don't know," replied the Doc. "Not knowing, I wouldn't care to say. I've not been out there since."

"He's all ribbed to get up," continued Johnny. "An' there's this about things: Folks that act square with me allus find that I act square with them. An' I'm tellin' you that them fellers will mebby be plumb lucky durin' th' next few weeks. I've been foolin' a lot down here—

holdin' back, sort of; but I quit foolin' th' day I went down an' dug Wolf out of his outfit. I'm aimin' to be serious these days. You said you don't know about Arnold—but it ain't much of a job to make shore, is it? You only got to take th' rough goin' dead east of this shack for a little ways until you get into Green Valley— an' from there on th' ridin' is easy. There's too much confusion along th' reg'lar trail with them touchy Double X punchers ridin' around up there. An' if you left right away you could get back in plenty of time for yore supper. Looks like yo're movin'?"

"I am," replied the other. "I might go down to High-bank, and start practicing."

"You might," admitted Johnny; "but I'm sayin' that you don't have to go to th' Bar H ranchhouse to keep out of trouble. I've passed you my word—you play square with me an' you'll mebby find this shack is safer for you than that ranchhouse ever will be if you don't play square. I'm meanin' this, Doc."

"I don't see where the question of safety comes in at all. I've found this place pretty lonely, sometimes, and I'm getting tired of it. What's more, I'm squatting on the SV range."

"I'm glad to hear you say that last, an' I reckon mebby it is lonely," replied Johnny, " 'though it shouldn't be. Yo're only a couple of miles from town, an' you got a good cayuse. There's some good boys up in town, too. You ought to ride in more often an' get friendly 'stead of holin' up like a bear dodgin' th' winter. An' as for squattin', why I'll say th' SV won't say nothin' at all to you about that, 'specially after you tells some of th' boys in town that you are only squattin' down here an' don't lay no claim to this land. Doc, th' time is shore comin' when nearly everybody on this range will be choosin' sides or settin' on th' fence—an' them as takes to th' fence should set awful tight an' still. But gettin' back to my reason for visitin' you: I reckon Arnold is plumb sick of layin' abed; I'm shore I'd be. You can't say when he should get up?"

The Doc was looking at him intently and his frown had

slowly disappeared. He was no fool, had no real affection for Big Tom, and he was beginning to see a great light. He turned deliberately, yanked the knot loose and let the blanket open and spread out over the floor. Picking up his bag, he considered a moment. "Hazarding a guess, I'd say that he has another week in bed. Did you notice any fever, any flush, or anything else that seemed abnormal to you?" he asked.

"Nothin' but stubbornness an' a grouch like a she bear with cubs," answered Johnny. "I reckon he stays on th' prod purty much when there ain't no strangers around. He must make life excitin' for his family. Now that he's gettin' ambitious, he'll be worse."

"Well, I'll go prepared for anything, anyhow. If you are riding down this way tonight drop in and I'll tell you how I found him. It was a clean break and everything was in his favor."

"I reckon I'll be too busy in town tonight," replied Johnny. "I got a job to do. If you ain't got nothin' special to keep you here an' feel like seein' th' boys, ride up an' spend th' evenin' with us. We'll be glad to see you."

The Doc listened intently. "Who's that riding up the trail?" he asked.

Johnny looked deep into his eyes, smiled cynically, banished his suspicions, and glanced out of the window. "I reckoned so," he muttered. "That's Fraser, goin' back to look for somethin' he's lost. He'll mebby find it tonight up in Dave's, if he looks hard enough. Times are shore changin' down here."

The Doc stepped forward and passed out. "When you leave, close the door behind you. The dust gets on my nerves and there will be plenty of it flying with this wind," and he walked briskly to the little corral.

Johnny watched him bridle and saddle the horse, mount, and canter away straight for the rough going east of the trail. Pulling the door shut behind him, he walked to the brush-filled hollow where he had left his horse, mounted, and set off at a lope for Gunsight.

"Mebby he means it," he soliloquized. "If he does, all right. I gave him a chance to go for that shoulder holster

when I looked out to see who was ridin' up th' trail, but
that don't mean much, for he might have figgered it was
too risky. Mebby he's aimin' to set on th' fence waitin' to
see how things'll settle down. That's all right, too—it's
his natural play—but I'm keepin' cases on him just th'
same. He's had his warnin' "—he shrugged his shoulders expressively and looked up the trail where he
thought he could distinguish Fraser's horse in front of
the Palace. "An' *that's* all right, too," he growled, "he's
where he'll be handy." After a moment he slapped
Pepper's shoulder. "Sorry, little hoss," he growled, "but
mebby you'll have to play pack animal for a while if I'm
goin' to watch them mavericks until after McCullough
gets that Bar H herd. Didn't I tell you we'd likely be
popular, an' unpopular? Well, it's shore comin' true."

I found him it was a clear, brush and even thing was in
his favor.

"I reckon I'll be too busy in town tonight," replied
Johnny. "I got a job to do. If you'll and got nothin' special
to keep you here an' feel like seein' th' boys, ride up an'
spend th' evenin' with us. We'll be glad to see you."

The Doc leaned intently. "Who's that ridin' up the
trail," he asked.

Johnny looked deep into his eyes, smiled cynically,
compared his suspicions and glanced out of the window.
"I reckon so," he muttered. "That's Fraser your back
to look for somebody he's not. It mostly had it tonight
in th' Palace. If he looks hard enough, Fraser are shore
shootin' down here."

The Doc stepped forward and passed out. "Then you
leave, close the door behind you. The dust pan on my
nerves and there will be plenty. If I'm big with this
wind," and he walked behind to the little corral.

Johnny watched him hurtle and saddle the horse,
mount, and canter away straight for the north going east
to the trail. Pulling the door shut behind him, he walked
to the bunk that notice where he had left the brass
concluded, and set off in a trot for Dunlady.

"Mebby he means it," he soliloquized, "if he does, all
right. I give him a chance to go for that shootin' holster

CHAPTER XXI

The Message

DAILEY, SEATED at a table, the everlasting pack of cards in front of him, beamed upon Fanning and Johnny as they entered. "Thought mebby nobody was goin' to show up tonight," he said. "Dave's scared of me."

"I never did care much for wild animals," retorted Dave. "An' I says that you shore go wild when you sees a deck of cards. If you'd only win somethin' once in a while, I wouldn't have a word to say."

"That's what makes him wild," chuckled Fanning. "Ben, how much has Nelson taken away from you?"

"Not very much, an' I more than got it back from th' others," retorted Dailey. "If I only had his luck with my skill—but what's th' use?" he asked, shrugging his shoulders.

"You shore has got to have plenty of luck with *yore* skill," jibed Dave, "or you wouldn't even have a shirt left."

"Lemme ask you somethin', seein' that you know so much about poker," said Fanning. "How far should a man back two pairs?"

"Them assassins? You get up to this table, you scoffin'

innocent, an' I'll show you when you ought to let loose of two pair," chuckled Dailey. "Who's this comin'? Fraser! Come over here, Bill, an' help me rope a couple of tenderfeet into a little game of draw. They're shy tonight."

"Who's th' other, besides me?" inquired Fraser, leaning against the bar.

"Huh!" snorted Dailey. "All right, then; help me rope in th' other two."

"If I'm goin' to be yore come-on, what do I get out of it?" laughed Fraser.

"Every cussed thing you can get an' hold onto, but you'd better sand yore hands. Here's another sheep: Hello, Gurley! Yo're just in time to get a seat—I allus did like a five-handed game. Come on! Come on! Don't be afraid of th' iron!"

"Make it four-handed for a little while," said Johnny. "That'll give Dailey a chance to stack it up in front of him all ready for me. I ain't as good at draw as some down here, but I can allus take it away from Ben, somehow. How's things on th' Triangle, Gurley?"

"Slowin' fast since them Double X fellers moved off. They made me wear out four cayuses a day. When will they finish up?"

"Purty soon, I reckon," answered Johnny, turning to Fraser. "You fellers are lucky. You don't get many strays over th' mountain, or through that canyon, I reckon."

"Not any that I've noticed," replied Fraser. "But we've been plumb lazy in our round-ups. We got an awful sight of brandin' to do next time."

"That so?" asked Johnny. "Been takin' life easy an' lettin' 'em go?"

"Shore; that northwest section is so rough an' full of brush that it's near impossible to get 'em out. There must be an awful lot of unmarked animals over there. We're goin' to have our hands full with 'em."

"Aimin' to tackle it this fall?" asked Johnny, carelessly.

"Mebby; mebby not. McCullough will save us from goin' up th' trail this year, so we might run a special combin' up out there."

"I'm runnin' one right here!" exclaimed Dailey, banging his fist on the table. "I'll run a brand on you fellers that'll smart so you can't sleep. Come on, let's get a-goin'. Hot iron! Hot iron! Ropers up!"

"I'll just take a bite out of you," said Fraser. "Anybody else hungry?"

"I just ain't never had enough to eat," chuckled Fanning, dragging up a chair, "not since I was a growin' kid—an' I ain't nowise shore that I had enough then."

"Which I says is frank, comin' from th' keeper of a hotel," laughed Gurley. "I've often felt th' same way when I ate in town. Turn it loose. I'm on."

"Let me see," pondered Dailey, "we deals five cards, don't we?"

"We do; but only one at a time," replied Fanning patiently. "Don't turn no trump."

"It's sorta comin' back to me," smiled Dailey, spreading out the cards to be cut to see who dealt. "It's sorta comin' back," he repeated.

"Then I'm sayin' it's due to be laig weary, for it's goin' to have a long journey," remarked Dave. He looked up. "Cuss it! Here's th' Doc! Hello, stranger! Shore, this is Gunsight. Hey, Dailey! he's got a whole satchel full; ring him into th' game."

"Bet he's got a wad of wool soaked with that there chloryfoam. Somebody ride herd on him," laughed Fraser, but he was tense. It was the first time anyone had seen the Doc and Johnny together since the kidnapping had been explained, and anything was possible.

"I'm not collecting buttons," retorted the Doc, smiling. "Hello, boys! Hello, Dave! Say, Fraser, I wish you would tell Big Tom not to send in the wagon for me; I've changed my mind. I got a hurt leg, and it won't be right for nearly a week. Set out a round on me, Dave; I'll drink mine and hurry along. I just rode up to get word to Tom. Dave, you should use something milder when you load this whiskey—ever try nitric?"

"Don't you do it, Dave!" expostulated Dailey in alarm. "I can't hardly taste it now."

The Doc looked at him, shook his head sadly, said good night, and went out.

"He didn't act like his laig was hurt," remarked Fraser wonderingly. "But you can't never tell nothin' about him; he's a queer bird. An' changeable? There ain't no cussed word for it."

"I've often wondered how he made a livin'," said Johnny curiously.

"Well, I'll be cussed!" snorted Dailey incredulously. "You have been here all this time an' don't know that? Huh! Th' Doc is a sort of self-actin' remittance man. He's got a wad banked back East, an' once a month I cash a check for him."

"Two pairs," muttered Fanning, scratching his head, and telling the truth to mislead his opponents. "That was what I was askin' about. Well, I'll see it an' add a blue."

"Any time *you* raise a blue, you got two pairs, all right!" snorted Dailey. "Two pairs, deuces up!" He held up a finger warningly. "I hears hosses' feets," he chuckled. "Move over, Gurley, an' give th' visitors a chance to edge in."

The sounds grew louder and soon stopped outside, and a laughing voice said, "There's Dailey, th' hoss thief, tryin' to learn th' game. He's a persistent dummy, for he's allus tryin'."

"He don't know one card from another," laughed a second voice.

"Hey!" shouted Dailey. "Come in here, you fellers, an' I'll show you how much I know!"

Slim appeared, followed closely by Larry and Arch.

"They ought to make you roll up yore sleeves, you mosshead," said Larry, grinning.

"Sit down there!" ordered Dailey, "an' I'll have *you* rollin' up th' bottoms of yore pockets!"

"Wimmin' an children first," quoth Fanning. "Come on, Larry."

"Did you hear that?" snorted Larry, staring at him. "I shore will, *now!*"

"This is goin' to be pay-day for me," said Dailey in great content. "Where th' devil are we at, anyhow?"

Over at the bar Johnny and Slim were carrying on a low-voiced conversation and figuring on a piece of paper, while Arch and Dave entertained each other at the other end of the counter. After a few minutes Johnny nodded his head in quiet satisfaction, put the paper in his pocket and, going up for a few words with Arch and Dave, wandered over to the table and sat down close to it, leaning back to enjoy the fight. He always found keen enjoyment in watching the storekeeper play, for Dailey's red-brown face was suffused with wrinkles of good nature, quite independent of how his fortune tended; his high, shining forehead and the bald spot above and behind it reflected the light and glistened. The eternal cigar he chewed on, cold, stale, and odorous, bobbed animatedly and his shrewd black eyes peered out from under bushy eyebrows, glittering, glinting, and alive with his emotions, like twin mirrors on which were reflected the subtle complexities of a nature enriched by a life crowded with experiences. He had no poker face, but knowing the sad fact, he had made an adept liar out of the one to which Nature had given so much expression.

He glanced at Johnny, his eyes dancing. "Yo're comin' nearer th' candle all th' time, little moth," he laughed. "I'll singe them wings of yourn—you see! My flush takes *this* game. Deal 'em up, Dailey," he grunted, raking in chips and cards.

"Come on, Nelson," said Fanning. "Better get in this. Th' old hoss thief is stackin' 'em up for you."

"Huh!" Johnny remarked. "It ain't as big a pile as I was hopin'. Oh, well," he sighed, "I'm like th' SV round-up: I take 'em as they come."

"How'd they come to start that so early?" asked Fanning. "It's plumb warm for workin' hard."

"Wanted to know how many head they had," answered Johnny. "An' what do you know about workin' hard?"

"He's seen me lots of times," cut in Dailey. "Did they find out?"

"Shore. They've got twelve hundred an' twenty, which

would be fourteen hundred an' fifty-five, if Arnold hadn't sold two hundred an' thirty-five head."

"That's good, considerin' how things has been let slide over there," remarked Fraser.

"Th' old figgers of three years ago," said Johnny, "when Arnold took possession, were sixteen hundred an' eighty-five, in th' fall. Now, lemme see—do I need two or three?" he mused. "Reckon there ain't no use of throwin' away a nice, high card, so I'll take two. I'm plumb fond of holdin' up a sider." He glanced at the two cards, slipped them into his hand and looked around. "Now, I was askin' th' Double X what factor they used to figger natural increase—an' they says one to five. That right?"

"That's allus been sort of gospel down here," said Fanning. "For th' Lord's sake!" he snorted, in playful pretense. "You takin' eight cards again?"

"You ain't got no right to ask nobody but th' dealer how many cards he takes," retorted Dailey. "As a matter of fact, I only took seven. I'm h—l-bent to get me a pair."

"You *are* dealing," declared Gurley. "How many did you take?"

"Three jacks," answered Dailey. "If I only had th' other three mebby I'd *have* a pair."

"Which same I calls enlightenin' an' 'lucidatin'," muttered Gurley. "I demands a count of th' deck. But, speakin' of factors, I'd say one to nine was nearer right, over on th' SV."

"Let him count th' deck," growled Fanning, "before he gets worse. One to nine! I'm sayin' one to five is close whittlin' down on this range. It'll come right eight out of ten. Well! well!" he chuckled, as he looked at his card. "Welcome, welcome, little stranger; how I wondered what you was! But I'm not pressin' my luck too hard. I sees, an' trails."

"I'm passin'," sighed Johnny. "Now I says that th' natural increase of them sixteen hundred an' eighty-five cows th' next year would be three hundred an' thirty-nine, usin' that gospel factor. Th' herd would finish th' second year with two thousand an' twenty-four. Usin' that gospel factor again, it would increase four hundred an' five, an' finish th' third year with twenty-four hundred an' twenty-nine. This is the summer of that third year, an' that twenty-four hundred an' twenty-nine ain't there. There's only twelve hundred an' twenty, which added to them that Arnold sold, makes fourteen hundred an' fifty-five. Now I figgers that fourteen hundred an' fifty-five from twenty-four hundred an' twenty-nine leaves nine hundred an' seventy-four head. That's what is missin'—nine hundred an' seventy-four head. Call it nine hundred seventy. Cimarron O.K.'s th' last tally figgers. Everybody but th' Bar H allows one to five is right. Where did them cattle go to?"

"I call," growled Gurley. "Kings up!"

"You can't never trust assassins," chuckled Dailey, laying down three tens.

"An' three tens ain't no good tonight," said Fanning, revealing an eight-full. "Two pair ain't no good to bet on hard, but they're plumb fine to draw to. What you got, Fraser?" he demanded.

"A headache," grunted Fraser, throwing down his hand.

"Deal 'em up, Fanning," said Dailey. "Where *did* they go to?" he asked Johnny.

"I've gone over everythin' I can think of," replied Johnny, leaning back. "I've figgered hard winters, wolves, fever—there wasn't none of them. Strayed off? Where to? Would they leave Clear River for an arid stretch forty miles wide—an' *stay* away? They have to drink, don't they? Quicksands? Those that wandered in wouldn't be many, an' them that was drove in we'll count part of that nine seventy. Where did they go?"

"Mebby they heard them angel voices callin'," said Fanning, grinning.

"I'm sayin' somethin' is plumb wrong down here," replied Johnny. "Somebody has been ridin' th' line careless, an' a lot of mavericks has got across. Fraser, how many riders has Big Tom kept on his northwest lines?"

Fraser looked serious and pretended to ponder deeply. "Only one—Wolf. An' he was allus payin' more attention to th' west line, facin' th' Snake Buttes country than

he was to th' north line, though. All he could think of
was rustlers. Cussed if he didn't near sleep with 'em, he
had 'em in his mind so strong." He did not see Slim's
sneering smile or the look he exchanged with Arch. Slim
was beginning to regard that outfit very much in that
light.

"That's what I thought," replied Johnny, triumphantly.
"He wasn't ridin' sign at all—he was only lookin' for
rustlers. An' while he was prancin' along that west line
lookin' for Nevada, them mavericks was driftin' off th' SV
to get in that brush where th' flies wouldn't bother 'em
so much. That accounts for a lot of them unmarked
cows you was speakin' about."

"Does look like mebby there's somethin' in that,"
cogitated Fraser. "As I said, we never paid much attention to th' cattle out there; but it don't sound reasonable
that all them SV mavericks would drift over onto us. An'
why only mavericks?" He thought for a moment. "I'm
sayin' nothin', but there's somethin' plumb wrong,
somewhere. Want me to ask Big Tom about it? Mebby it
was rustlers—they're plumb active."

Johnny considered. "Well, you might," he said, slowly,
leaning slightly forward in his chair. "Tell you what,
Fraser; I'm dead shore about them nine hundred seventy. Suppose you tell him to brand that many mavericks, takin' 'em as they come, with th' SV mark, an'
throw 'em over to Arnold when he holds his fall round-
up? Th' SV will provide stampin' irons, an' a couple of
men to help. As to rustlers, they'd have to drive across
th' Bar H an' th' Double X to get to Arnold's ranch—any
rustlin' that was done would be done on th' fringes of th'
Double X. Why, you fellers ain't never been raided; an'
to get to th' SV would be worse than gettin' to th' Bar H.
That's what we'll do; we'll have him throw over nine
hundred an' seventy head this fall, an' that'll make
things right."

Fraser boiled inwardly, but controlled himself. There
had been no accusation, nothing to call for defense, and
to take it angrily or as an accusation he felt would be to
play into Johnny's hands. Being guilty of the very thing

which the other had gone so carefully around, made him find the hidden meaning in the heavy circumlocution, and keep quiet about it for fear of revealing the real meaning of the words to the others in the room. He knew how Big Tom would take it, for he knew that his foreman was smouldering like a volcano, charged with the cumulative anger caused by recent events; and he felt sure that the news he would take back to the ranch that night would cause an eruption, and a great one. This was another reason for remaining calm: not knowing what Big Tom might decide to do, it would be well to give Johnny no cause to exercise any unusual caution, or to strike hard and suddenly. So he growled a little as he resumed the play.

"That's shore a whole lot of cattle to throw over to anybody, free, but, h—l!" he said, "it ain't no funeral of mine. It's Big Tom's business, 'though I reckon it'll sort of take his breath. Did Arnold say that?"

"He's sayin' it through me," answered Johnny quietly. "I'm workin' for him, an' actin' for him, an' I'm usin' my own judgment."

Slim lounged into an easier position against the bar and grunted. "Well," he drawled, "we're comin' to th' conclusion that th' round-ups down here has got to be general, spring an' fall. This here maverick business allus is a bad proposition, an' it's worse in th' kind of country that's plentiful on parts of this range. Sherwood is standin' out, set for a general drive. He says for all th' ranches to join hands, sweep th' whole range, do our brandin' an' divide up an' brand th' mavericks accordin' to some fair plan. I suggests dividin' 'em in proportion to th' number of cattle on each ranch, but that's only *my* idea. He goes even further, an' says that th' runnin' iron an' this brush brandin' we all have been doin' down here has got to be done away with, on th' Double X an' every other ranch in this section. Anybody knows that chutin' 'em, an' stampin' on th' brand is easier, an' that there ain't no honest reason for th' straight iron no more. Texas threw it into th' discard ten years ago or more. We're discardin' it, an' we're goin' to raise th' devil with any outfit that don't foller suit. That's flat, an' goes as it lays, regardless, to th' SV, th' Triangle, an' th' Bar H, with Sherwood's compliments."

"What about that nine hundred an' seventy, then?" asked Gurley.

"We've got nothin' to say about them, but if they are throwed over, th' rest will be divided," answered Slim. "Bein' th' biggest ranch out here, we stand to lose more than any other by throwin' over them cows to th' SV; but we admits its title to 'em. Tell Big Tom to think it over, an' see us about it before fall."

"One to five is figgerin' too strong," remarked Gurley, thoughtfully. "One to nine is nearer th' real figgers."

"There ain't no reason that I can see to change figgers that have proved themselves, time an' time again, down here," replied Slim.

"Havin' been talked plumb weak," growled Dailey, "suppose we rest ourselves with a nice, quiet game? It's yore deal, Fraser. Comin' in, Slim?"

"No, I ain't; I'm goin' out," answered Slim. "I got more than twenty miles an' I'm tired. Comin', you fellers?" he asked Larry and Arch.

"Shore," said Larry, arising. "Glad to escape. Better come along, Arch—what's a few more miles?"

"I'd like to," replied Arch. "Cuss it, I will! I can go to town th' next day. Good night, fellers."

They made a noisy exit and soon their banter and laughter grew silent down the trail. Fraser stretched, and yawned prodigiously, and his friend Gurley became restless.

Dailey, sensing the break-up of his beloved pastime, made an effort to save it. "Don't bust up th' game, boys," he begged. "I got a feelin' comin' over me that I can clean up th' whole pack of you. Let's see if I'm right."

"Try it on th' rest of th' boys," growled Fraser. "I'm cashin' in what's left, an' dustin' up th' trail for my little bunk. Comin', Gurley?"

"As far as th' partin' of th' ways," smiled the Triangle puncher, "unless you aim's to ride home by way of our house, so I won't be lonesome. It's only a few miles out of yore way."

"I'm likely to," retorted Fraser. "So-long, fellers," and he preceded his friend to the horse rail.

The remaining four smoked and talked for a little while and then Johnny arose. "Put them supplies in th' shed, Dailey?" he asked.

"Shore; in a strong sack, like you said," replied the storekeeper. "I put in a few more cans of tomatoes, seein' as they're handy when there ain't no drinkin' water near."

"Yo're usin' yore head," commended Johnny, and turned to Dave. "I'm goin' to th SV to let Cimarron's boys know that there's trouble comin', shore. You don't know when I'll be back or where I'm goin'; but I reckon mebby th' whole town will *hear* me, when I do come back. Somethin's goin' to bust loose tomorrow. I ain't no blind fool. Good night."

CHAPTER XXII

The Ultimatum

THERE WAS movement on the Gunsight trail at an early morning hour. Five men rode to within half a mile of the town and then halted for a final consultation, which was soon over. Three rode westward at a walk, another went on, bearing slightly to the east, while the fifth, dismounting, led his horse from the trail, picketed it in a steep-walled ravine and went north on foot.

The eastern sky paled, grew silvery, and then became tinted with red and gold. A man crouched behind the hotel shed, swearing softly because he heard no sounds of a horse within it. He snuggled close to a knothole, peering at the hotel wall not far from him, and the rifle in his hand was full cocked. Behind the saloon shed another man had thrust his rifle through a crack and as the light increased, he cuddled his cheek against the stock and peered along the sights into an open window in the rear wall of the hotel. Lying in a clump of weeds north of the saloon and near the trail was another rifleman, who could see Dave's north wall and the front of the saloon as well. A fourth had settled down in the end of a shallow gully across the trail from Dailey's store, his Winchester needing but to move over a short arc to cover the door of the saloon. It was point-blank range for him, and in this matter he was no better off than his three friends. The fifth, the angry and determined foreman of the Bar H, not finding cover as close as he would have liked, was forced to ensconce himself over two hundred yards from the front of the hotel, and a little to the right of Jerry's shop, where he kept turning problems over in his mind. Desperate ailments called for desperate cures, and if Gunsight objected as to methods, then it would have to object in the persons of the three easy-going inhabitants who were likely to be offended. The actions of the Double X were far more serious, but had to be risked if life were to be worth living for the outfit of the Bar H. With the coming of dawn Big Tom pondered less and looked more, his rifle at his shoulder, ready for instant use.

Back on the trail there was silent movement as an indistinct and bootless figure crossed it and paused, waiting for light. The darkness thinned and the figure moved forward again, bent over close to the boot marks on the ground, which it followed with slow sureness. The stockinged feet made no sound, avoiding twigs and dead leaves, and not an out-thrust branch whipped or scraped as the man worked forward. He carried a heavy Sharp's, the heel of his hand over the cocked hammer, his fingers covering the trigger guard as an extra precaution against accidental discharge.

The few buildings in Gunsight appeared as though a curtain were slowly rising and finally stood revealed in their entirety. The sun rose and threw soft, delicate shadows from the bases of all standing objects, too weak to mark their patterns far, melting into oblivion. A door slammed, sounding irreverent and out of place, and from the hotel chimney curled a timid wisp of smoke, this way and that, finally climbing straight up and losing its identity against the gray-blue of the sky, while its supporting column twisted and turned and danced as it hurried to self-effacement. Dailey's chimney sent up a skirmishing film, which died out; and then, as if in stalwart support of the fainting advance, there came a darker, thicker column, telling all who cared to read that Dailey put his trust in kerosene. The hotel door opened, causing a quick movement of Big Tom's rifle, and George, sleepy and unpleasant in looks and disposition, glanced idly around and went back again. From far off in the west the quavering, long-drawn wail of a coyote, mercifully tempered by distance, arose to greet the rising sun. Birds sang with delirious abandon and the soft noises in grass and sand and brush told of a waking world. In the vague grayness of the hotel, framed by the open door, something moved, steadily growing plainer and soon took the form of a towel in the hands of George, who drove winged pests before him and, with a final, frenzied waving, took hold of the door and slammed it shut. As it closed Big Tom relaxed, eased his hold on the rifle and reached back to remove a stone which was beginning to assert its presence under him to his growing discomfort. Turning his head, he looked back, and froze, his groping fingers rigid. Ten feet behind him and to his right was the black muzzle of a heavy rifle, and behind that a pair of gray-blue eyes regarded him malevolently through narrow slits in the bronzed face. For a tense, appreciable interval eyes looked into eyes, and then the foreman squirmed.

"Don't move, only as I tell you, an' slow," said Johnny's clear, low voice. "I got you just th' way I want you—ambushin'! Don't touch that gun, an' don't make no noise. First, put yore hands up even with yore armpits, palms down, on th' ground. Now inch back, away from that gun. Keep on—more—more—all right—stop! Slide 'em forward, straight out ahead of you, an' then lay still. You can admire Fannin's front door, an' imagine me in it, careless an' easy prey for a pot-shooter, if it'll do you any good. Don't look around till I tell you to, an' don't make a sound, blast you!"

Not being able to do anything else, Big Tom obeyed and soon felt his Colt leave its holster. A hand felt up under his coat, to see if the back-strap of his trousers held a gun. Being right-handed, the foreman would hardly choose to carry a six-gun there under ordinary circumstances, but this situation was not in that category. The back-strap was guiltless.

"Roll over on yore back," came the next command, and when it had been obeyed the same inquiring hand passed lightly and quickly over waist-band and shirt bosom, the left hand holding a six-gun now instead of the rifle. "All right, wiggle down in that gully, and then head for where you left yore cayuse, keepin' low down, like yore nature, an' out of sight of town."

"What do you think yo're doin'?" wrathfully inquired Big Tom, but obeying as he protested.

"Huntin' for an excuse to blow you apart, you ambushin' dog," came the metallic reply. "Shut yore mouth, an' keep on goin'. I'll give you a chance to talk later. Any harm that comes to you will be of yore own makin'. Keep on!"

They reached the brush at the edge of the trail, waited a moment, and then crossed swiftly, and when they stopped again it was at Pepper's side. Johnny quickly mounted and urged his captive on again. Coming to a picketed Bar H horse he ordered the foreman to mount it, and as the helpless man obeyed Johnny revealed their objective.

"Head for yore ranchhouse," he said. "Ride on my right side, yore stirrup even with my pommel, where my Colt will have a fair view of you from under my coat. If we meet anybody, pass 'em on yore side, an' don't make no remarks that ain't needed. We go at a lope; hit it up!"

And so they rode, except at a few places in the canyon, where the narrowness of the twisting trail made Big Tom go ahead. Arriving at the ranchhouse they rode around on its farther side, tied the horses to a stake, and went indoors.

"Sit down," commanded Johnny, indicating a chair in the middle of the room. "Here, look at this," and he handed the foreman a piece of paper which was covered with sprawled figures. "I don't know what Fraser forgot, or what he got tangled up, so I'll go over it again.

Them top figgers are based on th' tally sheets of th' SV in th' fall of th' year that Arnold took possession. They ain't like th' figgers Ol' Simon could 'a' showed, for th' ranch had been on th' slide for some years, an' plenty of its cows went on th' drive trail to give money to th' heirs. Th' lowest figgers are based on th' tally Cimarron finished yesterday. Natural increase, figgered as one to five, shows what they ought to be, minus them that Arnold had to sell to get grub. It's all there."

"Th' h—l with 'em!" blazed the foreman, crushing the sheet in his hand and hurling it from him. "What do *I* care about any figgers belongin' to th' SV? Take yore figgers an' get out—I'm advisin' you to leave this part of th' country, an' cussed quick. I ain't playin' godfather to th' SV, an' I'm runnin' this ranch without no help from you, Sherwood, or anybody else."

"When I leave this range I'll go of my own accord, an' there won't be no pushin'," retorted Johnny. "Sherwood can 'tend to his own business; I'll 'tend to mine; but I've got time to look after a little of yourn. If you ain't godfather to th' SV, yo're shore goin' to act like one. There's nine hundred an' seventy head clean missin' from it, an' there's plenty of big ranches down Texas way that would yell for th' rangers, an' holler calamity if they had lost that many. For a little ranch to lose 'em it is shore enough calamity. If anybody would put that many cows on th' trail for me I'd show 'em a lot of money at th' other end."

"SV calamities don't mean nothin' to me," rejoined Big Tom. "It was allowed to run itself, an' it run itself into th' ground. Why wouldn't it lose a lot of cattle?"

"It shore might do just that," conceded Johnny, "if it wasn't for one thing. Yo're an old hand in th' cattle business, an' you know that a bunch of cattle can run wild an' grow amazin'. An' they'd shore do it on a range like th' SV with that valley an' them brush-filled draws for winter shelter. There ain't no natural enemies to cut down th' calves—an' that ranch is good grazin' all year 'round. There wasn't cows enough to eat it down."

"There's them quicksands, an' there was a lot of gray wolves runnin' down here th' last couple of years!" shouted Big Tom, red with anger. "They never even kept up th' wire fence around th' quicksands. Why wouldn't they lose cows?"

"The quicksands would get a few," rejoined Johnny. "They would get more if th' cows was drove into 'em like I caught Lang doin'—an' them will be figgered in th' herd to be throwed back. I've asked about wolves an' everythin' else—there wasn't nothin' to keep 'em down. An' as for that fence, th' less you, or any of yore gang have to say about that, th' better it'll be for you."

"Then yo're callin' me a liar," blazed the foreman. "There *was* wolves down here! An' I never touched that fence, neither."

"Mebby you didn't personal; an' I ain't callin' you a liar while you ain't got a gun," retorted Johnny. "But I am admittin' that yo're plumb mistaken. Comin' down to cases, pleasant an' friendly, I'm sayin' that th' Bar H owes the SV nine hundred an' seventy head of cattle, as they come in a round-up, all kinds an' conditions. When do you aim to start deliverin'?"

The foreman sprang to his feet. "When do I aim to start deliverin'?" he shouted, staring into the calm, gray eyes of the man whose Colt covered him. "When do I aim to start deliverin'?" he repeated, his neck swelling. "I ain't aimin' to at all! Nine hundred an' seventy! That would plumb ruin us!"

"It ain't ruined th' SV," replied Johnny evenly. "Not quite, anyhow," he added. "An' it won't ruin you, because they can all be figgered as extras. We all know they ain't never been put on th' tally sheets with th' other cattle, for th' owners to know about. They're strays, you might say, that have been eatin' up yore grazin' scandalous. They've wandered over on you an' are likely to eat you into some kind of ruin. You ought to be able to do better without 'em, an' you shore ought to be glad to get rid of such a hungry bunch of cattle that you can't prove title to."

"I've got all th' title *I* need—they're on my ranch, an'

that's good enough," shouted Big Tom. "It's good enough for me, an' it's good enough for everybody else, you included."

"Not for nobody else," corrected Johnny, "me least of all. That title is questioned now by more than a dozen men. You can't keep 'em, nohow, for th' general round-up will cut 'em four ways. Th' times are changin' down here like they changed some years back on th' older ranges. Th' runnin' iron is dyin' fast, an' for good reasons. Maverickin' is goin' out of style—an' nothin' can stop it. An' with it goes that title you was mentionin'. Why not get ahead of 'em, an' throw them cows over onto th' SV before anybody gets insultin' you?"

"I'll have somethin' to say about any styles changin' down here," retorted the foreman. "Mebby more than some folks think."

"You ain't got a chance, not a chance," Johnny assured him. "You'll be like th' Injun that tried to push back th' first, an' last, engine he ever saw. It was goin' strong when he tried it."

"An' I ain't got th' authority to give away a cow, not even a single dogie—not to mention a herd. I'm not ownin' this ranch; I'm workin' for it. How can I straighten out my tally sheets to cover th' loss of a herd like that? They don't belong to me—they belong to th' ranch, to th' owners." He was wasting as much time in argument as he knew how in the hope that his outfit would return.

"Pshaw!" laughed Johnny. "They can all be accounted for. Didn't I just say that they never got on th' tally sheets at all? You shore found you had been feedin' a hull passel of cows that didn't belong to th' ranch in case they did get on th' tally sheets. You found it out, an' it was so plumb careless of yore line riders that you up an' fired them that was responsible. That won't bother you, because you got three names off yore pay-roll right now. There ain't nothin' we can't get around if we pull together."

"But th' title to 'em wouldn't stick," objected the baited foreman. "Every one of them cows could be took away from Arnold. I ain't got th' authority to make it stick. An' th' only reason I'm wastin' time talkin' to you over a fool thing like this is because you got a gun on me, an' I can't help myself." His brain seized upon and rejected scheme after scheme for getting out of the situation, one of which he recalled and examined anew. It was not a bad one, if bad came to worse, and he nursed it, sorry that so much time would have to elapse before he could carry it out.

"I just said we could get around anythin'," replied Johnny, pleasantly. "There's an awful lot of mavericks runnin' around on this ranch, most of 'em under four years old. They wouldn't show any Bar H brand. They'd only have a SV. There wouldn't even be a vent brand to single 'em out; an' cattle ain't tellin' where they come from, or we'd 'a' heard a lot of scandals long ago."

"Nine hundred an' seventy mavericks!" snorted Big Tom. "A fine chance I'd have of roundin' up that many! Yo're plumb loco."

"That is a lot, I'll admit," conceded Johnny, apparently balked. "Of course, if you owned this ranch, you could make it up with Bar H brands. But you don't. You can't give away nothin' that you don't own. I can see where that would put you. Anythin' that was yours you could give away; but not no Bar H belongin's. That yore idea?"

"Yo're gettin' th' drift, slow but shore," sarcastically rejoined the foreman. "Anythin' I own I can give away; but not nothin' I don't own. A kid can understand that. An' there ain't that many mavericks on this ranch."

"I still say we can get around anythin' an' I ain't no kid," muttered Johnny. "Lemme see: First, we'll consider cash. Got any?"

"Nothin' but my wages," answered the foreman, a sarcastic smile playing around his lips.

"Too bad," mused Johnny, "wages ain't a patch. If we could have you ownin' a nice pile of money—but you can get money!"

"Look here!" snapped Big Tom, aggressively. "I can't sign no checks over a certain amount a year—th' bank wouldn't cash 'em. An' they've all been signed for this year, all but th' pay-roll. An' I don't own that money, neither. That belongs to th' ranch."

"Well, failin' in cash," said Johnny, crisply, "I'll take a note. Will you gimme one?"

"I will; you can have it," nodded Big Tom, his pet scheme coming more vividly into his mind. "I'll make it out right here, an' now."

"I don't want yore note," objected Johnny. "What good is it? Now, if it was endorsed by somebody that could make it good, why that would be different. You said you'd gimme a note; then gimme that one for three thousand dollars, of Arnold's, that *is* endorsed by somebody that can make it good. An' also a receipt for it. That'll cut down that nine hundred an' seventy an amazin' lot. Th' difference won't be too many to get right here on th' Bar H, an' all of 'em mavericks."

Big Tom was staring at him as if doubting his senses. His face flushed and the veins on his neck and forehead stood out like serpents. He stepped forward involuntarily, but the gun stopped him. He was incapable of speech for the moment and could only make inarticulate sounds.

"That'll help a lot," said Johnny, lightly balanced and leaning slightly forward. "We'll let th' Double X say how many cattle, takin' 'em as they come, they would sell for three thousand dollars. Then we'll take that many away from that nine seventy. You can easy round-up what are needed to make up th' difference, brand 'em with th' SV stampin' irons, an' throw 'em over where they belong. I'll take th' note *now*."

'You'll take h——l!" yelled the foreman. "You'll take h——l!"

"You'll *get* h——l!" snapped Johnny, his eyes narrowing; "an' you'll get it *pronto*! Hunt up that note, an' without no more cussed nonsense. It's yore play, an' you shore want to play fast!"

"You won't get no note!" shouted Big Tom, his face twitching with rage. He seemed about to spring.

"Don't!" ordered Johnny, softly, but with a cold ferocity in his voice that carried conviction. "I'll shoot

you like I would a coyote, you pot-shooter, for you are a coyote! Get that note!"

Big Tom, seething with rage, swayed in agonizing hesitation. He had courage, plenty of it; but he also had common sense. Unarmed, he could do nothing against the gun which had killed his two-gun man in an even break; and his common sense came to his rescue, and barely in time. Glancing out of the window, he detected no signs of his outfit on the trail, and craftily attempted to begin the argument all over again.

"That'll do," said Johnny. "We've finished that. My time is valuable, even if I ain't lookin' for company; an' if they come, you'll be th' first to go under. Get—that—note!"

Shrugging his shoulders, the foreman stepped forward, but Johnny slipped aside and snarled a warning, so venomous and tense that Big Tom gave up the desperate idea, and slowly turned, a beaten man. He walked toward a metal-bound box in a corner of the room, Johnny close at his heels, the gun against the foreman's back. Unlocking it, he slowly raised the lid, and felt Johnny's breath on his neck, the gun pressing solidly against his spine. As the cover went up it revealed a derringer lying on top of a few papers, and the foreman's hand slowly passed by it and fumbled among the contents, reluctantly withdrawing with an unsealed envelope. Shutting down the lid he turned the key, and arose to his feet as his captor, alert as a cat, stepped aside.

Johnny took the envelope, backed off a little farther, opened it, glanced at the note and nodded. He looked around the room and then ordered Big Tom to the table. Taking the pen and ink from a shelf, he placed them before the foreman and then handed him the envelope, telling him what to write. When the pen ceased scratching he took the receipt, read it, and held it out a moment for it to dry.

"This saves you a lot of brandin'," he remarked. "Somewhere around two-thirds, I reckon, 'though th' Double X will set its value in cattle. Now, you listen close. There ain't goin' to be any round-up or brandin' on th' northwest section of this ranch till th' SV gets its herd. When we know how many will be needed you will have till th' general round-up to use th' SV irons. Send for 'em when you get ready, an' an SV puncher will come with 'em. I'm warnin' you fair: A Sharp's will talk to anybody runnin' a brand or round-up out there unless a SV man is on th' spot. An' there's goin' to be some SV men right soon—good ones—an' they'll be plumb touchy about wire fences comin' down. Now I'm takin' you for a little ride with me, so you won't be tempted to smoke up out of a window while I'm ridin' off. Come on; I'm shore in a hurry."

In a few moments they rode westward, Big Tom leading the way, and it was not until more than an hour had passed that he was free to ride back again, or to Gunsight for his outfit, as his fancy dictated.

He chose to return to the ranch and while he rode he elaborated the plan which had come to him, and rubbed his hands as its details unfolded. Since Nelson had admitted being the man who was responsible for the mysterious events which had puzzled the country, Big Tom had remembered Lang's report about having seen Margaret and Johnny riding together. The foreman had not given her up, although pretending to have no interest in her. Having lost the note he had to change his plans, and go about it in a different way. Now his rage and jealousy fanned the flame of his impatience, gave a keener edge to his scheming wits, and added zest to what he purposed to do; and before he knew it he arrived at the house. Entering, he saw the crumpled piece of paper and, kicking it across the room, laughed sneeringly.

"You've been proddin' th' wrong man, Mr. Nelson," he growled. "I'm slow to start; but when I *do*, there ain't nothin' that'll stop me."

CHAPTER XXIII

Range Activities

ON THE day following Johnny's message to Big Tom, Gunsight had awakened expectant, and had remained so all the morning, but to no end. Not a Bar H man had come in, so far as they knew, and the trio in Dave's changed from the belief each had retired with and discussed the situation from a different point of view.

"Big Tom is a wise ol' owl," said Dailey. "He'll move when he gets ready. Just now he's on a nest, hatchin' out somethin' that is mebby tender, bein' so young. He ain't layin' down so easy. I know him."

"He reckons, mebby, that th' man that dealt th' hands has got an ace in a hole," replied Fanning. "It's an old sayin' that you never want to buck another man's game. I don't know that Nelson has got an ace laid away, but he don't have to have any; Big Tom figgers he has, mebby, because them Double X *hombres* are so friendly with him; an' it's what Big Tom thinks that counts with him. Mebby somethin' will happen today, an' mebby it won't; but it's goin' to happen, just th' same, some time."

"I'm favorin' th' ace idea," said Dave, thoughtfully. "If I

was Big Tom I'd be plumb suspicious of any man that made th' suggestion that Nelson made when he knew there was an outfit ag'in' him. I'd figger he was either a cussed fool or knowed just exactly what he was doin', an' all th' time. Nobody down here believes that he is a fool, not now, anyhow; an' I'm dead shore he wasn't bluffin'. He's got an ace, all right—an' I'm admirin' Big Tom's waitin' game. When he thinks he's figgered out how far th' Double X will go we'll hear his answer. Besides, th' Bar H has got to round up an' brand that herd for McCullough. That may be holdin' him back some."

"Slim's remarks slid in like they was made to fit," commented Dailey. "An' *he* wasn't bluffin', neither. If th' Double X is backin' Nelson all th' way, he'll win; if they ain't, he won't. But I'm shore waitin' to see, an' hear."

Down on the Bar H dinner was over before the foreman had much to say, and he was careful not to reveal his personal experiences of the morning. He counseled patience, and gave good reasons for it. They had until fall to start on the SV herd, and many things could, and would, occur before then. The first thing to do was to get ready for the round-up of the trail herd, and in order to lull suspicions they would not work on the tabooed section. There was to be no branding done out there, and in order to show their fairness in not too noticeable a way, they would help the Triangle with its five hundred head. This over with, the Triangle punchers would have to hold the herd together until McCullough came along and, not being able to call on them for aid, the Bar H would have to appeal to the Double X for the loan of some of its men, who thus would be on the ground and see what cattle were to be cut out for the trail. Nelson was to be ignored until the herd was sold and the money put in the bank at Sherman, after which he would be taken care of.

"Nelson is a good man," Big Tom assured them; "but he ain't good enough not to never make mistakes, an' no man can take every trick. He's goin' to miss one, th' last he'll ever miss, or win, for that matter, but there ain't no use of any of us gettin' killed unless we have to. We can get him without it, an' without gettin' any of his sudden new friends on th' prod. I promise that. I know how we're goin' to play it—an' it's so easy it makes me laugh. He's a good man; but there are older heads than his'n. You foller my orders an' set tight. I'll handle this when th' time comes, an' it ain't here yet. Stay out of Gunsight unless you can go in peaceful, keep yore mouths tight shut, an' stay sober. I've said enough about him.

"Now, we got work ahead of us, an' we start at it on th' Triangle day after tomorrow. I'm goin' over to see Hank Lewis now. There'll be somebody from Twitchell an' Carpenter comin' up any day now to select th' cattle an' stay with 'em till McCullough counts 'em into his herd. After I see Hank I'm ridin' to town to leave word at Dave's for Sherwood to see if I can borrow some of his boys when we start our own round-up. Look over yore gear an' be ready for workin'."

His prophecy regarding the representatives of Twitchell and Carpenter was fulfilled at mid-afternoon, when two strangers rode up to the bunkhouse and inquired for him and, being told that he could very likely be found in town, they explained who they were and rode on to Gunsight, accompanied by Fraser. To the saddle of each were fastened three stamping irons bearing their road brand.

Big Tom was in Dave's when they arrived and after a few rounds of drinks they settled down to discuss the herds and range topics in general.

"Th' T an' C sendin' many over th' trails this year?" Dave asked during a lull in the talk.

"Shore," replied the older and taller visitor, who answered to the name of Ridley. "We've been busy since winter. We looked over a big herd of beeves south of th' Grande for th' first herd. There was over thirty-five hundred head and they was three- an' four-year-olds. They went up north of th' Yellowstone, on government contract. Another herd of three thousand two- an' three-year-olds went past th' Platte, bound west for new ranges. There was two more big herds went up to

Dodge—one of 'em bein' sold without th' new owners even seein' 'em. This bunch is goin' to new range north of here, some of 'em. I don't reckon there'll be many more this year. There ain't an animal in them that McCullough's bringin' up that's more than two years old, an' those are th' ones goin' to range. We took 'em from four different ranches to get 'em choice, an' they're all long-laigged longhorns an' a purty sight to a cowman. I'm bettin' Mac won't lose a single head neither. He's a trail boss that *is* a trail boss. He knows every river an' ford, water hole an' dry section from here to Montanny. He took that first herd north this spring, an' here he is back in time to swing this drive. He has a knack of pickin' good men for his trail outfits, an' he's daddy to 'em all from th' jump, without nobody knowin' it."

Big Tom arose. "Well, friends," he said, shaking hands, "yo're welcome to stay at either ranch while yo're here; but I reckon Fanning can make you more comfortable. We start on th' Triangle day after tomorrow—come down when you get ready. I told you how to get to th' Double X. If you go over there before any of 'em come to town, let 'em know that I'm countin' on usin' three of their men when I start my own round-up. See you later."

Dawn found activity on the range. The Double X, having rounded up its hundred head the day before, with a few additional to make up for possible rejections, held them apart from the SV herd, which also had extra cattle to offset any not up to the required standard. The majority of them, those which were certain to be accepted, had already been branded. The C and T inspectors watched the cutting out and indicated their choices as the cattle left the round-up herd, those rejected being turned aside and allowed to go back to freedom on the range, while those accepted were driven to the beef cut, which grew rapidly. A hundred and five finally were accepted, the odd five to make up for possible losses on the trail. Then the SV herd went through the same proceeding until four hundred and ten had been thrown into the beef cut. Because of Cimarron's discriminating judgment in making up the herd there were but few rejections; and, besides, the standard was not high, for, broadly, a cow was a cow. The remaining SV cattle were not returned to their ranch, but were set free to wander where they would. The general round-up would find them later and throw them back then if Arnold wished, although with the coming of the new round-up conditions there would be no great reason to throw them over—the brand would protect his interests, no matter where it was found. There was some talk about the SV cattle, but Johnny was credited as representing Arnold, and the matter was settled by agreeing that the T and C should pay Arnold, direct. Then the road branding began, and when it was over the consolidated herd was held to await the arrival of McCullough. It was then that Sherwood turned to three of his men.

"Th' Triangle ain't asked for no help, but you boys go down an' give 'em a hand," he said. "We're introducin' th' comin' of th' general round-up out in this country, an' we're doin' it gradual. There won't be no thought of us watchin' out for Arnold's interests over there, because these inspectors will do that anyhow. Go down an' show that we're friendly; an' from there go to th' Bar H.

On the Triangle the following morning things were running in full blast. After a breakfast eaten by firelight, the outfit was in the saddle at the first flush of dawn, and rode far out on the range. At an agreed-upon point it spread out in a thin line, the riders spaced at irregular intervals, depending upon the nature of the ground, and as they turned and moved back in the direction of Rock Creek they were joined by the Bar H contingent, which took up its position on one end of the line.

Draws, brush, and coulees shed cattle before the advance. A cow with a big, husky, and friskily independent calf arose to its feet and looked wonderingly at the disturbance. Gardner espied her and galloped forward, shouting and waving his hat as he rode. "G'wan, you! Get goin'!"

The cow stood irresolute, debating between the

lessons of experience and her own wishes, and the pugnacious counseling of her indignant offspring. Deciding in favor of the former, she wheeled and moved away, the rebellious calf protesting by kicking up its heels and by the defiant erectness of its tail.

"Th' devil you say!" grinned Gardner, watching them depart. "Yo're big enough to be weaned, you overgrown baby—an' yo're shore goin' to be, for yore ma's goin' north."

Out of a clump of brush popped a group of two-year-olds, heads up, curious and mildly frightened. They stood defiant until Gardner was nearly upon them, and then his sudden whoop sent them whirling and off toward Rock Creek, discretion overbalancing valor. He gave them no further thought, for they would continue to travel unless crowded too much, and he was too old a hand to do that. A cow with a dogie he let slip through, pity joining hands with common sense in their behalf. It was not his purpose to bother with sickly, stunted youngsters, nor to take from them the maternal care so necessary to their sense of security.

By this time the outpouring of cattle had put a respectable number in front of him, and as others were routed out they more willingly went forward, for the gregarious spirit urged them to join the little herd. Occasionally one having more spirit than the others would wheel around and attempt to escape, but in all instances, except one, the speedy dash of the trained cow-horse headed them off and sent them on the about-face. The exception was a five-year-old steer, crusty and sullen, his hide bearing mute witness to his combativeness. He planted himself on rigid legs, lowered his sweeping horns and without even a grunt of warning charged straight for the watchful horseman.

"Blasted mosshead," muttered Sam, avoiding the rush, and watching some of the cattle which had turned to see how the affair came out before making up their minds to duplicate it. Too old for the drive, Sam would have let him go, except for the bad effect it might have on the rest of the cattle, and except for his own aroused spirit. He swung his rope and it darted up and out, and caught a hind leg of the "mosshead" as the pony settled back. There was a blur of overturning steer, a bellow of rage, injury, and surprise, and a resounding thump. Riding forward and taking up the slack as he went, Sam suddenly took two quick turns of the rope around his pommel, checked the horse, and grinned. Down went the mosshead again with another thump, and before the animal could get on its feet the rope was slipped off his leg, and when he arose he found himself alone. Gardener had seen the waverers start back to freedom and had to leave the craggy fighter to check a catastrophe. Hard riding won out for him and again he went forward. Several weaners shot out of a draw and took great credit to themselves for outwitting the puncher; but Sam saw no use of collecting infants only to have them turned loose at the cut-out. One cow arose, spread its feet apart and moved its low-held head slowly from side to side. He gave it a pitying glance and let it alone. "Locoed," he muttered, and as he spoke it shied at a weed swaying in the wind and went cautiously around it. There came a sudden bellowing ahead and he dashed forward at the pair of bulls who were pawing streams of dirt into the air as they met in the dust cloud, head on, and locked for the fight, their great, muscular backs bowed under the power of straining legs. This was no time for masculine duels and he broke it up with quirt and hat, driving the testy combatants apart and sending them on their ways. Dust arose over the moving herd, under which was turmoil, confusion, the lowing of cows, and the bawling of calves; but it rolled steadily westward, slowly but surely. A rattler coiled swiftly and launched its venomous, dart-shaped head at the horse, which reared up with a snort of terror. Sam, stirred to sudden anger and recklessness, spurned a gun, and leaned over as the horse dropped to all four feet. His quirt whizzed viciously and a headless, splotched body writhed in the dust.

"I'm purty bad, myself, when I'm riled," he told it, and rode on. Shortly afterward a gray streak flashed from a heavy bit of brush, and Sam's Colt leaped into action, but in vain. The coyote punched a hole in the air and disappeared almost as though it had shrunk into nothing. He grinned: "That slug will catch you when you stop, less'n you turns out," he said.

Rock Creek coming into view, the long line of horsemen became a crescent, the ends moving forward as the center slowed, and soon a circle of riders held the herd on all sides. It slowed, grew compact, and stopped, shifting like a kaleidoscope, the different colors weaving in and out like patches of some animated, changing crazy-quilt. There was good grass here, plenty of water, and no more urging riders. Calves went bawling their panicky ways in frantic search for lost mothers, butting and worrying through the herd, receiving rebuffs and impersonal chastisements as they disturbed their elders. One stood outside the press and bawled like a spoiled child, its defiant tail as high as its sinewy neck and more erect. There came an answering call from the herd and a frantic mother shot out, nosed the squaller, and then both grew instantly silent, contented, and at peace with the turbulent world.

"G'wan back!" ordered Lefferts, grinning from ear to ear. "I'm sayin' that it's a great thing to have a ma, you bellerin' cry-baby."

The round-up had taken less time than had been expected and it was decided to go ahead with the cutting out. The riders took turns in going to the horse wrangler's flimsy rope corral, made by lariats strung from the wheels of the chuck wagon to the pommels of saddles on the backs of old, docile, and well-trained horses. Selecting from their best cutting-out animals, saddles were hastily changed, a quick meal eaten, and then the men rode back to the herd to relieve others, who duplicated the performance. The herd was gently made more compact so as to cover less ground and need fewer riders to loaf in their saddles and hold it, the inspectors rode out in front of it and the cutters-out went to work, trying to pick from the outer fringe of cattle. Cows and steers lumbered from the press and went either to the beef cut, or to freedom, according to the signal of the inspector. Quickly the round-up herd shrunk and the beef cut grew. At first there was some trouble to get the chosen cattle to leave the herd—they tried to rejoin it; but as the beef cut grew it drew more and more until it was hardly more than necessary to start the individual cattle for it. When night fell the original herd had disappeared, its more fortunate units ranging free upon the ranch. The beef cut, allowed to graze and not bothered more than necessary, was headed for a rise, where in due time it bedded down and prepared to spend a quiet, peaceful night.

A passer-by would have come upon a picturesque scene on the banks of Rock Creek that night. The cook's fire, blazing high, was surrounded by the men off watch, squatted, seated, or reclining as they swapped stories and told jokes. The chuck wagon was magnified and made grotesque by the firelight and shadows, saddled horses tied to it or picketed a short distance away, and the flimsy rope corral running from wagon wheels to stakes driven in the ground, was ready to hold a change of mounts in case of a sudden need. In the distance was the bedded herd, lying on the top of a rise where it could catch any passing breeze, the cattle chewing their cuds and blowing and grunting contentedly.

A yearling bummed among them, filled with the mischievous deviltry of youth, making life miserable for its elders as it stumbled and butted its erratic way. It left a fight or two in its wake and finally fled, abandoning all dignity when a crusty steer arose to chastise it. But the chip on its shoulder remained there until it tried to butt a calf from its warm bed, whereupon the indignant mother scrambled to all fours and sent the disturber on the run for safety. The calf was there because it bore no brand, which would be taken care of on the morrow. The bummer had no excuse to create any trouble over a warmed bed because the night was warm. Finally, the edge gone from its exuberant deviltry, it began to look for a place to sleep—and after barely escaping several thrashings it worked out of the herd and sought a place by itself, doubtless to ruminate upon the cruelties and indignities endured by yearlings.

The four night riders of the first shift went slowly, lazily around the herd, keeping a score or more yards from it, singing and carrying on chanted conversations as they met and passed each other. Gone was the dust and turmoil of the day and in its place had come rest and quiet. Over all the crescent moon, nightly to grow fuller, worked its alchemy on earth and cattle, shedding its soft silvery light. The distant camp fire grew steadily lower and finally glowed like the end of a great cigar, winking as gentle breezes fanned its embers and passed on. Somewhere out on the silvery range a lonely coyote poured a burbling plaint to the moon and passed on like a shadow in search of food to stop the clamoring ache of an empty stomach, gradually approaching the winking fire, where choice titbits might perhaps be found.

"I want a big chew of tobacco," chanted Gardner, as he drew nearer to Reilly, "An' I want it bad, for mine's all gone."

"It allus is," sang Reilly. "Don't bother that spotted yearlin' over by them bushes. He's finally quit his bummin' an' has bedded down all by hisself outside th' herd. You'll know where he is even if you went blind. He's real friendly an' lonesome, an' likes to converse with everythin' that passes."

'I know th' scamp," sang Gardner, returning the plug. "He's had one gosh-awful time today keepin' out of a lickin'. I'm sayin' he earned a dozen." Soon he made out Lefferts' song, who mourned a long-lost love.

> Her hair was th' color of 'lasses,
>   As soft as a bundle of wire;
> An' birds made their nests in its fastness:
>   If they didn't I shore am a liar.

Gardner was stirred by the melody and burst into song out of sympathy:

> Her eyes was as bright as old saddles,
>   An' crossed on th' end of her nose;

> *Her hands was as shapely as paddles*
> *An' hung down almost to her toes.*

Lefferts retaliated promptly:

> *Her cheeks was as smooth as th' cactus,*
> *An' pink as a big hunk of mud;*
> *At primpin' she was allus in practice,*
> *An' she was daintily shaped, like a tub.*

From across the herd came Reilly's natural tenor, a little ragged, but still a tenor:

> *Her voice was as sweet as a longhorn's,*
> *It sounded as soft as a scream;*
> *I'm scared to roll up in my blankets*
> *For fear that of her I will dream.*

The song was too much for the coyote, and he paused to yield to the craving for harmony reawakened in him.

"He's imitatin' you, Jim," chanted Gardner as he passed Lefferts. "Which same I says is well done."

"Go to th' devil, an' join yore tribe," sang Jim in delicate repartee, and forthwith began the mournful lay of Clementine:

> *In a hut a-mong th' bushes, all a'long th' foamin'*
> *   brine,*
> *Lived a min-er, 'forty nin-er, an' his daugh-ter,*
> *   Clementine.*
> *She was fair-er than th' ros-es, an' her for-m-m,*
> *   it was di-vine;*
> *Two dry-goods box-es, without their top-ses, made*
> *   gaiters for-r my Clementine.*

At half-past eleven Gardner rode in to the wagon, aroused the next shift, sought his blankets and was sound asleep before his three shift companions reached the camp. At three o'clock the second shift was relieved by the third, and last, which would stay with the herd until it was taken over by all the others, after breakfast.

The new day brought further developments. Several fires burned not far from the herd, irons projecting from them. The cattle were again cut out and driven away to a new herd, one by one, but this time they were taken close to the fires, and because of their weight and strength two ropers joined in the efforts of branding each animal. The glowing iron bit deeply through hair and into the skin on the left flank, filling the air with bellowing anguish, surprise, and indignation, and the odors of burning hair and flesh. There were fights; balkings, charges, but the hard-working, hard-riding punchers, the deftly cast ropes, and the trained horses, together with waving hats and an occasional revolver shot close to the nose of refractory, pugnacious bulls, and an occasional waved slicker or coat, won out, and the work proceeded at a good pace in spite of the general and apparent confusion. But whatever aspect of confusion there was, very little really existed except among the victims themselves, for the men proceeded along well-established lines, and the work went on as though it were running in a groove. Horses were changed every hour or two, depending upon the rider's judgment, and the inspectors, with the Triangle foreman, checked off the branded animals as they joined the road-branded herd. This herd grew rapidly and its guards were increased as needed from the ropers and iron men as they became too tired to hold the pace set. All day long the busy scene continued in the dust and the heat of the sun, with a bedlam of noise, an endless weaving and shifting, with lathered horses, sweat-and-dust-grimed riders, shouts of "Hot iron! Hot iron!" "Tally one!" "Ropers up!" and cries of warning and bursts of laughter. It were well that the Double X had sent three men to help; ten would not have been too many. Even with their help there was only one pair of ropers working at the fires and only three cutters-out, the rest being used to hold the two herds of restless cattle; and when night finally put an end to the operations less than half of the trail herd had been branded.

"Two more days," growled an inspector. "It's time you fellers throwed this worn-out, ancient way aside, an' got up even with th' times. You can build a chute that'll hold eight head an' by usin' stampin' irons you can turn out from sixty to eighty, yes, sometimes even a hundred, an hour, after you get th' hang of it. This handful should 'a' been done by noon. If I was you, Huff," he said, turning to the Bar H foreman, "I'd get on th' jump an' make a couple of them chutes, an' lay in half a dozen irons. One iron will do two or three with one heatin'; sometimes, if th' iron handlers work fast, two irons will stamp th' whole eight. You'll laugh when you see 'em comin' 'out, all branded, eight to a clip; an' th' work ain't near so hard. There ain't no holdin', nor ropin', nor throwin'. Here we've toted half a dozen Question Mark irons up here, an' they ain't hardly saved us any time. You've got plenty of time to put up a chute before we start on yore thousand—if you don't, we'll be a week on 'em, an' a week's too long."

His companion nodded emphatically, and offered to superintend the work. "Ridley can handle th' tallyin' for us out here. They've all been selected, an' comin' as slow as they do, it ain't no two-man job. Mebby th' Double X will lend a couple more men to help—they're finishin' a pair of chutes up there, an' know what's wanted. What you say about it?"

Big Tom considered, and grudgingly gave his consent. Gus Thompson, tired as he was, volunteered to go to his ranch with the request, and started as soon as he had eaten. And by the night of the second day following, when the road-branded Triangle herd was being held to await the coming of McCullough, two eight-cow chutes were ready on the Bar H for the handling of its thousand head.

The round-up on the Bar H went forward with a swing and when it came time for the road branding the chutes proved their worth. The cattle, driven up in groups of eight, were forced into the long, narrow boxes as fast as the branded group went out at the other end. A bar dropped past the nose of the leader, and another bar dropped behind the last one in. Two men standing on a platform running along the side of the chute, each was handed a freshly heated iron and hurried from animal to animal, stamping the brand on each in turn. All morning the long chutes filled and emptied, the men changing places as they tired, the iron handlers so bothered by the stinging odor of burning hair that none of them worked longer than two or three hours without being relieved.

"I'm backin' this here magazine-action brandin' with a hundred an' fifty pounds of fightin' Irish," declared Reilly, chuckling at the almost automatic working of the chutes. "Eight in, stamped an' out again while we'd be workin' on one slippery cuss. Seventy th' last hour for Sam's chute, an' Fraser crowdin' him close; an' us tenderfeet at it—I'm bettin' th' last hour does ninety to th' chute. We're gettin' th' hang of it, an' gettin' it fast."

"Slippin' along like water down hill," laughed Slim, borrowed from his bed and board to help the Bar H. "Hey, Ridley!" he called to the busy inspector, "got any new-fangled improvements that'll make these chutes do it themselves, so th' hard-workin' punchers won't have to loaf in their saddles, but can set around an' gamble? Holy Maverick! Look at him tallyin'! He's shore workin' harder than he was yesterday."

"Who's loafin', you fool?" snorted Sam, taking breath while the chute was being refilled. "I've stamped close to eight thousand since I climbed up here. An'—*Hot iron! Hot Iron!*" he yelled as the front bar dropped. "Wake up, you tramp!"

"You've got a lot to say, you has!" snapped Lefferts, running up with the irons. "All *you* got to do is push 'em ag'in' their hides—I'm near wore out!"

"Why use any bars at all?" queried Reilly, grinning at the hard-working Sam. "Just let 'em filter through, stamping 'em on th' run. We're wastin' time, this way."

"You've got near as much sense as Sam has!" retorted Lefferts, stirring his fire. "Which ain't payin' neither of you no compliments," he grunted.

Big Tom could not deny the advantage of chute and stamping irons, and the ocular demonstration took from him his last reasonable objection to them, although he found fault with them because the herd had to be driven to the same place each round-up, and because he did not believe them to be suitable for calf branding; but when it was pointed out that the cattle had to be driven somewhere before the herd would be worth bothering with, and might as well be driven to the chutes, and that it would be a saving of time to do that, or to build more chutes on the ranch rather than to revert to the old methods, he could not deny it. Regarding the branding of calves there was a division of opinion; but calf branding was not nearly as hard or slow as the branding of grown animals. He knew, however, that the styles were changing, and changing under his eyes, and that for him to become stubborn and set against the change would be to appear ridiculous, and to become a source from which much levity would spring.

The branding done and the tallies compared, the visiting punchers departed for their ranches, the inspectors accepting Big Tom's invitation to spend the night with him, and rode to the ranchhouse; and the herd, restless, sore, and in sullen mood, was watered well at the muddy pond and thrown upon the high bed ground, and would remain a herd until delivered to McCullough, and for some weeks thereafter.

CHAPTER XXIV

On the Trail

AFTER BREAKFAST the following morning Ridley and his
companion saddled their horses to ride back to Highbank, where they would wait for the trail boss. As they
finished cinching up, Big Tom strolled into the corral
and smilingly watched them.

"I suppose you want Mac to bring you a check, as
usual?" queried Ridley, swinging into the saddle.

"This is th' one time I'd rather have cash," replied the
foreman. "With cash, in th' next week, I can make a
quick turnover."

"Cash it is," said Ridley. "Gold or bills?"

"Make it bills," answered Big Tom. "I'm glad I met you
boys—come up again next year. If yo're lookin' for good
cattle then I'll have plenty."

"Then I reckon we'll be here. So-long."

"So-long," replied the foreman, watching them ride
away. As they dropped from sight over a rise he smiled
cynically and went back to the ranchhouse. Pausing at
the door, he looked out over the range in the direction of
the northwest section and the Double X, and slowly
turned his head, his gaze passing along the horizon,

behind which lay Gunsight, Green Valley, and the SV ranchhouse.

"I said it was easy," he growled. "*Me* throw over a couple of hundred head of mavericks to Arnold, an' split up th' rest four ways? It makes me laugh! An' when I hit Nelson he'll wonder what kind of brains he really *has* got. There's a jolt comin' to this section, an' it'll be Big Tom that springs it. About one week more an' *I* play *my* hand!"

Four days passed and then, in the afternoon of the fifth, a great dust cloud appeared far down the Highbank trail. Fraser discovered it and called Big Tom from the ranchhouse. The foreman glanced south, told the puncher to ride off and get the herd started, and then hurried to his horse, sprang into the saddle, and rode toward McCullough's sign. He had hardly more than gained the regular trail when he saw seven men riding toward him at a good pace, and no second glance was needed to identify the one who rode in the middle and slightly ahead.

The trail boss was a character to demand attention wherever he might be. Over the medium height, he was so heavily and solidly built that he appeared to be well under it when standing alone; he had the barrel-like chest that stands for strength, and his sloping shoulders were a little rounded from a careless saddle seat of many years. His rugged face was brown, the skin tough as parchment, and the faded blue eyes peered out in a direct, unwavering gaze between lids narrowed by the suns and winds, rains and dusts of a life spent in the open. His head was massive and the iron-gray hair, falling almost to his shoulders, gave it a leonine appearance. He wore no chaps, for his riding took him into few thickets and there was no reason for him to bear their discomforts. His clothing was simple and loose: black, heavy, woolen trousers thrust into soft, high boots with moderate heels, and bearing no spurs, for he depended on his quirt; a black, woolen vest, buttoned at the bottom, from an upper pocket of which protruded the well-chewed stem of a pipe; a heavy, faded, blue flannel shirt, open over the bronzed, hairy chest and throat; a faded blue kerchief, knotted loosely about his neck; a heavy, gray sombrero, moderate in height of crown, but with a wide brim. He rode a Cheyenne saddle, devoid of ornamentation, its housings covering the horse from rump to withers, and the reins of the bridle, contrary to the prevailing fashion of that southern range at that time, were short. A .44 Winchester lay in its sheath under his right leg; a braided hair lariat was coiled at the pommel; a heavy, plain six-shooter rested in an open holster; and behind him was rolled the everlasting yellow slicker. He rode a magnificent bay horse whose spirit was shown in every movement, and which would follow him about like a dog. Over all was dust, gray, thick, impalpable dust.

"Hello, Huff!" he bellowed. "Come down to see if I got lost? Join up with us; I'm figgerin' that Triangle herd may be up at this end of th' crick, an' if it is, it's got to move. Them long-laigged cattle of mine ain't had a drink since yesterday mornin', an' they'll shore rush that crick. We'll have some cuttin' out to do if th' other herd is in their path. How 'bout it?"

"You can pull up, then," replied Big Tom. "They're well to th' south of th' bunkhouse—you got plenty of room for ten times that little bunch yo're so peart about. I heard they are th' leavin's of four Greaser ranches."

"Glad to learn they ain't there," said McCullough.

"They're such leavin's an' scourin's," smiled one of his companions, "that I'm advisin' Mac to double th' night guard while he's within' forty miles of this bunch of ranches."

"We'll count that Triangle bunch right away," said the trail boss. "Where's yourn?"

"It's on its way," answered Big Tom. "It'll be on hand soon enough. Goin' to count that, too, tonight?"

"Shore. An' throw 'em together, an' bed down on Clear River, so we can get a two-hour jump-off in th' mornin'. Is th' Double X holdin' its bunch in th' same old place?"

"I reckon so," replied Big Tom, and soon they passed the Triangle ranchhouse, where Hank Lewis rode forth to join them.

"Get yore boys, Lewis," shouted the trail boss. "We'll count that herd right away."

"They're with it now," replied Lewis, as he drew nearer. "Glad you brought some of yore boys along—I'm short-handed for quick work."

It was not long before they reached the herd and it was slowly crowded into a more compact mass, and became wedge-shaped. McCullough, one of his men, and the two foremen stopped before the point, the trail boss and Huff on one side, the others not far away and facing them. The herd started slowly forward, narrowing to an animated ribbon which flowed between the two pairs of counters and kept them busy. McCullough and Lewis counted on knotted strings fastened to their pommels, Huff used his fingers to check off the tally, fifty head to each digit, while the fourth man threw a coil of his rope over the pommel of his saddle at each hundred. The counting was finished well under ten minutes and the results compared. Lewis said five hundred and five, the other three announcing five hundred and six.

The Triangle foreman laughed. "Here is where I get paid for a missin' cow."

"Three to one bein' good enough for me," replied the trail boss, grinning, "I says you do. It's worth that to see you again; an' what's a cow between friends?" He turned in his saddle. "You might move 'em up closer to th' trail, boys," he shouted, and added with a chuckle, "they'll disappear when my long-laigs come along."

His prediction was justified, for the long-legs, having run the last mile or two with the scent of water in their red nostrils, poured into the creek and soaked themselves inside and out. By the time McCullough and his group reached the scene, the Bar H herd was crossing the trail. The counting was gone over again, the tallies agreeing to a single cow, and the Bar H herd was allowed to join the strangers along the creek. In due time the enlarged herd was thrown back on the trail, and when the Triangle five hundred joined it they were, indeed, swallowed up.

The trail boss and Big Tom rode off to the Triangle ranchhouse, figured for a moment and then exchanged cash for a receipt. The foreman shoved the bills into his pockets and went with McCullough back to the herd, picked up the squad, and had the Double X contingent counted before the trail herd reached the river.

As the herd came along it made a fine sight for a cowman to look upon, the cattle strung out for three-quarters of a mile in length and spread well out on both sides of the trail, well watered and fed, and making under these conditions four miles an hour. The chuck wagon, drawn by four mules, rolled far ahead of it, the caviya of a hundred and thirty saddle horses to one side and also ahead. Each of the two point men was followed by four swing men, five to a side, and they had nothing to do now but look out for stragglers and to keep local cattle from joining the invading host. The bed ground was well chosen and the night promised to be a good one, notwithstanding that clouds were forming and the moon would be more or less obscured.

After the Double X contingent had joined their trail mates for the long journey and the great herd had bedded down, half of the trail outfit, together with the punchers from the ranchers, headed for town, McCullough electing to remain with the herd. Big Tom and Lewis shook hands with him and returned to their ranchhouses, riding together part of the way.

Just before they separated Lewis looked up. "I heard that Arnold was ridin' today—one of th' Double X boys met him at th' trail. I reckon it must feel good to be in th' saddle again after such a long siege in bed."

"I'm bettin' it does," smiled Big Tom. "I had a dose of it when I was a young man, an' once is shore a-plenty."

"He must think so, for he's aimin' to ride to town every day, an' spend some of his time gettin' acquainted with Dave an' his friends. Well, I'm leavin' you here. Good night."

"Good night," replied Big Tom, riding on with a sinister smile on his face.

The following morning was cloudy, which suited the Bar H foreman, who had a long ride ahead of him. He opened the south door of the ranchhouse, looked out and caught sight of a movement near the right-hand corner. A full-grown rattler was crawling slowly across a sand patch, and the foreman watched it idly. Then he grinned.

"Wonder how good my gunplay is these days?" he muttered, and his Colt leaped from its holster and roared. The snake writhed swiftly into an agonized coil, its flat head moving back and forth, its tongue darting angrily, and its rattles buzzing steadily. Huff growled at himself and fired again. The flattened, venomous head sank down, twisting and turning on the writhing coils.

"H—l!" growled the marksman, walking slowly forward for a closer look, which showed him that his last shot had cut through the vertebra and half of one side of the neck. It was good enough, and he turned and walked along the side of the house. Passing a window, he suddenly stopped and looked closely at the ground just under its sill, where boot prints were plainly visible. Before doing anything else he reloaded his gun, and then followed the prints with his eyes until the corner of the house cut them from sight. He stepped back until he could see the bunkhouse door to learn if anyone was coming up to investigate the shots, and his gaze followed the prints straight toward it until they became lost on harder ground. No one being curious about the shooting, he went back to the window and peered in. He could see nothing because of the curtain, and had about decided that he had enjoyed secrecy the night before, when a sudden thought struck him. The interior, being dark now, was not right for a test, and he went around to the door, opened it, threw up the other shades, and hastily returned to the window, where he smothered a curse as a small hole in the curtain let him see quite plainly. Again returning to the house, he closed the door and slipped his extra Colt into the waist-band of his trousers, where one side of his open vest covered it, put on his coat and, going out the rear door, sauntered toward the bunkhouse, his eyes finding and losing the boot marks as the trail passed over varying ground. Before he reached the house his four men emerged from it and began the regular, humorous, morning wrangle as to preference in the use of wash basin and towel. They grinned at his approach and he smiled in return, his eyes missing nothing in their expressions, and it was Fraser at whom he looked longest when he spoke.

"Throw my saddle on th' big bay, Bill," he smiled, pleasantly. "I'm goin' up to Sherman to fatten th' balance at th' bank. I may be back tomorrow night, but if I hear of any cattle that can be got cheap I may go on an' look 'em over. You boys have plenty of supplies, but if you run short go up to Dailey. If he's got any cigars, get a box—I reckon we can afford that much of a celebration, in view of that herd. But don't drink too much. You know why."

Fraser got the saddle from the storeroom and went out to put it on the foreman's best horse. As he came out of the door he nodded toward the north. "There's Mac's sign already; he must 'a' passed around Gunsight. He's well on his way."

The others looked at the faint thickening in the air beyond the town and past the east end of Pine Mountain, where the dust from four thousand cattle rose heavenward.

"He's a wise bird, gettin' to th' crick last night," commented Carson. "He's been movin' since dawn; an' I bet he's glad it's cloudy, with that dry stretch ahead of him."

"Shucks!" snorted Dahlgren. "Thirty mile of dry trail ain't nothin'."

"Not much," admitted Carson; "but, still, it's better cloudy than boilin' under th' sun."

"I reckon Mac ain't thinkin' as much about it bein' cloudy as I am," smiled the foreman, turning to take the horse Fraser was leading to him. He had asked Fraser to get and saddle his horse in the hope that the puncher would stand on his dignity and, perhaps, provoke a quarrel, out of which anything might come; but Fraser paid no attention to the request, unusual as it was, and grinned as he stepped back.

"It's fifty miles to Sherman, an' I'd ruther have it cloudy, all th' way," smiled Big Tom, mounting. "Well, so-long, boys!" and he was off.

He chose the trail over Pine Mountain, not so much for its saving in miles, but because it gave him a high, distant point from which to look back over his trail, and it avoided the Doc's shack and Gunsight as well. Reaching the top of the mountain, he turned and closely scrutinized the trail, finding nothing to bother him; but he was bothered, nevertheless, and he determined to pay as much attention to the trail he covered as to that which lay before him. Setting out again, he went well to the west of Gunsight and struck the Sherman trail ten miles beyond the town.

Back on the Bar H, Fraser was thinking. He had been doing a lot of it the last week, and he had not been alone in it. When his foreman had ridden off he leaned against the door and watched him until he was lost to sight. Dahlgren and Carney passed out, joked with him and went to the corral, soon riding off to the south. Dick Carson passed out a little later, paused, retraced his steps and leaned against the other door jamb.

"Wonder if yo're thinkin' th' same as me?" he quietly asked.

Fraser looked at him closely. "I don't know; I'm thinkin' of a gamble," he replied, hooking a thumb in an armhole of his vest.

"Shore; so am I," nodded Carson, carelessly. "This here range is shot full of holes, for us."

"It is," admitted Fraser. "We been driftin' them mavericks for three years—an' now they're goin' to be throwed back, branded, an' th' rest cut four ways. How are we goin' to stop it?"

"I'm figgerin' on driftin' myself; but I hate to drift alone, an' empty-handed," growled Carson. "I come down here to work for Huff, for fifty a month, an' pickin's. I've been gettin' th' fifty—but there won't be no pickin's, less'n I run some off with me. I'm tired of this blasted country, anyhow. Why, I'd ruther take chances, like Nevada, than go on this way down here. H—l!" he snorted in angry disgust. "I'm sayin' I fair itches to gamble," he added.

Fraser shifted to a more comfortable position.

"What do you think th' boss has got in his pockets right now?" he asked, cynically.

"A big, fat check, that won't do him nor us any good," replied Carson.

"Check!" Fraser laughed sarcastically. "Check? He allus used to have a check, after delivery; but he ain't got one now. He's got bills, wads an' wads of bills. Quite some over six thousand, I reckon, in bills. I saw his pockets bulgin', an' I wondered why he didn't take a check, same as usual. I wanted to make shore, so I did some scoutin' up around th' ranchhouse last night—I *saw* 'em. Wads, an' wads. I was shore tempted."

Carson was looking off toward Pine Mountain, an evil expression on his face, and he moved restlessly. "There's only one reason for that," he muttered, and turned to his companion. "Are you still thinkin' of a gamble?" he demanded, all thought of cattle out of his mind. "Th' herd money is shore worth while—what you say about it?"

"I was sort of turnin' it over in my head," Fraser admitted. "It's a lot of money; a powerful lot of money for one man to tote."

"It'll still be a lot of money if it's split in two," suggested Carson. "Do you figger he's goin' to bank it? All that cash? Why didn't he take a check? Why did he change, just when things was gettin' worse down here all th' time?"

"I don't know; but he's allus been purty white to me."

"Has he been three thousand dollars' worth?" asked

Carson, smiling evilly. "I'm figgerin' he's lettin' us hold th' sack, that's what *I'm* figgerin'. An' if he don't come back, who's goin' to sign checks for our pay? We're losin' our share of all them mavericks. There won't be no nice bunch of cattle goin' up th' trail for us fellers, not now. But there's one whoppin' big bunch of *cash* goin' up a trail for us, if we go after it. How's yore nerve? What's th' use of playin' for buttons, when there's *bills* to be had?"

"If I reckoned he was goin' to bank that money I wouldn't touch it, not if I was shore he was comin' back to stick with th' ranch," muttered Fraser. "But I reckon he's throwed us down. I reckon we're holdin' th' sack, all right. An' if he aims to keep it, then we has as much right to it as he has. Cuss him! he's chicken-livered! Come on: I'm with you," and he led the way into the house to get some of his personal belongings.

"He's got a start on us, an' a cussed good hoss," growled Carson as they hastened to the corral. "We can't save nothin' by cuttin' across, neither."

"No, we can't; but we can take a lead hoss apiece," said his companion, "an' ride without carin' what happens to th' ones we start on. He won't be pushin' hard— he don't like hard ridin', he thinks too much of his hoss, an' he ain't got no reason to be in any great hurry. He's serene as a snake full of birds, chucklin' at how easy it is."

Down on the southern part of the ranch, in a draw, there was another conference, where Dahlgren and Carney also were mourning the deplorable state of affairs on the range.

"Three years' work gone to blazes," grumbled Little Tom, resentfully. "I'm near on th' prod."

"Gettin' near on th' prod ain't worth nothin'," replied Dahlgren. "It's gettin' on one, a good one, an' stayin' with it, that counts. I figgers we still got a lot of interest in them mavericks, an' I'm dead shore there ain't nobody watchin' 'em this side of th' Double X line."

"There's a lot of 'em away south of there," said Carney. "There's a couple of herds hang out closer to th' water hole in West Arroyo. I've seen 'em often when I rode that way. We could round up near three hundred, hold 'em in that blind canyon till evenin', an' then run th' whole bunch over th' Double X southwest corner an' get 'em well away tonight. It's cloudy, an' there won't be much moon showin'—just enough light to see what we're doin', an' not enough to show us up for any distance. Th' four of us can swing that herd in bang-up style—an' Big Tom won't never catch us, once we get into th' Snake Buttes country. An' what's more, I know where unmarked cattle can be sold, with no questions an' at a fair price. Th' game's up for us, down here, anyhow."

"You aimin' to let them two in on this?"

"I'd ruther let 'em in on it, an' swing more cattle, than have 'em trailin' us tomorrow. An' four ain't too many for drivin' through th' Buttes."

"I don't like splittin' 'em four ways," growled Dahlgren, but he grudgingly gave his consent. "All right. Go up an' feel 'em out, while I start roundin' up. Don't give nothin' away before you know how they feel about it."

"I'm off. They wasn't goin' to ride out till late, an' mebby I'll catch 'em at th' house," and Carney was off like a shot. He was not gone long, and when he returned he spread out his hands expressively.

"They've pulled their stakes, I reckon," he reported. "Their blankets an' 'most everythin' they owned, of any account, was gone. My extra gun is missin', an' our stuff is spread all over th' place. I rustled some supplies, an' found they had been there, too. Let 'em go!"

"Cussed glad of it; now it's halves, instead of fourths," replied Dahlgren, cheerfully. "Come on; let's push this work. Don't get any more branded cattle than you can help; but we ain't goin' to waste no time cuttin' any out."

Up on the Sherman trail Big Tom was swinging along within ten miles of town when, passing a particularly high, abrupt hill, he turned out, rode along it and, dismounting, went up on foot until he could peer across the top of it. He did not have long to wait, for soon two horsemen appeared far back on the trail, where it crossed a wide, open space. Going back to his horse, he led it into a thicket and tied it to a bush, took his rifle and returned to the hill top, where he chose cover close to the bank at the trail's edge, and settled down comfortably to wait.

As the two riders drew nearer he recognized them by their ensemble, and by the way they sat their saddles, and it was not long before he could make out details. They were riding hard, both keenly alert, peering along the trail ahead of them. Nearer and nearer they came, pushing ahead at a fast, hard pace, eager to overtake him before he reached the town. Sweeping past the steep bank, they shot around a bend and went on.

Big Tom watched them until they had passed from sight, and then arose and nodded. "It's a good thing for you that you missed me!" he growled. "I hate to lose th' pay-roll money; but what's got to be done has got to be done. My interest in Sherman has plumb faded. Now for a smash at Nelson that'll hurt him to his dyin' day, d—n him!"

Darkness had fallen on the range and the night riders of the west section of the Double X were Slim Hawkes, Tom Wilkes, and Cimarron, who had the first shift. They were back on the old three-shift plan and would be off duty at half-past eleven. Cimarron had ridden south and had reached the end of his beat, the north side of a shallow arroyo. He softly gave the night's signal and, receiving no reply, decided to wait for a while, for Slim was due to reach and stop at the other side of the arroyo at any minute. He could faintly discern the outlines of objects at quite a respectable distance and wondered how soon the moon would break through the filmy clouds. Suddenly he listened closely and thought he detected the noise made by a herd. Slim's signal came faintly to him and he replied to it with a double one. In a few minutes Slim loomed up out of the dark.

"Are you hearin' that, too?" asked Slim in a whisper.

"I am," replied Cimarron. "That's a herd, an' there's

work for me an' you. It's comin' up from th' south, bearin' a little west, I reckon. How do you figger it?"

"West, bearin' a little north," answered Slim. "But it's shore comin' *from* our range, which is enough for us. I'm askin' no questions tonight. Th' last time I sung out Nevada shot me up. I'm doin' my talkin' tonight with my gun. An' I'm hopin' it's Nevada, personal: I *owe* him somethin'."

"Don't separate, or we'll mebby shoot each other," growled Cimarron. "If we hit 'em from this side we'll mebby turn th' herd so it'll stampede back where it belongs; an' if it does, th' fellers on th' other side will have plenty to do for a couple of minutes, an' give us a chance to get to 'em. It's closer. Are you ready?"

Slim loosened his left foot from the stirrup and then lay forward along the neck of his horse, Cimarron doing likewise; and then the two animals moved forward at a walk, innocent of any silhouetted figures sticking up in the saddles. Louder and louder grew the sound and soon the two clinging riders could plainly distinguish the rattle of horns from the hoofbeats. A few minutes more, and then a mounted figure became vaguely outlined. The herd was being moved at a walk, possibly to avoid greater noise until it was well across the Double X line, and now its bulk could be guessed at.

The herder leaned forward suddenly to scrutinize two moving blots he barely could make out against a rise of ground behind them, and the movement was the beginning of the end, for him. A sudden stream of fire poured from the left-hand blot and he slid from his saddle without a sound. The blots let out yells and dashed for the front ranks of the herd, which wheeled like a flash and thundered across the range over a course at right angles to the one which they had been following. The two night guards spurred toward the place where they hoped to come in contact with other rustlers, but found no one to oppose them, and they then set out to follow the herd. Far ahead of them they saw two flashes, followed at certain, agreed-upon intervals by another and then a fourth. Cimarron fired once, counted twelve and then sent two more shots into the air as close together as he could make them, which left nothing to be desired on that score. When he and Slim neared the herd again the moon shone down faintly and let them see what they were doing.

"Where'd you get 'em?" yelled Matt Webb. "There ain't a brand on 'em, that I can see; an' I can see plain enough for that."

"Where do you suppose we got 'em?" retorted Cimarron, "from Europe?" He rode at one end of the front rank and had the satisfaction of seeing it falter.

"I see a Bar H mark!" shouted Rich Morgan. "An' they're stoppin', thank th' Lord!"

In another ten minutes the herd started milling and soon afterward became sensible.

"I say we have been made a present of some of Huff's pets," chuckled Rich. "He says mavericks take title from th' ranch they're on; an' I'm gamblin' these are on th' Double X!"

"If they was ours I'd say to let 'em wander," spoke up Cimarron. "Seein' as they ain't, I reckon it'll save a lot of work if we beds 'em down an' keeps 'em together. I'll go on in an' let Lin know, so he can turn out th' off shift. We shot somebody out near that dividin' arroyo between Slim's section an' mine; you might take a look out that way. Slim's hopin' it was Nevada; but I'm sayin' mebby he'll be surprised when he finds out who it is."

"I'm guessin' right about th' outfit he belongs to, anyhow," replied Slim. "An' I'm not goin' in till I sees which one he is. Comin', Matt? I'll ride out with you."

Leaving Cimarron to go to the bunkhouse for the off shift, Slim and Matt rode rapidly toward the scene of the fight, and when they reached it they saw a figure on the ground. Dismounting they bent over it, and then looked at each other.

"Dahlgren!" breathed Slim.

Matt nodded. "They wasn't waitin' for their mavericks to be split four ways," he said, covering the upturned face with the dead man's sombrero. "They was stealin' a march on Big Tom while he is up in Sherman. Well, anyhow, he was on th' rustle—an' there ain't no harm done. Go on in, an' get yore sleep. As to th' herd, I reckon Arnold has got th' best title to it—but that's for Lin to say. If he does throw 'em over to th' SV it'll save Big Tom th' shame of doin' it hisself. Good night."

CHAPTER XXV

Still a-Rollin'

ARNOLD FINISHED his breakfast and, telling Margaret that he was going to Gunsight to see Johnny and Dave, the hiring of another puncher being uppermost in his mind, went to the corral and soon was riding along the trail, gratified by the entire absence of pain in his leg and with the stimulation which came from the easy motion, the sun, and the crisp morning air. When Margaret turned back into the house her brother had slipped out of the front door and had gone, eager to shirk his few duties and play scout. Since he had found an old, broken rifle in the deserted and disused bunkhouse it formed the foundation upon which he based his play. As she called to him, vexation in her voice, he was wriggling through a clump of brush not far away, his part of his scouting being earnest and real. Wiping dishes was woman's work, as he firmly believed, and he detested and scorned it. His pony had been saddled and picketed in a draw south of the house before breakfast, and when the opportunity offered he intended to get to it and ride off over the ranch until hunger forced him to return. Lying quietly in his cover he kept a keen watch until, the beds made, his sister should begin the kitchen work and give him a chance to cross the open space between him and the pony. He was growing more and more impatient when he caught sight of a horseman riding down the slope of a hill north of the house, and his anger and curiosity flared up when he saw that it was Big Tom.

The Bar H foreman rode leisurely past the corral, noting the absence of Arnold's horse and the pony, and stopped before the door. Swinging from the saddle he sauntered up to the kitchen door and knocked. Margaret wondered who it could be, a sudden thought of injury to her father coming to her, and she hastened to answer it. When she saw who the visitor was she stopped and recoiled a little.

"How-do-you-do?" she said coldly.

"Glad to see you, Ma'am," came the answer. "I rode over to see yore father about some mavericks of his that are eatin' up my grass."

"You have just missed him," replied Margaret. "If you return by the way of Gunsight you can see him there."

"Now, ain't that just my luck?" regretted the foreman, stepping inside. "Might I have a drink of water, Ma'am? I wasn't aimin' to ride back that way. Of course there ain't no chance at all of his comin' back soon?"

"Why, · no," answered Margaret, handing him the dipper. "He may not return until evening. But you can leave a message for him with me."

"It's somethin' we has to talk over," Big Tom replied, giving her the empty dipper. As her hand touched it he grabbed her to him, her screams muffled by his hand. Struggle as she would she was helpless against his bear-like strength and soon was limp with exhaustion and partially suffocated. Holding her with one arm and hand he took a clothesline from a peg on the wall and quickly trussed her with it until she was powerless to move. Gagging her with a towel he carried her to the corral, caught her horse, and threw her on it and cinched up the saddle which lay at the gate. Hurrying back to the house he collected provisions and ran out again, and in another minute he rode rapidly for the brush and rough ground west of the house, leading her horse. Bound, gagged, and tied to the saddle she could do nothing, every beat of the horses' hoofs increasing her terror.

Back at the house Charley wriggled around the corner, his curiosity overcoming caution, and he stared in amazement as he saw them crossing the open, his sister bound with rope. Suddenly cursing the useless rifle in a burst of rage, he dashed for his horse, mounted and rode for town to tell his father, keeping to the low levels until the hills and brush formed a screen behind him. The little pony ran at top speed, shrewdly guided over the rough trail, and the nine miles did not take long. Dashing up to Dave's, Charley shouted at the top of his lungs and pulled up at the door.

"Peggy's kidnapped! Dad! Peggy's kidnapped!"

A chair crashed in Dave's and three men jammed in the doorway, Johnny forcing his two companions back as he fought his way past them. "What's that?" he demanded.

"Big Tom's stole Peggy, d—n him!" shrilled the boy, tears of helpless rage in his eyes.

Johnny needed no further proof than the words and Charley's earnestness. "Where was it? Which way did he go?" he snapped, leaping to the black horse standing at the tie rail.

"At th' ranch—they went west. Oh, Peggy!" he sobbed. "Oh, Peggy!"

"Come a-runnin'!" shouted Johnny over his shoulder, wheeling his horse. He spoke to the black thoroughbred and she struck into a gait she could hold for hours, and one which was deceptive in its smoothness. As he rocked down the trail three Double X punchers rode in from the south.

"Keep a-goin'!" Dave yelled to them, apoplectic with his emotions. "Foller *him*! Big Tom's run off with th' Arnold gal!"

Slim's brief remark is better left unrecorded. Three sets of hoofs rolled out of the town and sent the dust swirling high along the trail. The punchers overtook and passed Arnold, who cursed the slowness of his mount, shouted profane reassurance at him and left him their dust. Dailey led Fanning around the corner of the saloon and aroused surprised resentment in his horse, which heretofore had regarded him as a sane being. Fanning's gray felt a touch of its youthful spirits return; if it had to race, all right; it wasn't much for speed, but it expected to be better than last at the finish.

Big Tom, having passed the boundaries of the ranch, pulled up long enough to remove the gag. "If you behave yourself I'll untie you," he said. "You can't get away—if you try it you'll learn what a rope feels like."

Margaret managed to nod and the rope came off of her.

" 'Twon't do no good to yell," he told her, "nor to hold back. You won't be missed till supper time, an' then nobody will do much worryin' till dark. They'll search th' range first—an' by th' time they finish that we'll be so far away that they'll never find us. Yo're thinkin' they'll trail us? Huh! Let 'em, then. Once we get into *my* country they can trail an' be d—d! You might as well make th' best of it. I got th' herd money in my pockets, an' we can have a nice little ranch an' live like th' story books say— happy ever after. Yo're goin' to live there with me. If yo're sensible you can do it as my wife. I'm going to give you that chance. But, yo're goin' to live there with me, just the same."

"You are even more of a beast than I thought," she retorted. "You'll never reach that ranch; and if you do, I'll kill you while you sleep."

"I'm chancin' th' last," he retorted. "Yo're thinkin' of that Nelson, huh?" he grinned. "When Big Tom *does* play his cards it takes more'n a fool like *him* to win th' pot. An' I'm sayin' I stacked this deck. I've been stackin' it for a long time, figgerin' everythin'. He's cold-decked, Ma'am; beat clean when he'd reckoned he'd won. Thinkin' they'll trail us, an' get us because we're not pushin' hard?" He laughed ironically. "Didn't I say I've been plannin' this a long time? There ain't no use of wearin' horses out when it ain't needed. With twenty hours, or more, start, ours will be fresh when we need speed—which we won't. You'd do better to begin practicin' callin' yoreself Missus Huff—it'll come easy before you know it. I'm givin' you that chance, an' I'll not bother you till a parson is handy. Then it will be yore move. You've got three days." Receiving no reply he looked around the range and thenceforth ignored her.

A black thoroughbred swept across the little SV valley, passed the corral, and rocked westward along a plain trail. The rider, his sombrero jammed tightly down on his head to baffle the pull of the whistling wind, cold with a rage which had turned him into the personification of vengeance, felt an exultant thrill as the double trail sped past him, for his quarry had but eighteen miles start, and he felt sure that it had been cut down by the speed at which half of it had been covered. There was nothing on hoofs on all that range that could keep an even lead against Pepper. She flashed past mesquite, around chaparrals, her great heart beating with a gameness which excelled even her love for the race; her trim legs swinging rhythmically, the reaching of her free, beautiful stride eating up the range and sending it past like the speeding surface of some great rapids. A Gila monster moved from her course barely in time, and a rattler coiled and struck too late. Off in the brush a startled coyote changed its mind about crossing the open and slunk back into cover, following the black with suspicious gaze. The great muscles writhed and bunched, rippled and bulged under the satiny skin, the barrel-like chest rising and falling with a rhythm and smoothness which graphically told that it was a perfect part of a perfect running machine. Down the slopes at top speed, up them at a lope, the undulating range slipped swiftly past. Brush and scattered mesquite, chaparrals and lone, sentinel cacti; hollows, coulees, draws, and arroyos went behind in swift procession. Still the double trail lay ahead, now lost as it crossed hard ground, now plain with small, shallow basins where the sand had slid back and hidden the outlines of the roofs, and then clear and sharp and fresh in soils possessing claylike cohesion.

The rider gave no thought to ambush. There was a

time for everything, but hesitation or caution would not claim its turn until the ride was done. If an ambush lay ahead, what mattered it? Others were coming along that trail, and only one need survive. The picture which he carried in his brain was not one from which counselings of safety could arise. Its message was to ride, ride, ride; and kill, kill, kill; and it turned the thin-lipped, narrow-lidded rider into an agent of Death, merciless and untiring. The ages rolled back from around his soul and stripped it of the last, pulsating film of civilization's veneer. No gray wolf ever ran a trail, no wolverine hunted in its northern fastness that was more coldly savage or cruel than this man whose grim confidence gave no thought of failure. Mile after mile he rode, motionless in the saddle save for the rhythmic rise and swing of a saddle poise superb. Neither to right nor left he looked, nor back where the billowing dust swirled suddenly high to roll spreading over the drab earth, slowly settling. Straight ahead he set his gaze, to the far-therest new-made mark on the winding, twisting trail, a trail which twisted and wound as though vainly seeking a place to hide until that flying Death were past. A high ridge of limestone poured into view and the swinging black was pulled to a walk, for a breathing spell wise in its length, and canny in its shortness. Then up slowly and off again on her far-reaching stride, the noonday sun blazing down unheeded.

To the west the ribbon-like trail was widening. Behind Johnny it was bigger by one more strand; behind Slim, a furnace of rage, was another strand; Tom Wilkes, grimly determined, made another; half a mile behind him rocked Cimarron, vengeful and silent, and added the sixth. Certain memories, returning to the *segundo*, caused him to ride off and make a trail of his own, confident that it would be a chord in a great arc and lead him past his two ranch mates. There was a certain pass far to the northeast which he vaguely coupled to the Bar H foreman, and with three men ahead of him to follow the certainty of the tell-tale trail, he could afford to gamble. Two hours later Slim became indignant and wondered if

Cimarron's black-and-white had grown wings, for his *segundo*'s dust did not suit his mouth and eyes.

"He can do it with me," muttered Slim, "but that Pepper hoss won't be seen by any of us till she stops. I hope Nelson ain't killin' her."

The Pepper horse was neither stopping nor being killed. She skimmed along with no faltering in her stride as though she remembered a day in a quicksand. There was a debt to be paid, and if heart held out and the heaving sides did not prove false to her thoroughbred courage, the lengthening shadows would see it canceled before they became lost in the day's deepening twilight. Down a narrow valley she sped, the hills rolling the tattoo of her drumming hoofs as though they liked the sound and were reluctant to let it die. Taking a brook at a bound and scorning her rising thirst, she swirled around a sharp bend, and twitched her ears suddenly forward, the quick pressure of her rider's knees telling her that he had seen.

Johnny slipped his Sharp's from its long sheath and, holding it at the ready, stood up in his stirrups, his horse somewhere finding a reserve power that fairly hurled her forward, the trim black legs whirring under her like flashing spokes of jet. The rider's lids narrowed to thin slits and the tight-pressed lips pressed tighter. Yard after yard he gained, second after second. The half mile became a quarter, steadily lessened and then, Pepper pounding over a stretch of rocky ground where the hammering of her hoofs rang out loudly, there was a quick turning in the saddles ahead, and a roar from the saddle behind, a ragged cloud of acrid smoke tearing itself to filmy bits and blending with the suddenly tenuous dust cloud in the rear.

Big Tom cursed in sudden rage and whirled his horse behind Margaret's, his rifle spitting past her shoulder. His shelter bolted from in front of him as a Sharp's Special stung the SV horse, its rider barely able to keep her seat during the convulsive lunge. Big Tom leaped down behind his mount and rested the gun across the saddle. Before he could pull the trigger another Special passed through the animal's abdomen and, its force spent, struck his belt and doubled him up, gasping for breath as the agonized animal leaped forward. The cantle of the saddle, striking the barrel of the Winchester, tore the weapon from its owner's hands and left him, slowly straightening up, with a Colt for his only defense.

Coming at him like a skimming swallow sped Pepper, her rider, having slipped the rifle back into its long sheath, standing erect in the stirrups, each hand holding a Colt. For a moment they were held aloft and then as the Bar H foreman drew his six-gun they chopped down and poured jets of flame and puffs of smoke over Pepper's head. The foreman twisted, fired aimlessly, lurched, fired again, and plunged forward, face down on the sand. Johnny slid his guns back into their holsters and raced for Margaret, who was fighting a pain-crazed horse.

Slim and Cimarron, neck and neck now, jumped the brook, sped along the little valley, keyed to fighting pitch by the sound of distant shots, and flashed around the bend, where they pulled up sharply and looked across the level pasture.

"H——l!" growled Cimarron. "I thought we was ridin' to a lynchin'! This here looks more like a weddin'. Get back, around that bend, you fool!"

"It shore does," said Slim, grinning. "A weddin', huh? Well, then, I says he's still a-rollin'."

TOR

Award-winning authors
Compelling stories

Please join us at the website
below for more information
about this author and other great
Tor selections, and to sign up for
our monthly newsletter!